JASPER FAULKS

AND THE PASSAGE OF TIME

MILAN OBRADOVIC

To my mother, who has always supported me
beyond reason.

Acknowledgments

This book has been a long time coming. I first mulled over a time-bending adventure spiraling out of a quaint Los Angeles neighborhood while pushing my son's stroller around our little corner of the Westside. He started middle school last year.

First and foremost, I would like to thank my wife Micky for her indispensable help, patience, and encouragement. I'm also grateful to all my beta readers, especially Joshua Hime, Abby Weber, and Julia Martens, as well as Christi Catalpa for help with the art direction, Kimberley Marsot for the final cover, and all the good folks at Snowy Wings Publishing.

It is a small part of life we really live.
Indeed, all the rest is not life but merely time.

Seneca, "On the Shortness of Life," AD 49

Table of Contents

Chapter One

A Better Tomorrow

UCLA Medical Center, Two Years Ago

"Our time together was a gift. A miracle. You're my miracle. You know that, right? I love you so, so much."

"Mom..." Overt displays of affection embarrassed Jasper under the best of circumstances. "You'll be fine. It'll be just like it used to be."

"Of course." Mom smiled enigmatically. "Come here."

Jasper leaned down to her. She still smelled like Mom, despite everything.

"I have to ask you for a favor," she whispered, barely audible over the background noise of a busy ICU. "You know how forgetful Dad can be. Be lenient with him. He loves you now and forever. Can you keep an eye on him for me? Can you do that?"

Jasper nodded. She pulled his head down to give him a long kiss on the forehead, imprinting it with motherly love. It left a tingle on his skin.

"And, Andy," she said. Since she spoke very softly, Jasper took a half-step back to let his father bend down.

"Promise me, let him be a kid. Let him have a normal life."

"It can't be normal without you," Dad murmured, squirming. "They'll fix you, don't worry."

"You know what I mean. Promise me."

"There's things he needs to know—"

"Not now, not tomorrow." Mom's voice held the hint of a sharper edge. "Promise me, love. Don't forget, he's still a kid. Don't. Forget."

"Yes, still a kid. I promise," Dad whispered. "I promise." He held her hand as she closed her eyes.

Jasper stepped forward to put his hand on top of theirs. "Mom? Mom…?"

Santa Monica, CA; Present Day

Jasper didn't know anyone who walked as much as he did, but then he also didn't know anyone else at his posh high school without a car in the family. Hopefully that would change soon—tomorrow was his sixteenth birthday. But on this gloomy June Sunday, the first weekend of his summer break, he still walked.

At the pet food store next to the cemetery, he bought a giant bag of *Outdoor Formula* cat food. Barely two minutes later, he regretted it already. The narrow plastic bag handles cut into his hand.

The Sunday crowd populated the cemetery, and on his way back home—cutting through the memorial park, as usual—Jasper felt self-conscious schlepping the thirty-pound bag past somber people bringing flowers for grandma.

He set the bag down next to his mother's grave and massaged the red streaks on his palms. "Should have brought my backpack. Or gotten the smaller bag, but how are thirty pounds barely more expensive than fifteen? Makes no sense. Anyway, don't tell Dad, or he'd freak out. Gotta go for now."

Other families might have marked the second anniversary of a loved one's passing with more decorum, but Dad wasn't big on anniversaries in general. Or anything marking the passage of time, really.

Jasper held out hope his father wouldn't forget his birthday tomorrow, but it grew slim. Dad hadn't even mentioned the anniversary of Mom's death.

A ten-minute walk later, Jasper dropped the bag on the ground to fiddle with the crooked gate to his front yard when a booming voice rang out on the other side of the street.

"Whatcha got there, Jasper? Cat food?" asked Jimmy, the stout adult son of their across-the-street neighbors. He stood on a telescopic ladder that reached into his grandma's avocado tree, trimming branches and picking fruit. Not the sharpest knife in the drawer, but a kind soul, who still lived with his parents and mainly helped out his nana next door. "Didn't know you had a cat. I'm allergic to cats."

"No worries, Jimmy, I don't have a cat. Just shopping, uh, for a friend." Jasper gathered his bag. "Save me some of your grandma's avocados, will you?"

Jimmy wagged an avocado at him before dropping it in his basket. "Will do. Come over some time!"

Waving goodbye, Jasper proceeded to the driveway side of his house.

A small hatch, left ajar, led to the crawlspace under the house, where a pitch-black feral cat he called Midnight nursed her two kittens, Panther and Shadow. He might have gotten carried away a little when he named them all.

Weeks ago, Jasper had found the adult cat under the house, barely clinging to life, or at least so he thought. Dad would have called animal control, but Jasper felt responsible and fed her milk. Days later, Panther and Shadow came into the world. Midnight already looked much stronger now. She had even let Jasper pet her once.

Better not to advertise to the neighborhood that he fed feral cats, but no way he'd abandon this little family now. Jasper filled a small bowl with water and a second one with the new cat food. He stored the bag in a large plastic cooler in the garage, already filled to the ceiling with old planters, garden supplies, and cardboard moving boxes chock-full of books and obsolete electronics.

Jasper entered the house through the side door. He took off his shoes in the hall when Dad walked out of the home office that doubled as his bedroom, himself looking like a feral cat—sunken eyes, scruffy five o'clock shadow, unkempt hair. Behind him, stacks of books piled up high in front of already fully stocked shelves of rotating inventory. Dad was a bookworm, a translator, and a principled shunner of e-books.

"Morning, Jasper."

"Morning?" Jasper checked his phone. "It's 2 p.m." Shouldn't he be the one sleeping in and crawling out of bed in the afternoon looking like the walking dead? Instead he had spent the morning cleaning the kitchen. Well, that and a couple of hours at the PlayStation, but still.

"Look at that. Gotta…" Dad tapped an imaginary watch on his naked wrist. "Gotta leave soon. Work. Excuse me." He walked into the bathroom.

"Uh-huh. Work. Today. Sunday," Jasper called after him. *Always something with you.* Dad simply couldn't stand spending any time at home with Jasper. At least not in the last two years. Jasper barely saw him, except when he moved another box to the garage. "You really have to go today?"

Dad re-emerged from the bathroom, looking refreshed. "Sundays don't mean anything to my deadlines."

"Not because it's Sunday," Jasper said. "Two years ago, today? Does that ring a bell?"

"Two years ago, what?" Dad looked puzzled, then indignant. *He had forgotten.* "Of course I remember. Two years—"

"You remember what she said, too? Because I do. Is this a normal life, Dad? I honestly couldn't tell. This is the longest I've seen you in a week, and you're about to leave again. You contribute nothing here." Despite the harsh words, Jasper's voice carried little anger. He did his best, but maybe he'd be better off on his own? At least he wouldn't have to worry about anyone else. *Be lenient with him.*

"I…" Dad seemed lost. "I'm trying to honor her wishes, Jasper." He sighed. "It's not as easy as you think. I wish I could explain—"

"Explain what, the word 'normal?' Usual, typical, expected. I'll be sixteen tomorrow, I thought we could, you know, talk about some things. As adults."

"Things, what things? Do you have questions about your body again? I thought Dr. Bender explained—"

"Dad! No, I mean, like, me getting a license and us getting a car again. And maybe you should see a doctor, or something." Jasper had tried to remote diagnose his father, but according to the internet, Dad either had depression or cancer. Annoyingly, so did everyone else. "Most days, you look like you sleep under a bridge."

"Huh," Dad grunted. "Thanks, but I'm fine."

"Well, we can talk about that too if you want," Jasper said.

"What did you say, sixteen? Tomorrow?" A smidgen of mischievousness flashed over Dad's face.

Jasper rolled his eyes. "Yah."

"Good age, if I recall correctly. So, you actually remember what Mom said to you, that night? Tell me."

Talk about being put on the spot. "That I should be lenient with you." Jasper lowered his voice to a whisper. "And that I should keep an eye on you for her."

"Huh. And what did she say to me?" Dad asked, with eyes more alert than Jasper had gotten used to lately.

"'Let him be a kid. Let him have a normal life.'" Jasper would never forget it. "She made you promise not to forget."

"And I didn't!" Dad rubbed his chin. "But it certainly seems like you're not going to be a kid for much longer. Maybe we'll have to make some changes around here." He left to get his trademark checkered blazer from his room.

Despite the balmy temperature, he always seemed cold. Jasper blamed his weight loss.

"Uh… Dinner tonight?" Dad asked when he returned.

For a second, Jasper had feared his father had forgotten all about their conversation. "You mean it?"

"It's a date. Pinky swear." Dad stretched out his right pinky finger.

"Oh-kay…" Jasper entwined it with his pinky, stunned by the throwback gesture.

Dad put on his blazer and reached for his briefcase. "Chef's choice, eight o'clock." He hesitated. "Unless you wanted to hang out with your friend, or friends."

"No, no, Clarence has got a thing early tomorrow." Jasper waved it away. "Dinner, eight o'clock."

"See you later then." Before he left, Dad smiled at him in a convincing imitation of a proud parent.

"Don't fall asleep at the desk," Jasper shouted after him, before muttering, "And don't walk into traffic, or something." He'd seen it, a couple of months ago. Dad walking across seven lanes of Santa Monica Boulevard, oblivious to the heavy traffic around him. Fool's luck he didn't get run over that day.

Jasper dismissed the memory. *Dinner with Dad. A talk between adults. Adults who pinky-swear, but hey…*

Chef's choice—today, that could only mean homemade pizza—one of Mom's specialties. Then it struck him—*it's a date*—and he found himself more nervous than he had been since his first and last real date: *Becky.*

A year older than him, great hair, even for a Becky. His debilitating anxiety as the evening went on had turned the date into such a disaster, just mentioning her name still sent his best friend Clarence into fits of laughter.

The rest of the afternoon, Jasper spent in heightened anxiety, following up an impromptu grocery shopping trip with an hour of unscheduled personal hygiene. He even threw in an afternoon shower, focusing strictly on the cleaning aspect of it, including a brave but futile attempt to tame his dirty blond mane.

He'd never surfed in his life, but with a summer tan and limited haircare, he couldn't help looking straight out of surfer casting central. According to conventional wisdom, it shouldn't hurt with the ladies, but he had yet to reap the rewards. Grandmothers seemed to find him irresistible, though.

After seven, Jasper prepped the pizza and set the table. When eight approached, everything was perfect. *Mom-perfect.* He picked an olive from the unbaked pizza and covered the gap with extra basil. A pizza stone in the oven filled the house with the aroma of family dinners long past.

Eight o'clock came and went. Understandably, Dad wasn't going to magically turn into a Swiss watch. A missed bus, a late phone call—a little delay could be anything, really.

Jasper turned off the oven and played a game on his phone, losing track of time for a while. Over an hour later, he messaged Clarence: "Cooked dinner for Dad and myself. Guess who's MIA."

Clarence didn't answer. Apparently an early night for him, before the first day of his basketball camp. Otherwise Jasper could always count on him. Clarence was the kind of friend who brought over chamomile tea and zwieback every day for a week while Jasper thought he was dying of the bird flu, and his only living parent translated toaster oven manuals from dusk till dawn. Good times.

About that living parent… Jasper called Dad's cell. Straight to voicemail. *Screw this.* He let his phone drop to the floor in anger, albeit knowing the protective case would do its job, and fired the oven back up. *Bake at 450 degrees, ten to twelve minutes.* An eternity for a hungry teen. By the time the pizza was done, Jasper had lost his appetite.

He lay down on his bed in his street clothes. Whether out of anger or sadness, the situation called for a few tears, but both of those wells ran dry. Instead, utter disappointment put his mind in a state of aimless agitation until a muffled clang from the driveway commanded his attention.

Dad?

Jasper rose with a sigh and scuffled to the hall to survey the scene through the little side door window. Midnight calmly licked her paws next to their metal watering can that she had apparently knocked from a small table in front of the garage. False alarm.

Inside, the house remained completely quiet. Jasper opened the door to Dad's office—nobody home, of course. Only little towers of neatly packed boxes full of books, ready to be moved to the garage.

Odd. Jasper could have sworn there had been stacks of books in front of the shelves earlier today. But since burglars obviously wouldn't break in just to clean house, he went back to bed, cranked up his white noise machine, and fell asleep to ocean sounds a little while later.

Chapter Two

Girl, Interrupted

"He's one of us. Hide!"

The last words Maya's mother had said to her. She'd never been more terrified in her life. *One of us.* The Bastard—Maya had no other name for him—never noticed her under the bed, but she saw enough. Too much.

Nearly a year later, Maya hid again, this time waiting. For him. Krishna said it was a sin to commit injustice, but a greater sin to tolerate injustice.

No more.

Every time her stomach rumbled, the crosshairs of her sniper scope trembled. When she had started her training regimen—young, angry, and with a belly full of bile and righteousness—she couldn't have imagined it would ever feel tedious to point a sniper rifle at a potential target, ready to snuff out a human life in a split second.

Yet here she was, still young and angry, but also restless and hungry, while the human life she wanted to end was nowhere to be seen. Krishna had surely said something about patience, too, but right now she couldn't remember what.

From her well-concealed ditch, Maya had a good view of

the vast city block. What was left of it, anyway. Less than a mile to the east, demolition crews gnawed their way through the city like a hungry caterpillar, clearing space for the new Metro Expo Line connecting Santa Monica to Downtown Los Angeles. At most, this whole area, currently surrounded by a solid fence topped with razor wire, had another couple of months before it would be devoured, too.

Maya's scope pointed at a panel on the south side, the only entry point to the entire block. After several eternities, the loose metal flap finally eased open.

A skinny middle-aged man in an antiquated checkered blazer stepped through the opening. The wrong man, again.

Maya took her finger off the trigger and rolled her eyes. *Stupid tick-tock.* He crossed the urban wasteland toward the only remaining building not a ruin, an abandoned auto body shop. The sun setting against the backdrop of graffiti-covered concrete gave his form an otherworldly sheen.

He didn't look like he belonged here, but he came every day, wearing the same suit, carrying the same beat-up leather briefcase. What was he doing in the shop for hours?

Nobody else had been inside the fenced area all week— a week that had left Maya with a month's worth of sore knees, elbows, and hipbones. The whole place still felt like a trap, but she longed for a hot shower, a warm meal, and cold, hard answers.

Decision time.

When the man reached the door, Maya put down her rifle and got up. Hopefully, Krishna had said that patience was overrated.

Just a peek. Two seconds, tops.

She tightened the black shawl around her head to match her snug, black outfit, leaving only a narrow slit for her to look through. Being naturally small and slender helped, but minimizing visual footprint was key to remaining unseen.

The moment the man stepped inside, Maya charged the seventy yards to the body shop, jumped to get a hold of the window ledge, and pulled herself up effortlessly in barely a second and change. It always gave her a rush whenever all that training paid off. She peered inside through dirty, cracked glass.

Strangely, the man had already made it to the other side of the room and stood next to a shiny metal door in front of a numeric pad. Maya had a clear view over his shoulder as he pushed buttons.

He typed so fast, she strained to keep up. This should be impossible, unless she had inadvertently transitioned back into Real Time. No, a fly in her line of sight appeared frozen in place, as if trapped in amber. Still the man casually shifted his weight to his other foot.

Another time bender like herself! He must have transitioned to Accelerated Time once he went into the garage.

The magnitude of the revelation left Maya dizzy for a moment. When she focused again, the man's shoulder blocked her view of the keypad. On and on he went mashing buttons until—

Click. The lock unbolted. The man pushed the featureless door open and stepped into a small, empty room. How could anyone spend hours there every day, especially as a time bender? This changed everything.

The door started to close on its own.

Maya dropped down and rushed to the garage door, peering inside. Walls tagged with graffiti, a couple of bolted-down work benches, a lifting platform, decrepit metal shelves covered in rust—everything left in here appeared too heavy or worthless to steal.

Only the metal door the stranger had stepped through sparkled, the day's final rays of sunlight bouncing off it.

She had left her rifle in the ditch, only wanting to take a quick peek, but the man always stayed for hours of Real Time, so she felt safe tiptoeing across the room on her thin-soled flats.

Click. The door relocked the instant she arrived in front of it. The sun had set outside, but she could still make out dozens of superficial dents, possibly sledgehammer or bullet marks, marring the shiny surface.

Somehow the numeric pad had disappeared. With a soft touch, she ran her gloved hand along the doorframe, but froze at a car noise outside. *Too close.* Someone was inside the fenced area. Now, of all times.

She turned away from the door and climbed onto the workbench to look through the broken window.

A black SUV parked in front of the garage. The loose fence panels on the south side stood open like a gate, revealing late rush hour traffic in the distance.

The driver wore black tactical gear and approached the garage on foot, moving at a time bender's pace. He appeared ageless, with thin lips, white-blond hair, and clear aviator glasses.

Maya ducked behind the wall.

It was *him*, the Bastard, her target. She'd been waiting all week, and now her sniper rifle lay outside in the dugout.

A *click* came from the door behind her.

The skinny man's leaving already? Karma mocked her, surely. A year of training, justice on her side, and now this. The trap was sprung, the jaws snapped shut around her.

Maya jumped down to the floor and lunged into the darkness behind the lifting platform, her mind racing. She looked up at the window… No, she'd be completely exposed while crawling through shards of broken glass stuck in the window frame.

The blank steel door opened, and the skinny man exited the empty room, showing no sign of having noticed her. After a few steps, he stopped to scour his briefcase.

When Maya's mark stepped into the garage, the men eyed each other for a fraction of a split-second. The Bastard moved first, drawing and firing a square-barreled Taser from a thigh holster with the rapid smoothness of experience.

What the hell? Maya battled the impulse to just step forward, unarmed, and join the fray.

Two darts flew toward the skinny man—thin wire unspooling behind them, tracing their flight paths into the thick air. Not the ideal weapon against a time bender. Anything slower than a bullet shot from close range carried the risk of being dodged.

The thin man raised his briefcase to catch the darts and charged forward. In the blink of an eye, he crossed the distance and threw an awkward punch.

Surprise flashed over the Bastard's face. He ducked just

in time and spun around in a crouching leg sweep.

The skinny man jumped and aimed an uncoordinated kick at the Bastard's head, but missed.

The two men traded attacks and parries. The bulky soldier was economical and professional in his movements, but the bookish, almost sickly-looking skinny man moved faster, as though he saw every move coming ahead of time.

Finally, the Bastard jerked his head back to dodge a right-hand feint, only to get clumsily front-kicked in the sternum with the force of a rearing warhorse. The strike hurled him all the way across the garage, pounding him into the wall beside the lifting platform. He bounced off the cinder blocks and landed in front of Maya, crumpled like a broken toy.

She stared at his face, angular and perfectly symmetrical, with a strong chin.

The skinny man stooped forward, hands braced on his legs, and gasped for air.

Would he finish the job or run away? Should she reveal herself now?

Before Maya made up her mind, the Bastard's eyes snapped open. He kipped up to his feet, no worse for wear from his crash. He drew a second, much bigger Taser-like gun from his thigh holster and pulled the trigger. With a crackling, a bright electric charge shaped like a spider web projected out of the device.

The skinny man raised his arms, but the payload hit him as fast as a bolt of lightning. He collapsed to the floor, his extremities twitching.

Maya pressed herself flat against the wall behind the

platform, not daring to breathe. Regret washed over her. She should have stayed in her ditch and picked the Bastard off from a distance. Revealing herself now would be suicide.

When the shuffling of feet had stopped, she risked a peek around the corner. The Bastard crouched on one knee, injecting something into the other man's neck that made the twitching stop. He put the empty syringe in his vest pocket, picked the unconscious man up like a sleeping child, and carried him outside.

Maya jumped onto the workbench and looked out the broken window. The Bastard dumped the other man into the back of his SUV and closed the door. This was her chance. Driving would slow his getaway down to Real Time.

She leaped toward the door, exited the garage, and raced to her ditch, not caring one bit if the Bastard saw her. Either he'd be busy driving, or he'd be too slow to catch her anyway. She jumped into the little trench she had dug herself and brought her rifle into position, trying to control her breathing at the same time.

The scope wobbled across the right and rear side of the black SUV that slowly drove off. She steadied the crosshairs on the front seats. Headrest… B-pillar… Her target?

No.

Too late. The SUV had joined traffic.

Maya closed her eyes. She had dedicated what felt like years of training to bring justice to this man. Justice that the police could never deliver to someone with his abilities. Had she blown it?

No, today was a setback, but the battle went on. Self-doubt didn't help. No more injustice. She wouldn't—

couldn't—tolerate it.

She unwrapped the black shawl that covered her face and turned it around. The other side was blood red with intricate gold embroidery. She put it on her head, ends hanging straight down, then crossed them behind her neck and brought one to the front to cover her face. After unfastening the broad strip of black cloth wrapped tightly around her upper body, she threw it over her shoulder, letting it hang down to her knees.

On her way out, she noticed something on the ground where the Bastard had parked his car: the skinny man's wallet.

Andrew Faulks, Santa Monica, California.

Maya allowed herself a smile. First, a shower and a meal, but after, she would finally get some answers. And eventually—revenge.

Chapter Three

Adulting

Jasper pressed his face deep into the pillow until his whole world became floating shapes in the darkness, faint construction noise in the distance, and the smell of hair gel residue.

Definitely awake. Damnit.

He rolled onto his back and reached for his cell. A few early morning *HBDs* on the usual social media channels, but most of the people he barely knew. He got up and checked the driveway on the off chance there'd be a big bow-wrapped Prius or something.

Nah.

Still the only driveway in the neighborhood without a car at all. Inside, Jasper searched the shrine and the office, but judging from the untouched bed, Dad hadn't come home yesterday at all.

Happy birthday to me, happy birthday to me, happy birthday, dear me-hee, happy birthday to me.

Since he was conveniently still dressed, Jasper proceeded straight to a birthday breakfast feast consisting of an energy bar chased by diet soda from a half-gallon bottle. He casually flicked the energy bar wrapper to the floor and took another swig. Seconds later, the doorbell rang. Jasper picked the wrapper back up and opened the door.

Clarence waved in greeting. "Happy birthday! You look like twelve."

"And you're dressed like twelve," Jasper said. "Did your mom pick that hideous polo?"

"I like mauve." Clarence grimaced and straightened his shirt before they bro-hugged. He set a small gift bag down on the empty dining table. "So, your dad ditched dinner yesterday?"

Jasper rolled his eyes. "Worse, he didn't even come home. After he promised, no, pinky-swore it." Jasper ignored Clarence's puzzled expression. "Told me we'd make some changes around here, all excited about my sixteenth birthday suddenly. Excuses, whatever." Jasper reached past the gift bag for the big soda bottle. "He can't even stand to be in the house with me on my birthday. It should've been him, not Mom. He was driving, after all."

"Don't say that, it wasn't his fault," Clarence said. "Did you call him yet?"

"Hell no. Not gonna call on my own birthday." Jasper shook his head and took a giant gulp of soda.

"Don't drink that, the stuff's poison. I can't even look." Clarence put a hand in front of his eyes.

Jasper burped and took another swig. "I'll take my chances."

"I'm serious. Hole in your stomach, just saying. At least eat something with that stuff," Clarence said. "Ulcers, obesity, stomach cancer—"

"I think I'm going to ask for formal emancipation,"

Jasper said.

Clarence whistled. "No way he's going to agree."

"He doesn't have to, I googled it."

"Oh, you googled it. Well in that case you're clearly all set," Clarence said. "He doesn't hit you, doesn't starve you, your grades are great for the laziest person on the planet. A judge would laugh you out of court. Being weird isn't illegal. Yet. Thankfully."

"Sure, take his side. He's only known you for two years and thought you were a burglar."

"I'm not taking his side," Clarence said. "But that's forgetful, not illegal. Although it does hurt my feelings."

"He attacked you with the fire poker."

"Maybe he's paranoid? I look intimidating."

"Not in a mauve polo you don't. And if he's paranoid, why does he always leave the front door unlocked?"

Clarence shrugged. "It's a safe neighborhood."

"He asked me if Mom's in the bathroom the other day. It's been two years." Jasper could keep the examples coming all day. "He's lost it."

"Dementia then? Alzheimer's or something?"

"He translates a whole book like that." Jasper snapped his fingers. "The next day, he thinks I'm in fourth grade."

"Maybe he saw you naked," Clarence deadpanned. Jasper suffered from a rare skin condition that caused him to be completely hairless from the chin down. Some adults paid good money for hair removal like that, but locker rooms full of teen boys hadn't been as appreciative. Clarence had put the kibosh on the teasing, but unfortunately exempted himself from that.

"You suck." Jasper flicked the energy bar wrapper at Clarence, who feigned being knocked from his chair.

"Open your present." Clarence pushed the gift bag toward Jasper.

It was a body hair grooming kit for men. Jasper punched Clarence in the arm but had to laugh for the first time all morning.

An alarm went off on Clarence's cell phone. "Gotta go, don't want to be late to orientation."

Clarence's father had signed him up for this basketball day camp. Total waste of a perfectly good summer starting on day one. Clarence didn't even like basketball, but apparently being a six-foot-six black guy at a mostly-white school raised certain expectations, as did Clarence's father. Jasper had given up trying to get Clarence to push back.

They bro-hugged farewell.

With emancipation hearings practically looming, Jasper had some seriously exciting adulting to do, like shopping for tin foil, toilet paper, and headache pills, so off to Target it was.

He locked the front door behind him and, on his way across the yard, gave the ladder up to the treehouse in their big oak tree a kick in passing. Dad had built it ages ago. Jasper immediately felt a pang of regret but couldn't well apologize to a ladder.

At the front gate, he composed himself and turned around to look at the treehouse.

A shadow flickered in the treehouse window. Someone up there, watching him?

"Dad?"

Jasper walked back and looked straight up the ladder. *This is stupid, why would anybody be in my treehouse?* He put his backpack down and climbed the ladder, making it a point not to hesitate when he reached the top.

"Hello?"

Nobody there, of course.

Good. But chasing shadows in a kiddie treehouse didn't seem very mature, so Jasper climbed back down to return to his adulting ways.

The Target run emulated the boredom of adulthood perfectly. He followed it up by overspending horribly for a blended iced coffee. Okay, so maybe Dad wouldn't have ordered the venti peppermint mocha Frappuccino with extra whipped cream, but his birthday warranted the indulgence.

Clarence had been harshing his mellow by periodically texting to encourage him to phone his dad. Even more annoyingly, he had a point.

Jasper finally made the call. Straight to voicemail. Dad's proper office then. "Andrew Faulks, suite 721, please."

The West L.A. high-rise contained a cluster of one-person offices with changing receptionists at the switchboard. Naturally, the call bounced back. Visions of his dad's lifeless body slumped over the desk crept into Jasper's head. "Could you knock on the door please, it's important."

A little while later, the receptionist returned to the line. "I'm sorry, Mr. Faulks is not in his office."

Whatever. Jasper hung up and texted Clarence but didn't

like the response: "You should probably call the police."

Maybe he should rather show everyone he could take care of himself? He doubted the police would let him live alone.

"And the FBI!" Jasper texted back. Clarence didn't answer, so he added, "Just kidding." Sometimes, Clarence could be a bit literal-minded.

When Jasper returned home, the front door was unlocked, and—as much as he was committed to this whole adulting business—he couldn't help being a tiny bit relieved that his dad was back after all. He dropped his backpack and took off his shoes.

"Dad?"

No answer.

The hardwood floor squeaked somewhere in the back of the house. His parents' bedroom?

Jasper's heart beat in his throat. He grabbed the big iron fire poker from the hook next to the fireplace and marched through the living room and the hall, past his room, to the master bedroom. Having only socks on his feet made him feel strangely vulnerable.

Don't be stupid, nobody's going to stomp on your pinky toe.

"Dad?" Jasper opened the door, but the shrine looked untouched as always.

He returned to the hall and peered into the study.

Niente, nada. The house was completely still. Had he really locked the door on his way out? He felt foolish carrying a fire poker around the house. He started to bring it back to the living room but paused when something caught his eye—the cuff of a white dress shirt sticking out from the door of his parents' closet.

Clutching the poker with his right hand, he used the left to fish his cell phone out of his right pocket. Still staring at the shirt stuck in the closet door, he called Clarence.

"Yo, Cee, got a situation over here," Jasper whispered. "There's a shirt sleeve stuck in the door of my parents' closet."

A moment of silence passed.

"Is that some kind of code?" Clarence asked in his deep baritone.

"There might be someone hiding in my parents' closet. I need some backup before I check."

"Dude, call the police. Right. Now."

"No, no, no…" Jasper strained to keep on whispering. "I don't know if someone's here, and if there is, it might be my dad. I'm not even sure there's anyone in the closet, but there's a shirt stuck in the door, and there's never anyone in this room, like, ever, so—"

"Are you high?"

"I'm looking at the shirt right now, it's definitely here."

"It could have been there for weeks. When did you last look into the closet?" Clarence asked.

"Not in forever, you never know who might be coming out of it."

"Hilarious. I'm hanging up."

"No, wait, I really need you," Jasper said. "Please?"

Clarence sighed. "Okay, I'm gonna see if I can get away a little early. Don't do anything stupid."

"Awesome. Front door's open. Bring a weapon." Jasper hung up.

Chapter Four

In the Closet

"An aluminum practice bat? Are you kidding me?" Jasper's voice almost cracked.

"First of all, it should be alu-MIN-ium, not a-LUMI-num, and second, I had to pick something from your neighbor's front yard. The other option was a pink tricycle. And third, Jay, what the hell?" Clarence sounded a good deal less mellow than usual.

"Keep your voice down."

Clarence didn't. "You can't be crazy enough to think there's actually someone in your closet, and if so, I hope you wouldn't be crouching in front of the room with a fire poker."

"My parents' bedroom's been a shrine for two years. Dad lives in the study. Now look at it." Jasper pointed at the shirtsleeve stuck in the closet door.

Clarence walked into the bedroom, his large frame dwarfing the furniture. Jasper abandoned his tense half-squat in the hall, stretched his legs, and followed his friend in.

"Could've been here for months," Clarence said and tugged at the shirtsleeve before reaching for the closet door.

"No, wait…" Jasper raised the fire poker with alarm, but

Clarence matter-of-factly opened the door. Dress shirts swayed on their hangers inside the closet.

A draft from the closet gently brushed Jasper's underarm. "Did you feel that?"

"Feel what?" Clarence asked. "Look, wow, it's a closet. Get some quality shut-eye, and if your dad's not back tomorrow, please call the police, or I will." He turned to leave.

"Hold on." Jasper pointed to the closet floor. There was a loose flap in the white carpet. He pulled it aside to find an in-floor safe underneath. "See."

"See what? It's a safe. My parents have one too," said Clarence.

"That's what they were looking for."

"They? There's not even *one* person in the closet."

"Ha!" Jasper said triumphantly.

"You're a dick."

"No, look." Jasper pointed at a footprint in dust on the snow-white carpet.

"Probably an old one of yours."

Jasper stepped beside the print, his foot at least three sizes bigger.

"Do you really think this has been here for years?" Jasper asked, then brushed the carpet with his hand. The dirt came off easily.

"Now what?" Clarence asked.

"We should open the safe."

"What? Why? How would you even do that? No, we should call the police."

"Nothing was stolen. And I can't even prove anyone was

in here. They're not going to take fingerprints and put a guard at the door like in the movies, but I'm sure they'd ask a lot of questions about my father."

"They should. You should've called them already."

"I'm not going into foster care or something, period," Jasper said. "I have to show them that I can do it alone."

"What are you talking about? Show who?" Clarence asked. "There's nobody here."

"You're right, I'm all alone, Captain Obvious. Show myself then, for God's sake. Now you're the dick."

Clarence sighed. "Don't make me regret this."

A short while later, Jasper turned the safe handle and the lock opened with a satisfying *click*. 071869: Mom's birth month, Jasper's birthday, and Dad's birth year. Pathetic, really. He'd have to talk to his dad about password security.

He laid the contents out on the carpet. Jasper didn't know what he was expecting. He'd never given any thought to what people kept in their safes. Their eighty-five-year-old neighbor probably had the same things in there. No need to worry. Or get excited, for that matter.

But then why did he feel a black hole in his stomach threatening to swallow him from the inside?

What was really all that special about:

> — *A handgun (Glock, 9mm), loaded, plus two spare magazines, loaded?*
> — *A thick envelope of cash, around $8000?*

— *An envelope with two passports, his and his dad's?*
— *A locked aluminum case, about half as big as a standard briefcase?*

They all seemed like perfectly reasonable things to keep in your safe, if not for the handwritten note on top of them. The note read:

Jasper,

I hope I was able to tell you what you needed to know.

Dad

P.S. Remember to water the bougainvillea.

Jasper and Clarence sat at the dining room table, eating yesterday's pizza that a hungry Jasper had nuked in the microwave.

"What do you think I needed to know? It's gotta be really important. He said the same thing after the accident, when we talked to Mom, before they took her into the OR. 'There's things he needs to know,' he said." Jasper held up his father's note from the safe. "I wonder when he wrote it. The bougainvillea died last summer."

"No idea," Clarence said. "I knew I was going to regret this. Maybe not as much as eating this microwaved artery clog, but still. We shouldn't have opened the safe." He dabbed his slice of pizza with a paper napkin, took a hesitant bite, and washed it down with some unsweetened iced tea Jasper kept around just for him.

"Stop complaining, it's not that greasy. You can go back to your kale smoothies later." Jasper took a swig from his soda and picked up the locked case. "Maybe what I needed to know was how to open this box?"

"Then he would've told you where to find the key. But he didn't even tell you about the safe, so he didn't want you to find the gun or the money, let alone open a locked box in a locked safe. That's kind of sending a message right there, don't you think?"

"If he's dead, it's all mine anyway." Jasper stuffed his face with a whole slice of rolled-up, mushy pizza. "We haf a thledgehammer in the garash."

"This is a Halliburton case, just forget about it. Contrary to popular belief, people rarely just leave the house and go die somewhere. You should worry about putting all of this back the way it was before your father comes back," Clarence said between nibbles.

"He probably told someone about the safe and the box, though, right? What's the point, otherwise, if no one finds it when you're gone?"

"He doesn't have any friends, you said it yourself."

Yes, a depressing thought. Maybe he should just put it all back and go to the police after all. Jasper set the case back on the table and looked around. If his dad didn't come back—missing, dead, whatever—this would remain his house. It had not felt like home in a while.

"Uncle Martin!"

"What?"

"Uncle Martin." Jasper got up and got his parents' wedding picture from the fireplace mantel. It showed them smiling with his dad's best man, and best friend, Uncle Martin. Jasper had grown up calling him that, even if he wasn't a blood relative. "If anyone, Dad told him about this stuff. Maybe even what I needed to know."

"The crazy guy?" Clarence put down the pizza crust and vigorously wiped his fingers with another napkin.

"We should ask him. Let's take this stuff and drive up there."

"You know I can't take you in my car. Plus the gun? No, no, no. No way, absolutely no way. I gotta be home by eight anyway. My parents—"

Chapter Five

Follow Your Passion

Maya had been watching the front door for more than an hour before the boys finally stepped outside and headed out on foot, leaving the tall kid's car behind.

She had a date with a ditch she was already late for, but curiosity got the better of her. The day had taken an unexpected turn. She shadowed the two boys on foot, keeping a respectful distance, but not really bothering with proper pursuit tactics. No need. They bickered non-stop, completely unaware of their surroundings. *What a life.* Had she ever been like that?

The unlikely duo cut through an empty back alley. She could probably pick Faulks junior's backpack right here in broad daylight. When she peeked through the window during her stakeout, they sat at the dining table eating pizza, studying items she suspected they had found in the safe.

No, another day would give her a better opportunity. Despite her time bending and the boy's obliviousness, today had brought two close shaves already, first in the treehouse, then in the closet. For a bit of a klutz, the boy had decent instincts.

Whatever had been in the safe was her best bet to shed some light on the auto body shop situation yesterday. Two time benders fighting? They said the enemy of your enemy is your friend, but the Bastard had abducted this Andrew Faulks, and nothing in the house hinted at his time bending skills, let alone some great criminal conspiracy. Apart from a quantity of books no human could read in a single lifetime, but some people were collectors more than readers.

Faulks' son appeared to be a standard issue surfer kid. From the way he hadn't even suspected time bending during her narrow escapes, she felt certain he wasn't only a tick-tock but remained completely ignorant of his father's abilities.

The boys reached a bus stop, continuing to argue over food. Something about kale.

A couple of minutes later, they boarded a big blue bus with large white letters proclaiming it to be what everyone could see it was—a "Big Blue Bus." Was this art? People here had a strange sense of humor. She was still a Midwestern girl at heart.

The bus headed east, away from her next destination. Pursuit would mean missing the time window when the Bastard had shown up yesterday, so Maya remained behind to resume her original plan.

She transitioned to Accelerated Time and hurried back to the scooter parked around the corner from Faulks' house. A twenty-minute motorbike ride followed by a stealthy approach on foot later, she settled back into her dugout with view of the auto body shop.

It had been a bit of a gamble, to spend most of the day trying to figure out how Faulks fit into the picture after her target had shown up for the first time yesterday. She had put up a camouflaged motion sensor on the dirt road to the shop, but it had its limits. A possum would trigger it same as her mark. There hadn't been any alerts in her absence, but now she'd gone into attack mode again, sniper scope pointed at the gates.

Time passed, and her thoughts circled back to yesterday—the Bastard. He had been here, at the trap she'd been sure had been set for her, but it certainly didn't seem like he had even considered she might be around. Faulks was his target, and he got his man in the end, despite the struggle.

The gun that put Faulks down had also killed her parents, or at least debilitated them, she had no doubts about that. There had been distinct circular electric burns across both their torsos.

But what was it—a lightning gun? Electrobeam projection? With a wide area of instant impact, this electrified spiderweb was the perfect weapon against time benders.

She kept her scope pointed at the entry point to the fenced-off block. Hours passed, yet Maya's mind kept wandering. Why would the Bastard show up again if he had achieved his objective, and she wasn't even on his radar? Why wouldn't he expect her, anyway? After killing her parents, the Bastard had left a note, trying to lure her here, to Los Angeles, to this abandoned auto body shop.

Maya's eyelids grew heavier as the sun went down. After she caught herself momentarily nodding off, she packed up for the night and retreated to her safe house.

Somehow this strange place was key, and she didn't like to leave it unwatched, but even time benders had to get a good night's sleep. Especially since she'd now have to make time to pursue the connection to Faulks, too. But more importantly, she couldn't, *wouldn't*, lose sight of justice. The Bastard still had to die.

Chapter Six

Crazy Train

Almost two hours after they had left the house, Jasper and Clarence found themselves walking up a steep hill to Uncle Martin's house in Echo Park.

Clarence hadn't budged on the driving, so they took the bus. The ride lasted forever, and the seats smelled of pee. Jasper answered Clarence's accusatory stare with a raised eyebrow of innocence. Not only was he innocent of the olfactory assault, *he* would have taken the car, given a choice.

The gun had stayed at home. Clarence made a convincing case that it getting stolen beat anything that might come from taking it on the bus or parading it around Echo Park. He could be very persuasive in these matters.

At least he had tagged along at all, telling his parents a rare lie about dinner with his basketball buddies. They needed a cover story for Clarence's parents, the Wrights, who didn't like them spending too much time together.

After Jasper had filled Clarence in on some of Uncle Martin's quirks, like never wearing anything but sweatpants regardless of the occasion, he suspected Clarence regretted his decision already.

"And he never answers the door?"

"Nope," Jasper said, "it's a duplex. Any time someone visits, he just pretends he's living in the other half. He's erased his name from public records too."

"Sure, good luck with that in this century."

"Dad used to tease him about this stuff, but they've always been best friends. At least until my mom died. Uncle Martin didn't come to the funeral."

"Did you ever see him again?" Clarence asked between deep breaths as the climb became steeper.

"Once. Dad took me. They just kind of scowled at each other. I went to the bathroom, and we pretty much left right after. Uncle Martin gave my dad a gift, but he never opened it. It was all very awkward."

"So why do you think your father would've told him about the safe? Or that he'd help you now?" Clarence asked.

"Because he's the closest thing to family I have left."

"Then we better hope this doesn't apply to us." Clarence pointed at a single sign on the fence around a nondescript, slightly shabby duplex: "Keep out."

From the roofs here, they had a view of Dodger Stadium in the distance, but the neighborhood couldn't have been less glamorous.

Jasper rattled a locked gate that didn't have an intercom or doorbell. "Uncle Martin? It's Jasper."

Nobody answered.

"Maybe your uncle doesn't live here anymore."

With all blinds closed, the property appeared abandoned.

"No, this is how it always looks," Jasper said. "Uncle Martin!"

Still nothing.

"Let's climb the fence."

"Here's an idea: let's not," Clarence said.

"After an hour-and-a-half in the pee bus, you don't think I'm turning around now, do you?" Jasper punched Clarence in the shoulder. "Come on, give me a leg-up."

A minute later, they knocked on the first front door, but still didn't get an answer. Jasper walked from one barred window to the next, knocking on them in passing.

"Uncle Martin? Are you there?"

"Hello!" Clarence joined in and knocked on a bathroom window too high for Jasper to reach. "Mister Higgs, are you home?"

"Uncle Martin, it's about Dad. Andy. Your friend. He's missing."

Maybe the duplex stood empty after all. Should he stage a mock emergency to draw Uncle Martin out? Pretend someone attacked him? Clarence would probably veto that. Still, one more try.

"He's missing, my dad's missing, and we found something…" Jasper had reached the second door. "We found something in the safe."

The blinds of the window next to the second door snapped apart. Bright lights flashed on and backlit Uncle Martin behind metal window bars, his trademark stubbly beard and oily black hair barely discernible.

"What did you find? Did Greasley tell you to come here?" he asked.

Jasper's mind went blank. What did he find? And what's a Greasley?

The dark figure of Uncle Martin loomed over him, looking down expectantly. He got the unsettling feeling that the bars over the windows had been intended to keep someone inside rather than outside.

"I don't know a Greasley. Nobody told me to come here," Jasper said, composing himself. "We found a locked metal box. And money, passports. I need your help—"

"Locked box, eh? Don't open it. Put it back. Wait for your dad. He's…" Uncle Martin grimaced. "You know, a loner. Okay, bye then." The blinds twisted shut. A split-second later, the light inside went out again.

"Wait, how do you know? Dad didn't come home yesterday. We came a long way." Jasper took off his backpack and pulled out the aluminum box. "We brought the box. There was a message from Dad. That I needed to know something. He said the same thing right before Mom died. Maybe you—"

"Jay, forget about it, he doesn't seem well." Clarence put a hand on Jasper's arm. "Let's go home, sleep on it, figure it out tomorrow, what do you say?"

Home. Sleep. That sounded excellent. It had been a draining day, but Jasper needed answers. "We also found a gun. With the box and the cash and the passports. A gun."

The light inside went on again, and Uncle Martin opened the blinds. "Glock? Nine millimeter?"

"Er… yes—"

"I gave that to him. He should be carrying that. It's not safe out there. Idiot." Uncle Martin adjusted his glasses and examined Jasper from head to toe with dark brown eyes that seemed more alive than before. "You should be carrying that. Are you?"

Jasper shook his head.

"Idiot."

"See, I told you we should've brought it," Jasper said to Clarence.

"You're going to take advice from him?" Clarence pointed to the man in his stained white t-shirt behind thick metal bars.

Uncle Martin seemed to notice Clarence for the first time. "You brought a friend. Okay, so why don't you and Hakeem the Dream here bugger off then. I have, uh, things to do. Yes. Tell your dad I-told-you-so when he comes back. Bye." With that, the blinds closed for a second time.

"But what is it that I needed to know?" Jasper asked.

His question remained unanswered.

"Hakeem the Dream? Because I'm, like, black and tall? Ha ha, that's real funny. What decade does he think this is anyway?" Clarence said after a while.

The kids didn't talk much on their way back. When they arrived at Jasper's house, Jasper assured Clarence he was going to be okay and sent him home. He didn't look forward to being alone, but still preferred it over dealing with the Wrights tonight. That thought Jasper kept to himself.

Before going to bed, Jasper didn't put his new treasures back into the safe. The envelopes went under his pillow, the box under the bed, and the loaded gun on his nightstand. Despite being dead tired, he twisted and turned, unable to sleep, until he remembered he had forgotten to feed the cats.

He went outside, where Midnight greeted him by coiling around his legs for the first time. *Happy birthday to me.* He petted her for a while, then left food and water in the crawlspace for the kittens. Back in bed, a deep sleep took him seconds after he turned off the light.

Chapter Seven

The Box

Jasper opened his eyes and saw green. His cheek chafed against something other than his pillow, something scratchier and a bit… moldy?

He sat up straight and looked around. Dozens of bills from the envelope, adorned with fresh drool stains, were spread out on his pillow and mattress.

The smell still filled his nose and coated his tongue. *Yuck.* He tried to work up some spit, but his mouth was parched. Blindly reaching for the water bottle next to his bed, he almost knocked over his nightstand. The gun fell to the floor with a loud clang.

Thank God Dad didn't come back and see me like this.

He set the gun back on the nightstand, stuffed the money into the envelope vowing not to leave it under the pillow ever again, and put the aluminum case on the bed.

He'd get to the bottom of that box today, one way or the other. Uncle Martin warned not to open it, but Clarence had been right, why would anyone listen to Uncle Martin?

He suppressed the thought that not opening the box was the one thing Clarence and Uncle Martin agreed on.

Anyway, he still needed the key.

Two hours later, he had opened and emptied all drawers, shoe boxes, piggy banks, and wallets he could find. No keys.

Next step: picking the lock.

After three more hours, his fingers hurt from prodding the box's lock with paper clips, sewing needles, and screw drivers, and if he had to read one more website on lock picking, he'd smash his laptop with the box and set both on fire.

The hard way then.

Yet two more hours later, the box was pockmarked by a small hammer, dented from a bigger hammer, unharmed by a fall from the tree house, and completely unaffected by slamming the garage door on it. Multiple times. A tactic destined to fail, but Jasper did feel a little better after trying.

He sat on the garage floor, the box opposite him, wedged between the door and the concrete floor.

With a groan, he lay down and stared at the exposed wood beams under the roof, taking inventory of his life. Mom dead, Dad missing, his only ersatz relative crazy. *So far, so good.* Drooling over hundred-dollar bills in your sleep and spending seven hours trying and failing to open a box you found in your missing father's safe? *Room for improvement.*

He read his dad's note again. "I hope I was able to tell you what you needed to know."

What did I need to know? How could you leave me hanging like this after what happened to Mom?

The car wreck had been horrible, yet somehow Dad didn't have a scratch on him. Over time, Jasper still felt he hadn't lost one parent, but two.

He looked at his father's handwriting. Tidy, without any indication how long ago it had been written.

"P.S.: Remember to water the bougainvillea."

A couple of years ago, they had planted a bougainvillea in a three-foot-high pot on the side of the house where the driveway led to the garage, hoping it would climb over the trellis and shade the driveway. Instead, it had died a few months after the accident, right before Jasper took over the housekeeping duties.

Frustrated, Dad had thrown out the plant and put the expensive Aztec-patterned pot here in the garage.

Jasper sat up and looked around. Flanked by ceiling-high stacks of Dad's books, the pots sat in the corner of the garage, the biggest at the bottom. He opened the garage door fully to let more light in and nearly threw out his back trying to get to the bottom of the pile, the glazed bougainvillea pot, as fast as he could.

Jasper didn't know what to expect, but there had to be something in that freaking pot at the bottom. Balance.

God, fate, the universe, the Force, the great spaghetti monster, they all owed him something in that damn pot down there. Something he needed to know.

Please…

He lifted the final pot. Empty.

The second-biggest pot still raised high above his head, he let out a primal scream and threw it against the garage wall. In his rage, time seemed to stand still when the pot burst into a thousand pieces that appeared beautifully suspended in mid-air before showering the garage floor.

"Why me?" he wanted to shout from the top of his lungs,

but the words didn't come out.

He slumped to his knees in front of the giant flowerpot, rested his head on the rim, and finally found a few silent tears from wells he thought had dried up long ago.

A little while later, he lifted his head and wiped his eyes. The teary veil gone, he looked straight down into the drain hole in the middle of the pot. *Uneven edges.*

Jasper reached down into the hole. The surface felt smooth, yet sharp-edged underneath in one spot. He pried an object from the wall of the drain hole.

A small key, wrapped in clear tape.

Jasper looked on as Clarence parked his Prius in the Wrights' driveway. He sat on the steps to the impressive front porch of the Wright House, as he called it to Clarence's chagrin, and had been waiting for less than five minutes. A giant purple bougainvillea in full bloom provided him with shade in the afternoon sun.

Between his legs stood his backpack with all its precious cargo—the box, the money, the passports, the gun.

Months ago, when he first got it, Jasper had given Clarence hell for the Prius, but of course, he was more than a little envious. Unfortunately, driving laws didn't allow Clarence to take Jasper with him without an adult in the car, and Clarence took most laws seriously.

"I thought you might be interested in what I found," Jasper said while Clarence locked the car.

"I know what it's not. You were wearing the same rags yesterday." Clarence fanned himself with his hand in mock disgust.

"No. And you're an ass."

"Guilty as charged. So what is it? Another mystery box?"

"Better." Jasper held up the key.

Clarence looked at his watch. "C'mon in, we don't have that long."

The Wright's house was gigantic, a real out-of-place McMansion with five bedrooms, a pool, a pool house, and endless smooth surfaces. This being Santa Monica, it must have cost a fortune. The bathroom gleamed so bright it almost required sunglasses. From the tiles to the windows to the floors to the appliances to the pool, everything shone.

Except Clarence's room, which looked like the inside of one of his old PCs—dark and dusty, with lots of electronic parts of unclear origin and purpose, interconnected by more cables than you'd find in a space shuttle. He had no posters of basketball players on the wall.

"Where did you find the key?" Clarence asked.

"'Remember to water the bougainvillea.' Found it in the pot."

"Obviously. What next? The 'X' marks the spot?" Clarence chuckled at this own joke. "What's in it?"

"Haven't opened it yet. I thought we should do it together."

"But is it the right key?"

Jasper's face got hot all of a sudden. "What else would it be?" He opened his backpack and got out the box.

"Are you kidding me?" Clarence asked. "You brought

the gun?" He jumped up from his chair.

"I didn't think it would be—"

"Damn right you didn't think! Do you have the slightest idea what's gonna happen if my parents see it? They're gonna call the cops. They'll never let me near you again. And what are the cops going to do with you? Underage, carrying a gun, dad's missing?"

Jasper didn't have an answer. It wasn't like he volunteered for his present situation.

Eyes closed, Clarence took meditative breaths.

"I'm sorry. I shouldn't have brought the gun," Jasper said.

Clarence exhaled slowly. "All right." He opened his eyes, shrugging off a dark cloud. "Sorry for yelling. You're in a tough spot. Let's just make ab-so-lutely sure my parents don't find out." He sat back down.

"If you don't tell 'em, I won't." Jasper gave him a cheesy wink.

His friend reached for the box and softly ran his fingers over the scratches and indentations. "This looks like it survived a mine explosion. What the hell happened?"

"Long story. I didn't exactly find the key first thing in the morning." Jasper took the box back and pushed the small key into the lock. Tape residue made it difficult, but with a bit of firm pressure it slid in. He turned it—

"Open sesame." A moment of elation, then the black hole in Jasper's stomach stirred once more. Again, he took perfectly ordinary looking objects from a hidden place and laid them out:

— An old notebook.
— A large folded blueprint.
— A list of student names and UCLA college records.
— Three square black sheets of plastic with holes in the middle and some manner of shiny grey-brown material visible in a narrow slit.
— Seven old photographs.

Clarence leafed through the notebook. "This is from before you were born. Here, on the first page, 1990. Kinda looks like a diary."

His father's handwriting, definitely, but only the first part had diary entries, apparently written when he still went to college. "Prof. Kruzman got upset that we didn't finish our assignment over the weekend…" The rest of the pages had tables of values that didn't make any particular sense to Jasper, annotated schematics of electric circuit boards, and complex wire diagrams in mixed handwriting.

"This isn't any better," Jasper said, "it's even older." He pointed to the header of one of the lists of student names. "Independent Studies 176, Fall 1989. Students: Banerjee, Medha; Faulks, Andrew…"

"That's your dad," Clarence pointed out helpfully.

"Must be his college records, but look here: Higgs, Martin."

"*Uncle* Martin, great." Clarence's voice couldn't have been flatter.

"Yep. And here, Renée Durant, that's my mom's maiden name."

"I didn't know they went to college together. Why is her

name crossed out?"

"No idea." Jasper put down the papers and picked up one of the strange black plastic squares. "What are these?"

"Five-and-a-quarter inch floppy disks. Used for data storage in the eighties. Every PC had a drive for these."

"Do you have one?"

"Yeah, right over there behind the VCR." He pointed in the general direction of where a gnarl of cables congregated.

"Oh, cool," Jasper said.

Clarence rolled his eyes. "I'm kidding. Nobody has one anymore. And even if we had, like, a big-ass external reader for that, we'd probably need a program we don't have to access the data."

Jasper shrugged. Undoubtedly, Clarence's online buddies would come to the rescue if that really happened. Tech nerds loved challenges like that. He turned his attention to the blueprint. "Just a bunch of rooms or a cluster of bungalows or something. Certainly not our house."

Clarence sat on his bed nearby to take a closer look. "Doesn't look like a house at all, more like a tunnel. These stairs go down, not up."

The blueprint had some small scribbling in the bottom right corner. Jasper squinted. "The Passage of Time. Fourth draft by M. Higgs."

"Is he an architect?"

"I don't even know what he is," Jasper said, "but I'm gonna have to pay him another visit. Maybe we just didn't ask the right questions."

"He's not an oracle, he's—"

A knock on the door as it opened interrupted Clarence

before he could finish his sentence. He stood up straight so fast the rebounding mattress nearly catapulted Jasper from the bed. "Mom! A little privacy!"

Clarence's mother was in her early forties, with toned, muscular arms and less warmth in her voice than Siri. She spoke as if Jasper wasn't even there: "Your father will be home in ten minutes."

Jasper could tell she tried not to raise her eyebrows and nod in his direction, but he didn't need the hint. "Hi, Mrs. Wright. I was about to leave anyway."

He got up and tickled Clarence right under his armpit.

"Jay? What the hell?" Clarence blushed and swatted away Jasper's hands.

"Oh." Jasper laughed. "Don't be like that now." He turned to Mrs. Wright and folded the papers they'd been looking at. "Can't be too careful with the homework." He flashed a goofy smile hoping she didn't remember it was summer break. "Let me see if I have enough space in my backpack—"

"Be quick about it," Mrs. Wright said and left.

"What are you thinking?" Clarence straightened his powder blue polo.

"I'm just trying to have some fun with it, excuse me. I'm the one they can't look in the eye." Jasper handed Clarence the floppy disks. "Keep these. I'll try to find something useful in the notebook."

"If this doesn't lead anywhere, you'll go to the cops, promise me."

"I promise," Jasper said, fully aware he hadn't specified how long he intended to follow his leads. Something out there he needed to know, and he didn't plan to give up before he found out what.

When he left, Jasper punched Clarence in the ribs a little harder than strictly necessary. In a good-natured, boys-will-be-boys way, of course.

Chapter Eight

First Contact

By the time Jasper got off the bus, a California sunset had painted the sky a reddish purple so beautiful that even the locals couldn't help but notice. All but one.

Jasper mechanically put one foot in front of the other, unable to think of anything but the contents of a certain plain aluminum box.

There had been the requisite family pictures, but also others from his dad's university days. Group pictures. Those, plus college records, lists, the strange blueprint—it didn't feel like a time capsule or the yearbook you keep to laugh at your hairdo.

All of it had been important to his father, beyond fond remembrances, but could it be relevant to his disappearance? Or had he simply walked off a bridge somewhere? Checked into a motel on the freeway to Vegas and forgot his identity?

Obviously, sarcasm wouldn't help find him, but it wouldn't hurt either. Jasper had already tried disappointment, tears, and indifference, all equally useless. No choice but to keep going, even if the backpack just got a little heavier.

He also still had the damn gun to deal with. Uncle Martin should be able to make sense of it all. Too bad he couldn't make sense of a weather forecast for SoCal in August.

Jasper turned a corner into a cul-de-sac, leaving behind the sidewalks and the three people who bothered to walk more than from the front door to their hybrid SUVs. At the end of the cul-de-sac, he cut through an unfenced backyard to his street.

A figure passed in the corner of his eye. Or did it? More an outline of someone. He turned around—a deserted street.

Just what he needed, hallucinations. *Does your family have a history of mental illness?* Yessiree, completely crazy, the whole lot. Well, at least the few still alive. No, sarcasm didn't help, but it didn't hurt either.

Something tugged on his backpack. He whirled around, the world a vivid blur.

A small, slender figure, wrapped in black from head to toe, stood behind him, arms raised to grab his backpack, which had come loose during his spinning maneuver.

Instinctively, he reached for his bag and tore at it.

The other person shied away, but as soon as Jasper had pulled it free, the thief reached for it again, faster than the eye could see, starting a tug-of-war.

Jasper had an advantage in height and build, but simply couldn't yank the backpack free. They spun in circles, Jasper staring into his dance partner's eyes, dark and bottomless.

The outside world became a CG background to a blockbuster superhero fight, sharp and colorful, but somehow appearing unreal. Only instead of leaping from building to building, they struggled for a ratty JanSport backpack in the middle of a residential cul-de-sac.

"Let go," Jasper yelled and took one hand off the bag to flick an awkward punch at his enemy's face.

Way too slow.

The answer arrived fast, a palm strike aimed at his ribs. He couldn't get out of the way without letting go of his bag—an unacceptable price.

The impact made a thumping sound straight out of an old kung fu movie, but he didn't fly back thirty feet on a cable rig. Instead, he dropped to one knee and gasped for breath as searing pain shot through his chest.

The outside world came crashing back and confused his senses. Somehow, he still held on to something, had his arm wrapped around the shoulder strap of his backpack. But nobody tried to take it away anymore. Instead, a shimmering black figure reached into the open main pocket.

"No!"

Jasper lunged, swinging his fists wildly, and wrenched at the backpack. The gun, the documents, the box—everything—spilled on the pavement. The figure grabbed his father's diary with incredible speed while he dove after the box in desperation.

His adversary slowed and came into focus, standing out sharply from the background. The mask was just black cloth wrapped around the face, only exposing big dark brown eyes, but a loose piece draped over the right ear.

The box tucked under his arm, Jasper reached for the flap and tore off the fabric. The inside had a colorful pattern.

A girl, maybe a couple of years older than him, with dark skin and long black hair tightly pinned to her head to fit under the hood. On her forehead, she wore a black dot.

She frantically tried to replace her face cover.

Jasper used the distraction to scan the ground for the gun. He had difficulty seeing things as clearly as moments ago, but he did spot the weapon a couple of steps away.

Go.

Two steps, take a knee, pick up the gun, turn—

"Uhhhh." The girl sounded disgusted rather than worried and disappeared from sight as if she'd been edited out of a film.

Instinctively, his eyes tried to latch onto any movement. Right when he thought he'd lost his mind and imagined the girl, his gaze locked onto her thirty feet away near a big ficus tree at the end of the cul-de-sac.

"What the hell?"

Instead of leaving, obviously within her power, the girl hesitated, still in shooting range, but Jasper couldn't have hit her from there. Or anywhere, most likely.

This was no ordinary robbery.

"Where's my father? What have you done?"

"I haven't done anything to your father," she answered.

"Liar! What do you want? Where's my dad?"

"I don't know where he is, but he was taken."

"I don't understand. Taken by who? Does it have anything to do with all this?" Jasper pointed at his backpack on the street.

She paused for a moment before continuing a little quieter: "Look, I'm not your enemy, but I can't explain. You wouldn't understand. Everything you know is useless."

"Where is my father? What's going on here, tell me, or

I'll shoot." It felt like something people said in these situations, but she didn't seem terribly alarmed.

"I'm going to borrow this for a while." She held up his father's notebook. "Next time you threaten to shoot someone, make sure the safety is off." She pointed at the gun he awkwardly aimed in her general direction.

He looked down and didn't see a safety. Did this thing even have one?

When he looked up again, the girl had vanished.

Jasper felt unbelievably alive. Excited, confused, worried, a little afraid, but so alive, despite his chest pain. For a smallish girl, she packed a hell of a punch.

He realized he still held the gun and stuffed it in his backpack before gathering the rest of his belongings. Everything was accounted for, except the diary.

The nearest houses all had their blinds and curtains closed. Jasper wondered how long the whole fracas had lasted. It felt like forever but couldn't have been more than a couple of minutes. Good thing nobody had seen them or called the police.

Really, what would he say? Granted, she had attacked him, but he had a gun, a lot of cash, and a missing father he hadn't reported. *Yes, officer, she kinda teleported over there and told me my father was taken.* They'd drag him to a drug screening.

He decided to go home first, then call Clarence. At least

he had to be on the right track. These things from his father contained information of value. Why else would the girl have tried to steal them?

He cut through the unfenced yard at the end of the cul-de-sac and walked one more block to his house. People gathered in their front yards for some reason. He recognized quite a few faces, some had been around the neighborhood all his life. Some spoke to him as he passed, but he didn't answer.

"So sorry."

"Let us know if we can help."

"We called 9-1-1 as soon as we saw it."

He heard some whispering, too, not intended for his ears.

"The poor boy…"

"First his mother…"

"Doesn't surprise me…"

When he arrived at his house, finding the tree house in the front yard just as he remembered it relieved him.

Maybe he shouldn't have been so focused on the treehouse since flames engulfed the main house, already well beyond saving.

The roof had partially caved in, exposing charred framing that creaked and crackled. A constant stream of embers and fragments rained to the ground. The front door still held back flames on the inside, but smoke pushed through the cracks. The windows facing the yard glowed.

Twilight had given way to dusk and an orange blaze reached toward the dark blue sky. Sirens wailed in the distance.

Jasper's reality shifted.

The flames stopped crackling and growing; they solidified and wrapped the house in a protective red, orange, and black foam layer. The debris hung suspended in midair, the roof beams frozen mid-collapse, the smoke turned into tiny clouds.

Stillness.

Everything was going to be all right after all. He'd have plenty of time to rescue his most important possessions. The family pictures, his laptop, all the toys and tchotchkes that would be horrible to lose, but he couldn't quite remember right now.

Surely, it was safe to enter. Did the house really burn anymore? He should take a closer look at the frozen flames.

Jasper strode toward the front door. A warped noise reminiscent of a worn-out tape recorder gave him pause. He turned toward the noise. His neighbors, all lined up on the street in front of his house, stared at him with frozen grimaces illuminated by the static glow of the burning house.

They seemed too vivid to be dead, too rigid to be truly alive.

He tried to scream, but the world came crashing down on him—the roar of the fire, his neighbors' yelling, the heat of the flames, the suffocating smoke. His legs gave out. Could he be aware of himself fainting?

Someone picked him up like a doll.

Chapter Nine

Eva and Adam

My name is… she wrote: "Eva Zeiger."

I am — she filled in "nine" — *years old.*

All morning, Eva practiced her English, her Italian, and her French. She had read her workbooks so often, nothing remained that she could learn from them, but they reminded her of happier times, when she had read them together with Adam and *Fräulein Ochs*, her former teacher. They treated her so badly in the beginning, but they all cried when they said their good-byes, most of all *Fräulein Ochs*.

Eva could really use a friend, with Adam gone too.

My favorite color is "pink."

My dog is called…

She wished she had a dog, a golden retriever. She'd call her Missy and they could go for long walks outside.

From the window of her study, Eva had a view of countless snow-covered mountain peaks that had taken *Fräulein Ochs'* breath away when she first saw it.

"Oh my, oh my," she had said, "I bet you two don't even know how incredible this is."

Eva and Adam had shrugged. All mountains looked alike to them.

The view from the other side of the Zeiger estate intrigued them considerably more. Not the driveway, the forecourt, the garage, the helipad, or the gardens, remarkable as their splendor was, but way in the distance, a city nestled in a valley. Eva could see it when the skies cleared. Her heart beat faster just thinking about it. A real city with people and shops and schools and a pretty lake. She could take Missy for a walk around the lake—that would be the happiest day of her life for sure.

Forget the dog. You'd hate being outside. It's cold and wet every day. And the mountains are boring, and the people in the city look at you mean. And besides, you're probably allergic to dog hair.

Adam, her twin brother, would say that. She wished he would stop being so negative, but he always had a point. A lot of things gave her allergic reactions, probably dog hair too. Easy enough for imaginary Adam to say these things; the *real* Adam surely had his second ice cream of the day in Davos right now. She tried not to be too envious. It was an unbecoming emotion.

Davos, the most fabulous city in all of Switzerland, nestled in the valley that she could see from her house sometimes. Their mother lived in Davos. Lived with Adam now, Eva presumed, but didn't dare pester Father with her questions.

Eva had last seen her mother a year ago. She used to visit more often. Now, Eva barely remembered her face. Would it be easier or harder to hate her if she remembered her face?

Oh, Eva hated her plenty without remembering her face. To this day, she just didn't understand. Why take Adam? He needed Father's care as much as Eva did. More so, even. And why only Adam? If she took him, why not Eva too?

A line of thought too upsetting to contemplate. She focused on her workbook.

I like to eat "pizza".

My favorite band is "Rip Current".

When I grow up, I want to be "a doctor".

Father said he'd get Adam back, but Eva had almost stopped believing. Something, something, something, lawyers, custody, courts. Mother had taken Adam in the middle of the night, like a thief while Eva had slept. She couldn't even say goodbye.

Feeling sorry for yourself again? Stop whining, you have it so good.

Adam again. He had a point, as always, but he had drawn the wrong conclusion.

"I don't feel sorry for me, I feel sorry for you!" Eva said out loud.

Hopefully, their mother had continued his treatment. What if he got worse and Father couldn't help? Eva worried about him often.

Feel sorry for me? Who's been a vegetable last weekend, shriveling up in the shower? You! Father's worried, he's working day and night.

"You know I didn't do it on purpose," Eva said.

Of course she knew she was alone in the room. She wasn't crazy or anything, she just clearly heard in her head what he'd say if he, her twin, after all, was still here. What harm did answering him?

Sometimes—no, let's be honest—frequently, she didn't like what she heard, but she had no company other than

Father. Sadly, Adam had gotten crankier and crankier lately.

Eva got up and walked over to the bookshelves that covered most of the wall on the far side of the room. Father said information equaled power. There were 1792 books on the shelves, including twenty-eight dictionaries, thirteen atlases, and 131 encyclopedias, if you counted the volumes individually. Eva had read every single one, apart from the dictionaries and encyclopedias, more than once. She had tried re-reading the *Brockhaus Enzyklopädie* but got bored and stopped after the final entry for "A"—*Azzurri ("the Blues; nickname for Italian national teams, e.g. the Italy national football team")*.

She took out the National Geographic Atlas of the World. It opened naturally at North America, because her favorite band, Rip Current, came from California, and also because she had hidden the magazine from Father in that spot.

"RIP CURRENT. 'Meet the band!' 253 new pics. 1000 facts. 3 HOT!!! Posters."

The magazine was well worn, so she turned the pages carefully. She had tried to take good care of it since her mom had secretly given it to her on her last visit, but it lacked the sturdiness of those bound encyclopedias. She might have read it a couple hundred times more often, too.

"I'd shave my head to meet RC! (And 99 Other Fan Confessions!)"

Of course that woman would shave her head; it would grow back. She hadn't figured out why that would make her more likely to meet the band.

"Your Lips Here! — First Kiss Confessions."

An arrow pointed to the smiling mouth of Julian, baring

two rows of straight pearly white teeth. Gross! Sure, a cute boy (although not as cute as Robbie), but still… What if one of them accidentally kept their mouth open just a little? Everyone knew nearly one thousand different types of bacteria lived in the human mouth. And one hundred thousand individual bacteria on every tooth. *Just, no.* She turned the page.

"Which RC Boy Is Perfect 4U? Take Our Quiz!"

She already knew: Robbie. Nothing in this world did she feel more certain about. He was a perfect match. Like her, he loved reading, pizza, chocolate ice cream, and dogs. He didn't care for tattoos, broccoli, or mean people. Moreover, he had to be the best-looking boy in the whole world. His dreamy hazel eyes, his rascally smile, that unruly tangle of sun-streaked hair! If he didn't love music so much, he would have become a surfer.

How exciting that would have been. He said he went to the beach every day at home in Los Angeles. When they didn't tour Japan, Portugal, Argentina, or any of the other exotic places they visited all the time. What fun, to see the whole world like that. Or to see the ocean from your window, not only stupid mountains all the time.

I bet he can't even surf. You read the whole dictionary, didn't you? Remember "M?" As in "marketing?" They make that stuff up for stupid little girls like you, who'll never see the ocean.

"You don't know that. You're just being mean, shut up," Eva said.

She wondered if her mother had taken Adam to see the ocean. Sometimes, she wished it had been her instead of Adam. A terrible thought, she chastised herself. Father worked so, so hard to make her healthy again. He knew what was best, and her place was here.

What if she had one of her episodes *outside*? Anything could happen outside, everyone knew that.

"I Was Grounded For Sneaking Out To See Rip Current —
Totally Worth It!"

The girl in the story didn't tell her parents she went to the concert and had to climb out of her window. Eva's rooms on the fourth floor had sealed windows, but she knew how to get out another way.

After her mother had stolen Adam, Father installed an electronic lock on the door, but he didn't know how fast Eva had become. She could just walk out of here. If she wanted.

Maybe.

No, probably. For sure.

She looked at her digital watch: 11:59:57 a.m. At noon, Father would bring lunch.

Father took the best care of her, although he had to be terribly busy with more important matters, being the richest man in the world and all. He had to be, since he was the richest man in Switzerland, and Switzerland, with all the banks, the richest country in the world. Eva put the *Rip Current* magazine back into the atlas and returned it to the shelf.

Noon.

As always, Father wore a black turtleneck sweater and carried a tray with her lunch. Grilled chicken breast, steamed broccoli, cooked lentils, a tall glass of water, four colorful pills. Every day. Plus green tea in a small thermos and a cup of fruit for dessert. It aided her digestion. It was for the best.

When he left, Eva watched the door take forever to click shut. When the familiar metallic sound of the lock finally arrived, she sighed and looked down at her plate.

Eat your broccoli, silly girl. It's good for you. We both know you're not going to sneak out and run away.

"I don't *want* to run away," Eva said. The real Adam had never been this nasty to her. But imaginary Adam did have a point. She sighed and took a bite of broccoli. It was for the best.

Chapter Ten

The Wright House

Cold water ran down Jasper's neck and back. A hand patted a wet towel to his forehead. He blinked and squinted up at his elderly neighbor from across the street, Janice. They sat on a bench in her backyard. He had spent quite some time here as a young kid, less and less in recent years.

"Here, my dear, take a sip. Your favorite, I think."

She handed him a Capri Sun. His tastes had changed, but this wasn't the time to point it out.

"Thanks, Jan," Jasper said. "How long was I out?"

"Oh, just a couple of minutes. Jimmy carried you here. You gave us quite a scare."

"What happened?" Jasper couldn't make sense out of his own memories.

"You sprinted toward the burning house like a crazy person, then turned around and screamed like a banshee before you fainted. Jimmy carried you away right before the roof came down."

Jimmy, of all people. Now Jasper felt even worse for the jokes he'd made behind his back when they were younger.

"The house?" Jasper asked.

Janice shook her head, got up, and looked around the corner toward the street. "Oh dear, I hope you feel better. I'm pretty sure everyone will want to talk to you."

Jasper got up and peeked over the fence. Neighbors, firemen, EMTs… A police car just pulled up right in front of Janice's house.

Despite the cold, wet towel around his neck, Jasper got hot flashes. *Think. Think!* The house, forget about the house. What's important? Dad. The box. The girl. What's going on in my life? It all came rushing back.

A deep voice out front asked, "We're looking for the owner. Where's the owner of the house?"

Yes, where is he? Jasper wondered. Maybe he should tell the police everything. Let them figure it out. Finally file that missing person report.

And then, what next? No parents, no relatives, no house, and no answers. Get bullied in an orphanage? Go back to school as if nothing happened? There had to be another way.

The backpack—where is my backpack?

Panic gave way to relief when he saw it under the bench. Good old Jimmy hadn't left it behind.

"He's in my grandma's backyard," Jimmy's booming voice carried from the street to Jasper's ears. "I saved him, I did!"

Seconds later, the police knocked on the gate, but Jasper had already come to terms with his best option: to find his father and figure out what was going on in his life he had to lie—about everything.

Thankfully, as a teenage boy, he had some experience in the matter. Leave out what you can, keep it simple, keep it plausible, divert attention. When the lies get too big, call in reinforcements.

He got out his cell phone and messaged Clarence: "House burnt down. Police r here. Come quick & bring yr folks."

With nothing left to lose other than the clothes on his back, he asked Jan to keep an eye on his backpack, before he opened the gate to perform his song and dance.

Later that night, the Wrights drove him to their house in their hybrid Escalade. Clarence and Jasper sat in the back, silently.

Detective Keane, the friendly police officer, had been relieved the Wrights conveniently volunteered to take Jasper in for a few days, until his dad returned from the business trip.

Yes, of course Jasper would continue to try to reach him on his cell phone.

No, he really didn't know which hotels his father was staying in since they only communicated via cell phone. Who calls a hotel desk these days?

Yes, he had stayed home alone before. Many times, in fact.

No, he didn't know how the fire might have started. He was at his friend Clarence's house all afternoon.

It had all been very convincing. And was good enough for three days, apparently. After that, Keane would put in a missing person's alert and reassess Jasper's living arrangements.

Clarence had given Jasper disapproving looks throughout the charade but didn't bust him. Not that Jasper knew how the fire had started. He didn't even have time to think about that yet.

The Wrights generally thought Jasper was a corrupting influence on Clarence, but he had gambled they'd feel obligated to help in front of the authorities, and they agreed to take him in.

Right before everyone had left, Jasper badgered the last remaining firefighters into checking for the cats in the crawlspace, but no trace of them remained. Better than most alternatives, but he still hated having no way of confirming they all escaped unharmed.

At the Wrights', Jasper stayed in the pool house. He knew they had a proper guest room next to Clarence's in the main house, but he actually preferred the isolation for the rest of the night. He didn't have a private moment with Clarence, so he simply said, "We'll talk tomorrow."

In his new temporary bedroom, Jasper put on borrowed Spiderman PJs that turned out to be comically large and went to bed. The sheets smelled of bleach.

My backpack!

Jasper jumped out of bed like he'd been stung by a scorpion, accidentally sending the oversized pajama pants down to his ankles. It took him a second to realize his backpack remained where he had left it, leaning against the nightstand. He had picked it up at Jan's yesterday after the police left.

He whistled in relief. Jasper hadn't been able to tell Clarence about the girl yet, although objectively speaking, her antics constituted the more newsworthy development of yesterday evening. A teleporting ninja pickpocketing him in the street? *Sure, why not.*

He stepped out of the pajama pants and looked for his clothes. A knock on the door interrupted him.

"Jasper?" asked a childlike voice.

Condi! Clarence's sister, an eleven-year-old, pig-tailed straight-A student had recently taken to annoying Jasper by hovering whenever he visited Clarence. Just what he needed while traipsing around bottomless.

"One second!" Jasper struggled to step back into the Spiderman pants as the door swung open.

He yanked the pants up, getting stuck in one leg with both feet. Thankfully they still covered the important bits, even if it looked like he had put on a mermaid tail.

"Hey, why even ask if you're not going to wait for my answer?" he barked.

After a wide-eyed look at his situation, she giggled. "I brought you some clothes. And breakfast's ready."

"Those aren't mine," Jasper said after one look at the pile she carried.

"Mom threw 'em out. Beyond saving, she said. Sorry. And sorry 'bout your house. You must be really sad."

"Yeah..."

Condi seemed to expect him to continue, but when he

didn't say anything, she finally put the clothes down on the bed. "These were the only ones in your size."

Mom jeans, a mustard-colored polo, and tighty-whities, all straight from Clarence's closet of about three years ago.

"Hurry up, everyone's waiting for you. And Clarence is leaving soon," Condi said before she left.

The clothes smelled like the very definition of borrowed—unfamiliar detergent mixed with the staleness of years in the closet.

Jasper peeked through the curtains to make sure Condi had really gone back to the main house before he dropped his mermaid's tail and reluctantly put on Clarence's old tighty-whities.

Someone owed him for this, big time; he just wasn't sure who.

Breakfast brought new ignominies.

"Something smells burnt," Clarence's dad said.

Condi sniffed her plate. "It's not the bacon."

"No, that would be me," Jasper said. He had noticed it on the way over to the main house. No time to shower yet, not if Clarence left soon. "My luscious locks." He shook his head dramatically.

Locks didn't quite capture Jasper's current mop situation. On a good day, it might have looked like a sun-streaked surfer do, but lately bad hair day had become the new normal, even before he had singed the tips. "Apologies, I got a bit crisped up yesterday."

Only Condi chuckled.

When he had finished his plate, Clarence's father didn't waste any time in dissolving the festive gathering.

"Clarence…" He tapped his golden Rolex. "Camp. Don't want to be late."

"On my way soon," Clarence said and headed to the bathroom.

"I am so stuffed!" Jasper lied and got up right after. He chased Clarence to the bathroom just in time to put a foot in the door and follow him in. The room gleamed of white marble from top to bottom.

"You can't leave, we have to talk," Jasper said.

"You know how Dad is. I have to go," Clarence said. "I think my parents agreed to take you in because they felt they had to, but we shouldn't rock the boat."

True. And if the Wrights threw him out, he had nowhere to go, but he couldn't hold his story in for a whole day. "Yesterday, before I got back to the house, there was this girl. She tried to steal my stuff. My dad's stuff. We wrestled for it, and she, I don't know, turned invisible and took my dad's diary."

"Invisible? What do you mean, she wore camouflage?" Clarence asked.

"No! She vanished. And she knew things. About my dad. She said he'd been taken. D'you know what I'm saying?"

"I really don't, but, man, you've been under a lot of stress." Clarence took a half-step back. "Maybe you should just rest for a while."

"I just slept for ten hours, I'm not seeing things. She tried to steal my stuff," Jasper said.

"Let's talk later, I really have to pee, and then I gotta go to camp."

"At least try to get this card reader. I need to know what's on those flop pies, or whatever," Jasper said.

"Floppies. Disks. Floppy disks. And now get out of here before my parents see us." Clarence opened the bathroom door.

Jasper left the room and ran straight into Clarence's mom. She folded her arms and turned down the corners of her mouth as if a misbehaving puppy had disappointed her.

"Look, honey, we're very sorry about your house and you're welcome to stay, but while you're here, there'll be no shenanigans." She raised her eyebrows signaling she expected him to know what kind of shenanigans she meant. "No. Shenanigans. Is that clear?"

She really expected a response.

"Crystal!" he said and flashed a comically wide smile. "Just needed to borrow some deodorant. My hair's all singed, hate when that happens." He stupidly patted his empty pant pocket as if that explained his nonsense excuse, then squeezed past her and headed to the pool house for some privacy.

Jasper locked the door, sat down cross-legged on the bed, and carefully laid out his treasures.

"I hope I was able to tell you what you needed to know." What did he need to know?

The gun. Uncle Martin had thought Jasper's dad might need it someday, but he didn't know why. It certainly hadn't helped Jasper with the girl. It annoyed her more than frightened her. Not that he'd shoot someone anyway. The gun seemed more a problem than a solution. He had to hide it, but he had no privacy here, and taking it with him wherever he went would be quite risky.

The money and the passports. At least they didn't burn in the house, but they didn't really help him find his father either. Although he should really buy some new clothes. These mom jeans traveled up his crotch and chafed in the wrong places every time he sat down.

He tried to remember details about the notebook the girl had stolen—diary entries, tables, notes, schematics. Nothing stood out in his memory.

What was the girl's angle anyway? Did she set the fire? They had fought barely a minute earlier, but if she could turn invisible, who knew what else she could do?

Then it hit him—the footprint in Dad's closet. She had tried to steal from him before. And if she could turn invisible, she could be here in the pool house with him right now.

He sprang up and paced back and forth, scanning the empty room. No, there had to be limits, otherwise he'd never have caught her trying to swipe his backpack. Whatever she could do, there had to be a rational explanation. He'd still have to take his next shower in his underwear, though.

Back to the blueprints, the student records, the floppy disks, and the photographs—a building he didn't know, names that didn't mean anything to him, obsolete tech he couldn't access, and old pictures. Obviously, a total slam dunk.

He sighed and leafed through the pictures. Baby Jasper with his parents looked to be the most recent one. A creased one of college-aged Mom and Dad seemed to be the oldest.

His father had carried it in his wallet for many years.

The others had to be taken in the time between the two. One showed Mom, Dad, and Uncle Martin, all laughing, with Dad and Uncle Martin out of focus—definitely not taken with a digital camera.

Another featured a group of eleven people, including Mom, Dad, and Uncle Martin, in front of a huge sign like the ones in driveways of company headquarters: *BioDein*, 100 BioDein Way. Everyone smiled.

In another one with the same group of people, everyone stood in a lab, with only Mom missing. One man in a lab coat stood apart from everyone. Older than the others, he might've been their professor.

Ten students, plus their professor. Then nine students, Mom missing.

Jasper looked at the student records.

"Independent Studies 176." Ten names, Mom's crossed out.

On a picture taken at a funeral, Jasper didn't recognize dozens of the people in the background, but in the foreground, again: a group of nine now-familiar students, this time without their professor.

The final picture focused on a construction site: the bare bones of a one-story building with a flat roof and a wide garage door next to a smaller normal door. A car shop? He didn't know the place.

Two of the students posed in front of it: Uncle Martin and one other. They smiled moronically and held a sign between them that read "POT 1991." In the other hand, each of them held a cigarette. No, not a cigarette. Much too thick for that.

Jasper threw the pictures down. *Useless.* So Uncle Martin used to smoke big blunts? What a shocker.

"What do you make of this stuff?" Jasper asked. "What do you think I needed to know?"

Clarence, back from camp, laughed out loud, something that didn't happen all that often. "How to operate a shower? You still smell like you put your head on the grill."

Jasper had decided to de-emphasize personal hygiene for the moment but wasn't too keen to elaborate in front of Clarence. "You know what I mean. Can we find my dad with this?"

"Jay, this is crazy. Look at this stuff; ancient family pics, maps, passports, money? A gun," he added in a whisper. "I mean, your father's missing, and your house is burnt out. You're staying in our pool house. Is this the time for a paper chase?" Clarence picked up the photo from the construction site. "1991's a long time ago, there's just no point."

"What would you have me do? I *have* to find him. He wanted to tell me something, something I needed to know. He wanted me to have this, but something happened. Do you think the police will believe me about the girl? Do you believe me?"

"About the *vanishing* girl?" Clarence grimaced. "You said it yourself. You said you felt weird these last few days—"

"Are you gaslighting me? She could turn invisible. I saw it. I don't know how, but I swear to you. I really need you to believe me."

"I believe that's what you think you saw."

"Don't be a dick." Jasper gave his friend a hammer fist to the top of the head.

"Ouch." Clarence rubbed his noggin. "Okay, okay, I believe you."

"Thank you. Now can you please look at this stuff? This is kinda your thing."

Clarence was a sucker for riddles and adventure games. When he started brooding over Jasper's treasure, picking items up and laying them back down reverentially, Jasper knew he had him.

"Let's take a step back," Clarence said. "I don't think this is the treasure. This is the map. At least the stuff that was in the box. The gun, money, passports, anyone could have that in a safe, so let's disregard it for now."

"How does that help, calling it differently?"

"As a way of thinking. What's the treasure we're looking for? Your dad, right, or at least to find out what happened, what he wanted you to know? For that, we need a map."

Jasper handed him the blueprint.

"I meant that metaphorically, but we might as well." Clarence put the blueprint on the floor next the old photos and the college records. "It has the obvious advantage that it's a location. Unfortunately, we don't know what or where it is. We could do a web search for the dimensions." He traced the outline with his finger. "Looks pretty unique. If there's something in public records, we might get a match. Or call a local architect, maybe they heard of your uncle." Clarence tapped Uncle Martin's name under the drawing before shifting his attention to the records.

"This is definitely the group in the pictures. We could start with a normal web search. Or run facial recognition and see if we can match faces and names." He put the group pic on top of the records. "I know someone who says he can do that on the open web pretty efficiently. And finally"—he picked up another group picture—"if we contact UCLA, I'm pretty sure they'd at least put us in touch with this guy." He pointed at the professor.

This sounded all perfectly reasonable, but talk about long shots. Jasper furrowed his brow. There had to be a better way, an easier way.

"What is it?" Clarence asked. "Makes too much sense?"

"Nah, but the blueprints, they say 'Fourth draft by M. Higgs,' right? And he's on the list of names, he's one of the students."

"Right…"

"And he's like, in five of the pics. More than my mom and dad."

"No." Clarence crossed his arms in front of his chest. "It's useless."

"I know Uncle Martin blew us off last time and kinda insulted you, but he'd have to be a giant douchebag to turn me away now."

"Turn you away *now*? We already know he's a douchebag and won't even open the door for you."

"Only one way to find out. Desperate times and all that. Bus or Prius?" Jasper asked. "One way or the other, I am taking the gun this time."

Chapter Eleven

Shared Secrets

They rode mostly in silence as Clarence's discomfort with the driving arrangements radiated through the car. You could've powered the Prius's battery with the negative energy, but Jasper didn't fancy leaving any of his things behind, especially not the gun, not after yesterday. The faint smell of burnt hair still clung to him.

Jasper looked out the window, trying hard not to let his thoughts go to dark places. On the bright side, this was certainly the biggest adventure of his life. A vanishing girl, a gun, a safe, a map, a mystery, what more could anyone want? He could do without the missing father and something else, what was it again? Ah yes, his house had burned down, and he had no home, no family, and absolutely no idea whether the only person who could shed some light on everything would even open the door for him.

An adventure sounded great, but the movies got away with all sorts of bullshit. Somehow, stumbling over the charred remains of your loved ones could be the twenty-seventh most significant thing to happen to you in two hours, if the original Star Wars was any indication. Talk about creative license.

Thankfully Jasper's adventure had not featured the charred remains of loved ones. Or anyone, really. Yet.

"We're here," said Clarence.

They found Uncle Martin's house exactly as they had left it, utterly uninviting.

"I know, I know." Clarence folded his hands to give Jasper a leg-up over the fence.

Once inside, they walked straight to the window where Uncle Martin had talked to Jasper the day before yesterday. It seemed a lot longer ago.

"*Uncle Martin!*" shouted Jasper.

Screw games or subtlety. He knocked on the window with barely enough restraint not to break the single-pane glass behind the thick metal bars.

"We really need to talk to you. It's very important."

Jasper knocked even harder, finally causing a hairline crack in the window that raced toward the frame.

"I don't think the problem is that he doesn't know we're here," Clarence said.

Jasper reached back to give the window another firm knock when he noticed a Post-it across the crack. It read: "Please don't break my window. Go home. Talk to your dad."

Clarence shook his head disbelievingly.

Jasper leaned in toward the window. "He's missing, remember?"

No answer. And no Post-its.

Go home? There was nothing Jasper would rather do, but right now he didn't even feel like smirking at the unintended irony.

"Uncle Martin, I know you have some issue with my dad, but I really need your help. He's still gone, and our house burned down. Someone tried to steal the things I found in the safe. There was a note from Dad, something I need to know." The first time they talked, the safe had brought his uncle out of hiding. "Remember, we found a box and a gun. The gun you gave Dad." He whispered now. "I have the gun with me, just as you said, but I need to know what's going on, what I need to know."

Another Post-it appeared on the inside of the window, seemingly out of thin air. Jasper and Clarence leaned in to read it: "Only your father can explain."

This time Clarence couldn't restrain himself anymore. "Great party trick with the Post-its, but did you listen to anything he just told you? It's sad enough you're the only one who can help him, so why don't you just open the damned door and—"

Jasper raised his hand and Clarence closed his mouth grudgingly. As much as Jasper would have liked to join his friend in some cathartic berating of Uncle Martin, it couldn't be the most promising tactic to draw a recluse out of hiding.

Jasper continued, quietly, "Uncle Martin, the box? I found the key. We opened the box. Your name is all over the stuff we found. College transcripts, pictures. There's a blueprint, too. It says, 'The Passage of Time,' by Martin Higgs."

The window opened and Uncle Martin's visage, framed by his scraggly beard and unkempt hair, appeared behind the metal bars. His piercing gaze turned from Jasper to Clarence, then back to Jasper.

"What do you know about the Passage of Time?"

Uncle Martin's eyes held an alertness in marked contrast to his careless appearance. Jasper felt in his bones the man would know if he lied.

"We have these blueprints. You drew them, that's what they say."

"Yes, yes, yes, I know that I drew them. Do you know what it is? Where it is?" asked Uncle Martin.

"No, but—"

"Good." Uncle Martin closed the window so fast that the force should have taken out the cracked glass, but nothing even rattled. The last Post-it still read: "Only your father can explain."

Stunned, Jasper composed himself for a moment, then sat right in front of the window and put his head in his hands.

Clarence sat next to him and put his arm on Jasper's shoulder.

"This whole thing sucks even without charred bodies," Jasper said.

"What?"

"Never mind. Let's go, I'm tired. I need a quiet place to go insane. You hear that, Uncle Martin? Maybe I'll end up like you… I'll go to the police. I need help. I'll tell them about the invisible girl—"

The door to Uncle Martin's house opened. "Invisible girl? Doesn't sound like something the… *po-lice,*"—his enunciation dripped with disdain—"would be interested in."

After all the window knocking and the behind-iron-bars

cameos, after Jasper had finally given up hope, there he stood—Uncle Martin, in all his sweat pants-clad glory.

"We should talk." He held the door open. "Not him." Uncle Martin nodded toward Clarence.

"We have no secrets," Jasper said.

"Oh yes, you do." Uncle Martin chuckled, then leaned forward conspiratorially. "More importantly, I do."

Clarence pointed at the door. "And they're *in there*?" His sarcastic tone mimicked Uncle Martin's enunciation earlier.

"No, you fools, in here." Uncle Martin pointed to his head. "If you think I'm insane, you can leave now before you waste any more of my time."

"Look, Clarence is my best friend, more than a friend, and whatever you tell me, I'm going to tell him later anyway, so why don't you let us both in?" Jasper said.

"You know nothing about secrets. Secrets are weapons. And if there's two people and one of them has a gun, when the world is going to hell and there's one cookie left, who is going to have that last cookie? You let someone in on your secrets, you're handing them the gun. And you'll never get that cookie. And if you tell him anyway, then maybe I should keep my secrets to myself."

"If the two people are true friends, it doesn't matter who's got the gun, they are going to share the cookie," Clarence said.

Uncle Martin flashed a wide, sarcastic smile, showing two rows of surprisingly shiny white teeth. "It's a metaphor, boy. Forget about the cookie."

"I know it's a metaphor, and a particularly stupid one at that," Clarence said. "I'm just saying that between friends, secrets aren't weapons."

"Then I'm just saying you haven't had friends for long enough. Jasper?"

Uncle Martin still held the door open, but Jasper hesitated.

"What if they both have secrets? Then it's like the Cold War, no one can use them."

Uncle Martin sighed. "I guess, but that's not the point…"

"Clarence is gay, but, like, totally in the closet," Jasper blurted. "And when he accidentally left his computer on one day, his parents found, uh, some explicit stuff and got super mad. I was with Clarence all afternoon the day before, so I took the fall and told his parents it was mine. They totally bought it, and now they think I'm trying to seduce and corrupt their innocent baby boy or something, while he's actually the one in the closet."

"Jay, what the hell?" Clarence said wide-eyed, shaking his head in disbelief.

Jasper continued, "So there, nobody knows. No one but me. I know his secret and now you know, so it seems just fair that he should know one, too."

"You really did that for him?" Uncle Martin looked back and forth between the two of them, baffled and amused at the same time, sizing them up in a new way.

Jasper nodded.

"This is so utterly inappropriate, I don't even know where to begin." Clarence shook his head. "How could you possibly think I'm okay with this?"

"If we had talked first, he would've thought it was a trick. Why do you care if he knows?" Jasper asked. "It's not like he's going to call your dad."

"Oh, that's the way it's gonna be, huh? Then you probably won't mind if I tell him that you're a hairless freak who looks like a ten-year-old from the chin down? That you threw up three times before running away from your first date because you were so terrified anything would happen in the downstairs department, and the girl would make fun of your whole-body Brazilian? That your nickname in the locker room was mole-rat—"

"Nice, very nice. Of course you have to bring that up. Sure, just tell the whole world. I guess I should count my blessings that your tastes go in the opposite direction judging from—"

"You need a reality check, my friend. You can be so selfish. I can't believe you. After all I've put up with over the last couple of days—"

"All *you* have put up with? Excuse me? I think—"

"Everyone just shut. Up. I implore you! Come in, both of you, just please stop talking." Uncle Martin stood straight, put his left arm behind his back, and wiggled his right index finger at them. "If either one of you bring up any part of this conversation ever again, I will end you. I mean it."

A huge, fresh mustard stain on the right leg of his sweat pants somewhat undermined his attempt at authority. He frantically waved for both of them to step inside.

Jasper squeezed by Clarence, elbowed him in the ribs and whispered, "See, it worked."

Clarence rolled his eyes. "This can't possibly be worth it."

"Cell phones?" Uncle Martin held open a cast-iron casserole dish in front of them.

Clarence defiantly stuck his hands in his pockets, but Jasper stared him down, and they both put their cell phones into the pot. Uncle Martin turned them off, covered the dish with its lid, and invited them to sit down on a green, deep-buttoned plush couch.

The sparse living room looked long lived-in, yet rarely used at the same time.

"Wow, you still have a tube TV," Clarence said.

Uncle Martin smirked. "If you knew what I know, you'd have one too." He sat on a plush footstool opposite Jasper. "Tell me about this invisible girl."

Jasper told him. About his walk home, the girl, the burning house. And he showed him what they had found in the safe and in the box.

At the beginning, Uncle Martin seemed to listen intently, then more and more often checked out mentally for a few seconds, his eyes rolling back into his head before snapping forward to focus on Jasper once more. He massaged his thighs and arms, but never interrupted to ask questions.

"What does it all mean? What's happening?" Jasper asked. "How could she be invisible?"

Uncle Martin continued to look straight ahead for a few seconds, seemingly asleep with open eyes, then appeared to notice Jasper had stopped talking. He cleared his throat to break the silence, got up, and walked a few steps over to the barred window.

Clarence rolled his eyes at Jasper.

"Uncle Martin, were you listening? Is everything all right?" Jasper asked.

More awkward silence followed before Uncle Martin finally turned around and attempted a smile with mixed success. "Everything is very far from all right, sorry to say." He dabbed at his sweat-covered forehead with his shirtsleeves and laughed nervously. "It's not really my place, you know, gotta keep my trap shut. Your mom and dad were very, very explicit back when..." His voice trailed off.

"Mom's dead and Dad might as well be, one way or the other," Jasper said bluntly. For two years, his father had been an impostor of the person he used to be.

"Yes, that would do it, I guess." Uncle Martin shivered and looked around his house forlornly. "Your dad and I... How to put this? We share a certain condition. A secret, if you will." He paused, his eyes again taking on his trademark absent-minded look.

"Yes, a secret..." Jasper prompted him after a few second.

"We don't experience time quite like other people." Another pause stretched long enough to become uncomfortable.

Finally, Clarence forced a laugh to break the silence and looked at his wristwatch. "No kidding! It's almost six o'clock, maybe we should be on our way."

"Shh," Uncle Martin said and held up Clarence's watch, still standing about eight feet away while Clarence looked at his naked wrist.

"Whoa, what the?" was all he could shout while he scrambled to his feet.

Uncle Martin seemed to teleport from his spot at the window to the couch they were sitting on and pushed Clarence back down into the cushions. "Ready to listen now?" His eyes twinkled. Whatever just happened had reenergized him.

Jasper and Clarence nodded, dumbfounded.

"Then let me tell you a real secret," Uncle Martin said, "one that's a lot more titillating than your sexual proclivities or your pubertal status."

"It's actually a skin condition," Jasper mumbled. "Everything's, like, fully functional—"

"Shh," Clarence hissed and gestured for Uncle Martin to continue.

Uncle Martin turned to face Jasper. "When your father and I were in university, there was an incident. A group of ten students, including your parents and yours truly, plus our professor, visited BioDein, the pharmaceutical giant up in the desert by Palmdale. Our professor had research privileges and could come and go. We were in this sealed lab when a gas pipe burst. Everyone unconscious, nobody was looking for us. When we woke up, we had changed, although we didn't immediately realize what we could do."

"Ack!" Clarence interjected. "Don't you just hate those radioactive spiders?"

"It's all funny until something happens to you," Uncle Martin said.

"But what do you mean, changed?" Jasper asked. "What happened?"

"What happened exactly, I—we—still don't know, and it's not from a lack of trying to find out. It's hard to explain. There's no precedent. Over time, we figured out that—"

"Didn't you go to a hospital?" Clarence asked. "What kind of gas was it? Did you get poisoned?"

"Are you the Spanish Inquisition? Do you want to hear the story or not?" Uncle Martin asked. "They have medical facilities on-site at BioDein, better than any public hospital, and of course they examined us. We all stayed overnight. But what could we tell them? We were fine. They investigated the leak. Some experimental oneirogenic anaesthetic that never made it to market. What we caught was them disposing of the leftovers, basically. A dead end beyond that."

"Hold on," Jasper said. "What's un-aero-genetic—"

"Oneirogenic anaesthetic," Clarence repeated. "Sleeping gas, basically."

"Correct," Uncle Martin said. "On our way back to UCLA, people started coming forward, talking, sharing experiences, weirdness. Finally, we tried out our new…" He waved his arms around mock-pompously. "La dee da, *powers*, for lack of a better word. Our professor set up a lab for us. We ran tests on ourselves, blood work, cognition, CT scans, bone marrow, the works. We tried to find out as much as we could. You have to understand, this was a group of incredibly smart students, all prodigies, all with different interests and backgrounds. This independent studies class was an interdisciplinary genius lab, Professor Kruzman the smartest person I've ever met to this day. We were freaked out, but this was by far the most incredible thing that ever happened to us. There was nobody who could have helped us, or who knew more about it than us, so we went on to—"

"What is it that you can really do?" Clarence asked. "Besides magic tricks? 'Experience time differently… a new world…' Sounds conveniently vague."

"Well, I can't shoot spiderwebs out of my ass, if that's what you're asking. One of our group with a flair for the dramatic called us the time benders."

"Time travel? Nice," said Clarence sarcastically. "So who is going to win the NBA Finals?"

"Don't be ridiculous. Nobody can travel back in time. It's impossible."

"Back in time? That implies that you can travel forward in time," Clarence said, sounding pleased with himself. "And last time I checked, game seven was still in the future. So, if you can travel forward in time, who's going to win?"

Uncle Martin rubbed his temples. "Everyone travels forward in time. You, me. That's the nature of time. Provided we don't die, we're all going to find out who's going to win. But to tell you who will win would require me to be able to travel back here from the point in the future when I find out, and that's what's impossible."

"But if there's no going back, what's a time bender supposed to be?" asked Jasper.

"Time bending doesn't change the direction of time, only its duration, so to say, or in my personal opinion, actually only its perception. I can access Accelerated Time while you two are in what we called Real Time."

"How would you be able to change my perception of time?" asked Clarence.

"Yours? I can't. Obviously, I'm talking about my perception of time."

"Why does it matter to us how you perceive time? How does that affect reality? And how did you get my watch?" Clarence asked.

"I was speeding up in Real Time," Uncle Martin said, closed his eyes and took a few deep breaths with his hand over his stomach as if he'd become nauseous.

"But you were invisible, you teleported like that girl," Jasper said.

"This is harder than I thought," Uncle Martin mumbled, looking unwell. "I wasn't invisible. I was so fast you couldn't see me."

"So basically you run fast like the Flash or something," Clarence said. "I don't buy it."

"Well aren't you Mr. Smarty-pants? I don't run, trust me. Gentlemen don't run. It's like an extra dimension of time. Or possibly space, we could never agree—" Uncle Martin disappeared right in front of their eyes. When he reappeared, he held a bottle of water in each hand. "Anyway, here, drink. I'm a terrible host. But then I don't entertain much lately. Except myself." He cackled, seeming livelier again.

"What just happened?" Jasper asked.

"I got a couple of waters from the fridge. And trust me, I didn't run."

Clarence contorted his face in pain, struggling to square what he had seen, or not seen, with his firm belief in the order of things. "But time doesn't work like this."

"Like what? What do you know about time? There's only

one law. You can never go back. The constant, regular passage of time is an artificial construct, a way of thinking. All the things in the universe stand in relation to each other. The next moment their relation to each other has changed. That's time. Do you think there's anything constant about a measure of time, a second, a minute, an hour? What about black holes?"

"Actually the theory of relativity—" Clarence started, but Jasper shushed him.

"What about the beginning of all things?" Uncle Martin asked.

"Jeez, is it time for a *Big Bang Theory*?" Clarence made exaggerated air quotes with his fingers.

"Everyone's a comedian." Uncle Martin sighed. "Whether you believe in God, or a god, or no deity at all, at some point there was nothing, and then there was something. Is there any artificial measure of time that could meaningfully capture that change? A split-second? An eternity? It's irrelevant. We are constantly rearranging on a molecular level at incomprehensible speeds. The cat that jumps is not the cat that lands."

"That doesn't explain anything," Clarence said, "that's just banal."

"That's life," Uncle Martin said. "The things that comprise us change constantly, but for a while, it all holds together as a person, constantly rearranging. Maybe what is me is changing just a little bit faster while still holding together, who knows." Uncle Martin paused, but when neither Clarence nor Jasper reacted, he seemed annoyed. "Whatever. The thing is, we don't know how shit works, deep down. How do planes fly? Why does the sun rise in the East? What's the speed of light?"

"Actually we know all of these things," Clarence said.

"So you're paying attention, but you know what I mean. What was before the Big Bang?" said Uncle Martin.

"Forget the Big Bang," Jasper said. "You just turned invisible. Does that mean you can do whatever you want, whenever you want it, and no one can stop you? Like, walk into a bank, take all the money, walk right out? Win the hundred-meter dash in the Olympics without running? You're practically Superman."

Uncle Martin snorted. "What is it with all the superheroes? No, I can't fly or lift an airplane. Besides, my back hurts like hell. And how many banks has Superman robbed? Nonsense."

"Still, I mean, look around your house. Why this life? Why doesn't the world know about this?" Jasper asked.

"Because there's only ten people in the world who can do it, and believe me, none of them ever wanted anyone else to find out. Now at least two are dead." Uncle Martin sighed. "And I can't imagine the rest are much more sociable than me. Interaction like this, I mean talking to you in Real Time, is very difficult. Your dad tried the normal life..."

"When you say, 'two are dead,' you don't mean my parents, do you?" asked Jasper. "You think my father's still alive, right?"

"I don't know, but I didn't mean your dad. We're hard to kill, you know. See things coming. But our professor died in a plane crash less than a year after the incident. Years later, one of our friends took his life and..." He cleared his throat.

"We went our separate ways."

"But what about my mom? Don't you mean three are dead?"

"Your mom? Never affected. Only one in our group who remained normal, stuck in Real Time like you two. Brave woman, to marry your father knowing what he was."

"What do you mean?" Jasper asked.

"What do you think life is like with someone who reads three books while you do the dishes? Who does a month's work in one evening? Not one of us was blessed with superhuman memory. Do you remember what you had for lunch four weeks ago? What you talked about? If you have too much time, you spend a lot of it alone in your head. Excuse me," Uncle Martin said and left to use the bathroom.

Jasper could imagine exactly how living with a person like that felt like. He had been doing it for his whole life without realizing it. And was this talent why his dad didn't even have a scratch on him after the accident that cost his mom's life? How could his father keep all this from him?

When Uncle Martin returned moments later, a look of wide-eyed surprise flashed over his now puffy and reddened face before he grimaced and sat back down.

Clarence cleared his throat. "So, while this is all fascinating, Jasper's father, any ideas? Do you believe the girl? Was he taken? And who could even do that?"

"Yes," Jasper said, "The girl. She was too young to have been affected by your incident."

"What girl?" asked Uncle Martin. "And what do you know about the incident?"

"Uncle Martin!" Jasper said. "The invisible girl, she's

why you let us in in the first place. And you just told us about the incident."

"I…" He looked around with milky eyes, searching for something he couldn't see. "Your father will explain, yes. I shouldn't have…" He walked to the window and stared intently toward the quiet street. "I really shouldn't."

After long, uncomfortable seconds of silence, Clarence kicked the sole of Jasper's shoe and raised his hands in a questioning manner.

"Shouldn't what?" Jasper asked.

"Yes, the coast is clear." Uncle Martin closed the blinds and turned around. "You have to leave now. I trust nobody followed you here. You can't be too careful out there. Do be careful."

"Dude," Clarence said to nobody in particular, sounding exasperated.

Jasper felt the visit derailing. "The girl, who was she?"

"I don't know. If she's a time bender, someone has been experimenting." Uncle Martin snorted, then coughed. "Bad news. Horrible. Nobody should inflict…" He didn't finish. "You can't trust anyone. Avoid her, avoid everyone."

"But my dad! Is there anyone else who knew who my dad really was? Who would try to harm him? Why did you give him a gun?"

Uncle Martin slowly looked him up and down. "Did you listen to anything I said? Are you the village idiot? He's an ass"—he pointed to Clarence with his thumb—"but at least he's not an idiot."

"No, I'm not," Clarence said. "And I think it's time for us to go."

"Past time," Uncle Martin said and burped. "I'm a busy man."

"But you can't throw us out now," Jasper said, "I have so many more questions. I have to find my dad. What's the Passage of Time?"

"How do you…?" Uncle Martin hesitated, then seemed to remember. "A stupid pun. I was young. Long abandoned, much too dangerous. Who knows what—" He stopped himself. "Do you know where it is?"

"I already told you—no," Jasper said.

"Good, excellent. Go now. I can't help you." Uncle Martin looked down and muttered to himself, "Milky space sauce."

"What?" Clarence asked.

Uncle Martin looked up, and the fog seemed to clear again for a moment. "You wouldn't understand, boy."

"Please don't call me 'boy,' sir," Clarence said.

"If you leave now, I'll gladly call you Your Majesty." Uncle Martin opened the casserole lid and gave them back their cell phones. "Don't turn them on until you're a mile away. And don't come back, I won't open the door. Good luck with… Whatever. Good luck with whatever."

Chapter Twelve

Far From California

"*R*obbie Top Secret! His Greatest Fears (And How He Conquered Them)."

Whenever she felt anxious, Eva turned to her Rip Current fan magazine to feel less alone in the world with her fears, although she couldn't quite relate to all of Robbie's. Classmates who made fun of people's acne ("*a disorder of the skin, prevalent chiefly among adolescents, caused by inflamed or infected sebaceous glands*")? That seemed unrealistically cruel.

Eva also didn't mind spiders. Maybe California spiders were particularly scary, but she had looked it up, and the encyclopedias didn't say so.

One thing she could relate to all too well, though—Robbie had been terrified to leave home for Rip Current's first world tour, *Drowned Out LIVE*. He was afraid he'd miss his parents and his friends. Who wouldn't! And who would take care of him if something happened? Say, in Japan, or Portugal, or Argentina? But his love of the music, his band mates, and especially all of his fans convinced him he had to go.

She'd read the article often, but it struck her now that she had missed the forest for the trees—leaving home was somehow the best decision he ever made! Not that she'd ever contemplate such a thing. Yet, she couldn't stop thinking about the sound her door made when it clicked shut. A high-pitched *click* followed by a brief scratching sound, then a deeper *click*. She had tried to replicate it all afternoon.

Between browsing her magazine and re-reading the Encyclopædia Britannica entries for "C," that is. Not all entries for "C," just the ones after "California." She looked up California again after reading about Robbie being homesick and just kept reading for a while absentmindedly until she remembered her experiment.

The closest she had come was to tap the tip of the golden pen Father had given her for her ninth birthday on the door handle, then slide it down the handle for the scratch and tap the bulbous end cap on the door plate for the final deeper clicking sound.

Nerd. Wanna look that up in your precious encyclopedia, too? "A foolish or contemptible person who lacks social skills or is boringly studious." Sound familiar?

Eva ignored Adam. And besides, that's what the dictionary said, not the encyclopedia. He should know better since he had read all of them as often as she did.

He had become a real meanie. She wanted a friend, a bit of freedom, an adventure. That couldn't be too much to ask. Father meant well, but so did Robbie's parents when they didn't want him to go on a world tour.

And it's not like she wanted to leave home, she knew about the size of the estate. She'd been to the garages and Father's quarters, yes, long ago even to the shed by the helipad. But a slice of leftover pizza in the kitchens? Or a cat in the courtyard? Was that too much to ask? The possibilities seemed downright endless.

After dinner, Father and Eva played a game of backgammon. He won, as he always did, before he briefly left while she got ready for bed.

She put on her nightgown in the bathroom and went back into the library to put her hand on the spine of the *National Geographic Atlas*.

"I'll do it tonight, Robbie," she whispered. "My own world tour. Wish me luck."

You'll freeze and die before anyone finds you.

"Why do you have to be so cruel?" Eva hissed at Adam. Why should she freeze then, exactly? She didn't have that many episodes and she'd only be gone, what, minutes? A couple of hours at most.

Father would be furious. You should stay here.

"Robbie would want me to go," Eva said. "He says sometimes you have to face your biggest fears. He'd want me to be happy. Why don't you want me to be happy? Why are you not my friend anymore?" That shut him up. Her brother had always been her best friend and confidant (*"a person with whom one shares a secret or private matter, trusting them not to repeat it to others"*). Now, he seemed only to undermine her.

After Father tucked in her comforter, he kissed her on the forehead.

Eva could barely remember the last time he had given her a kiss. "What is it, Father?"

"Nothing. Just… Maybe I'll have good news soon."

"Is Adam coming back?" Eva asked.

"No." He got up abruptly. "New medicine. Maybe. But it needs more time. Tests."

"What tests? Why?"

"To make sure it works, of course. Sleep well."

New medicine? A year ago he had said the same thing, right before Mom took Adam.

Despite the exciting news, Eva had other worries right now: the door was closing. Father had to be halfway down the corridor already, but she couldn't take any chances, and waited and waited until the door almost hit the lock.

She reached under her pillow and pulled out the golden pen she had practiced with alongside a thin cardboard coaster she had kept from lunch. Father didn't notice its absence.

Eva got up, tiptoed to the door, and gingerly pushed the coaster between the latch and the plate right before it would have snapped into place. Then, when the door normally would have clicked shut, she used her pen to tap, then scratch the door handle. Finally, she turned it around to strike the lock with the end cap.

This time it didn't sound right at all, and Eva held her breath.

The corridor outside remained silent. Either Father had already left, or he didn't notice.

Phew. She gently pulled on the coaster. It remained securely between door and lock. Careful not to make a sound, she opened the door as slowly as she could bear and stuck her head out into the corridor.

Dark and deserted.

She stepped outside her room and enjoyed the cool floor

under her bare feet. Using the coaster to prevent it from locking, she closed the door behind her.

Robbie didn't have to sneak out of his room like this for his world tour!

She waited for Adam to say something nasty, but he remained mute as a fish.

Eva took a step forward and inhaled deeply. The air had a faint flowery smell to it. An open window in the corridor maybe?

It smelled… intoxicating (*"to elate to the point of enthusiasm: 'the intoxicating touch of freedom'"*).

Chapter Thirteen

Planned Obsolescence

Jasper's cell phone alarm woke him in the morning. He turned it off, pulled the sheets over his head, and slept for another three hours. He didn't care if Clarence left for camp, he didn't care if the Wrights thought he was a slacker, and this Thursday morning, he didn't even care whether he made any progress finding his dad. Three days had already passed. A few hours more would make no difference.

He didn't know if it had been Uncle Martin's revelations per se, but a deep fatigue had seeped into his bones yesterday evening, which had only now begun to lift.

He crawled out of bed and finally showered for the first time since the fire. If any invisible girls decided to watch, so be it. Hopefully they enjoyed the show. Afterward, he put on another set of Clarence's ridiculous hand-me-downs and ate a couple chocolate bars.

The Wrights had all left and locked the main house, so he stayed in the pool house and looked down at the floor. Beige carpet. His backpack taunted him with its secrets.

My whole life has been a lie.

What do you do when it turns out that your missing

father, your crazy uncle, and their college buddies were actually members of a secret group of time benders? Freaks who didn't live according to the same universal laws everyone else did? What do you do when you find out that the person closest to you hid the very core of his existence from you? The piece of the puzzle that would have explained everything?

Do you keep looking for him? After all, nothing had changed except the laws of nature—and why bother dwelling on them? Jasper drew comfort from that thought.

Was it just his father's secret that he "needed to know?" Or the location of this Passage of Time? In any case, Dad remained missing and Jasper only had today and tomorrow before the police would set the wheels of bureaucracy turning.

Clarence had the afternoon off before their first big game day on Friday, so Jasper didn't have to wait long for him to be back home.

"Let's go to my house, have a look around," Jasper said.

"I don't know, what's the point? Feels like gawking."

"It's not gawking if it's your own accident." Besides, Jasper was fed up with the Wright's backyard and pool house. "And I need to find the Passage of Time. The blueprints aren't enough, the floppies are useless, we need some other clues."

"Not to be too negative, but what are these clues supposed to look like?" Clarence asked. "You've lived there all your life and didn't notice anything. Now it's burned down, and you think you're going to find some mysterious clues? Like directions to a secret underground lair under a floorboard or something?" The flatness in his voice made the idea sound absurd.

"Why is that so unlikely? You heard everything Uncle Martin said. It might rain unicorns tomorrow for all we know."

"I'm still not convinced he didn't trick us with that disappearing act," Clarence said. "I mean, do we have any hard proof? The guy's a loon, that's the only thing I know for sure."

"I know what I saw, and I know you saw it too. Are you coming with me or not?"

Barely twenty minutes later, they stood before the ruin that had been Jasper's childhood home. Yellow tape marked *Police Line – Do Not Cross* crisscrossed the charred frame that remained of the front door.

"It's not even as bad as I thought," Jasper said. "Let's go inside, what's the worst that could happen?"

"Let me think, uh..." Clarence stroked his chin mockingly. "We could die if the walls collapse, we could die if the rest of the roof comes down, or we could be arrested for breaching the police tape. Just off the top of my head."

"Well, you don't have to go in." Sure, the roof remains looked a bit dodgy, but Clarence's objection sounded suspiciously like a dare. "Let's start with the garage. That looks stable enough."

They walked down the driveway along the left side of the house. Jasper checked the hatch to the crawlspace, but as on the day of the fire, there was no sign of the cats. At the end of the driveway, the garage appeared untouched. He filled bowls with water and cat food for the kittens and left them in the crawlspace, same as before. Maybe they'd return.

"Do you have a cat you didn't tell me about?" Clarence asked.

"They don't belong to me. They don't belong to anyone."

"Excuse me, 'they?' There's more? You're feeding feral cats? C'mon man, you know better."

"Well, maybe I don't." Jasper didn't feel like justifying himself.

"The cities are trying to get rid of 'em because they eat all the birds, y'know," Clarence murmured.

"And do you want rats? Because that's how you get rats. By getting rid of all the cats," Jasper snapped before trying to change the topic. "Look, no police tape on this one." He pointed at the side door to the main house.

"That's only because the door is locked," Clarence said. "Anyway, you're still not supposed to go in there."

"Says who? It's *my* house." Jasper unlocked the door with his key.

"Fine, whatever, but I'm not going." Clarence put his hands in his pockets. "Look at the state of that wood."

True, its blackened appearance didn't exactly inspire confidence. "Then take the garage. I'll be quick." Jasper stepped inside.

In the home office that doubled as his father's bedroom a roof beam had smashed his desk, but not his computer. His dad took his laptop with him to his rented office, so now it had to be with his dad or whoever had taken him. Half the room, including the bookshelves, lay buried under roof and attic debris.

The hallway remained clear, but Jasper walked straight past the door to his bedroom. At this point, he didn't need to see the charred remains of his childhood to mark the end of an era.

A wood beam that had smashed his laptop had, quite literally, dashed the one hope of rescuing something of value. He'd left it open on the living room table, and it lay in scattered pieces.

Maybe it wouldn't have been as bad had he closed it before he left. The floor itself still seemed stable, although it looked badly charred.

Jasper sighed at the destroyed laptop, examining the fragments. When he crouched, he noticed the floor had only partially charred. The most severe burn marks on the hardwood floor formed a distinct pattern. They curled from the table over to the fireplace and the window in definite trails, far from random. Someone had drawn them in gasoline. Someone had set fire to his house.

The girl? As a time bender, she would've been able to disappear from their fight to start the fire, but how could the fire have been as big as it was when he got here? If a time bender started a fire, did it burn faster?

A shiver ran down Jasper's spine. What else could these people do?

He looked out the half-molten window toward the street—and up to the tree house.

The tree house!

The morning after his dad hadn't come home, he thought somebody had been in the treehouse. He remembered the feeling of being watched, but at that point, the thought of invisible people hadn't crossed his mind.

Unable to get the front door to open, he ran to the side door. Clarence already waited for him outside, a cardboard moving box in hand.

Jasper blurted, "Tree house," and ran to the front yard.

He climbed the ladder and looked around. The treehouse looked as empty as the day his father had disappeared—with one exception: a simple red brick on the floor in the far corner.

"Ha!" Jasper's excitement turned his exclamation into a squeal. He cleared his throat. "Come up here."

"You know I hate heights," Clarence said while he climbed the squeaky ladder.

Jasper pointed excitedly to the brick.

"Oh, a game," Clarence said, "I know, it's… a brick."

"Yeah, but I didn't put it here." Jasper raised his eyebrows.

"Pick it up, you drama queen."

Jasper lifted the brick, revealing a neatly folded piece of notebook paper with a few lines of tidy handwriting. "If you're reading this, you're not as thick as I thought. I still have the notebook. If you want to compare notes, put this brick in the tree house window and I'll find you."

Jasper handed the note to Clarence. "From the girl. Not as thick as she thought? She doesn't even know me."

"Yet she really gets you," Clarence said.

"Do you think it's a trap? It has to be a trap," Jasper said. "She wanted to steal it all when I caught her. She might have done this for all we know?"

"What do you mean, 'done this?'" Clarence asked.

"Someone set the fire. There were burn marks on the floor."

"Oof. Let me see that again." Clarence took the note and held it up to the light. "Handwritten, no special marks. Either she doesn't have access to a computer and a printer, or she just doesn't bother. The paper is a page of the notebook, proof that she has it. She says she wants to compare notes, pretty non-threatening language. She says she can just find you, yet she hasn't tried to steal anything else. Maybe it's a peace offer?"

"You're getting an awful lot out of that paper," said Jasper. "She tried to rob me! More than once."

"You pointed a gun at her." Clarence shrugged. "Maybe she's as desperate as you are? And what do you mean, more than once?"

"Remember the small footprint in the closet? Before we found the safe? That must've been her." Jasper picked up the brick and weighed it in his hand. "What if there's nothing useful in the notebook?"

"What if the notebook has the juicy bits?" Clarence asked.

"I'm not risking it." Jasper put the brick back down on the floor. "I have to find the Passage of Time myself."

Back at the Wright House, Jasper and Clarence had the place to themselves for once. The parents were at work, and Condi at her day camp.

Clarence set the cardboard mover's box he had found in the Faulks's garage down on the floor in his room and showed a metal box wrapped in cables to Jasper. "The rest is useless. Old CD and DVD writers, camcorder stuff, charging cables, but if this works…"

"What is it?"

"An old internal five-and-a-quarter inch floppy disk drive." Clarence disentangled the drive from the cables. "If I can get it to play nice with my setup, we should be able to read the disks you found in the safe."

"Can't you just plug it in somewhere?" Jasper asked.

"Let's see, this uses a thirty-four pin IDC connector. Maybe I can melt that down and pour it into my USB connector mold? No, I can't just plug it in somewhere."

"So what are we gonna do?"

"Well, I did buy a three-and-a-half-inch floppy disk drive enclosure with a USB connection at a flea market once," Clarence said. "If I can use the internal pin connector for your dad's drive, we might be able to use it as an adapter."

"So basically you can plug it in somewhere."

"Yes, you can plug it in somewhere, maybe you want to try? I have a very specific suggestion where exactly you can plug it in."

"Oh, I get it now," Jasper said. "This is hard, you just happen to be able to do it. You da man!"

"Why do I even bother?" Clarence dug into a large pile of unidentifiable electronics until he found the disk drive enclosure.

Using a tiny screwdriver, he opened the case and, after

some fiddling, pulled out the end of a flat broad cable with a black connector. It slid right into the connector at the back of the drive.

"Ta-dah." He smiled broadly.

"But does it work?" Jasper asked.

"I have no idea, but the cable fits." Clarence plugged the USB connector into the hub on his desk. After his system auto-installed the corresponding driver, the drive appeared on his desktop. "And we're in business. Hand me those floppies. We should make a copy first."

Jasper passed him the floppies, and Clarence put the first one into the drive. He secured the wobbly disk in place with a little switch that covered the disk slot.

The drive made a loud scratching noise when it started to read the disk.

"Holy crap, get it out of there," Jasper said and reached for the drive.

"Don't." Clarence slapped his wrist. "That's normal. If you rip it out, you might destroy it."

Several file symbols appeared on the display. Clarence copied and pasted them to his desktop, and the drive resumed spinning noisily. A couple of minutes later, Clarence repeated the procedure for the second disk while Jasper prayed silently that the drive wouldn't croak.

When Clarence put the third disk in, the noise changed pitch from the now-familiar scratch to more of a rasp.

"Uh-oh," Jasper said, but the noise changed back a second later and a single file appeared on the computer desktop.

"That didn't sound too healthy. Who knows how long

this thing has been in storage? But doesn't matter now, we have all the data," Clarence said and copy-pasted the file.

An error message appeared: "Failed to copy data. Permission denied."

"Odd," Clarence said and tried to drag-and-drop the file symbol. The message repeated.

"What's the file?" Jasper asked.

"An executable, 'nmpad.exe,'" Clarence said. "A program. You'd think my OS would ignore any ancient copy protection. Maybe I can clone the whole drive and work around that later."

"Can't you run it from the disk as long as this thing's still working?" Jasper asked.

"I could try a DOS emulator," Clarence mused.

Whatever that is. "Computer voodoo. Sounds great." Jasper held his breath when the drive started its raspy rah-rahing again.

After a few seconds, the normal reading sound returned. A new window opened, with crude graphics, green on black, displaying an image of a numerical pad, like from an ATM. The only keys were 1, 2, 3, 4, 5, 6, 7, 8, 9, and 0. Below the pad were three underlined spaces.

"Three digits? Try 1-2-3," Jasper said.

"You're the boss." Clarence typed and pressed enter. The drive spun the disk up again. After some brief croaking, the numerical pad reloaded. "I don't know if we have enough time to try a thousand combinations. Every time it reads the disk, it gets worse. This thing might give up any minute," Clarence said. "We should get a new drive."

"And when will that be? Tomorrow? Next week? I have

no time," Jasper said. "Let's try a few more. Nothing random, something with significance."

"That's difficult with three digits. Usually you have four. You know, month and day, or a year. What was the safe combination again?"

"Too long, six digits," Jasper said and looked at his dad's college records. "Their student IDs are seven digits."

"I should try to copy it again. If it's on my hard drive, it should be easy to crack."

"You said the drive might break at any time. The copying made a lot more noise than trying the numbers," Jasper said. "Try this one; it's the only three-digit number on here."

He pointed to the header of the student list, "Independent Studies 176."

Clarence typed 1, 7, 6, and hit enter.

The drive spun up again, but the scratching didn't stop, and the floppy disk kept on spinning.

Jasper jumped up from his chair. "Eject, it's eating the disk."

"No, it works. Look."

The numerical pad didn't reload. The screen remained black for a few seconds until a little, green-glowing "1" appeared in the top left corner.

Scratching transformed into a tapping noise, and the drive started chattering like a sewing machine. The screen filled with ones, as if the key had become stuck.

"Do something, it's dying. Eject the disk!" They couldn't lose all their progress.

"That'll rip it. It has to stop reading first." Clarence furiously typed away at his computer, but the drive wouldn't stop needling the disk, judging from the noise.

The endless stream of ones continued to fill the computer screen while the drive hammered faster and faster.

"Pull the cord before this thing is toast," Jasper pleaded moments before the needling noise died down and a faint mechanical squeal took its place. The disk stopped spinning and the stream of ones dried up. "Too late."

"I'll make a screenshot. We can let it cool off and try again," Clarence said. He unplugged the drive and ejected the disk.

Jasper held it to the ceiling light. The thin inside layer showed a spiraling crease with intermittent tiny punctures in it. Beyond saving.

When Clarence plugged the drive back in, it wouldn't even power up. He opened the enclosure and found several loose pieces of solder. "Yeah, this is above my pay grade. At least we have a copy of the other files on my hard drive, and maybe the screenshot was showing some program code. It all went so fast."

"Nah, only ones." Jasper had seen it clearly and the screenshot proved him right. Lines and lines of ones. Whatever the numeric pad once guarded was lost.

Why does the universe hate me?

With Jasper's luck, the data Clarence copied from the other two disks would turn out to be a copy of Pac-Man. At least no stupid numerical pad, code, or dying drive prevented them from reading the rescued files.

The first disk had five folders. Clarence opened the first and randomly picked one of the files. It opened as a text document.

"Look, an actual address!" Jasper jumped up from his chair. "On Olympic, here in L.A.!"

Google Maps showed an office high-rise on Olympic Boulevard, not too far from the Wright House by L.A. standards. But their excitement waned. The other documents also contained actual addresses in or near Los Angeles. And each folder had multiple documents with drawings of floor plans, diagrams of power grids, copies of construction permits, soil analyses, and earthquake risk assessments.

A strip mall in Inglewood, a bank building in Glendale, a medical building in Koreatown, a gas station in Hollywood, none of them looked remotely like the blueprint of the Passage of Time.

They flagged all of the locations on a map app.

"Looks like these are actual addresses and buildings, but I can't see a pattern," Clarence said.

"Maybe the second disk is more helpful." Jasper tried to stay positive.

The second floppy's files contained lists and invoices for building materials—cement, lumber, drywall, nails, etc., all made out to Baumgarten & Sons Construction, Inc.

"Hey, that's the name of one of Dad's friends." Jasper reached for the list of student records. "Here, Alexander Baumgarten."

"Maybe one of the 'and Sons?'" Clarence searched for it online but found nothing on Baumgarten & Sons

Construction. However, a Rüdiger Baumgarten had sold a California-based construction company in the late nineties for a sweet one hundred and seventy million US dollars.

"Try the delivery address," Jasper said. South Barrington Avenue, around the corner and one block south of the office building on Olympic from the other disk. They looked at the area in Street View—a Pooch Hotel. This turned into another wet dog kind of day.

"We have to put this information together the right way," Clarence said. "Someone was constructing something, maybe that strange Passage of Time."

"Or any of these other buildings," Jasper said, "and not one of them looks like what we're searching for."

"It's not that many places." Clarence pointed at the map of Los Angeles on the screen where he had flagged all building locations. "Maybe tomorrow you can take a look in person and find a common denominator?"

"Me, alone? Without a car and in one day? The girl may be looking for the same info, and I have one day before the police declare my father missing and send me who knows where. I can't go sightseeing in Inglewood for hours while—"

A firm knock on the door interrupted his speech. They had completely missed anyone coming home.

Without missing a beat, Jasper stuffed his things into the backpack while Clarence minimized the computer windows. Before anyone said, "come in," the door opened and revealed Mr. Wright, his trademark stern expression even sterner today.

Clarence sensed it too. "Is everything all right?"

"Jasper," Mr. Wright said in a steady baritone, "the police are waiting for you outside."

Jasper remained calm on the surface, but most of the blood in his body had shot straight to his head. *Not Dad!*

"They're here to pick you up," Clarence's father said.

Chapter Fourteen

Nothing to See

The police had not found Jasper's dad. In fact, Detective Keane said their main concern was locating him and asked if Jasper would mind accompanying them to the station and answering a few questions.

"Hold on, shouldn't there be a lawyer present if he doesn't have family with him? He's still underage," Clarence said.

Underage maybe, but he could speak for himself, thank you very much. "It's okay, no problem." Jasper couldn't think of anything he had legally done wrong and didn't want to stir the pot. "I'll call you when I'm done, no big deal. Or should I be worried, Detective?" He faked a laugh.

Detective Keane had been very amiable the night after the Faulks's house had burned down. "Of course not, we want to get to the bottom of this for you."

They rode to the station, Jasper in the back, listening to classic rock radio. After a while, Keane turned down the volume. "It was arson, you know?"

"Excuse me?" Jasper pretended he'd been distracted, but he had heard the detective quite clearly. *So they knew.* Not all too surprising considering the state of the living room floor, but what did it mean for his present situation?

They stopped at a red light, and Keane looked at Jasper in the interior rearview mirror. "The fire. It was arson, we have no doubt."

"That's..." Jasper squirmed in his seat. What did they expect him to say? "Wow, who would do something like that? And why?"

"That's what we're trying to find out." The cop turned the music back up.

Once they reached Keane's office inside the police station, Jasper's ears became hotter with every question.

"How often does your father go on business trips? How often do you communicate? Is there anyone who might wish you harm? Has anyone ever threatened you? Have you noticed anything strange around your house lately?"

Jasper did his best to stay close to the truth, but soon enough the grilling really started.

"Do you have a good relationship with your father? Do you love him? Does he get upset? Do you get upset? What happened to your mother? Do you blame your father for the accident? Did you ever just want to start over again?"

Detective Keane had copper hair, blue eyes, and very pale skin. The red patches on his face only seemed to grow as the interrogation went on. He sensed Jasper held something back, but how could he possibly have guessed what?

"How would you feel if your father never came back? What did you do on the day he didn't come home? And the day the house burned down?"

The question went on and circled back. More than once,

Jasper wondered if he should simply tell the police what he really knew. The time benders had hidden their talents for decades. Could he justify spilling the beans when nobody would believe him anyway? They'd want to question Uncle Martin and who knew how that would go down. And even if the police didn't believe a word Jasper told them, everything would go into an official file and he straight to a psych eval. *No.*

"How long does it take to get home from your friend's house? Did his parents see you leave? Did you know that eighty-seven percent of all arson is committed by someone who lives or works in the building…?"

After what felt like hours later, Keane released Jasper back into the wild. He had stuck with his story, not that he had much of one. If they could, they would have probably microchipped him. Instead, they had to settle for asking him to notify them in case he wanted to leave town.

Jasper imagined this was what it felt like to have taken a good beating. And yet, he had still dodged a bullet, at least until tomorrow evening, when they'd declare his father missing, and Child Protective Services would take responsibility for him.

He looked at his phone. One message from Clarence. "Hope you're ok. Dad offered to pick you up when you're out."

Thanks, but no thanks. He'd rather walk naked all the way

west on Sunset to the sea than spend alone time with Clarence's dad.

No, he only had tonight and tomorrow. Moping around the Wrights' was a waste of time, so he started walking.

He had left his backpack in the pool house. Obviously, he couldn't have taken a gun into a police station, and he hadn't been keen on risking anything else either. He felt unmoored without it, free to do anything tonight, whatever tomorrow would bring.

And whatever tomorrow brought, he'd have to face it alone. Clarence couldn't miss the first big basketball meet of the summer.

Jasper texted back, "I'm ok, but they're making me wait. I'll take a cab later."

He found a spring in his step. Only a few blocks to Olympic Boulevard. He'd check out that office building tonight.

A personal training gym took up most of the building's ground floor. Behind an unmanned granite desk, a maze of glass and mirrors housed enough fitness equipment to combat the whole nation's obesity epidemic.

Jasper went in, hoping for a discreet look around, but a tan blonde in her early twenties darted out of the break room to take up position behind the massive desk.

"Hey, are you looking for someone?" She exuded the tentative friendliness of someone who hasn't yet determined whether they have to treat you well or can safely ignore you.

"Uh, not really, I was just, uh, looking around," Jasper said, buying time while he came up with a cover story.

"Are you looking for a gym? I'm sorry, but we're adult-only."

Jasper hated that she hadn't even asked if he was eighteen, but with his loaner kiddie clothes, he couldn't blame her. "Nah, not looking for a gym, these twenty-four inch pythons are all I need." He threw his hair back and flexed his rather unimpressive bicep.

"You're funny!" She smiled.

Sometimes you had to play the cute kid. "I'm writing a paper on the impact the metro rail will have on local business," Jasper said. "Blah, blah, it's all very boring. I'm mainly interested in what sort of businesses have been in here over the years. Can you help me with that?"

"In this building? Dozens." She shuffled her papers. "There's tons of offices upstairs, check the directory."

"I'm focusing on retail." Jasper grinned. He had already checked the directory outside, he wanted some gossip. Not that he expected Time Benders Incorporated, but he had to start somewhere.

"Well, our manager will be back next Monday."

"Oh, bummer. My paper's due on Monday morning." He laughed nervously. "Maybe you can help me. What's been in this space before the gym?"

"How should I know? Look I'm really busy…" The way her voice rose at the end let more than a little valley girl shine through, but it was late, and nobody else worked here. Well, maybe except for the guy in the gray overalls prodding an electric panel at the other end of the lobby.

"Sure, thanks. One last question, who's fixing the power over there?"

"Oh, that's only the janitor. Ivan or Igor or something." She shuffled her papers some more.

"Got it." Jasper walked over to the electric panel.

"Excuse me, sir, can I ask you a question? Have you been working in this building for a long time?"

The janitor turned to face him and answered with a mild Russian accent through a walrus-like mustache that reached all the way down to his lower lip, "Yes, yes, over twenty years, since it was built."

Bingo! "Sorry to keep you from your work," said Jasper, "but do you remember the stores and companies that were in here before this gym? Anything unusual?"

"Unusual? What do you mean?"

"I don't know, maybe a… private club?" Jasper asked. "Something that didn't make sense to you?"

Without hesitation he answered, "No. Just different gyms, for many years a bank. Before the bank? No, I think the bank was first."

"Someone told me this building had a strange history, but maybe it was a prank. Do you remember if there were any other plans, I mean before the bank?"

The janitor thought for a couple of seconds, and his Russian accent became more noticeable. "I don't know if that's strange, but when this was built, in ninety-one I think, it was empty for a while. They already hired me, you know, the company, but nobody moved in. Everything was done, finished, but they always had problem with the power.

Zhou-zhou." He waved up and down with his hands. "Like wave, up and down. Lights flicker. Once power was down for three days. All other buildings had power. I sit in my little room with a flashlight…" He acted out the memory with his screwdriver. "Empty building. When they repaired it, put in extra generator, it's working since. Well, more or less." He chuckled and pointed at the bunch of cables hanging from the wall panel he was working on. "But strange company or club, no, I don't think so."

"Thank you," Jasper said, "Igor, is it?"

The janitor's face lit up as if Jasper had given him a gift. "Yes, yes, Igor! How did you know?"

"You're famous." Jasper winked at him. At least he had made someone happy tonight, even if his investigation had been a bust. He looked around left and right as he exited the building. Nothing seemed particularly strange or unusual. An anonymous high-rise like any other.

It sounded weird for this office building to remain empty for a couple of months after completion. Did that happen often before the offices and stores got rented?

The locations from the floppy disks had to be connected to the Passage of Time, but it couldn't be everywhere at the same time. Uncle Martin said it had been long abandoned, but on the internet, it had looked like the office tower, the mall, the gas station, the bank, and the medical building were all in use.

And sure, Uncle Martin had also said the Passage was much too dangerous, but his judgment clearly couldn't be trusted in all sorts of ways.

Jasper put one foot in front of the other without a clear

destination. Why did L.A. have to be so big? He couldn't take a little roundtrip to Glendale and Inglewood and back.

Even only going to the Wright House from here, he'd have to turn on Barrington to cut through to Ocean Park and wait for a bus west. Everything took forever.

The money from the safe would allow him to rent a taxi for a day and drive to all the locations, but Friday traffic would take him hours. When he kicked a soda can to the curb in frustration, a huge green neon sign caught his attention.

"Pooch Hotel: Doggie Daycare, Boarding and Spa." The place had come up on their internet search for the delivery address. It looked newly finished, that would've been obvious even without the big *"now open"* sign above the entrance. To the right, a driveway led to an underground parking garage.

Jasper peered in through the glass front at an empty desk. It was well after regular office hours. A small sign at the door read, "Please ring bell for service after 6pm or on weekends."

Should he ring?

A bright spotlight illuminated the house number: 2268. *Not 2269.*

Street View had shown them the Pooch Hotel. The wrong house. He was absolutely certain the delivery address had said 2269. Turned out a crude sense of humor could be useful after all.

Jasper looked around. The uneven numbers had to be on the other side, but the whole block was fenced off and the buildings razed for the Metro-Expo-Line.

Since Jasper's dad didn't drive any more, Jasper had followed all public transportation development with special curiosity. Actual construction in this area was scheduled for later this year.

He crossed the street to take a look behind the fence. Sturdy plastic fabric shielded the construction area from public view. Half a block to the west, he managed to pry away a little fabric and peek inside.

The whole block had been abandoned and mostly torn down a while ago. Nature already overgrew piles of rubble, dirt, and trash. High grass sprung up in the cracks of old driveways and sidewalks. Someone could shoot a zombie-apocalypse movie here without building a set. This being L.A., maybe someone had already done that.

No complete buildings remained standing, except a single one about twenty-five yards away from the curb. It wouldn't have been visible from Barrington if whatever originally stood in front of it had still been there, but with the whole block torn down, Jasper could make it out quite clearly, even in twilight: a one-story building with a flat roof and a wide garage door next to a smaller normal door.

He had seen it before, on one of his dad's pictures in the box. Uncle Martin and someone else had held up a sign: POT 1991. Jasper had thought it meant something else, but now it made more sense. He had found the Passage of Time.

Score!

A rush of blood to the head. Almost dizzy with excitement, he forced himself to keep walking calmly, checking for a gap in the fence.

Don't get cocky, kid.

Emotional high or not, he could do without shredding his limbs on razor wire. Luckily, one of the panels on the south side wasn't properly fastened. He pried it open and squeezed through.

Inside the old auto repair shop, Jasper used his cell phone display as a source of light. The flashlight app on his ancient Android had stopped working a while ago.

Looking around, he saw nothing but unremarkable trash, except for a solid steel door without lock or handle. Considering all the dents and scratch marks, someone had already tried to get past it.

He traced the area around the steel doorframe with his phone.

Thanks to the feeble glow of the display, Jasper had to get close to the wall. So close in fact that he could make out a subtle change of the wall texture in an area to the right of the frame. In bright daylight, he never would have noticed.

He brushed it with his fingertips and gave it a knock. It sounded different from the regular wall, metallic and hollow. He found the edges and applied a little more pressure.

A three by five-inch hidden panel swung open on hidden hinges. It had appeared seamless with the rest of the wall, an impressive feat of engineering.

Behind it, a numeric pad with sturdy metal keys was the spitting image of the digital one on the floppy disk—no screen, no writing, no keyholes. He took a picture of it with his cell phone.

This had to be it. The answer to the mysteries of the safe, the key to finding out what happened to his dad.

Another code. Clarence and Jasper had figured it out before, for the numerical pad on the computer: 176.

Jasper took a deep breath and firmly pressed 1, 7, 6. The keys didn't make a sound when pushed down, or after he entered the code.

He listened for any hint that a lock or mechanism moved behind the panel or in the doorframe.

Nothing.

What had been the combination to his dad's safe again? Mom's birth month, Jasper's birthday and dad's birth year. Bringing his cell phone up to the numerical pad to illuminate the keys and make sure he didn't accidentally push the wrong button, he pressed: 0, 7, 1, 8, 6, 9.

Again he listened, again nothing happened.

Jasper gave the door a good kick, not denting it even a little bit. He searched the room again, but it didn't give up any more mysteries. He had found the lock already, he simply lacked the combination. Clarence could help figure out the code, but he must have been in bed already, in any case unable to leave home alone right now.

Outside the repair shop, the part of the north and east walls enclosing the area behind the metal door didn't look any different than the regular walls, with one exception: no windows. The walls themselves were solid concrete and nothing currently in Jasper's power could bring them down.

Reluctantly he headed back to the Wright House. The Passage of Time would keep its secrets for another day. Tomorrow, he'd have to find a way in.

Chapter Fifteen

A Box of Pain

"Look, it's the exact same thing." Jasper showed the picture of the numerical pad on his cell phone to Clarence. "Same as the one on the floppy disk."

"It's a numerical pad. They all look like numerical pads," Clarence said.

"Come on, what are the odds? It's a metal blast door without a handle in an abandoned dump. With a numerical pad!" Jasper tapped his cell phone display for emphasis. "What else would it be but the Passage of Time?"

"Say you're right. Now what? It's a metal door without a handle, and we have no idea what's behind it. Your uncle said it was too dangerous."

"So that's the one thing he said that you believe? I have to get in there today!"

Jasper hadn't been able to catch up with Clarence until after breakfast. When he had arrived at the Wright House yesterday evening, the Wrights wanted to know what the police said. When he told them about the arson and that CPS would start checking in tomorrow, they had fallen quiet.

"Well, they must have experience in these matters. I'm

sure they'll have suitable accommodation for you," Mr. Wright had said before he added, "but your father will be back by then anyway, right?" He sounded neither convincing, nor convinced.

Jasper didn't think the Wrights suspected him of setting fire to his own house, but at this point, they couldn't know what to think anymore. They'd be glad to see the last of him.

And if he needed any more evidence of that, the clothes Mrs. Wright had laid out for him this morning could serve as exhibit Z: a yellow SpongeBob t-shirt.

Buying new clothes sounded very tempting, and he still had the eight grand in cash, but damn it, he had other worries first. So he sat in Clarence's room, resignedly sporting his tall friend's elementary school-era SpongeBob t-shirt, a little too small even for him.

Mr. Wright simultaneously knocked and opened the door, something Jasper wouldn't miss wherever he wound up.

"Come on, champ, big day today," Mr. Wright said cheerfully.

Ah yes, the first big meet of Clarence's basketball camp. A mini-tournament against the SaMo Hammers and the Brentwood Thunder or something ridiculous like that.

Clarence's enthusiasm knew no bounds either. "Dad, do you think maybe I could stay here today? Jasper is having a rough time, and he's my friend and our guest, so—"

"Clarence, we talked about this. Camp isn't optional. You don't want your broadband privileges revoked again. And I'm sure Jasper will be able to entertain himself, in his room, for one more day."

"I'm right here," Jasper said under his breath.

If Mr. Wright heard him, he didn't show it. "You should be proud of your athleticism and be happy to get out of this…" He looked around Clarence's room. "This nerd cave. See you outside in five." With that, he exited, but left the door open behind him.

"I'll help you when I can, but you know my dad," Clarence whispered and got up.

"See you later," Jasper said. "What are you gonna do?" *Except tell him to go play the stupid tournament himself if it was so damn important?*

What had Mr. Wright done for Clarence lately? Bought him a freaking Prius and expected him to LeBron it up at some irrelevant high school basketball meet. How about adding some actual understanding and empathy to that parental love? The guy didn't know the first thing about his son.

Much like Jasper hadn't known the first thing about the father he tried to find.

The same father he had been so frustrated with for the last two years, he considered emancipation.

The same father he had silently blamed for his mother's death for years.

The same father who led a double life so strange, less than ten people on earth would believe you if you told them.

But still his father and he loved him.

A realization crept up his insides. It made him so nauseous, he tried to think of something else, but it wouldn't go away.

He might already be an orphan.

Panic squeezed him. A desperate need for the familiar sights and sounds and feel of home—*now.*

He grabbed his backpack and started walking, happy to leave the Wright House behind.

A good thirty-minute walk later, the sight of the charred remains proved a harsh reminder that what had made his house his home had been destroyed.

Nothing looked different than yesterday, let alone more inviting. Police tape still crisscrossed the front door.

Foolish nostalgia, a waste of precious time.

He retraced yesterday's steps past the house to the unburnt garage, where Clarence had found the floppy disk drive and where he had found the key in the flower pot at the beginning of this crazy goose chase. But standing in the garage, the last undamaged remnant of an earlier life, his surroundings felt alien.

He looked over to the house. From the side, if he squinted and didn't see that the roof had caved in, it almost looked like it had for the last fifteen years, but even then, the smell of burnt wood wafted over.

This had been a bad idea. He looked around the garage. These were all just things. He had come for the wrong reasons.

He had to worry about finding his father, not this empty shell of a house.

Can you keep an eye on him for me? Mom's words echoed

in his mind. I'm trying, Mom.

But could he be—a hero? His gaze fell on the bag of cat food. He checked yesterday's bowls in the crawlspace and felt euphoric. They had been emptied. The cats still had to be around somewhere.

Jasper refilled the bowls and walked back to the front yard with renewed purpose. No more moping, he'd be all action from now on, starting by tracing his dad's steps from here to the Passage, then trying more combinations at the strange door.

He looked up to the tree house, where the girl's message still lay under the red brick. Or did it really?

Better to check. The brick was still there, but the neatly folded handwritten note underneath had been replaced. The new one, written on the same kind of paper from the stolen notebook, read: "You've seen my face. 2+2=176. Let's meet."

Enough with the riddles. And why'd she think he'd change his mind? After all, she attacked him, even stole from him. But why the new note anyway? Clarence—he had drawn five conclusions in sixty seconds from the first note.

Jasper looked at his phone for the time. No, Clarence would be playing his first game. He couldn't call him now. But if he wanted to get past that steel door later, a little mental exercise couldn't hurt. He sat down on the floor in the tree house and looked at the note again.

What would Clarence say?

Firstly, she'd left a new note, which meant she knew he had rejected her previous proposal. Which meant she knew he had been here and didn't put the brick in the window. Most likely she followed him around, surveilling him—a deeply disconcerting thought. The yellow SpongeBob t-shirt seemed like an even worse choice of garb than this morning.

But he had caught her earlier when she tried to steal from him, so maybe she kept her distance. She could have also set an alarm somewhere here. He looked around the treehouse. Maybe a Wi-Fi camera?

Down on the floor, his fresh footprints sat atop the prints he and Clarence left yesterday. They hadn't even thought about trying to conceal that they had been up here. The smoke from the fire had coated the treehouse in a thin layer of soot. Anyone with eyes would know they had been up here.

He was clearly overthinking this.

The message itself then. "You've seen my face. 2+2=176. Let's meet." Yes, he had seen her face, briefly. A pretty girl, whatever. Perfectly symmetrical, oval-shaped face with dark brown eyes and all that, but what was "2+2=176" supposed to mean?

That fateful college class his parents and Uncle Martin had attended—"176." She must have gotten that from the notebook. But "2+2"? "Let's meet"? Like he'd change his mind because she reminded him that she was pretty or something? He had other worries than meeting girls right now.

His mind went back to their single encounter. How surprised she'd been that he caught her. How she turned invisible in front of his eyes.

Hell—how *would* he know if she followed him around?

No, right now he couldn't ally himself with someone like that. If he found his father and knew more about time bending, he could think about taking the precautions necessary to meet another time bender. 'Someone has been experimenting,' Uncle Martin had said. 'You can't trust anyone.'

I have to find Dad. Alone.

He'd have to take a few detours to get rid of anyone who might be following. As for today, if she was so desperate to meet him, he might as well use that to distract her.

He took out a pen and wrote his response on the note: "4pm today. Here." After a couple of seconds he added "(Friday)," then folded the note and put it under the brick in the window.

He'd sometimes thought about being watched or followed in the abstract, about losing a tail, like on a cop show on TV, but halfway down the ladder, Jasper felt someone watching him as strongly as he'd feel someone physically bumping into him. And it gave him the creeps.

He turned around for the last few rungs and scanned the neighborhood before jumping down to the ground. Hopefully, that had looked natural enough even if someone was watching.

As usual at this time in the morning, the streets and front yards in this neighborhood were empty. Only a few parked cars and a plumber's van across the street.

Unfortunately, that didn't mean anything if his watcher could turn invisible. But invisible didn't mean vanished into thin air, so if he could only make sure he got away alone, he'd be in the clear.

Jasper took out his cell phone and called Westside Taxi Service, a number he had on speed dial ever since his dad had sold the car. "Five minutes, great. Thank you." He'd just make sure to be alone in the car; that should do the trick for now.

A man's voice right behind him interrupted his train of thought. "Heads up!"

Jasper turned around. For a split-second, he caught a flash of pipe coming at him. Right at his eye, to be precise.

"Ahhhhh-ouch!"

It hit him in his left eye, barely missing the eyeball. The socket bore the brunt of the impact. Searing pain flashed through his skull as a hit knocked him down on his butt.

"Sorry," someone grumbled.

Sorry? What the hell? Tears shot into Jasper's good eye. Through the veil, he tried to make out what had just hit him.

Ten steps past him, a man in a dark blue overall carried a long, rigid plastic pipe across the street on his way to the plumber's van.

Jasper still sat on the sidewalk, disbelieving. "Dude, what the hell?"

The plumber kept on walking to his van and put the pipe in the back.

"Hey, you hit me in the eye!" Jasper yelled.

The man closed the back door and walked to the driver's side. He looked straight at Jasper but didn't say anything.

Jasper still couldn't focus very well, but the man was broad-shouldered and had white-blond hair. He opened the door and reached inside right as a familiar face appeared in the front yard of the house behind the van.

"Jasper, is that you honey?" called Janice. "I've been worried, are you all right, did you just scream?"

The plumber looked from Jasper to the elderly woman, a glint of sunlight flashing from his clear aviator glasses. He hesitated.

"Jimmy, come outside for a moment, will you?" she said. "Jasper here needs some help."

At that, the plumber got into his van and drove away.

Jasper flipped him the bird when he rolled by but didn't notice any reaction.

"I'm fine, Janice, thank you," Jasper said. "Gotta go right now, I'll explain some other time." He got up from the sidewalk. His knees still felt a little wobbly, but he managed to give Janice and Jimmy, who had just emerged from Janice's house, a thumbs up right before a cab turned the corner and stopped in front of him. Jasper waved at his neighbors and got into the car. It took him a little while to remember where he wanted to go.

"You look like hell." Clarence handed Jasper an ice-cold sports drink.

Jasper had caught the last two minutes of Clarence's first match, then intercepted him on the way back to the locker room. They huddled in a corner to the side of the door while everyone else had gone in.

"Thanks, Captain Obvious," Jasper said and took the bottle, "and, uh, thanks for the drink." He pressed the bottle to his left eyebrow that had swollen to half the size of a ping-pong ball.

"So the guy didn't even check on you?" Clarence asked.

"Nope, just kept on walking. Total dickhead." Jasper rolled the bottle over the whole side of his face now. "Ahh, that feels so good."

"Why did you even go back there?"

"Because I'm an idiot, but at least I put that girl on the wrong track. I hope. Any idea about the message?"

"Hmm. She wants you to work something out. She's trying to gain your trust, she wants you guys to meet, but there's gotta be a reason why it's in code, and it's gotta be because she wants to hide your connection from anyone else. For some reason, she thinks this is enough for you to figure it out. Obviously, she doesn't know you as well as she thinks."

"Maybe she thinks I have a smart friend, who it turns out isn't quite as smart as he thought he was," Jasper said.

"Touché. But seriously, there's gotta be enough there. Something to make you trust her."

The coach's voice boomed from the locker room "Wright, get your ass in here!"

"One minute, coach," Clarence shouted back at the locker room door, then turned back to Jasper, "but you can still worry about that later. I've been thinking about the door. There's no handle, right?"

Jasper shook his head.

"No handle, no display, no keys except for zero to nine,"

Clarence said. "I think that means you can try as many combinations as you want. Think about it, you can't get in there any other way and anyone walking by could just try any combination at any time." Clarence was in his element now. "It can't re-lock or unlock after a wrong combo, and you can't reset it or anything. There's no override, it just opens on the right combo, period. I don't see how it could work any other way, unless there's another door or mechanism."

"But that's great news, right?" Jasper said. "I can just keep on trying until I find the right one." If there was nothing to figure out, all he'd need was patience.

"Unfortunately, it's highly unlikely that the combination would just be four or five digits, let alone three," Clarence said. "That would make the lock way too vulnerable to chance. And just six digits would make it a million possible combinations. And it might be more than six digits. Well, you do the math."

"Wright, do you want to sit out the next game?" The coach yelled again, his voice holding a sharper edge.

"Gotta go," Clarence said to Jasper. "You staying? We can talk after the game."

"Yeah, I'm staying," Jasper said, "but I don't know why if all you have is bad news. Got another bottle for my eye? I think I'm gonna drink this one."

Despite his snark, Jasper was happy to stay. In addition to the mother of all black eyes, the mother of all headaches brewed. Way too many mothers for a half-orphan.

He didn't go up to the grandstand, if you could call the staggered pullout benches that, but instead sat on the ground next to the locker room from where he could see the middle of the court and the scoreboard, but neither of the baskets.

The ref started the game, and Clarence's team had the ball. They moved forward out of Jasper's view.

He tried to ignore the pain migrating deeper and deeper into his head and focused on the silver lining in Clarence's conclusions. A million possible combinations or more, but no limit to how many he could try. It would take too long to try 000001, 000002 and so on, but at least he could try all combinations that made some sense.

It had taken only two tries to figure out the combination for the program on the floppy disk: the fateful 176. Too bad the disk was broken, whatever the 176 had unlocked could have helped him now.

Clarence's team scored and moved into defense and out of Jasper's view again.

He couldn't think anymore. A pounding red ball of pain nestled in the center of his brain.

Many years ago, he once had a headache on a long road trip with his parents. They didn't have any meds with them, over sixty miles from the next pharmacy. Dad told him to imagine the pain as a little ball in your head. Move all of the pain inside that ball, put the ball in a box, and think of something else. It hadn't worked then, but maybe he had been too young.

He tried to put the ball of pain in a box. *Have to think of something else…*

He took his cell phone out of his pocket and loaded a game, hitting arrow keys in a trance-like state, just going through the motions. *Don't think of the pain.*

But the ball of pain in a box in his brain still hurt. He put it in another box.

And another box.

He let go of his phone and put his hands over his eyes.

Black boxes swallowed more and more black boxes, but in the center, the red ball of pain refused to go away.

He let go of his surroundings and fell into the boxes, one after the other, blackness swallowing blackness, never ending.

Until he realized that the red ball of pain had disappeared, and he stopped falling, his pain gone.

He opened his eyes and picked up the phone that he had dropped. It appeared more real than before, an object of importance.

He lightly brushed the smooth phone display with his thumb, feeling sticky resistance where his button mashing had left smudges on the surface.

Of course, use marks.

He opened the photos app and looked at the picture he had taken of the numeric pad yesterday evening. The flash had fired so you could see the metal keys very clearly. All appeared new—except one.

Finally a stroke of luck? Jasper bit his lip and took the folder with all the Passage of Time materials out of his backpack.

He was looking for a combination that wasn't random, but it couldn't be too personal either, since it would be used by a group of different people. A very, very specific group of people, with a lot of time on their hands and an impish sense of humor, if Uncle Martin was any indication.

He found the piece of paper he had in mind and started counting. The result made sense. Too perfect to be random.

He looked up just as Clarence lumbered past him up the court. According to the scoreboard they still only led 2-0. No way Jasper could wait for the end of the game.

He pushed the folder into his backpack and got up. He'd call Clarence from the Passage of Time. He had no time to lose.

Chapter Sixteen

The Passage of Time

Jasper stood in front of the keypad next to the steel door to the Passage of Time, the piece of paper he hoped held the combination in his hand as a good luck charm. He didn't need to read from it.

In the broad daylight, the numeric pad blended seamlessly into the bare concrete wall. He had to feel for it and even knowing its rough location, it appeared like magic when it smoothly swung open and exposed the polished metal buttons.

He looked closer to confirm what he had seen on the cell phone pic: all the buttons were free of scratches or use marks. All, except one. *The* "1." The sturdy metal wasn't scratched up or worn out. The difference was subtle, like when you look at a newish computer keyboard, but you can tell that there's more A's in the English language than Q's.

"Please let me be right," he whispered to himself and pressed the "1" button over and over again.

He clutched the piece of paper in his hand—a printout of the screen grab Clarence had saved right before the floppy disk drive gave out.

They had thought it gibberish, produced in error. Now

Jasper gambled it wasn't gibberish, or code, but rather *the* code.

Twice he had counted. There were exactly one hundred and seventy-six ones there.

It made perfect sense. The people coming here could bend time, so it wouldn't take them any more Real Time than a normal person needs to press the button a couple of times. And you could never possibly forget it. You just kept pressing ones. Silly, sure, but ingenious too.

But only if it actually works.

1, 1, 1, 1, 1, 1, 1, 1, 1, 1, 1, 1, 1, 1...

After Jasper pressed the key one hundred and seventy-six times, a deep *click* came from the wall.

Success. The kind you're after for your whole life—delivering under pressure.

He busted out a big, goofy smile, usually reserved for moments like riding a death-defying rollercoaster, but when he pushed open the big steel door, his joy turned into something different entirely.

Behind the door a small, square, completely empty room with a rectangular hole in the floor right in the middle of it greeted him. Bare concrete steps without any kind of railing led down to pitch black darkness.

The tracks of Jasper's rollercoaster had disappeared, and the only way to go was down. But did he have to go alone? He looked at his cell phone. One bar of reception. With this much concrete around him, downstairs would be worse.

He called Clarence. Voicemail. Damn basketball. He hung up again and texted him: "At the PoT. Figured it out. Going in now."

Then another one: "Look for my body if you don't hear from me in a couple of hours. Ha ha."

Jasper didn't trust the electronic locking mechanism, so he kept the steel door open with a brick from the garage before stepping forward into the hole in the ground, sincerely hoping for a light switch down there somewhere.

The light of his cellphone display was a small comfort as he descended the stairs into darkness.

Damn that broken flashlight app!

The smooth concrete around him didn't change all the way down the twenty-four steps until he found himself in a square corridor leading to another heavy steel door, this one round, like in a bank vault. The pristine surface reflected the light from his cellphone like a mirror.

He got closer and looked at himself. What a mess. A swollen eye and hair that screamed ten-years-in-the-wilderness more than cool surfer do. SpongeBob seemed to be mocking him. He looked like a freshly beaten up homeless kid. Well, technically he *was* a freshly beaten up homeless kid.

The massive vault door looked thick enough to withstand a grenade explosion, but Jasper didn't see a locking mechanism beyond the spinning handle. "Please, no more riddles," he said and turned the weighty handle carefully. The polished metal felt cool to the touch. He sensed the locking mechanism inside the door moving.

When the handle wouldn't turn anymore, he pushed.

Twelve inches of solid steel swung open smoothly without much resistance.

Behind it, the blackness stretched down another corridor and swallowed the light from Jasper's phone long before he could make out anything of significance. The air smelled stale.

He opened the door as far as it would go. With a series of clicks, a whole battery of fluorescent lights running along the middle of the ceiling all the way down the corridor turned on. Another *click* followed and faint fan noise announced an ancient air conditioning unit powering up. Jasper looked around at several louvers in the bare concrete near the ceiling, about halfway down. A door at the far end looked identical to the one he had opened.

After his eyes adjusted to the glare of the industrial lighting, he stepped forward and left the vault door behind him open. The inside also had a spinning handle, but he didn't dare entomb himself.

As expected, the phone had no reception. Hardly surprising twenty feet underground and behind a steel blast door. Jasper put it back in his pocket.

Apart from the lighting and the air conditioning, the corridor consisted of the same uninviting, endless concrete as on the other side, only broken up in the middle by a metal ring, about a foot wide, that ran up both sides and met at the ceiling where two inverted plastic bowls were mounted. They looked like motion sensors. Maybe that's what had triggered the lights and AC.

On the left side of the metal ring, several bundles of

cables in all colors of the rainbow ran behind a rectangular opening cut into the metal covering.

Someone had unfastened one of the bundles, cut several wires and bridged others. Since he couldn't even begin to make sense of this, Jasper took a deep breath of stale air and moved on to the next door. He turned the spinning handle and pulled. Like the first one, it opened smoothly.

Whatever he had expected, it wasn't… *this*.

Uncle Martin said the one thing you can never do is go back in time. *Wrong*. Jasper found himself in a large lounge straight out of the, what, 1970s? 1980s? 1990s? Whenever they had put the colorblind in charge of interior design.

A big round purple carpet stretched out in front of him with a frog-green sofa and armchairs grouped around the biggest tube TV he had ever seen. Next to it stood a big tower of stereo equipment topped with a fancy matte silver turntable.

To his right, three metal-framed reading chairs with accompanying glass side tables had been placed in front of rows and rows of bookcases filled to the brim with books with colorful spines. To his left, a large dining table with ten orange plastic chairs stretched towards the far end. A slightly lighter shade of purple than the carpet adorned the walls. At least the popcorn ceiling had been painted in a less eye-straining cream color.

Not even a distant hum disturbed the dead quiet, but the air didn't feel as stale as it had in the corridor. Jasper checked the closest chair for dust. It didn't look like decades' worth. All chairs were neatly set under the table except the one at the head, which stood at an angle. He checked, and it had no dust on it at all. Someone had been here not too long ago.

"Dad?" Jasper said aloud. He couldn't help himself.

No answer, of course.

The lounge had six doors leading somewhere else, seven if you counted the one Jasper entered through. "Idiot, idiot, idiot," he said and took off his backpack.

The blueprint! He already had a map of the whole place. *"The Passage of Time." Fourth draft. M. Higgs.*

He looked at it with fresh eyes. He was clearly in the "big room" at the center of the drawing. The approaching corridor had been much longer than in the drawing, that's why he hadn't thought of it before now. But the seven doors were unmistakable. The one to his left should lead to a small chamber.

He checked, it was a bathroom.

Another one should lead to another corridor with more rooms branching off, and it did. He'd have to check them later.

On the other side of the lounge, another small room contained supplies. Pink toilet paper. Who thinks of these things?

On to the other big room. The lounge was the heart of the Passage of Time, this was the brain. At first glance, it looked like a library with bookshelves lining the walls and several desks with reading lights on them, but the shelves were filled with dozens, no, hundreds of nearly identical-looking folders and notebooks in neat rows populating the shelves from floor to ceiling, only broken up by name tags in alphabetic order separating large sections of the shelves: Banerjee, Medha; Baumgarten, Alexander; Durant, Renee (there were just a few folders and notebooks for his mother); Faulks, Andrew; Hakin, Murat; Higgs, Martin; Jupiter, James; Misra, Nirav; Greasley, Floyd; Zeiger, Tranquillo. Jasper knew all the names. They had been the students of course 176.

Most of the desks had ancient beige IBM PCs on them, but one had a laptop and folders and notebooks strewn all over it. His father's laptop?

Jasper picked up one folder. The label read "Misra, Nirav XXIV - 11/4/91 - 12/16/91." He looked at a random page. "Hemoglobin 13.8; Hematocrit 43.8; MCV 97.3; MCH 29.0; MCHC 31.1..." He put it down again.

This was the mother lode of information about the "176" students, especially if someone happened to be interested in their hematocrit on 11/17/91, but to piece this together would take forever and still wouldn't tell him where Dad was now. About as useful as an encyclopedia when you're lost in the desert and out of water.

A loud metallic *click* followed by a deep hum interrupted Jasper's frustration.

It came from the next room, separated from the library by a wine-red plastic curtain on tracks.

Jasper peeked through the opening in the middle. This area had been completely trashed. A high pile of metal, wood, and shattered glass occupied half of it. Chair legs, table tops, a small cabinet, even a couple of stretchers peeked out from the rubble.

In the other half of the room, a huge freestanding refrigerator kicked on, humming. It was empty except for a six-pack of Diet Coke cans. Jasper looked at the expiration date. Still in the future.

Sweet.

He cracked one open, drank deeply, and pressed the ice-cold aluminum against his black eye.

A running fridge reminded him of how little he knew about this place. There had been more doors in the main room and he had already seen another corridor with more doors leading who-knows-where.

He took another sip of Coke and looked at the blueprint again. The "library" was just one big room without the room divider, but if the rest checked out, the main lounge branched off into two more rooms without any other entries or exits.

He walked back to the library and decided to check the remaining rooms before going up to call Clarence. The PCs were eighties junk, right up Clarence's alley. Jasper put the newish laptop that looked like Dad's into his backpack.

Back in the main lounge, he looked at his map while entering the remaining rooms. It made him feel a little more secure, like having a GPS in an unfamiliar neighborhood.

In the second-to-last room, large and elongated, the lights didn't come on automatically. Jasper found a switch right behind the door. It turned out to be a home theater with four rows of three seats each, an old two-reel film projector behind the final row, and a screen at the other end of the room. Shelves occupied the wall behind the projector with dozens and dozens of film reels. "Back to the Future," "Ghostbusters," "Raiders of the Lost Ark," "Batman," and more.

Pretty sweet, but not very helpful.

He turned off the lights and entered the final room, the third biggest behind the lounge and library.

A game room. No, the ultimate game room, with everything. A full-size pool table, a poker table, a darts area, a foosball table, two pinball machines and eight video arcade games. Even some fitness equipment in the corner (a treadmill and an exercise bike), although why anyone would want to use those over the games was beyond Jasper.

Surely, calling Clarence could wait until he had checked if that pinball machine still worked.

It did. The theme was Back to the Future, and *Great Scott* was it glorious.

Jasper had never played pinball before, but for a minute, his problems vanished as he smoothly thwacked the metal ball with the flippers, rewarded by the wonderful sights and sounds of a commercial pinball machine.

When the final ball fell straight down between the flippers, the machine abruptly turned itself off. Nothing in the world was more tempting than another round, but the game had gone dark.

With a sigh, he turned around to face reality again.

What the actual…?

Over the pinball noises, Jasper hadn't heard anyone approaching, but there he stood, about fifteen feet away, looking expectantly at Jasper as if he had already been waiting for a while.

The… plumber?

Short, white-blond hair, glasses, broad shoulders, blue overalls. Jasper hadn't seen him this clearly earlier, but he definitely stared at the same person.

"What are you doing here? You hit me right in the eye with that pipe," he burst out with before thinking. Of course this couldn't be coincidence. "What do you want? And where's my father?"

The man didn't say anything, he simply watched Jasper with cold, watery blue eyes.

He's studying me like an insect.

Near-instantaneously, the man had a gun aimed straight at Jasper. The weapon had practically materialized in his hand. A time bender!

"Sorry kid," the man said in an unnatural drawl that betrayed his words with an utter lack of empathy.

Jasper fell again, this time not into blackness, but into a vivid world of hyper-reality, despite the muted room lighting.

Jasper was keenly aware of the precise moment the plumber pulled the trigger fifteen feet away from him.

It was right now, and as the bullet left the barrel in a puff of smoke, there could be no doubt of its direct path to bury itself in Jasper's gut.

Chapter Seventeen

The Descent

For the third time in three days, Eva slipped the coaster between lock and frame after Father left, but tonight, she sat back down on the edge of her bed, wondering if she should take a little break from her adventures.

Exploring the homestead (*"a person's or family's ancestral home, which comprises the land, house, and outbuildings"*) still felt exhilarating, but she did long for some restful sleep.

Little Miss Adventure is tired, that's real cute. Told you, should've stayed here. Got lucky you didn't freeze. Got lucky Father didn't see you. You won't be lucky forever.

"Go fly a kite!" Eva snapped at Adam, surprising herself with the outburst. "I'll leave in a minute and I'm too fast for Father anyway."

She enjoyed the sense of freedom her nightly excursions gave her, but Adam's sudden silence once she stepped outside her rooms might have been the best part of it all. Back here, he had become even more negative. Just telling him off reenergized her already, and she knew exactly what to do next. She longed to explore one specific area since Father started talking about new medicine and tests the night she had first snuck out.

Last year, a few months before Mother had taken Adam, there had been construction noise in the adjacent building. Eva and Adam saw trucks come and go for a few weeks, but the building stood at an angle to the main residence, so they couldn't see any construction from their windows. When they asked Father, he talked about renovating a few rooms in the South Wing, "to run a few tests."

Finally Eva had a pretty good idea of the location of these rooms. She put on her ballet slippers. The cool floors had been enjoyable on her first night out, but being barefoot made her feel vulnerable.

For her trips, she had shifted into what she had dubbed her overdrive mode (*"Seven Cities in Four Days—Rip Current Conquer Europe in Overdrive!"*). Most of her knowledge of the world had come from books, but what she knew about her special abilities, about Real Time and Accelerated Time, she had learned from Father, and even *he* didn't know about overdrive. That she had figured out all on their own.

Most people, like Mother and *Fräulein Ochs*, were stuck in Real Time. Father (and herself and her brother, of course) could access Accelerated Time, but Father didn't know that when Eva went into overdrive, time stood practically still. Even Father appeared as slow as a tick-tock in comparison.

Unfortunately, her uniqueness didn't end there. If anything, overdrive mode was a small consolation price for her condition—the "freezing," her uncontrollable episodes of slowing down, the spasms and blackouts. Father kept her in isolation for her own good. Curing her was his whole raison d'être (*"the reason or justification for someone or something's existence"*), he always said.

You'll be frozen stiff somewhere out there like an icicle. Nobody will find you, and you'll starve and die. But go on with your little adventure if I'm boring you here.

"I will, thank you," Eva said and made for the door. Who cared what Adam thought? It took weeks to starve; everyone knew that. Who didn't love a diversion? She hadn't suffered any episodes in days. Or was it weeks even?

"No Risk, No Fun! Behind The Scenes—Rip Current On Tour."

Robbie and the other members of Rip Current did all sorts of dangerous stuff on tour, like bungee jumping and jet skiing. This was her tour, even if her world couldn't compete with Rip Current's.

She snuck out the door and replaced the coaster behind her. She had explored the main house on her last trips, steering clear only of Father's rooms. It didn't serve up any real surprises, not even the kitchen, where she had hoped to find some leftover pizza or a tub of chocolate ice cream. When she didn't find them, she chastised herself. "Silly girl, why would any of that be in the kitchen if Father doesn't like it?"

She had found the main house as she remembered, right down to the family pictures and portraits in the giant foyer. The picture of Father's father Xavier in front of giant tunneling machines had burned itself into her memory, probably because Father, who never talked about the past, had once pointed it out. "Without your grandfather, the idiots here would still be rolling cheese wheels up and down the mountains."

Eva didn't know what to make of it. She liked cheese. But

construction and demolition was the family business, so whatever he had done must have been good.

She didn't remember how it came up, but once she told *Fräulein Ochs* that Father was in the construction business.

Her teacher had chuckled. "If your father is in the construction business, Apple is in the keyboard business." She didn't understand it, but the quote stuck with her because it was delivered in a sarcastic (*"marked by using irony in order to mock or ridicule"*) tone by the usually sincere *Fräulein*.

There wouldn't be any family portraits where Eva wanted to go tonight. She took the stairs down to ground level and followed the corridors to what would have been a dead end if not for a small metal service door with a turning lock. She hadn't dared open it before, but a rush of wanderlust coursed through her tonight.

A cool whiff of air reached out of the darkness and coiled around her ankles. Her eyes took a few moments to adjust, but then, by the shine of a little moonlight, the room revealed itself as a large garage and delivery area.

Pity… She was about to turn around when a light at the other end of the garage flashed into action. An "up" arrow illuminated briefly, followed by a pulsating "-1" and a distant rumble, then stillness. A freight elevator!

Because of the wide horizontal doors she hadn't recognized it at first. She tiptoed over to the service door next to it and looked inside. A dimly lit staircase only led down. Eva's heart beat faster. She took a step forward.

This seems like a great idea. If you want to die a lonely death.

"Shh, be quiet," Eva whispered. Of all the times Adam

could have broken his silence! She listened intently, hearing nothing but faint distant humming. "I know you're only in my head. And you're not my boss." She took the stairs down, almost dizzy from the thrill of it all.

After two flights, she found the first exit door, marked "-1." She hesitated but kept on going. Two more flights brought her to "-2." She looked down but couldn't see the bottom of the staircase.

"SURPRISE!!! Five Ways To Party Like Rip Current—And Not Get Caught!"

With bated breath, Eva put a hand on the door handle.

Barely a minute of Real Time had passed when Eva already finished exploring the whole floor behind "-2" and took another two flights down to the next one, predictably labeled "-3." Less than another Real Time minute later, she proceeded to "-4," now thoroughly confused.

What was this place?

She had stopped counting the rooms after fifty. Some had strange machinery, some uncomfortable looking chairs or odd metal tables, others housed all sorts of supplies.

One of the floors had several rooms with beds on wheels in them, and weird mirrors where you could look into the room from the corridor, but from inside the room it was only a mirror. Some rooms had heavy locks on the outside, like cells. Or were the locks protecting the inside?

Eva had stayed in overdrive throughout. She would

have liked to spend more time to figure everything out but didn't dare linger.

This place was her *home*, or at least next to her home, or under her home. Could it be a hospital? Everything looked fully operational, just deserted.

She had seen one man, but the sight of him had startled her so much, she turned around still unsure if he was asleep or dead. The man had lain in a bed at the far end of one of the rooms with all the beds on wheels, his eyes closed. Then again, Eva moved so fast, anyone in Real Time would have appeared frozen.

Absentmindedly, Eva kept on descending the stairs until she almost stumbled because they had ended, "-4" was the bottom floor. Go back up or explore?

Eva, time to turn around. I'm afraid.

Adam had been quiet since she ignored him at the top of the stairs. How could she turn around now? Maybe this floor held the answers.

"I'm not afraid," she said.

You should be. Fear is good. There are monsters in the deep. Let's go back to our room.

"You have to conquer your fears," Eva said and thought of Robbie, who had arachnophobia. (*"PICS! Rip Current Visit The Zoo—How To Conquer Your Fear Of Spiders!"*)

This isn't about your crush or some phobia. Not all fear has to be conquered.

What to make of this newly philosophical Adam? He sounded more reasonable than miserable for once, but these last few days ignoring him had been the best days of her life since the real Adam had been taken by their mother. "Why should I listen to you now? You never want me to be happy!"

Is that so? Adam asked laconically (*"using very few words to the point of seeming rude, uninterested, or mysterious"*).

"Yes." She put her hand on the door handle. It didn't move, but not because the door was locked.

Oh no, were her last thoughts as she felt the first violent spasms come on. When they finally stopped, she was frozen in place as if encased in amber.

Chapter Eighteen

Between the Eyes

Jasper knew the bullet would hit him. It already had, in a way.

Compressed air marked its flight path across the room, ending right at his belly button. No chance to react, obviously.

People say time slows down and one's past flashes before their eyes right before they die.

Not so much the past in Jasper's case, more regret and surprise. Regret about having put the girl on the wrong track and not having waited for Clarence, surprise about the bullet spinning like a drill bit. He tended to think of bullets as flying straight like airplanes.

The bullet chipped away at the fabric of his T-shirt, drilling a hole into SpongeBob before it would drill a hole into him.

Nothing he could do about it really. Who is fast enough to get out of the way of a bullet? Who has the time?

Maybe someone who can read the inscription on the bullet while it's perforating his T-shirt?

9mm.

Jasper tried to twist his belly out of the way. Time

seemed to advance in super slo-mo since the bullet had reached him, but his muscle fibers hadn't adapted to the operating speed of his brain synapses.

Must. Twist. Out. Of. The. Way.

He managed to create an angle to the bullet, but it continued going forward, drilling.

The projectile pierced his skin and furrowed its way into his belly fat. *Baby* fat, Clarence would mock him.

Searing pain.

Jasper twisted his body farther, but the bullet kept on spinning, now parallel to his abdominal wall, lacerating skin and fatty tissue in its path.

Excruciating pain—

Keep moving. Jasper cried out in agony and collapsed to the floor, glass shattering behind him—the pinball machine. Truly unforgivable.

Had the bullet gone through him or past him? Jasper still felt oddly alive, his sense of reality now restored.

Across the room, all hell broke loose at the same time.

"Noooooooooooooooo…"

Someone screamed. The ninja girl? Where had she come from?

All dressed in black, her face contorted in rage, she charged the shooter. A final lunge and she knocked the gun out of the man's hand, her forward momentum sending them both tumbling over the foosball table.

Jasper sat up and checked the front of his shirt. It had two holes in it, bullet entry and exit, and a red skid mark connecting the two. The bullet had left a bloody trail running horizontally across his stomach, leaving poor SpongeBob looking like the sole survivor of a Japanese horror movie.

Behind the game table, the two combatants got up in an instant and tore into each other. The speed of their movements made it hard to follow what was going on. The girl maneuvered around the big guy like a black blur. As far as Jasper could tell, he couldn't get a hold of her. She darted in and out with stinging blows and kicks, while he tried to grab and swing, but mostly hit air.

Now they struggled to get a hold of some sort of... satchel? The bag broke away from the fight and flew across the room, banged against the dart board, and spilled its contents on the floor.

A split-second later, the girl appeared next to it, grabbed a handful of the darts from the board, and launched them at the man as he galloped at her.

He brushed them to the side mid-flight with his arm, but it took him the briefest of moments that allowed her to grab one of the items from the floor.

When the man reached her, she jammed a small black box into his chest, and he staggered back a step, twitching. A stun gun?

He didn't cry out in pain, but his face was all gaping mouth and flaring nostrils. His eyes full of contempt, he tried to take a step forward, but his knees buckled, and he keeled over unceremoniously, clutching his chest.

With the man's collapse came a moment of sudden stillness. The fight had lasted seconds, if that.

Jasper looked at the girl. She leaned over slightly, put her hands on her knees in exhaustion, and made unintelligible squeaky sounds.

"Are you okay?" Jasper asked.

"Quick, where's... the... gun?" she asked Jasper between deep breaths. Bruises and scratches covered the left side of her face.

"I don't know." The question caught Jasper off guard. "What gun?" *What gun? The gun I just got shot with. Was there a stupider question?*

She looked understandably confused.

She must think I'm daft.

"Let's get out of here," Jasper said. "We have to call the police."

"No!" She straightened her back. "Don't you realize what this place is?"

"But what about him?" Jasper gestured toward the motionless man.

"We kill him," she said calmly. "And fast, before—"

Movement at the edge of Jasper's field of vision... *Too late.*

It should have taken the man much longer to recover. It should have taken him longer to even get up, but he rushed forward already, crossing the distance to them in the blink of an eye.

The girl took a moment too long to find an extra gear. The man snatched her in a bear hug, his massive arms tightening around her like a vise—a death grip.

She cried out, and Jasper had no doubt that within moments she'd lose consciousness, have her innards turned to mush, and her spine snapped in two. His fear for her shocked Jasper into hyper-reality. Objects around him stood out like cardboard cutouts. He knew he had less than seconds.

The X marked the spot—two cues on the pool table. Jasper grabbed one and was back before the girl's cry had even stopped. He swung the cue with a kind of ferocity he didn't even know he had in him and landed it on the side of the man's head, right over his ear.

Splinters of the broken cue hung in the air, and a geyser of blood erupted in slow motion from a gash in the man's scalp. He let go of the girl and collapsed to the floor like someone had flicked his off switch.

Reality shifted back to normal again. Jasper rushed in and tried to hold onto the girl's arm, but she slipped through his grip and sat down on the floor, groaning.

"Can you walk?" Jasper asked.

"I…" She couldn't even keep her eyes open, let alone answer him properly.

Police or no police, they had to get out of there before the freaking Terminator woke up again.

Jasper doubted he'd be able to carry her all the way. "Hold on, I'll drag you." He stepped behind her, slid his arms under her armpits, locked his hands in front of her chest, and dragged her out of the game room.

She weighed less than he expected. How had she held her ground against that monster?

He dragged her out the door and to the big lounge. Jasper kicked the door behind him. It slammed shut but couldn't be locked.

Noises don't wake people up from being knocked out, do they?

Jasper had no idea what he'd do once they got outside, but with his would-be killer still down here, unconscious or not, they would have to figure out something fast. Even if they found a car, who'd drive it?

The girl opened her eyes.

"You're one of us." She smiled. "I knew it."

"I don't know what that means. We have to get out of here." Jasper continued to drag her through the lounge. Being underground had been cool at first, but with an unconscious killer seconds away from possibly waking up, it became oppressive.

"Wait," she said, "I think I can walk."

Jasper put her down gently on the purple flokati rug.

She cocked her head, held her jaw with one hand and the top of her head with the other, then twisted it to crack the vertebrae in her neck.

"Ouch!" Jasper's hand instinctively sought his neck.

"Better," the girl said. "Let's see…" She got on her knees, leaned back and arched her spine. "Should be fine. Let's go back and kill the Bastard before he wakes up."

"You can't. You can't just go around, like, killing people," Jasper stammered.

"You're right." She got up. "Only him."

It felt wrong, but Jasper had to laugh nervously. "Come on, I mean… You can walk. Let's get the hell out of here before we both get killed." Jasper noticed the disconnect in his reasoning, but still. You can't just kill people. *Even before we'll both get killed?* Things you thought you'd never say back when your life hadn't yet been thrown into disarray by disappearing fathers, time bending uncles, and murderous plumbers.

She grabbed his T-shirt. "I saw him shoot you, right here

in your soft belly." She poked him.

"Ouch." *Soft belly?* Sure, he didn't quite rock a sixpack, but that felt like a gratuitous slight. "The bullet did catch me, you know."

"You should be dead," she said matter-of-factly.

"Sorry to disappoint," Jasper said and took a few steps toward the exit door, "but I really think we ought to get out of—"

The *slam* of a door being kicked so hard it burst from its frame brought their chatty interlude to an abrupt end.

The Termi-plumber was back, and this time it was personal. Blood covered his neck and shoulders, and somewhere along the way he had lost his glasses.

Unfortunately, he had found his gun and opened fire from the doorway right away, spraying bullets in a fan-like pattern.

Jasper's world shifted again. The girl shouted something in a drawn-out, distorted way and waved toward the exit door. "Coooooooome ooooooooon…"

The bullets would miss Jasper if he didn't move, but the girl glided toward the door and right into the flight path of a bullet. Didn't she see?

The plumber let go of the empty gun. It fell in slow motion from his hand. He leaned forward, about to charge across the room toward them, but hesitated for some reason.

Jasper finally realized, whatever was happening to him, in this hyperreality *he* was faster than both of them. The girl didn't see the bullets, she just tried to get out of the room. And the man would be right on them if he could, but to Jasper, he looked like he tried to run through gelatin.

The bullets traveled faster than the girl, Jasper had to take care of her first. He weaved around the other bullets and pulled her close, squeezing together into a space between two bullets, holding her tight while the projectiles skimmed past them on either side.

Her eyes slowly widened.

Jasper let go of her and took another step over to the dining table. He glanced over his shoulder at the plumber, creeping closer, raising the splintered, bloody pool cue like a club. Jasper grabbed one of the orange plastic chairs and threw it at him, then another, and another.

Jasper ran toward the door, overtaking the girl after a couple of steps. He turned the spinning handle, pushed the door open, and waited for her to catch up.

The plumber avoided the first flying chair, but the second threw him off balance, and the third tripped him to the ground. His face compressed down on the concrete floor, nose first.

The girl cleared the open door. Jasper closed it behind them and spun the handle as far as it would go. Once back in the corridor, Jasper tumbled back into familiar reality.

The girl said something in a high-pitched Mickey Mouse voice. He didn't understand any of it. She rolled her eyes, then spoke normally.

"Why do you keep dropping back into Real Time?"

"I don't know how any of this works," Jasper said, "I'm just, I'm just a guy."

"Well, just-a-guy, *he*"—she nodded toward the door— "knows how this works, so run!"

And run he did. She overtook him so easily that he felt

incredibly vulnerable. He wouldn't even be able to evade a softball, let alone a bullet. The wound across his abdomen hurt when he ran, and the backpack that miraculously remained over his shoulder after all this commotion weighed him down. The corridor from the lounge to the second vault door felt even longer than on the way in.

The girl stopped at the hole in the strange metal ring that ran around the inside of the corridor and fiddled with the cables, her hands a blur.

"What are you doing?" he asked running past her.

She yelled a high-pitched "Go-go-go-go-go!"

Jasper opened the second vault door and stepped into the next corridor that ended at the stairs up to the garage and the final door with the numeric pad. He turned around. Whatever the girl was doing, she had finished and appeared next to him in an instant. In the distance, the handle on the inner vault door turned.

"Don't stop," she said.

He ran as she closed the door behind them. He wasn't even halfway up the stairs when she swooshed past him, egging him on in her sped-up voice: "C'mon-c'mon-c'mon…"

They emerged from the hole in the ground in the little square room. She opened the door to the garage and raced outside so fast that Jasper could barely see her black outline.

By the time he'd closed the code-locked door, she had already busted through the main door on a motor scooter.

"Leave that. Hurry!" she yelled in her normal voice and looked at her watch. "Ten seconds!"

Jasper tried to run one more time, but it turned into more

of a hobble. He looked down. SpongeBob, drenched in blood, now looked more victim than survivor of a Japanese horror movie.

"Ten seconds and what…?" he yelled as he made his way past the trashed hydraulic platform.

"Just hurry!"

Finally, he reached the scooter and swung one leg over to sit behind her. With a strained roar from its engine the little scooter jumped forward.

Jasper grabbed two handfuls of her black outfit to keep from falling over backward from the acceleration.

"Ten seconds and what?" he shouted as they rode out of the garage and across dips and ditches on the way to the fence.

Boooo-OOOOM-mmmmm.

A subterranean explosion shook the ground like one of the usual Southern California earthquakes, but a unique muffled thump with a follow-through rang in his ears, chased by the hissing and licking of flames and the soft clinking of debris bits raining on the surrounding area.

"What the?" Jasper ducked reflexively, not that it prevented anything from falling on him from above. Car alarms went off by the dozen.

The girl glanced over her shoulder, revved the scooter's engine, and steered for the loose fence panel.

Jasper peered back at the garage, shrouded in smoke, the surrounding area covered in rubble.

"Holy hell! That'll be on the news tonight," Jasper said. "We need to get out of here."

"The vault door should have held," the girl said. "Unless

it was open when it went off."

So she had been responsible. What happened in the tunnel?

"Heads-up!" she yelled.

They rammed the fence. The hinged panel swung open, but the impact rattled the scooter and sent Jasper hard to the right. She adjusted, and with a dangerous wobble of their diminutive vehicle, they spilled onto busy South Barrington Boulevard.

"Eek!" Jasper shrieked.

A big, black SUV rushed on from the left, certain to T-bone them and end his adventure right then and there. Jasper got a wonderful close-up view of the gleaming chrome grill, but with a most precise last-ditch turn, the girl narrowly evaded the truck and turned sharp left to go north.

They settled into traffic. The girl seemed less shaken than Jasper by this latest near-death encounter and turned around to him. "How on earth didn't you know that you were a time bender?" Something behind them caught her eye. "Look out!"

Jasper turned around. A smudge in the distance got bigger and bigger, slaloming around the cars behind them and gaining ground on their scooter.

Their old friend? It couldn't be...

Running faster than Usain Bolt could dream of, it was indeed the plumber. Jasper squinted as traffic around them slowed down to a crawl. Their pursuer looked worse for wear, his nose a pulpy mess, blood staining the front of his blue overall, and tattered strips of pants fluttering around his legs. Hard to believe he had survived the explosion, but here he was, running circles around moving traffic.

"Don't worry, we'll get away," the girl said, sounding a little squeakier than before.

"How?" Jasper asked. "He's faster than us."

The plumber gained on them, rounding another vehicle and running a red light.

"Good, at least you're not tick-tocking now," the girl answered. "Of course he's faster than this thing can drive."

"No kidding, we're practically standing still," Jasper yelled.

"Are we?" She pointed to the speedometer as she swerved, the scooter slipping sideways as if through syrup, to pass the car in front of them. Apparently, they went forty-five MPH, and the wind blowing through his hair confirmed it.

This is so weird.

She said, "He's actually pretty slow right now. People are watching."

A pedestrian pointed at the plumber, who continued to gain on them at a decent pace, but nowhere near fast enough to be invisible.

"Here's your first lesson. Everything you can do, you can now do faster, but you can't do anything that you couldn't do in Real Time, got it?"

"I… I think," Jasper said hesitantly. It might have made perfect sense, but he found the imminent mortal danger quite distracting.

"Son of a bitch," she shouted.

Fortunately, she meant the driver of a BMW convertible that had just started to change lanes right in front of them, not him.

Accelerated Time let her easily brake within a split-second to avoid rear-ending the convertible.

She honked, and it sounded like a fog horn.

"Just hold the Bastard off for another mile or so and he'll run out of steam. I'll explain later." She steered to the other side of the BMW.

Hold him off... hold him off? Bloody hell, how am I going to do that?

Avoiding the car in front of them had cost valuable yards. The plumber had caught up to barely five car lengths behind them. His face twisted into a mask of pain and hatred. Considering he looked as if he had been run over by a truck twice, Jasper couldn't blame him for the animosity. *But hey, you tried to kill me first.*

Four car lengths...

Would he try to knock them over if he got close enough? And would it hurt like falling off at forty-five MPH or be a leisurely impact to fit how everything appeared?

He needed a weapon, something he could use at a distance. If only he still had that pool cue.

The plumber already had a gun out. Why didn't he fire, as close as he was?

Three car lengths...

"He's got a weird gun," Jasper said. "It's, like, square. Don't know why he's not firing."

"Rats," the girl said, "the spider net gun. That'll bring us down. You have to keep him from firing it."

"What? How would I even—"

"This thing won't go any faster," Maya said, with a

sudden hint of desperation in her voice. "I don't care *how* you stop him, just do it."

Just do it. Sure. Keep him from firing the spider net gun, whatever that was.

Just another day at the office.

Firing. The. Gun.

Jasper contorted himself to take off his trusty, indestructible backpack.

Two car lengths…

The plumber raised the square-barreled gun. The spider gun. That'll bring us down, she'd said.

Jasper stuffed his hand down the backpack's main compartment and pulled out a gun, a real gun—his father's gun.

"Keep going!" he yelled, raised the gun, and aimed it at their tormentor.

"Shoot the Bastard!" the girl yelled, her voice back to a tone of determination. She had glanced back and seen the gun. "It's him or us, aim for the eyes, focus. You can do it."

Her words made his hair stand on end. There had to be another way. More Batman than Punisher.

The plumber steadied his aim.

Enough. Jasper pulled the trigger and watched a bullet exit the gun barrel toward their pursuer.

The plumber took flight, involuntarily, head over heels, and rammed a large metal trash container at the side of the road.

"Did you get him?" the girl asked.

"Yeah, uh… Yeah."

"We should turn around and make sure." The girl

slowed down the scooter.

Turn around? Screw that. "No, keep going. I got him. Right between the eyes."

"Are you sure?"

"Saw the bullet drill right in. Not pretty," he lied. "Go faster, people are staring."

Traffic cleared in front of them. The girl revved the engine, honked twice, and whooped into the wind before reaching behind her back to Jasper and squeezing his hand. They rode silently for a while.

"You might have remembered that gun a bit earlier," she said, "but at least you got him. Name's Maya, by the way. Hold on, it's not that far anymore."

Jasper wrapped his arms around her waist as they accelerated. He couldn't untangle the jumble of emotions he felt right now: fear for his life, gratitude for his rescue, queasiness about his lie, apprehension about her bloodlust, but more than anything—the thrill of it all.

No need to tell Maya right now that he had aimed for the leg, not the eyes.

The wind blew in his face. He might have asked where she headed, but he didn't care. Something stirred he couldn't quite put his finger on.

The wound tore at him, and the blood had seeped through the shirt down into his pants.

Never mind, he felt more alive than ever before.

"I'm Jasper," he said. "Jasper Faulks."

She turned her head just far enough to give him a roguish smile. "I know."

Chapter Nineteen

Hello Kitty

Their destination turned out to be Maya's temporary housing in Brentwood.

They left the scooter on San Vicente near the Country Club and walked the rest of the way, Jasper gritting his teeth for every step. Considering she approached an expensive-looking Spanish two-story by way of the guest bathroom window, he figured she didn't pay rent on the place.

"I can't believe you're stuck in Real Time right now," Maya said while she gave him a leg up. "How can it just come and go like that? I hope nobody sees us."

Jasper dropped down inside, then held out his hand to help her, but she pulled herself up effortlessly.

"I told you, I don't know how any of this works. I'm just a guy," Jasper said.

"Yeah, one who can dodge a bullet. Take off the shirt and let me look at that wound." She peeled her thin black leather gloves off.

"What, are you a doctor now, too?" Jasper instinctively crossed his arms and ignored the stab of pain in his midsection.

"No, but the next best thing for the time being." She

opened the mirrored doors of a small medicine cabinet. "Are you prudish? That's cute, but really unnecessary." She turned around and looked at him mock-sternly. "It's a medical emergency."

She was right, of course. And he definitely wasn't prudish, despite Clarence's protestations, so when she turned back around to pick things from the medicine cabinet, he took off the bloody SpongeBob t-shirt. The wound looked clean enough. It ran for about eight inches straight as an arrow across his midriff right under his belly button. He wasn't squeamish around blood, but he'd never seen this much coming out of his own body.

Maya turned around with a little bottle in her hand. "Do you prefer— Holy smokes, did you have a cesarean? It's like an open mouth!" She straightened her lips and mockingly opened and closed her mouth like a fish. "I was about to ask Motrin or Tylenol, but there's prescription stuff in the master bath upstairs. Why don't you lie down in the guest room, and I'll see what I can find?" When she closed the medicine cabinet, their gaze met in the mirror. "Look, matching black eyes."

Jasper lay down on the bed in the guest bedroom. The blood that had seeped into his boxer shorts and jeans had dried, and small flakes sprinkled the linens. He definitely needed new clothes. Not that he was particularly sad to see the last of Clarence's hand-me-downs.

Clarence! He had completely forgotten about him.

Jasper took his cell phone out of his pocket. Three missed calls. His last text message had been, "Look for my body if you don't hear from me in a couple hours. Ha ha." Now there were five replies.

"Are u ok? Got 1 more game."

"I'm outta here. Are u still there?"

"Guess u have no reception. I'll be there in 10."

"Are u OK??? Let me know."

"Police and firefighters everywhere. PLZ reply if u get this. Calling Mom and Dad now."

Jasper typed, "I'm ok…," then stopped. If Clarence had told the authorities he might be down there, he'd also have to tell them when he heard from Jasper. They might all be waiting together by Clarence's cell phone for a message.

He deleted his text. Cruel to Clarence, but it would be safer to stay missing for a while. He'd have to find a way to let his friend know he was still alive, but not tonight.

"Knock, knock…" Maya pushed the door open with her foot and entered the room with a glass of water in one hand and cradling a whole pile of medical supplies with her other arm. She handed him the water and a small orange prescription drug bottle. "Vicodin. Should do the trick for now."

Jasper put his phone away while she put a bottle of water, a towel, a bottle of disinfectant, a package of gauze pads, a roll of wound dressing, and a roll of tape on the nightstand.

"Have you done this before?" Jasper asked.

Maya laughed. "No. Have you?"

"No, I think I better take two of these." Jasper washed two Vicodin down with the water. "Whoa. What the hell?" He felt better in moments, if a little lightheaded.

"Opioids. Take the edge off fast," Maya said. "That's just

the tiny amount you absorbed through your mouth. You'll sleep well later."

Relaxed, Jasper flopped back onto the bed before Maya flushed his wound with a bit of water and carefully patted it dry.

"Maya, do you know what happened to my father?"

She hesitated for a moment. "He was taken, as I told you. By the Bastard."

"The Bastard? Do you mean the plumber?"

"Plumber? Because of the overalls?" Maya asked.

Jasper told her about the plumbing van and how the man had hit him with the pipe earlier.

"Yeah, not a real plumber, but yes, the guy you shot. I wonder if that was a test. Any conscious time bender would have ducked that pipe, but you didn't and then, later, when he felt safe, dodge a bullet and *boom*—pool cue to the noggin, thank you very much. Well done. Anyway, I called him the Bastard. He kidnapped your father last Sunday. Shot him with that spider gun. Some experimental electrobeam projection, most likely. Nasty stuff, not standard issue for any military in the world, I checked. You dodged a bullet earlier—impressive, I didn't think that was possible at that distance—but still nowhere near fast enough for that thing. The electricity hits you right away, more time doesn't help. You saw my stun gun earlier, but with that, you have to get close."

No wonder she had been so worried on the scooter when Jasper mentioned the square gun. "What happened after he shot my father with that thing?"

She soaked a corner of the towel in disinfectant. "You

might want to hold on to something."

Jasper lay down flat and grabbed the bed frame.

Maya softly patted the wound with the towel.

The Vicodin did its job, so instead of screaming like a stuck pig, Jasper only gasped and involuntarily curled his toes.

"Already done." Maya put down the towel. "The Bastard put him in the trunk and drove away. I don't know what happened to him after. I didn't see him again until today and I don't know where he's been."

She opened a package of gauze pads and gently pressed them one by one in a straight line onto the clean wound.

After the pain of the disinfectant, Jasper barely noticed the pads.

"So, this Bastard took my father who-knows-where almost a week ago and now—"

"Yes, and now the Bastard's dead," Maya said, flat.

"You should have told me before I..." Jasper hesitated. Before he *what*? He had not shot him, after all.

"Look, I'm sorry about your father," Maya said while wrapping his whole midsection in wound dressing. "Lift your butt up for a second if you can, so I can wrap this all the way around." He did as she asked. "If the Bastard wanted to kill him, he's already dead. And if he's not dead, the Bastard would've never told us where he was. You should be very proud that you shot him. I wanted to do it myself, but dead is dead, no more injustice, so I'm thankful for that, even if I didn't do it. And tomorrow, we can look for your father without looking over our shoulder."

Jasper bit his tongue. Why upset her now? "Are we safe

here? Whose house is this anyway?"

"Judging from the stash of prescription painkillers, anti-depressants, and laxatives in the medicine cabinet upstairs, I'd say entertainment industry types. According to the neighbors, they won't be back for another week, so rest up."

Maya finished dressing the wound by fixing everything in place with medical tape.

Jasper flexed his midsection a little. It felt much better than before, good enough to sit up. "Great. Thank you."

"You're very welcome. Now we only need to get you out of those pants." She burst into a bright smile at his nonplussed expression. "They're disgusting, look at all the blood. No worries, I'll let you take care of that on your own. I brought you some of my clothes. They're the biggest I have, I hope it's okay for one night."

She pointed to a small pile of clothes on the nightstand that Jasper hadn't noticed before.

"Thank you, Maya," Jasper said. "Thank you for everything. Without you—"

"No! *I* thank *you*," she said. "Today was a good day. A very good day, thank you for that, Jasper, Jasper Faulks." The corners of her mouths hinted at a small wry smile. "I'm Maya Banerjee Misra, by the way, but I'm sure you knew that already."

After that, her appearance shimmered, and she vanished in front of his eyes like the first time they had met. A split-second later, the door to his room closed from the outside.

Banerjee Misra. Of course! Her parents were Mehdi Banerjee and Nirav Misra, part of the original time benders with his father and Uncle Martin. Obviously, that meant she had inherited their ability, as he had his father's, even if he couldn't control it. Was he supposed to have already known that? Not known that?

Jasper felt drowsy. Better to try and make sense of it tomorrow. He got up and unfolded the clothes she had left for him. On her, they might be baggy, but to Jasper they looked like the tiniest pair of pants in the world. What was rolled up inside was even worse.

"You've got to be kidding me." He shook his head.

As he pulled down his bloody boxer shorts to put on tiny heather grey sweat pants and a pink Hello Kitty T-shirt, Jasper sincerely hoped Maya had indeed closed the door from the *outside* after she had vanished in front of his eyes.

Chapter Twenty

Morning Delight

Jasper woke to a strong smell of disinfectant and laundry detergent. On the nightstand next to his bed lay a stack of his, or actually Clarence's, jeans and underpants, freshly washed and neatly folded.

Would these invasions of privacy ever end? At least he wouldn't have to parade around in these tiny sweatpants that left uncomfortably little to the imagination. Sadly, the pink Hello Kitty t-shirt would have to do for now. Judging from his absence, SpongeBob had succumbed to his injuries.

On the upside, Jasper's wound felt less than lethal. The smell, disinfectant and some organic funk, was the worst of it for now. No blood had seeped through the dressing overnight. Even getting out of bed, the pain had lessened considerably from yesterday.

He put on the freshly washed pants and looked for the rest of his belongings. His backpack held everything he owned and looked untouched. Dad's laptop had a few dings from their escape, but the screen remained intact. He powered it on, and it booted up. Right up to the password screen. Jasper rolled his eyes.

071869… No.

176… No.

11111111111111111111… The computer stopped him at twenty digits. Still no.

A problem for another time. He closed the laptop, stuffed it into his backpack, and stepped out into the hall.

"Maya…?" No answer. What would he do if she had left? The possibility hadn't even crossed his mind.

"Over here."

Relieved to hear her voice, Jasper hurried to join her in the kitchen, where she sat at the table eating a sandwich and reading his father's notebook, which she had stolen from him, what, four days ago? It seemed like yesterday and an eternity at the same time.

She looked up when he entered. "Cool shirt."

"Yeah, um," Jasper said, "it's just my style. Lately anyway."

"I swear it's the biggest one I have."

"Have you looked upstairs? Maybe the owner has something a little less pink in his closet."

"I'm not a thief!"

Jasper looked down at the breakfast table and raised his eyebrows.

"I bought all of the food, and when I leave I'll put everything else just the way it was," Maya said. "Nobody will know we were here, unless *you* break something."

"The meds?" Jasper asked.

"Hello? An emergency… And they were for you, remember? Past the expiration date anyway. And in case you're wondering, I paid for the scooter."

Jasper cleared his throat and nodded toward the

notebook.

"Oh, yeah, sorry about that. At the time, it was quite clear you had no idea what was going on. I always meant to give it back to you. I am not a thief."

Only a would-be murderer… "Care to share some of your non-stolen breakfast? I'm starving," Jasper said.

They had breakfast and caught up on each other's story over the past week. How Maya had seen Jasper's father fight the Bastard, how she found the wallet and Jasper's house, how she first hid in the treehouse, then later in the closet when Jasper surprised her, how startled she was when he caught her with her hand down his backpack, and how she eventually followed him into the Passage of Time yesterday.

"How did you show up in the nick of time?"

"Actually, the Bastard must've arrived after me. I was looking at my parents' folders in the library room when I heard the shot. The Passage was one of the two locations I watched whenever I could. The most likely one to catch the Bastard, but both times he actually showed up, it turned into a mess with a Faulks family member for some reason. Oh well."

"Sorry," Jasper said. "What was the other location?"

"Your house, of course. That reminds me, I left you a second message in your treehouse. I was on my way there earlier, but you triggered my motion alert on the path to the auto body shop, so I turned around and you know the rest. Maybe we should swing by your house later and pick up the message before anyone else sees it?"

"No need, I saw it before I went to the Passage and, er, took care of it."

"So, did you decide to trust me before I saved your life down there?" Maya asked with a smile.

"Yeah, sure." Jasper looked at the notebook on the table, embarrassed that his original plan had been to send her the other way. Water under the bridge and all that. "Anything useful in my dad's notebook?"

"Some older diary stuff about the time benders, but the back end had all the wiring schematics for the trigger and the explosives in the Passage. That metal ring down there was full of C-4 and whatnot. You would have needed the notebook to get in safely, but the trigger was disabled already, exactly like in the drawings. I studied it on my way in and reconnected it on our way out. Pity it didn't bury the Bastard down there alive, but we did get him in the end, so I guess it doesn't matter."

"Except that I still don't know what happened to my dad, and all the information down there is now lost forever," Jasper said. His own lie about the Bastard's fate troubled him, but was this the time to come clean? *No*, not before he found a path to his father, or at least so a ruthless voice in the back of his mind insisted.

"You don't know for sure that all is lost," Maya said. "How did you end up in the Passage anyway?"

Jasper explained how he found the Passage and cracked the codes, what Uncle Martin told him about the time benders, and what information about their headquarters he gathered from his father's materials. Much seemed to come as news to Maya.

"Didn't your parents tell you all that?" Jasper asked. "I mean, you're a time bender."

"They taught me about time bending, when I first changed. I think they were just as surprised as I was. But they never told me about their past. What I wrote, about putting two and two together, that all our parents are time benders, I knew from the notebook. That was the first time I saw a list of all of them. I figured if you saw the two Indian names on there after you saw me, you'd know I'm their daughter, and you could trust me. I didn't know anything about the Passage before. They…" She cleared her throat and took a sip of tea before she continued. "We were very private, as you can imagine. I used to be very outgoing. After my, uh, transformation, not so much. It's not easy among the tick-tocks, you'll see. It's very hard to connect." She tapped her temple with two fingers, then pointed at Jasper.

"Tick-tocks?"

"People stuck in Real Time. Everyone but us, basically." She seemed amused, as if she'd just heard a joke that went over his head.

"Not only us two though, that reminds me…" Jasper showed Maya the pictures of the students. Three of them featured her parents and now that he had put two and two together, he saw the family resemblance.

When they looked at the old pictures, Maya teared up. She tried to hide it, but really, what were the odds that she'd gotten something in her eye that exact moment?

Jasper waited for her to compose herself. "So, your parents—"

"They're dead. I don't have to tell you who did it. Why he did it, I don't know. He left a message later, trying to lure me to Los Angeles, but I didn't take the bait. I stayed up in

Michigan, trained for a year, got ready, then I came here on my own terms. I won't tolerate injustice. Never again."

They sat in silence for a while before Jasper looked at the picture of the ten original time benders again. "It's an old picture, but the Bastard isn't one of them. How come he could bend time too? He's too old to be someone's son."

Maya sat up straight. "If this"—she pointed at the group pictures—"is what connects your father and my parents and the Passage of Time, but the Bastard wasn't one of the ten, he must be connected to one of them. How else would he know about all that stuff?"

"But what's the motive?" Jasper asked. "Why did he kill your parents and take my father? And where do I look for him now?"

"That's what I'm saying. He's connected to the ten. That's how we should look for your father," Maya said.

"A connection isn't a location. Blech. I'm running out of time. I can't go back to my house. I can't go back to my friend—" *Damn, Clarence.* Jasper had forgotten about him again. The poor guy probably thought he was dead. "If I don't find my dad soon, in the end, I might just run around like a homeless orphan chasing connections. What kind of a life is that?"

The sentence hung in the air when Jasper saw Maya's blank expression and realized what he had just said. "Sorry. You know that's not how I meant it."

"No, that's how you meant it. And you're right. What kind of life is that?" She took his hand. Her grip was delicate, her skin cool and smooth. "Look, for a long time I had a purpose—justice for my parents." She paused at the memory. "What you did yesterday... Let's just say I owe you. We'll find your father together."

Jasper squirmed inside, holding in the lie.

She picked up the picture of the ten students. "We're not chasing connections. This is the connection; we already know that. Ten people, that's all we need."

"Four people," Jasper said. "Ten minus our parents are six, minus one guy who killed himself according to my uncle, and minus, well, my uncle. Four people."

"Minus your uncle? Shouldn't we at least consider him?"

"He's got issues, but he's like family. He'd never do anything to—"

"Then maybe we should start with him," Maya said. "Who'd know more about the others than him?"

"Believe me, my friend Clarence and I, we tried. He's a dead end. Drugged, confused, totally paranoid. We'd have a better shot finding everyone through Google than through him."

"Don't bother. If they're anything like our parents, there'll barely be a trace on the whole internet."

"Our parents?"

"Have you never googled your parents? There's absolutely nothing," Maya said.

"I never googled my dad, but that doesn't surprise me. He's not the social media type."

"That's not what I mean. I mean *nothing* nothing. Like they don't exist."

"Well, there's always public records," Jasper said.

"Yeah, I used to think the same thing. You mean like real estate. I don't know who that is, but the house you and your dad lived in belongs to an Isabel Dujardin."

Jasper didn't know an Isabel Dujardin, but the name sounded familiar. His grandmother on his mother's side of the family was born a Dujardin in France, but they didn't have any contact with that part of the family. They certainly had never visited them in America.

"How do you know all that?" Jasper asked.

"What do you think I do with all my time? My nails? Do you remember what I can do? What you can do now? How much you can get done in one day, let alone months?"

"You know I can't control it. Maybe it was a fluke?"

"You seem to be doing okay," Maya said. "What time is it?"

She pointed at the vintage kitchen clock on the wall. It showed the time as 9:14 and 13 seconds, which seemed about right, but the second hand didn't move.

"It's broken," he said.

"Is it?" Maya asked innocently.

He looked again, really focused on it, and suddenly noticed how it stood out from other objects around it, like a beacon of some heightened reality, distinct from all other things in the universe.

Ever so slowly, the second hand crept forward. Time passed, and nothing happened in the kitchen, no, in the whole world, except the second hand of the kitchen clock making its way from 13 to 14. After an excruciatingly long moment, it came to rest in the 14 position.

Jasper still didn't know how to control his access to Accelerated Time, but the possibilities seemed endless. Not knowing what to say, he could only come up with, "Mind.

Blown."

Thankfully, Maya still laughed. "Come, I'll show you a few tricks."

She led Jasper to the private backyard, where she made him sit cross-legged on the grass next to the pool. Time bending, lesson one.

He had accessed Accelerated Time two different ways already: he had been sucked into it subconsciously in the presence of another time bender like earlier this morning, and of course, yesterday's plentiful excitement and fear of death had done the trick too.

For now, given a choice, he'd gladly do without being terrified for a while.

"Think of it as a state of mind, like meditation," Maya said. "Instead of running, you stand very still, until everything around you is also completely still. Then you can start running again, and everything else will remain still."

He tried, sincerely, but that way of thinking didn't work.

"Don't sweat it," Maya said. "My mother had this thing about a flower field, and she'd be the only one that grew. Everyone's different. The key is, uh, to find your own key."

So he couldn't access Accelerated Time at will, but what he could do was follow her lead. If he focused on her like there was nothing else in the world, easy enough for some reason, she would transition to Accelerated Time, and he'd be sucked right along without really understanding how.

Staying invisible to the tick-tocks turned out to be one of the tricks she had talked about earlier. No magic, just speed, no biggie. But then it was all speed here, distance there, size relative to the observer, duck here, stretch there, slow down, go fast, become the hummingbird wing… Ultimately, Jasper got so confused, he ended up running in circles in Real Time, flapping his arms.

"Screw the hummingbirds!" He dropped to his knees, gasping for air, before he bent over forwards and rested his forehead on the lawn. "I'm more of an ostrich."

Maya laughed so hard, she nearly buckled over.

Maybe she had orchestrated the exercises mostly for her entertainment, but Jasper enjoyed the instructions and her company. And the smiles and the laughter, even if on occasion he couldn't tell whether she laughed with or at him.

For the first time in a long time, he felt so contented, he would've volunteered to make a fool out of himself in a Hello Kitty T-shirt at the pool for the rest of the day. Or his life, for that matter.

But as soon as he had successfully jittered his way through the backyard in Accelerated Time a few times Maya turned very serious. She looked at her watch. "The only advantage we have is time, we shouldn't waste it. As long as your father is out there our job's not finished."

Jasper wanted to object that he felt nowhere near ready, but before he could open his mouth she put a hand on his shoulder, making him wish his pink tee was a little less sweaty.

"You'll be fine," she said, almost convincing him. "Let's take this show on the road."

Chapter Twenty-One

The Scene of the Crime

Jasper and Maya hid in the shadows of the entrance to the Pooch Hotel's underground parking garage. Maya had been incredulous that a doggie daycare could have its own underground parking, but why not? Maybe it was an L.A. thing.

The object of their interest lay on the other side of the street anyway, the Passage of Time they had so narrowly escaped with their lives yesterday.

"Accelerated Time or not, I have a bad feeling about this," Jasper said. "Why are there so many people?"

Police tape cordoned off the whole block, including the abandoned garage that housed the entrance to the Passage. The loose fence panel had been replaced, and traffic officers encouraged passersby to keep walking if they so much as slowed down anywhere near the fence. Vehicles from the Fire Department, LAPD, and the L.A. Transit Authority parked in a neat row south of the block.

"It's a much bigger audience than I expected, but that also means it's more likely that someone will be talking about what's going on in there," Maya said. "Maybe I should take this one alone, I also want to make sure they didn't dig up my ditch, although that's on the far end anyway. What do you think?"

"If that's what you want." Jasper tried not to sound too relieved. Messing up would mean being seen, maybe even getting caught, and he didn't think he could talk his way out of the situation this time.

Still, they couldn't write off the biggest treasure trove of information about their parents and the other time benders, not while his father was still out there somewhere. If the Passage could be accessed, they had to know.

"Look." Maya pointed to the parked cars. "They're using a small door in the fence. I can sneak in. Wait for me here and monitor the situation, but if you get into trouble, run and meet me at the hacienda later. Remember, in Accelerated Time, you're faster on foot than anyone here can drive." She pulled her black shawl over her head and headed into traffic to make her way across the street.

In Real Time, she moved so fast none of the drivers could hope to see her, but in Accelerated Time she didn't even run. The cars barely inched forward while she almost leisurely slalomed around them.

The tick-tocks didn't take any notice of her. Being small, slim, and dressed all in black helped minimize her visual footprint, but her movement was key. Perpetual, purposeful, chaotic, like a caffeinated prima ballerina tracing the flight path of a drunken mosquito. Even if the tick-tocks glimpsed a shape, their minds would never be able to put together enough information to call it to their attention.

Jasper couldn't hope to ever emulate her graceful movement. Maya twirled past the parked cars and trucks in front of the little gate in the fence when Jasper noticed a deep pleasant buzzing… in his pants?

His concentration broke, and he tumbled into Real Time, the cars suddenly zipping by at forty miles an hour. He felt a mix of disappointment and relief. At least he messed up still hiding in the shadows.

The buzzing in his pants stopped. A long text message from an unknown number. It had to be Clarence.

"This feels weird since u're probably dead. If not, screw u. I spent the whole morning at the police station. Told them ur father had mental issues and disappeared, u didn't want to go to the police and went into the 'Auto Body Shop' because u thought he might be sleeping there. They think u're an arsonist or sth, that u set ur house on fire & blew urself up in that garage. Maybe killed ur dad too. I don't know what else to say."

Well, that explained why this place teemed with cops. But how to contact Clarence? He couldn't leave him hanging like this.

The phone buzzed again. "The police said they'll try to trace ur cell phone signal, so I guess I'll know soon if u're buried in that garage or not. Later. (Or not.)"

Jasper almost dropped his cell phone. *Of course.* He had to get rid of the phone. No, the SIM card. Or did these things have a MAC address that could be tracked too? Who knew how exactly this stuff worked… Well, Clarence did, but that didn't help him now.

With trembling fingers Jasper opened the back of his cell phone and put the SIM card down on the bare concrete. He stomped on it, grinding his heel into the plastic and metal bits.

An elderly lady with an elaborately coiffed poodle on a golden leash walked by and glanced at him warily. "No signal." He forced a smile.

The lady turned away and quickened her pace.

Okay, so he trashed the SIM card, but what if the police had already traced it? Could he throw them off by dropping the phone at the Passage? Make it appear like a casualty of the explosion?

Jasper smacked his forehead. He'd been in Real Time for the last couple of minutes. Maya should be back already. Or was this Accelerated Time? A pang of panic hit. *Can you become unstuck in time? Is that what happens to Uncle Martin when he spaces out?*

No, the cars rolled by at normal speed. Where the hell was Maya?

No time like the present to find your own way. He'd never feel comfortable using this phone again, so he put it on the floor next to the SIM, stomped it into oblivion, and carefully collected the pieces.

Even in Accelerated Time, he could never copy Maya's invisibility dance, but he could certainly try to run in a straight line fast enough not to be noticed by unsuspecting tick-tocks. He took a deep breath and tried to trick his body into Accelerated Time.

Jasper closed his eyes, forcefully pressing his eyelids together. Geometric shapes formed in the blackness, grey and purple rectangular frames expanding, contracting, collapsing into themselves, into each other. Constant movement, his synapses firing in the blackness. He delved into the shapes and down the rabbit hole. Head first, he let himself fall into the blackness... Falling...

The shapes vanished; only blackness remained. He no longer fell. Everything just stopped. Jasper was very much alone in his mind. He opened his eyes. Accelerated Time. A sense of satisfaction washed over him.

He peeked around the corner.

The cars inched forward. He had done it. Run over there, lose the phone, look for Maya, get the hell out. Most importantly, always keep on moving.

The little door in the fence all the way over at the south side still stood open. A man in a gray suit walked onto the property. In Accelerated Time, it looked like he almost stood still. Jasper couldn't guarantee himself he'd be able to make it there before the door closed again, but he knew he had to start... *Now!*

He had always preferred walking to running, but a world on pause wasn't a 2K in P.E., but forbidden fun—simply exhilarating. After he had cleared the street, he knew he'd make the open door before it closed. It had barely moved while he had already crossed half the distance.

When he got closer, Jasper recognized the man about to inadvertently hold the door open for him: Detective Keane.

Jasper's wound started to hurt, so he slowed down from a sprint to a jog. It should still be fast enough to remain unseen and slip through the door. Better to conserve some energy. He couldn't allow himself to be sucked into Real Time on the other side.

The detective moved out of Jasper's view, and the door lurched a lot faster. He must have slammed the door shut from inside.

Jasper gritted his teeth and picked up speed again. At a full run, he pivoted sideways and pirouetted through the narrow gap.

He kept on running toward the ruins. The door slammed shut behind him. He peeked over his shoulder.

Keane headed for two uniformed police officers standing around a folding table at the side of the property.

Ignoring a beginning stitch in his side, he stayed on course for the Passage, or what remained of it—the back wall and a heap of rubble.

Jasper reached into his pocket and threw the phone and SIM card bits onto the pile. It vanished in the cracks. Whenever they'd get around to sifting through the debris, they'd find the phone and might assume him down there somewhere. If nothing else, maybe it would keep them from actively looking for him elsewhere.

The pain of his wound joined forces with the stitch in his side and turned his abdomen into a ball of pain. Gritting his teeth, he forced himself to keep going around the back wall of the garage, where he put his hands on his knees and caught his breath. The whole run had taken mere seconds in Real Time, but minutes for him. The gash across his abdomen had not reacted kindly.

He understood how the Bastard had been able to catch up to Maya's scooter yesterday, but also why she was so sure that they would outpace him in the end. You can only do what you're capable of doing in principle, even if you're doing it faster in Accelerated Time. Running had become too painful, at any speed.

He pulled up his Hello Kitty shirt and pushed down on the wound dressing. The pressure brought a bit of relief, but blood had soaked on the other side. He suppressed a groan, took off his backpack, and kneeled down to search for the bottle of Vicodin Maya had given him. He found it and popped a couple of pills in his mouth, chewing them despite the revolting taste. Hopefully they'd kick in just as fast as yesterday, even in Accelerated Time. He put the rucksack back on and crawled forward on his knees to sneak a look around the corner for a sign of Maya.

About twenty feet to the right of the entrance, Detective Keane looked at some papers on the table with the other police officers. All three appeared completely oblivious to the small, ninja-like figure dancing and shifting around them, staying out of phase with their reality, but listening in on their conversation—Maya.

Jasper pulled his head back. His worries had been for naught. She remained unseen and spying on the police, leaving him with a new problem—how to get out of here? He peeked around the corner again. The door was closed, and who knew when anyone would leave.

The fence behind him had no doors or openings along its whole length. No way he could climb it unseen in his current condition, let alone make it over the razor wire. Police guarded the big gate across from the Pooch Hotel, and he couldn't dance through it like Maya.

Back to square one. The way in had to be the way out. He'd have to wait for the door to open again, like… it just did?

In the blink of an eye, the door had opened and closed.

In the blink of an eye for Jasper in Accelerated Time, which made it imperceptible to the tick-tocks.

Only Jasper seemed to notice the tall figure dressed in black, including a ski mask over his face, surveying the scene while gliding over the ground in a jittery way similar to Maya's more elegant invisibility dance.

Another time bender, and it wasn't the man he knew as the plumber.

Maya had her back turned, oblivious to the man's presence.

When the masked man noticed her, he took cover behind a forklift parked to the left of the table everyone gathered around and scanned the area for prying eyes. Prying eyes like Jasper's.

He had been so transfixed by the development, he had forgotten to hide. No question, the man looked straight at him.

Instinctively, Jasper pulled his head back and jerked himself upright. Hard to feel more vulnerable than on your knees. Stabbing pain shot through him, like his belly tore open. When would these damn opioids kick in?

Jasper shuffled, looking for balance, but the rubble on the ground turned into marbles under his unsteady feet, and he slipped. With a loud *crunch*, he ended up flat on his back, squashing his backpack underneath him.

Shock replaced the pain. The fall had taken him beyond the corner shielding him from the police officers, and he couldn't see Maya or the other time bender anymore. The tick-tocks moved at normal speed and looked for the source of the noise. Jasper lay on his back like a bug.

"Freeze!" Detective Keane reacted first. "Jasper? Jasper! Jasper, don't move, we're here to help you."

Definitely Real Time.

Keane and the two others ran toward him as he scrambled to his feet. If he could transition back to Accelerated Time, he could outrun them all, but in Real Time? No chance.

Close your eyes, concentrate!

No, run away!

No, slow down!

Run faster!

Argh!

This time bender needed more time. Time to concentrate, time to focus. The one thing he couldn't do was let them arrest him.

"Stop!" Jasper yelled. "I have a bomb!" It was the best he could come up with on short notice. Regrettably.

"I have a bomb?" Idiot! How are you going to get out of that? They'll never believe anything else now!

On the upside, it did work in the short term. The police officers stopped about ten yards away from him.

"Jasper, don't make it worse," said Detective Keane. "Come with us now and I promise you, I'll do whatever I can to get you help. A lawyer, a therapist—"

"Don't..." Jasper said, "don't come any closer, or I'll blow us all up." He took off his backpack and pointed at it. "If I drop this, we're all going to die. Don't come any closer!" He hoped nobody remembered that seconds earlier he had fallen on it.

Idiot, idiot, idiot! Focus! He closed his eyes and pressed his eyelids shut. *Shapes in the darkness. Falling. Come on!*

It didn't work.

"Jasper, put down the bag!" The Detective lowered his voice to a calming pitch. When Jasper opened his eyes again, Keane raised his hands defensively. "Listen to me, don't make it any worse. I can still help you, but not like this. Put down the bag!"

No way out. Accelerated Time didn't arrive for Jasper when he needed it most. He'd have to take his chances with Keane.

"Whatttt arrre you doinggggg?" a voice droned into his ear. "Iiiii can'ttt carryyyy youuu, youuuu'lll havvvvve to runnnn."

Maya!

Jasper couldn't see her, but he suspected she hovered around him in Accelerated Time, while trying to whisper into his ear in Real Time. He couldn't even begin to imagine how difficult it must be to operate on two temporal planes at the same time. He barely functioned on one.

"Run where?" Jasper asked, not caring that the police heard him. They already thought he was crazy anyway.

"I'll disssstract zzzemmmm," the disembodied voice hissed into his ear, and Jasper thought he saw a shimmering figure glide past him.

"Run where?" it echoed in his mind, but before he had time to think, an invisible force tackled Detective Keane into his midsection and rammed him into the smaller of the officers, sending them both tumbling to the ground, where Keane's flailing elbow hit the other officer square in the family jewels.

"What the...?" Keane cried as he tried to get off his colleague, who moaned in pain.

The third policeman took a step toward his colleagues to help them up but fell victim to a forceful leg trip and landed on top of them, head butting Detective Keane on the nose on his way down.

Jasper ran. Or at least he tried his best in his present condition. His wound tore at his belly with every step. One of the police officers tried to grab his leg when he hobbled past the pile, but he barely avoided the grip.

The three policemen disentangled themselves from each other and ran after him. They didn't get far until an invisible force tripped them up once more.

"There's another one!" Detective Keane yelled behind him. "It's, it's..." Words failed him.

Jasper had almost reached the door.

He needed to run away, disappear into traffic, hide in a dark corner, get away to have privacy for a minute and a chance to dive into Accelerated Time. Unless he had completely lost his ability to bend time, in which case he was well and truly screwed.

Maya bought him time, and a surge of hope dulled the pain. He picked up a little more speed. Barely ten more yards and—

The small door to the street flew open, a sturdy police officer blocking Jasper's way out, his gun already drawn.

"Halt!" he commanded.

Jasper stopped and frantically looked left and right.

"Put down the backpack!" Detective Keane shouted behind him. The three officers advanced baby step by baby step, guns in hand.

Even unhurt, Jasper couldn't have evaded a swarm of bullets. And even Maya couldn't take out four people at once.

Game over—

Jasper couldn't even finish a thought that brief when the force of arms grabbing him from the window of a passing high-speed train hit him.

As the force carried him away, he caught the briefest glimpse of the police officers' faces behind them. They had not even reacted to his disappearance yet. One blink of an eye later, a leap and a jolt. He broke through the fence on the north side. Jasper caught single frames of the street, traffic, someone running after them, then an empty alley.

He didn't have time to process any of it, let alone struggle against the stranger, when the man in black already slowed down again.

The man opened a small back door to a large building and stepped inside a maintenance room, where he set Jasper down on the floor.

The door to the alley flew open again. Maya.

The man raised his hands apologetically. He had transitioned back to Real Time because Jasper could follow his motions.

"Leave him alone," Maya barked and assumed a fighting stance. "Are you okay?" she asked Jasper, serious concern in her voice.

Jasper looked down at the blood-soaked bottom half of his, actually her, pink t-shirt. "Just the old flesh wound. I'll live." He looked at the masked man and added, "I hope."

"Who are you?" Maya asked.

The man took off the ski mask and greasy dark brown locks fell down to his shoulders, framing an unshaven face.

"Uncle Martin!" Jasper said.

"*That's* your uncle?" Maya said. "You've got to be kidding me."

"Shh...," Uncle Martin whispered, but Jasper couldn't stop himself.

"Uncle Martin, what's going on? How did you know we were—"

"Just..." Uncle Martin composed himself. "Shh! What's so hard about that? Shh." He raised his index finger to his lips incredulously. When Jasper and Maya didn't say anything, he continued, "Good. My house, 3 p.m. Everyone makes their own way. Don't get captured, you fools."

He took off his black nylon jacket and tossed it to Jasper. "And for God's sake, man, put on something less conspicuous." He put the ski mask back on and walked away, mumbling, "Hello freaking Kitty."

Chapter Twenty-Two

Never Back Down

Once Eva's spasms started, every thought felt like wading through molasses ("*thick, dark brown syrup that is separated from raw sugar during the refining process*") until the whole of her came to a complete standstill. It did not feel like sleep, but like the world around you went on and you rejoined it at a later point in time. Eva's body didn't collapse, just like tick-tocks didn't collapse when she went into Accelerated Time.

She existed in a different time, one where she moved so much slower than Real Time she appeared frozen to everyone else. At least according to Father's hypothesis. And also where the danger lay: What if she froze while she swallowed food, while swimming, or while taking a step over an abyss ("*a deep or seemingly bottomless gulf or great space*")?

That's why she never left her quarters, why Father was so protective. She had awoken (although "wake" didn't quite describe the sensation correctly since her frozen state offered no sense of rest) in her bed more times than she could count. Usually, she last remembered reading, brushing her teeth, or looking out the window.

After freezing while taking a shower, her skin took days to recover from the soaking. Real Time marched on relentlessly. And sometimes, she rejoined the present right where she had frozen without Father finding her.

So when she rejoined the here and now, it relieved her that she still stood at the door at the bottom of the strange staircase.

Father hadn't found her! He had to be looking for her. Was it still night or the next day? Or… Her longest freeze lasted two days and two nights. Surely, he would have found her by now in that case. Unless he never came down here.

She let go of the door handle and hurried up the stairs, passing the "-1" floor that she had skipped on the way down. No time to explore. At the top of the staircase, she cautiously opened the door to the garage.

Small windows let in some sunlight and the garage turned out to be more of a delivery area, with pallets stacked at the far end, a massively oversized garage door, even a moveable conveyor belt machine.

Please let it be early morning sunlight! Eva threw caution to the wind. She barged into the main residence, weaved through the corridors, then up the stairs to the fourth floor, her floor. She relaxed upon discovering the sun had come up, but it didn't appear too late into the morning.

At 7:30:00, Father always brought herbal tea, yoghurt, a fruit cup, half a cheese sandwich, and a granola bar for mid-morning snacking. Every day. It was for the best.

It had to be before 7:30. It simply *had* to be! He couldn't know what she had done. He'd be furious. *Oh Robbie, what do we do if he's found out? What will* he *do?*

She turned the corner and knew it was 7:29:59, since she found herself looking at her father's back while he carried the breakfast tray. She took a step back, hid, and peeked around the corner.

He moved slow. Not frozen certainly, but slow compared to her. Still, only a few more steps to the door. She would have no problem reaching the door before him, but opening it, going in, closing it in front of his nose without him noticing? Never!

That's it, silly girl! It's over. All of it. Over. I told you so, I did.

"Shut up, Adam, unless you have something helpful to say!" she told her brother silently, but what could she tell Father?

He took another step closer to the door. Had he already seen the coaster that kept the lock open? Not that it mattered if he actually got to the door before her. But how to prevent it?

If I help you now, I need you to promise me something.

Adam was... negotiating? "How could you help? And what do you want?"

I never want to go back down there. You know, where you froze. Promise me. Never there, never again.

"If you help me now, I promise." Why would she want to go back to that spooky place anyway?

Turn around, go back down. There's another staircase at the end of the corridor, use that. You're so fast, you can do it. You'll be at the door before him.

"But he'll be looking right at me!" This was a terrible plan.

No, he'll be looking this way.

"Why would he be looking this way?" Eva whispered, then felt Adam guiding her attention to the window. No, the windowsill. No, the flowerpot on the windowsill. Then she understood.

She pushed the pot over the edge and ran back down the stairs, down the corridor one floor below, then up the stairs on the other side.

She sneaked a look around the corner. Father had almost reached her door, two steps more, at most. She wouldn't make it without being seen.

In the distance, the pot hit the floor. It took an excruciatingly long time for the sound to travel far enough, but finally Father turned around.

Eva took a deep breath and rushed forward. No time to second-guess her plan now. She reached the door the moment Father had completed his turn, carefully pulled it open just far enough for her to slip through, and caught the coaster that had begun to fall. She stepped into her room and spun around, then closed the door behind her as fast as she could while making as little noise as possible. The continuing cracking sound from the flowerpot breaking would hopefully conceal the noise from the lock.

She took off her slippers and jumped into bed. It happened rarely, but sometimes she'd still be in her nightgown for breakfast. She'd pretend she had slept in. As tired as she suddenly felt, it would be an easy story to sell. She pulled her comforter up to her chin.

Now did you learn your lesson, silly girl? Stay home, stay safe. Stay home, stay alive. If that's what you want, that is.

Adam had regressed to his acerbic (*"sharp and forthright in temper or tone"*) self, but for the moment Eva didn't care. What an adventure. Even Robbie couldn't have imagined half of it in his wildest dreams.

Chapter Twenty-Three

The Troll Cave

Uncle Martin had left them in a control room located at the back of the office building on Olympic that Jasper had researched the day before yesterday. He explained to Maya why and how he had ended up flat on his back next to the ruins of the Passage of Time and told her where Uncle Martin lived before they split up.

She went back out to get her scooter at the Pooch Hotel and Jasper snuck out through a maze of control and maintenance rooms that eventually led to a familiar lobby, where Igor the janitor fiddled with another electric panel. Jasper hid his face behind the popped collar of Uncle Martin's jacket and left the building.

Ninety minutes to get across town in Los Angeles—ambitious whether you could bend time or not. And all the time bending in the world wouldn't make the bus go east on Olympic any faster, that much Jasper had learned in the last few days.

He sat in the back row and tried to slip into Accelerated Time to no avail. At least the painkillers worked, and Uncle Martin's nylon jacket hid Bloody Kitty, so Jasper rode the bus like any other—albeit badly dressed—tick-tock. He reached the gate to Uncle Martin's house seconds before Maya pulled up next to him. The uphill walk had hurt, but he still felt a little competitive.

"Score one for public transportation." Jasper gave Maya a thumbs up.

"Not bad, but I did pick up a few goodies for you on the way." Maya held up a bag of supplies from the pharmacy.

Before Jasper could think of a witty comeback, Uncle Martin materialized out of nowhere behind the fence. He had changed into his trademark grey sweat suit and looked a far cry from the intimidating figure he had struck an hour earlier.

More than anything, he seemed to be annoyed to see them. "Now you show up? I would have thought you'd take your situation a bit more seriously, no?"

"Uncle Martin," Jasper said, "you said 3 p.m., and here we are."

Uncle Martin looked at his watch. "You're five minutes late. Get in here quick, I have, er, other things running." He held the gate open and scanned the empty cul-de-sac.

Nothing had changed from the last time Jasper had been there. He leaned his backpack against the sofa and turned to Uncle Martin. "This is my friend Maya, the time bender I told you about last week. She saved my life yesterday. Her parents are your old friends—"

"Medha and Nirav Misra," Maya shook Uncle Martin's hand. "Nice to meet you."

"Incredible, an unexpected pleasure." Considering how worried he had been about the existence of another time bender a few days ago, Uncle Martin seemed strangely relaxed.

"Thanks for saving my butt back there at the Passage," Jasper said. "You got there just in time."

"Don't flatter yourself." Uncle Martin waved dismissively. "I wanted to make sure the explosion sealed and buried the place. It was all over the police scanners. Being in time to see you make a fool out of yourself was the side entertainment. What did you even try to do?"

"I know this sounds silly, but I was trying to access Accelerated Time," Jasper said.

Uncle Martin laughed. "And how were you going to do that?"

At this point Maya interrupted their conversation in Accelerated Time. Jasper couldn't understand a word she or Uncle Martin said, but a lot of back and forth happened.

After a while, Jasper loudly cleared his throat, which brought their exchange to an end. "If you're caught up on our adventure now, the first thing we should do is—"

"Actually," Uncle Martin said, "the first thing we need to do is make sure you don't bleed all over my Persian rugs. Your friend brought some tools, and I'll stitch you up."

"No way." Jasper glanced at Maya. "Please do me a favor and just do what you did yesterday, that worked."

"It doesn't look like it worked well enough," she said. "I think you should let him do it."

Jasper sighed. He took the Vicodin out of his pocket. "In that case, I need another couple of these."

Uncle Martin took the box out of his hand and studied the label. "Aha, the culprit for the current impotence your lady friend told me about." He chucked the pills into the trash.

"Excuse me?" Jasper said, while Maya tried to hide a giggle with a cough.

"Temporal impotence. Opiates will leave you stranded in Real Time. Gotta stick to the over-the-counter stuff if you get a boo-boo. The good news is, as soon as they wear off, everything will be back to normal. Now lie down and let the professionals help you."

"I hope you've done this before." Jasper took off his t-shirt, lay down bare-chested on Uncle Martin's itchy satin couch, and wondered if going to jail with Keane might have been the preferable option. Bloody Kitty joined SpongeBob in T-shirt heaven.

"Oh, many times," his uncle said. "Suture kit?"

Maya handed him the suture kit.

"Thank you, dear." Uncle Martin opened it and examined the needle closely before turning his attention back to Jasper. "Just never on a live human. Now bite down on this and don't move."

When Jasper opened his mouth to protest, Uncle Martin shoved a wooden spoon between his teeth. "Shh! It'll be over in no time."

Uncle Martin turned his attention to the bloody gash across Jasper's belly and transitioned to Accelerated Time, making him appear blurry.

Jasper's wound stung for a moment, then Uncle Martin's appearance came into focus again, and he took the spoon from Jasper's mouth. "Now that wasn't so bad, was it? You'll be as good as new in no time. We heal fast."

Cleaning and neatly stitching up the laceration had only

taken seconds.

"Hold on." Uncle Martin shimmered again. Bandages materialized across Jasper's midsection.

"One second," Maya said, and a big smiley face magically appeared on the bandage.

"I like your new friend better than your old one." Uncle Martin gathered up the medical supplies. "Got a sense of humor."

"That's all real funny, but could you keep it in Real Time for me?" Jasper asked. "The meds haven't worn off yet and I'm not really looking forward to that anyway."

"Take whatever you want against the pain, just ditch the opiates. I remember our first transitions. Nobody could even talk to anyone. Nobody had the first clue. We were stumbling around like newborn fawn." Uncle Martin laughed. "But you two are naturals, it seems. Born with it, who would have thought? Tranq would have a coronary." He chuckled and took a small vaporizer from the big front pocket of his hoodie and took two hits. "A proprietary blend. To help slow everything down for a while. Keeps me functioning in Real Time, hopefully. I'm trying something new."

Jasper had more pressing concerns than Uncle Martin's self-medication as long as it kept him from going off the deep end. He got up from the couch and put on Uncle Martin's washed-out AC/DC T-shirt. It must've last been black at some point in the late eighties. "Born with it, pah. How did that possibility not even come up when I visited you the last time? Still don't know who kidnapped my father either. Or what they want with him. And you never got around to explaining how this all works."

Uncle Martin smirked bitterly. "Yeah, how it all works. That's the trillion-dollar question, innit? As I told you and your, uh, tall friend last time, after the incident at BioDein, ten very smart people could suddenly bend time. Whatever allowed us to do it must have been induced, but we didn't know how. Or what had physically happened to our bodies to allow us to experience time differently. Or if it could be passed on to others. Guess we know that much now, eh?"

He turned to Maya. "I'm very sorry about your parents. They were good people, decent people. I wish they had told you about us, our history, maybe even what they discovered after our group broke up. I refuse to believe researchers of their caliber and curiosity and special talent spent seventeen years in a Detroit suburb editing middle school science textbooks."

Uncle Martin and Maya's conversation in Accelerated Time earlier had left him well-informed. It had been a minute for Jasper, but who knew how much time that had given them to catch up? Sucked to be left out of the new club like this.

"In any case, you two certainly inherited the talent," Uncle Martin's voice ramped up to a Mickey Mouse pitch. "Excuse me." He closed his eyes and bit his lip, then took another couple of hits from his vaporizer, inhaling deeply before continuing in his normal speaking voice. "We filled folders and books and hard drives and diaries with our measurements, our research, our analyses, but in the end, we disbanded before we got to the bottom of it."

"And everyone went home? Just like that, none the

wiser? I should do that, too, smoke some whatever and turn on my tube TV. That's really helpful," Jasper said, with a harsher edge to his voice than he had intended.

Maya looked at him, thin-lipped, before turning to Uncle Martin. "I for one would like to hear what happened. Why didn't you continue?"

"Look, there were ten time benders, well, nine who moved into the Passage of Time, plus Jasper's mom, and we were all brilliant, but at different things. And we didn't get together because we were friends. Andy was a bookish idealist, often solitary, but a communicator when needed, my best friend too, but his earnestness could get on your nerves like nothing else. And your parents were brilliant analysts, but"—he raised his hands apologetically—"no offense, dear, they were very guarded, dare I say dour. Alex made everything possible with his father's dough, but he was like an enthusiastic Labrador puppy, always straining at the leash—and our accommodations the size of a porta-potty. With Nobel Prize-level obsessives like Tranq in there, always looking inside, probing how far we could push our bodies, you can imagine how well that went. And then Floyd, kind of a hanger-on, by-the book guy, the opposite of a free spirit. I couldn't stand the guy, but he and Andy got along great. I could go on, but you catch my drift."

He sounded weary and regretful. "We worked and lived together underground for a few years that were decades to us. We loved each other, we hated each other, and at the end we couldn't agree on anything anymore, least of all how to use our talent in the outside world. And then of course the Internet blew up and changed everything. There were fights, we sealed and booby-trapped the passage, and everyone went their separate ways. Bye-bye, the end, turn off the TV. Or on, you know."

A moment later, Uncle Martin vanished, but after a few seconds, he reappeared as if nothing had happened.

"And you," Maya asked Uncle Martin, "what's your thing?"

"Thing? What thing?" He nervously puckered his lips.

"You said you were all brilliant at different things?"

"Ah, yeah. I remember. I'm a bit of a renaissance man, I'd say." He chuckled and wiped his nose with his sleeve. "Had to do everything myself all my life, you know. Plus, I sleep only an hour or two a night, so I get a lot done."

"Yeah? So what were you getting done last Wednesday after you threw us out? Thanks for stitching me up, but maybe I wouldn't have gotten shot in the first place if you had helped me."

Sure, all this background stuff was intriguing, and at any other time in his life Jasper would've loved to hear every detail, just, like, not now. "The police think I set our house on fire and blew up the Passage of Time. I threatened them with a bomb a couple of hours ago!" A horrible idea, he had to admit. "And we still don't know what happened to my father, if he's even still alive. Where that Bastard took him."

Uncle Martin and Maya started a side conversation in Accelerated Time that Jasper couldn't follow. *Fine. Whatever.* "And since that guy is not one of your friends, who is he, uh, was he?" He hoped Maya hadn't noticed. "Why could he bend time? What did he want from Dad? Does anyone actually care about that? Clarence does, but he can't help me.

215

Maybe you could help, but do you care?"

That brought their side conversation to an end. Uncle Martin scratched the back of his hand, leaving bright red streaks on pale skin. "I'm sorry for last week. Lately, I've been having trouble with the peculiar rhythm of my life. By my latest calculations, I'm around two hundred and seventy-five years old. Not my cells, obviously, but I feel it upstairs. Dog years." He laughed, but it turned into a coughing fit. "Real Time is hard, and Accelerated Time is lonely. This is helping me interact with tick-tocks." He pointed to his inhaler again.

"Bullshit," Jasper barked. "Your best friend was kidnapped, and you didn't care. Look at yourself. You're a pathetic middle-aged junkie."

"Jasper, please," Maya said.

"No, he's right. At least mostly." Uncle Martin took another hit from his inhaler. "It seems our bodies age in Real Time, but up here?" He pointed to his head. "Sometimes I feel thin, like Bilbo Baggins." He caressed his inhaler and croaked, "My precious," before another coughing fit. "Lots of time spent in my head. Solitary confinement. It's crammed up there. Anyway…"

He ran his hand through his greasy hair, turned around, vanished, and reappeared at the door at the far end of his living room. From the way it swung open, Jasper figured it quite solid. "I've never shown this to anyone, but I guess it doesn't matter now. Let's see what we can do."

Jasper walked over and peered in at a narrow staircase leading down into a basement.

Here we go again. Jasper grabbed his backpack.

"Excuse the mess. My decorator went for a lived-in feeling." Uncle Martin plowed through empty beer and soda cans, clearing the way for Maya and Jasper. It looked like a family of ten had lived in his basement for a year—without garbage pickup.

Jasper found it easy to ignore the empty food and beverage containers, the dirty clothes, the stained couch, and the pervasive sense of yuck due to the centerpiece of Uncle Martin's basement: flat screen displays lined the entire back wall, floor to ceiling.

In front of them, a large desk spanned the width of the room, littered with multiples of the latest game consoles and flanked by expensive-looking carbon-fiber-wrapped loudspeakers. Under the desk, PC towers hummed side by side with cylindrical Mac Pros. Old gaming consoles, controllers, and cables stuffed wall shelves next to tall racks full of servers, hard drives, and more CPUs.

"Wow." Jasper had never seen anything like it.

"Why…?" Maya wondered aloud.

"You cannot possibly overestimate what a game changer high speed internet was for people like us," Uncle Martin said. "It was part of the reason we split up, but after we split up? Boy, you have to find a way to entertain yourself. Endless days, endless nights trying not to go crazy. Can't really do anything in public, and after we closed the Passage, there was nowhere to go but home. Gotta find something."

"Why couldn't you just lead your life in normal time,

Real Time I mean?" Jasper asked.

"I'm sure everyone tried. I always thought Andy did rather well considering Renée was a tick-tock. It's not easy." He took a hit from his vaporizer. "But it gets harder as you get older. It's like sleeping; you can only do so much of it. Like when you have the flu, you can't say, oh, I'll just sleep for ten days, and when I wake up, it'll be gone. That's not how it works. You have to pass the waking hours. So you set a few thousand high scores or rile people up on the internet to pass the time."

"Hold on, you're, like, a troll?" Jasper asked. Time bending seemed like winning the lottery. Was Uncle Martin the sad lottery winner on the local news who lost it all again a few years later?

"All those years, all that time," Maya said wistfully. "There must be a way to, I don't know, help humanity with that."

Uncle Martin laughed bitterly. "Yes, of course. Why don't we try to cure cancer? Like that's so easy. I remember the discussions. Do you believe there's life somewhere else in the universe? Older than us? More intelligent?"

"What does that have to do with anything?" Maya asked.

"Indulge me."

"Maybe. The numbers suggest it," Maya said.

Uncle Martin leaned forward. "Are you familiar with the Fermi paradox? Why don't they visit? Or at least communicate? Why the silence?"

"I don't know."

"Because they don't care!" he yelled and threw his hands up. "They could fly by and wave or send an email. Hi there, humans, it's us, highly-evolved space aliens, just saying aloha, nice to see you're not proto-slime anymore, and by the way, here's how you fix your climate and here's how you cure cancer..." Uncle Martin wiggled his index finger and pointed at them. "No, no, no, they don't do that. Here's my theory: They're so freaking advanced, they don't worry, they're not curious, they don't care about a-ny-thing at all. All they do is levitate in their milky space sauce, massage their pleasure centers, play on their PlayStation five hundreds, rub their little alien dicks, take their purple space drugs and scratch that itch! Scratch that terrible itch of existence all freaking space day long. They don't give a rat's ass about humanity and they never will. And after over two hundred years on the internet, forgive me, neither do I."

Uncle Martin's words hung in the air. Maya, who had so easily taken a liking to Uncle Martin, curled her lip. Jasper looked at the dozens of screens. They showed paused games, running games, news websites, TV channels, internet message boards, streaming services, more games, more messages...

The grime and stench of the leftover food and who knows what else were nauseating. And looking at the piles of crusty clothes on the floor gave him an itch in his borrowed T-shirt.

"Then why did you even tell me about time bending in the first place? Why save me at the Passage today? Why show us this?" Jasper looked his uncle in the eye.

Uncle Martin took another hit from his vaporizer and inhaled deeply. For a split second, his pupils dilated and contracted. A wry smile appeared on his face. "Well, maybe

I'm not quite as advanced as these alien assholes yet, eh?"

He sat on his swivel chair and pulled one of the keyboards closer. "Let's see if we can find out what's going on. It's a crime against the internet to let a twenty-four gigabit per second connection run idle." He started typing. "We gave our word not to keep tabs on each other when we went our separate ways, but I'm comfortable calling this an emergency. Let's run a few generic searches about yesterday, that Bastard, as you call him, and my old pals. Grab a drink and snacks; we're going to have to let these scripts run for a while."

Uncle Martin's fingers blurred over his keyboard. On seven displays in the center of his setup, numerous browser windows opened and added tabs by the dozen in seconds. Everywhere Jasper looked, search results, lists, texts, graphics kept on scrolling and scrolling, too fast for him to make out anything. Uncle Martin's head made small sharp movements like an owl's as he followed the information from screen to screen.

Jasper reached for a soda and wiped the top vigorously. When he cracked it open, Uncle Martin already turned his attention back to them. "We have powerful enemies. They're blaming yesterday's explosion on a gas line incident. Nothing about a car chase or shooting on Barrington. No pictures of anything. Or anyone."

"Can they just do that? Sweep a dead guy in the streets under the rug?" Maya asked.

It's easier if he's not really dead. He should really come clean about that part of the story, but he didn't want to lose Maya's help or trust. Or company, for that matter.

"Obviously, because they did," Uncle Martin said. "The question is, who did it? From what you told me, it seems the Bastard didn't know Andy personally, but he knew to find him at the Passage. Now did someone tell him, or did he extract that information, maybe from your parents?"

"No, he couldn't… I would have heard. There was no, uh, conversation before…" Maya stammered.

"That's okay, that's all we need to know. So, it wasn't your parents, Kruzman and Alex are dead, nobody blackmailed me, that leaves four people: Murat, Floyd, Tranq, and Jayjay. The crawlers came up completely empty on Jayjay—"

"Wait a second," Jasper said. "The Bastard. Whatever the plan is behind killing Maya's parents and kidnapping Dad, there's no way he's the brains of that operation. Right?"

"Agreed," Maya said. "There's something dispassionate, a soldier doing his job."

"Mercenary," Jasper suggested.

"I'll add a mercenary search." Uncle Martin typed, and three more displays to his left sprang to life with new windows and tabs. "But back to our list. Murat— There's an arrest record from three years ago in Turkey, inciting unrest. That's where I'm losing the trail. Someone bought a McMansion in Arlington, Virginia, under the name of Floyd's deceased parents. That's gotta be Floyd." He made gagging sounds.

"Tranq. He took over the family business, it seems. They're absolutely loaded." Uncle Martin clicked through a dozen browser tabs. "Donated thirty million Swiss francs to the University Hospital Zurich. He always wanted to be a doctor, brilliant mind. After the incident, he figured that wasn't quite ambitious enough anymore. That you guys inherited the talent would send him into fits. He always wanted to trigger the talent in Renée. He thought she was the key to everything. Why wasn't she affected et cetera, et cetera."

"Did he have a theory?" Jasper asked.

"I'm sure he did. He certainly tried to convince her to be his guinea pig, but she never let him, beyond blood draws and such. After she got cancer, she sought professional medical treatment and didn't come to the Passage often, except to pick up your dad. Annoyed by it all. Can't blame her, I wouldn't want a real-life Dr. Moreau handling my medical care either."

"I thought your mom died in a car accident?" Maya asked.

"Yes, way later. She had thyroid cancer before I was born, but she beat it," Jasper said.

Maya blinked. "Thyroid cancer, that's…"

"That's what?" Jasper asked.

"I don't know. Weird. Interesting. I don't have the word for it. It's probably nothing." Maya tightened the shawl around her neck.

"Nothing is nothing," Uncle Martin said.

Maya took a deep breath, then spoke quietly. "My parents… The Bastard, he mutilated their bodies." Her voice was barely a whisper. "I was hiding when it happened, and I couldn't see, but I saw the stains the next day. I couldn't sleep in that house anymore." Her voice rose again. "Anyway, I stole the coroner's report. It said the cuts appeared random, except in one area. Both of them had deep incisions right underneath their Adam's apple. Their thyroids had been cut out."

"That's, uh, I don't have the word either." Jasper put a hand on her shoulder. "Besides horrible, I guess."

"Thyroid, thyroid cancer, ritual murder, mutilation…" Uncle Martin opened more search windows. Tabs kept opening and closing. He took another hit from his vaporizer.

"Look at that." Uncle Martin pointed to a browser tab: "Thyroid Research Online Journal." The title of the article read, "University Hospital Zurich introduces new thyroid epithelial cell imaging process aiding in early diagnosis and treatment of thyroid dysfunction and carcinogenesis in the thyroid."

"There's a bunch of others." Uncle Martin scrolled through a few tabs. "Apparently, the Division of Endocrinology at UHZ is on the bleeding edge of thyroid research."

"So who exactly donated the money? Tranq, you called him?" Jasper took the old student records and pictures from his backpack and showed them to his Uncle.

"Tranq, a.k.a. Tranquillo Zeiger." Uncle Martin pointed at the name on Jasper's list. "Comes from old Swiss money. Construction and demolition. The father blew up half the Alps for their Gotthard Tunnel. Tranq was the first to realize the economic potential of the internet for people with our talent. He wanted us all to get into the for-profit business together. That didn't go down so well with Andy." He pointed out Tranquillo Zeiger on the group picture. "That's him, in the black turtleneck. Always wore one to cover scars on his neck."

Zeiger was clean-shaven, thin, of average height, with short dark hair and attractive, angular features.

"What would he want with my father after all these years?" Jasper asked.

"Let's not jump to conclusions." Uncle Martin turned back around to his keyboard.

"Stop!" Maya pointed at one of the screens to the left running the mercenary searches. "Scroll back up. There."

She had found a 2008 article about a military investigation in Iraq and skimmed it aloud. "Private Military Contractor Acquitted of Murder... Lethal Accident... Victim found with fourth-degree electrical burns... There's a picture. Yes, it's him."

Jasper would never forget the face of the man who shot him. In the picture, he wore the same model of steel-rimmed glasses as yesterday.

They had found the Bastard.

"You were right. Mercenary. Let me throw some facial recognition algorithms in the mixer." While Uncle Martin ran another data crawl, Jasper put the student records and the picture back into his backpack. When he pulled out his hand, he cut the back of it on a sharp piece of plastic sticking out of the laptop he had taken from the Passage.

"This is the laptop I found yesterday. I think it's my father's. I fell on it earlier, but maybe it still runs, and you can—"

"Hold on." Uncle Martin pointed at him. "You haven't turned that on, have you?"

"I couldn't get past the password screen, but with all the

stuff you have here—"

"So you did turn it on?"

"Well, yes, but it didn't boot all the way up. Why?" Jasper asked.

"If the Wi-Fi is on, it'll look for access points even before you sign in, which means it'll announce its MAC address to any network in range," Uncle Martin said.

"So what?"

"So what? If that's really your father's laptop, whatever he's done online with it has been matched to a MAC address by the big man in the sky, and I don't mean the one with the son and the holy ghost. As soon as you turn this thing on and it starts looking for Wi-Fi, it's a big fat blinking dot on someone's map, that's what."

"I don't know, how would someone know what to look for? And wouldn't we run the same risk right now?" Jasper asked.

"Look around you. Does this look like I'd run a Windows firewall and call it a day? Of course I take precautions." Uncle Martin nodded toward Jasper's father's notebook. "Your father, on the other hand, good grief, judging by this ancient piece of—"

"Guys, guys!" Maya yelled. "Top right, the paper."

She pointed at a PDF version of *Davoser Zeitung*, the local paper of Davos, Switzerland. The headline read, "Adam-Zeiger-Stiftung unterstützt Neubau von Spital Davos." A picture showed a stern Tranquillo Zeiger handing an oversized check to the smiling mayor.

"Adam Zeiger Foundation supports building new Davos Hospital," Uncle Martin translated. "More philanthropy."

"*Adam* Zeiger?" Jasper asked.

Uncle Martin shrugged. "His father, maybe."

"That's not what I mean," Maya said. "Zoom in on the picture."

In the background behind Tranquillo Zeiger, slightly out of focus, but unmistakable, stood the Bastard.

"Ugh." Uncle Martin snorted.

"Isn't this what we wanted? Find the man behind the Bastard?" Maya asked.

"Yes. And no. This is like finding your car has been stolen by the police." Uncle Martin sighed. "Who are you gonna call?"

"That car is my father. We have to steal him back!" How could finally knowing who was behind his father's abduction be a bad thing? "When was that picture taken?"

Uncle Martin tried to scroll up to look for the date on the newspaper, but the browser tab locked up. He tried to reload the page. The browser tab cleared the PDF but didn't reload it. "No worries, it's in my cache." He opened a file browser. "Let me… Holy crap!"

The program closed itself.

"Impossible!" squeaked Uncle Martin, unable to stay in Real Time.

He furiously typed away at his keyboard, but one by one all of the browser windows and tabs closed on all the displays and with them all their search results and information.

Jasper only caught glimpses of Uncle Martin for a while. He appeared under the desk, pulling the plugs of his PC towers, he appeared in front of his server rack flicking switches, then talking to Maya too fast for Jasper to understand, before finally collapsing on his swivel chair in Real Time.

"I've been breached. We have to get out of here. They might be on the way already."

"What happened?" said Jasper. "Who's they?"

"Who knows?" said Uncle Martin. "Who cares?" He got up again, and in the blink of an eye, hard disk drives that he pulled from the rack piled up on the floor in front of Jasper.

Jasper didn't know what to do. Leave and go where? And do what? Could it really be as bad as Uncle Martin suggested? All for a computer crash?

"It's Zeiger," said Maya. "He noticed someone was putting information together. Now he's covering his tracks."

"But how would he even be able to pull the information? That's, like, impossible," Jasper said.

"Exactly right!" Uncle Martin yelled. "Except, you're wrong. You two better hide far away from any network or camera for a few years."

"But my father…"

"Ah, yeah, I keep forgetting about him. May he forgive me. Loopy…" Uncle Martin twirled his finger next to his temple and continued piling up hard drives in the middle of the room. "You guys will have to go now."

Uncle Martin vanished for a moment. When he reappeared, he doused the pile of HDDs in gasoline from a large red canister. "I mean go now as in right now."

"But—" Events were moving too fast for Jasper. Just as he was getting somewhere, the rug got pulled out from under him.

Uncle Martin poured a trail of gasoline from the pile of HDDs to his desk, then back to the rack and the wall shelves.

"You heard the man." Maya picked up Jasper's backpack and handed it to him. "We have to go." She pushed him up the stairs.

Jasper turned around to argue, but Uncle Martin lit a match and dropped it on the pile of drives without hesitation. Jasper ran up the stairs, through the living room, and out the door. Maya, already waiting for him, got on her scooter.

"Hop on, let's go."

"Isn't this a bit of an overreaction?" Jasper asked. "He got hacked, whatever. Burning down the house ten seconds later?"

"It wasn't ten seconds for him. Come, we can talk later."

Grudgingly, Jasper put on his backpack and got on the scooter behind Maya.

A wisp of smoke rose from an air vent in the wall close to the ground.

"But where are we going?" Jasper asked. "Uncle Martin said—"

"Shh," Maya hissed. "Do you hear that?"

He did. Sirens, getting louder. Getting louder fast and racing up the cul-de-sac toward Uncle Martin's house.

"We have to go." Maya revved the engine, turned the scooter around and rode it to the gate at the back of the property, which led to a back alley parallel to the main street.

"Open it, they're almost here."

The sirens continued growing louder. They couldn't be far now.

Jasper got off the bike. A chain and padlock secured the gate. He kicked at it, but it didn't budge.

"I can't break this," Jasper said. "You can do your dance and get away. I'll… I'll take my chances with them."

"There has to be another way." She looked around. "Try the shovel."

"No." Jasper took off his backpack and pulled out the gun. "I keep forgetting this thing."

The chain or the lock?

The lock. A gut instinct.

The sirens ceased getting louder. The authorities had parked in front of the house.

Jasper aimed at the lock. What about ricochets? He positioned himself a bit more sideways, squinted, held his breath, and pulled the trigger.

The deafening shot muted the sirens for a moment. Jasper examined the lock. The bullet had ripped right through it. One kick and it came off. He pulled down the chains and forced the gate open.

Behind them, a policeman in SWAT gear took a bolt cutter to the chain on the front gate.

Jasper got on the scooter. Maya wrapped her scarf over her nose, revved the engine, and accelerated. They turned the corner as policemen ran toward Uncle Martin's house behind them.

He clutched himself tight to Maya as they sped down the back alley, kicking up dust behind them.

Chapter Twenty-Four

Under The Bridge

Maya zigzagged around Downtown for a while, careful to check her mirrors, parallel streets, and helicopters for signs of the police. Nothing. It looked like the authorities hadn't even picked up their trail after the bumpy dash out of Echo Park.

"Pretty sure we lost them." She steered her scooter south toward the L.A. River, the massive concrete channel that ran nearly dry all summer. On an empty little dirt road under a gigantic I-10 overpass, she stopped, and they got off the scooter. She hated what she'd have to do next. "I'm going to miss you, my friend."

Jasper looked at her quizzically. "Not you, stupid, the scooter."

"What do you mean?" Jasper asked.

The boy could miss the forest for the trees sometimes. "It's not safe. We have to leave it." Maya unwound some of the black wrap from her forearm and wiped down the scooter, starting with the handlebars. With the key in the ignition, someone would probably steal it before the end of the day, but better safe than sorry. "I know it's annoying, but we'll have to walk to a Metro station. It's not far. We passed one on the way."

"And go where?" Jasper barked. What had gotten into him? "If that rich Swiss dude is behind the Bastard, what are we even going to do? Fly to Switzerland and knock on the door? And Uncle Martin? He'll be gone by now. Who knows if he'll ever show up again?"

Like she had all the answers… "We'll figure it out. Let's get home first, let you sleep off the Vicodin and—"

"Home? What does that even mean?" Jasper dropped his backpack in front of him. "Here I've got my father's laptop and I can't even turn it on. My best friend thinks I'm dead, and the man who shot me is the only…"

"The only what?" she asked. The Bastard's demise was the only upside to this whole mess right now.

Jasper looked around, left and right, but it seemed more out of insecurity than anything else. All Maya saw was this dry artificial river and more concrete than in the whole city she grew up in.

"The only trail that's still warm, my only hope," Jasper said. "I'm sorry, Maya, I know I should have told you earlier, but the Bastard isn't dead. I didn't shoot him in the eye. I aimed for his leg, he stumbled and hit that container. I just wanted to get away."

A torrent of Stygian images flooded Maya's mind when she closed her eyes. Bright blood on the floor of her childhood home, the smell of burnt flesh, concrete walls closing in, squeezing the life out of her. She felt out of her own body, surrounded by unending blackness. It took a few seconds for the fog to clear. When she opened her eyes again, Jasper approached tentatively, but she stopped him with a wave of her hand.

She cleared her throat and swallowed dry before speaking calmly. "How could you lie about this to me? After how many times I saved your sorry ass?"

"I... I was afraid you'd turn around that day. And then, later, I was afraid you'd get upset and throw me out," Jasper said, his voice turning into a whisper. "And all that talk about killing him? Even if it's revenge, that's just murder. I mean—"

"Murder? I hope you never have to see murder." Maya remembered what murder looked like. The Bastard had to be put down like a rabid dog. *Murder... If anything, murder is letting the man go free one more day.*

"Look, I'm sorry I lied to you, but I have to find my dad," Jasper pleaded. "We could track the Bastard, or something—"

"Something what exactly? First, find him, then follow him around at a safe distance while he leads us to your father, that kind of something?" Maya asked, and Jasper shrugged apologetically. *What a grand plan.* "Give me a freaking break. If you ever see him again, you better shoot him in the eye for real this time."

Follow this animal around? How naive can you be? Maya felt sick. Her nemesis still lurked somewhere, probably even in this city. Yes, she would have to find him again, but there would be no following around.

"There has to be a way, a different way," Jasper said. "My dad—"

"I had a dad, too. There's no other way. It's not murder. It's not revenge. It's justice. It's a sin to let this monster live.

When you find your father and there's parts of him missing, you'll understand." Maya took a few steps away from Jasper. How could he not see this?

"So I was right, you're going to leave me?" Jasper asked.

Maybe I should. "Leave you? No. You're free to come with me or go wherever, but this savage is out there and will hunt us unless we find him first. You know what I must do, and you won't stop me from doing it." She wrapped her black shawl tightly around her head. "Are you coming or not?"

He looked at her, wordlessly. What the hell did he expect her to do?

"You know where to find me." She walked away, accessing Accelerated Time after a couple of steps.

After endless Metro and bus rides, Maya finally arrived at her hacienda again. She stepped into the alley across the street from her safe house and emerged in her stealth getup for the final approach through the bathroom window.

Over the last couple of hours, her stance toward Jasper had mellowed. If her parents were still out there, alive, she'd be thinking the way he did. Alas, they weren't. Jasper had to understand that some men couldn't be reasoned with. She'd have to make sure of that.

Still, she'd grown fonder of the boy's company than she liked to admit to herself. If he didn't show up here later today, she'd check the Faulks' house tomorrow. Neither of them had a string of useful allies and confidants lined up, to put it mildly.

In Accelerated Time, she pulled herself up to the ground floor bathroom, her private entryway. She unwound the hand and forearm wraps, then her head scarf before scrubbing the day's grime away at the sink.

Getting around this city took forever. She'd have to procure a new motorbike tomorrow. Maybe borrow one, after all. She ran a little low on cash.

Maya stepped into the hall and closed the door behind her. From the kitchen doorway, a crackling net of blinding brightness—

She raised her hands. Lightning struck her forearms. A debilitating electric current surged through every fiber of every muscle that kept her upright, robbing her of control of her body. She knew she'd fall before it happened.

What a strange sensation, her thoughts being ahead of her body's reaction to something that already happened.

Before she could crumple, her assailant hoisted her over his shoulder with ease. Maya's head dangled upside down from limp neck muscles.

Left, right, up and down, it made no difference anymore. For a fleeting moment, her eyes pointed in the direction of the large entry hall mirror. She only had time for one observation before losing consciousness: she had met her captor before, more than once. Every time, one of them had been lucky to get away alive.

She only knew him as the Bastard.

Chapter Twenty-Five

A Friend in Need

Jasper picked up a handful of pebbles from the Wright's perfectly manicured stone garden. Half past midnight. The house was asleep, but the night sky reflected the ever-present glow of the city and illuminated the Wright's property like the sun had set just minutes ago.

Second floor, third window from the right. After the third pebble had hit, Clarence drew back the curtain.

Jasper put his index finger to his lips, then pointed toward the back entrance. A minute later, a PJ-clad Clarence opened the door.

Jasper spread his arms and whispered, "Ta-da."

Clarence punched him in the breadbasket and knocked him down onto his behind. "You utter dickhead, I thought you were dead."

"Punch me once more and I might be. I'm happy to see you too." Jasper pulled up his T-shirt to reveal the bandage underneath. He grunted and held his breath until the worst of the pain passed.

"Damn! Sorry, I didn't know... But then, you know I didn't know... because you didn't freaking tell me what the hell is going on!"

Jasper rolled over to his knees. "Well for one, I got shot in the gut right where you just hit me."

"Aw man, I'm so sorry." Clarence extended his hand to help him up.

"What's another butt kicking among friends?" Jasper took his hand and pulled himself up. "It actually makes me feel a little better about what I'm going to ask of you."

"Crap, what do you need?"

"A place to crash, food, clothes, fresh bandages, and pain killers for now. And no one can know, especially not your parents. Or your sister. Or the police." Clarence's face looked almost as pained as Jasper's. "I should also tell you it's pretty dangerous to help me. And we need to access my father's laptop, but we can't go online. The internet isn't safe anymore. In fact, best to shut down your whole network now. I'll explain tomorrow."

Clarence closed his eyes, took a deep breath, then nodded once. "At the end of all this, I should get to punch you again."

Jasper had slept like a rock. After the last couple of days, coming back to the Wright House almost felt like coming home. He shuddered at the thought, but still enjoyed the good night's sleep, clean bandages, fresh clothes, and a bottle of painkillers.

Over the counter stuff, so he could attempt some time bending action. Clarence wouldn't believe a word otherwise.

Hell, at this point, he had to prove to himself that it hadn't all been a particularly weird dream.

All the Wrights had already left for the day, including Clarence for camp, but he promised he'd play hooky and be right back with breakfast. Jasper waited for him in the pool house, curtains drawn, reflecting on yesterday's events.

He hated to admit it, but Maya might have been right about the Bastard. Much too dangerous to follow him around. And how would he find him anyway?

Yet, how could Jasper join her hunt-to-kill mission with his father still out there? He missed her already, but his pleading alone obviously didn't suffice to bring her around to his point of view.

That left him with few options for now. He sat on the floor in the pool house and looked at his possessions spread out in neat little piles. *Déjà vu all over again.* The photos, the blueprints and university records, the notebook, the passports and money, the gun, and new in the fold: a broken laptop.

As a fugitive, his passport would be useless. Certainly, the police would have put him on a no-fly list or something like that by now. He needed to access the laptop, his last, best hope for new information, Uncle Martin's warnings be damned.

A firm knock on the door ripped Jasper from his thoughts. Instinctively, he lunged forward through a veil of dizzying blackness and, after always forgetting about it before, now found himself reaching for the gun.

The door swung open in slow motion.

Clarence, carrying a paper bag and two cups of coffee.

"Eeeeeaaaasssssyyyyy…"

Jasper realized he had been drawn into Accelerated

Time. He let go of it, and Clarence's voice reverted to normal. "Damn, don't shoot me before breakfast. Be careful with that thing."

"Sir, put the coffee down slowly and take a step back," Jasper quipped to cover for his overreaction.

They devoured crumbly, gluten-free muffins and washed them down with a pint of some soy milk-blended coffee concoction. Typical Clarence, but after the last couple of days, Jasper felt like hugging him just for the normalcy of hating his culinary choices.

Jasper tentatively started to tell his crazy story, first focusing on Uncle Martin's revelations, his warnings about the laptop, and how he got hacked when they tried to track down Zeiger.

"I'm sure that kind of hack is possible," Clarence said. "I mean, you were there, but are you sure he didn't put on a show for you?"

"The police were real enough. And why would he do that?"

"Because he's crazy?" Clarence shrugged.

"Just because he's paranoid doesn't mean they aren't after him. Besides, that's not nearly the most unbelievable thing that happened in the last two days."

"Tell me about it," said Clarence and opened his mouth to take a big bite out of his muffin when it suddenly vanished and reappeared in Jasper's hand.

"The hell!" Clarence scrambled to his feet and waved his arms through the air, swiping at ghosts.

"Relax." Jasper got up and took a bite out of the muffin before handing it back. "It's just your friendly old time-bending freak, Jasper Faulks. What else is new?"

Clarence's reaction blindsided Jasper. Everything that happened had been quite outlandish, and Maya and Uncle Martin were time benders themselves. He had seriously underestimated the impact of his revelation.

So he explained in detail how he had seen the bullet and twisted out of the way, described the high-speed slow-motion scooter chase, and how he had made his way back to the ruins of the Passage of Time before getting stuck in Real Time for the rest of the day.

Clarence also made him demonstrate his abilities. Hide this, fetch that, build this. In this low-pressure environment, Jasper had decent control over the process for the first time. He had found his crutch. Shapes floating in the darkness. They collapse into themselves to reveal a black sea of time, waiting for him to dive into it. He felt quite satisfied with himself. Maya would have been proud.

"I give up." Clarence lay down on the floor and looked at the ceiling. "That this happened to *you* is the most unbelievable, baffling, scary, amazing thing that's happened to *me* in all my life, I can't even begin to imagine what you must be feeling."

"To be honest, I haven't had much time to think about it," Jasper said, and they both chuckled. "I mean, I got shot, nearly shot a guy myself, got stitched up, almost got caught by the police, got kidnapped, hacked, and I think in the end I kinda got dumped."

"I understand completely," Clarence said. "You just didn't have a chance yet to ponder all the ways you're violating the nature of the space-time continuum."

"Screw the space-time continuum. I need to know what's on this stupid thing." Jasper slapped his father's broken laptop dismissively.

Clarence sat up. "Of all the things you could do now—"

"What? I'm still looking for my father. You got any better ideas?"

"No, it just seems so small in the grand scheme of things. I could disable the Wi-Fi manually and see if the whole thing runs as it is. Or we can just take out the HDD and hook it up to my computer."

"That seems… too easy?" Jasper raised his eyebrows. "You remember we can't go online, right?"

"Hard as it may be to believe, these things do run without the internet, you know." Clarence got up. "Let's go to my room, Condi will be back from camp in a couple of hours."

Minutes later, Clarence had removed the hard drive, put it into a USB case, and hooked it up to his desktop computer.

"When I turned it on, it was password protected," Jasper said. "I tried a couple of obvious ones, but—"

"Doesn't matter," Clarence said. "It's an old Windows 7 machine. We don't need to boot the OS, we can just take ownership of the files." He clicked away on his computer.

"We can?" asked Jasper.

"Man, compared to your Uncle Martin, your dad doesn't take cyber security seriously," Clarence said. "None of this is even encrypted." He pointed at a slew of folders he had copied to his hard drive. "And neither is the file with all his emails. Maybe I can even pull a few websites from the cache and see what he was looking at."

"Hold on, are you absolutely sure we're not online?" Jasper asked. "We have no idea what these guys are capable of."

"I can't get much surer than taking down the whole network. The bigger question is, what are we even looking for? This could take days to sort out."

"It won't take days," Jasper said, "although it might feel like it for me, from what I understand."

Clarence needed a moment to realize what Jasper meant. "Oh. Of course. I'll just stay out of your way then, I guess."

"All right, here goes nothing." Jasper closed his eyes and dove into the darkness. This could be really exciting or tremendously boring.

Boring or exciting? When Jasper had gone through the final document from his father's laptop, he couldn't tell.

In Real Time, only twenty-six minutes had passed. He didn't get hungry, thirsty, or tired, but it still felt like a whole day. He had no way to measure Accelerated Time.

Jasper rubbed his temples and slipped back into Real Time.

So tired. Not physically, mentally. He abruptly got up from his chair. "Let's go."

"Whoa, welcome back," Clarence said with a mouth full of muffin. "Did it work?"

Jasper had wanted to ask and show Clarence so many things along the way, but now back in Real Time, the last thing he wanted to do was explain everything. All this new information awaited processing, and Clarence had basically spent a whole day snacking.

"What do you think?" Jasper scoffed. "Get a move on. Maya. We have to find Maya."

Jasper kept his head down in the back seat of Clarence's Prius. "Go all the way up to San Vicente. She left her scooter at the Country Club after she saved me. I'll find the house from there."

"Why are we looking for the girl now? I'll take the CliffsNotes version," Clarence said and steered his Prius east on Pico, where it joined traffic at a brisk fifteen miles per hour.

"It was my father who left the note for her at her parents' house," Jasper said. "She thought it was the Bastard, who tried to lure her to L.A., but it was my dad. We have to look at this whole thing in a different way."

"Your father? How do they know each other?" Clarence asked.

"They don't. He was in Michigan to meet her parents, but they had already been murdered by the Bastard."

"Why would he go up there?"

"He saw how Uncle Martin had deteriorated and thought it was a long-term side-effect of the time bending. And after Mom died, he himself wasn't functioning properly in Real Time anymore either. It's like everyone's worst traits got amplified. My dad debilitated by anxiety and self-isolation, Uncle Martin drowning in paranoia and snark. He told Dad the real enemies are in Washington D.C. and all sorts of conspiracy nonsense. That's when he gave him the gun that we found in the safe. They had another big fight about something. Dad didn't spell it out in his notes."

"That was before Michigan?"

"Yeah, he tried to get in touch with the others, but when he tracked down Maya's parents, it was too late, and he retreated further into his shell, all self-doubt and procrastination."

"Stay down, police behind us, don't look now," Clarence said in a deliberately calm manner. "Just a patrol car, I think." A few moments of tense silence passed before he gave the all-clear. "They're gone. Where were we? The other time benders?"

"Dad left messages for the guy in Turkey but didn't hear back. Same with Zeiger in Switzerland. They ghosted him," Jasper said. "Then there was the one guy that vanished completely—"

"The one your uncle didn't find either?"

"Yes, Jayjay something. Just gone. The only one who actually responded by email was this Floyd Greasley that Uncle Martin hates. He said he was fine, had a career as a tick-tock and all, but only wanted to talk details on the phone. No notes about that."

"Hm," Clarence grumbled. "I still don't understand how your father and Maya are connected now."

"When he arrived up in Michigan, Maya's parents were already dead. But he found out locally that they had a daughter who had vanished, and he left a message. Maya told me the Bastard left a note for her as bait, so whatever my dad wrote, she misunderstood and came here to take revenge for her parents."

"By killing him in cold blood?" said Clarence. "That's crazy."

"That she is," said Jasper, "but whatever is Hindi for *cojones*, she's got 'em. You should have seen her charge the Bastard with her bare hands—"

"San Vicente, we're here." Clarence slowed down and knocked on the window.

Minutes later, Jasper found Maya's hacienda. He remembered the Spanish two-story well, but even if he had forgotten everything about the house, the big palm tree, the modernist front yard, or the little path to the window where Maya had helped him enter through the bathroom, there still would've been a telltale sign that gave away which house they were looking for.

With his luck, it just happened to be the one that had burnt to the ground.

"Maya!" Jasper sat up straight.

"Get down," Clarence said, but Jasper ignored him. They drove by the house at a crawl. The familiar black and yellow tape crisscrossed the ornamented gate and the front door of the house. The second story of the house had caved in.

"Stop the car," Jasper said.

"Get down, don't be stupid. The fire's been put out hours ago." *Clarence with his reason.* "If anyone was in there, they're in the hospital."

"Or the morgue." Jasper felt a sudden stab of fear. The

only person in the world who could relate to what he went through. It had only been a day, but he did miss her terribly.

"Don't be ridiculous. Does this look like a secured crime scene to you? A murder scene?"

True. No police, no firefighters, no crime scene investigators, just some black-and-yellow tape.

Jasper slid down to the back-seat floor again. "We should come back tonight and break in. There must be some trace of her."

"Don't be silly," Clarence hit the brakes a little harder than seemed necessary, and Jasper bumped his head on the back of the driver's seat.

"Duck," Clarence hissed. "Someone's crossing the street."

Jasper had nowhere to hide. A person standing next to the car couldn't miss him. "Just drive."

"I can't run her over," Clarence said.

Jasper risked a peek between the front seats. A small elderly lady stood right in front of the car. She smiled nervously and signaled to roll down the window.

Clarence shook his head and tried to wave her on. "Now she's pointing to her cell phone, I think she's trying to say something."

The woman's voice was muffled, but clearly audible. "It's your uncle. He says it's important."

"How is that possible?" Jasper opened the window, and the lady handed him her phone with a worried smile.

It was indeed Uncle Martin. "Took your sweet time showing up. I have exactly two minutes on this line, so listen closely—"

"What? How should I... How did you... Who's the woman...?" Jasper stammered.

"Ten seconds wasted. Listen, I talked to Floyd Greasley, remember him?"

"Yes, he's—"

"Good, that was painful for me, so pay attention. The lickspittle is a D.C. pencil pusher with some high-level ties to the CIA. Since he considers himself friends with your dad, he helped me with some flight data. That stuff's hard to come by. Anyway, a day after your dad was taken, a charter plane left Burbank for Puerto Rico. It refueled and flew to Engadin, a small airport about an hour south of Davos in Switzerland. Curious itinerary, but it gets better. Another charter left yesterday evening with the same itinerary. I hacked security cam footage from Burbank and guess who boarded the little birdie? No, don't guess, we don't have the time." Jasper heard Uncle Martin suck on his inhaler. "I think your little girlfriend called him the Bastard. He carried a big piece of luggage, if you catch my drift. About five foot four, a hundred pounds. I think the in-flight dinner will be curry tonight." He chuckled at his questionable joke, but it turned into a bellowing cough.

"What do you want me to do?" Jasper asked, but no answer came. They had been disconnected. Or Uncle Martin had hung up. Who knew.

What do you want me to do? Jasper asked himself as much as anyone.

Twenty minutes later, Jasper and Clarence sipped pints of chocolate milk shakes in the most remote corner of the closest In-N-Out. The news Uncle Martin had delivered called for a sugar high.

"Let's get real, what would you even do in Switzerland, hypothetically, if you could make it there?" Clarence asked.

"Look for Maya, I guess. And Dad," Jasper said.

"What does that mean on a day-to-day though? I guess it doesn't matter since you can't go anyway. The flight would be a couple of grand at least." Clarence pushed his half-empty milk shake to Jasper, who had already finished his.

"I have the money." Jasper reached into his backpack and pulled out a stack of cash. "And a passport." Strange, now that he thought of it, he didn't remember ever applying or signing for one. Could parents do all of that for their children?

"Yeah, good luck with that," Clarence said. "The police are trying to arrest you. Do you think you can use that passport to board a plane? Once they scan it, their security dashboards will light up like a Christmas tree."

Jasper opened the passport and studied the picture of himself. He looked straight ahead in front of a white background, but he didn't look right into the camera as you would in a photo cabin. It was a year old at most, yet he had no recollection whatsoever of taking passport pictures.

Don't these things have an issue date? Jasper squinted and actually read the fine print for the first time. "Forget the Christmas lights." He slammed the milk shake cup on the table in excitement. "They're looking for Jasper Faulks. This passport belongs to Jasper Durant, and he's going to Switzerland!"

Chapter Twenty-Six

Trusted Traveler

Jasper and Clarence drove back to the Wright House. Jasper needed to pick up some clothes and arrange for the next flight to Switzerland.

Tree trimmers blocked the street in front of the house, so Clarence turned around to try the other side.

"Stop the car!" Jasper yelled.

Clarence hit the brakes. "What did I run over?"

"Look, it's Keane!" Jasper pointed at a row of banana trees that separated the corner house from the Wright House. With a bit of imagination he could make out a police car in the Wrights' driveway. "Just keep going."

Clarence drove past their street, and they went unseen.

Jasper exhaled sharply. Clarence in his Prius would've never been able to get away from the police like Maya on her scooter. The thought alone belonged in the Hall of Fame of foolish ideas. After that, Jasper had Clarence drive him straight to LAX. Time to follow his dad and Maya into the lion's den.

By chance, they made it in time for the only direct flight from LAX to Zurich, leaving later that afternoon. He purchased a ticket at a Swiss Air service desk. A grim lady with a robust Swiss German accent raised her eyebrows when he pulled out a wad of cash, but she took the money without comment. After some more typing, she handed him his passport and the boarding pass. "Hef a safe flight, Mister Durant."

"Danke," he answered, exhausting his German in one fell swoop. He stuffed his ticket and passport into his pant pocket and slung the backpack over one shoulder.

"Maybe I shouldn't take the gun on the plane," he whispered conspiratorially, knowing he'd get a rise out of Clarence.

"You think, you genius?" Clarence seemed about to launch into a cautionary tirade when Jasper's smirk stopped him. "Oh no... No, no, no." He leaned in and whispered, "What if I get pulled over? Black kid with a stolen gun, do you know what's going to happen to me?"

"You won't get pulled over," Jasper answered. "You drive a Prius."

"And where am I going to put it? Can't you just dump it?"

"Here? Do you think they don't search these trash cans?"

"So what?" Clarence spoke up. "Let them find it. We'll be gone by then."

"Shh, be quiet." It had come to where Jasper had to be the voice of reason. Maybe Uncle Martin's paranoia had sensitized him. "When they find the gun, they'll check the security cam footage." He slightly inclined his head toward one of the cameras monitoring the terminal.

"Can't you just, like, do that time bending thing and dump it?" Clarence wagged his hand.

"One, I'd still be visible on the camera footage here and there, and two, who knows if Dad registered the gun to his name. I don't want that out there." Jasper pulled Clarence down by his shirt collar and whispered, "Hide it in the pool house. If your parents find it, it was obviously me who did it." He let go, and Clarence finally nodded.

Jasper bought a carry-on case, a bunch of garish T-shirts (I *heart* LA!), a travel guide, and an English-German dictionary. Working some time bending magic, he might be fluent by the time his plane touched down in Zurich. On second thought, probably not. Better to rest while he still had the chance.

The cell phones with the pre-paid SIM cards looked inviting, but he didn't dare tempt the digital overlords.

The backpack he gave to Clarence, save for the money, the passport, and a picture of all the 176 students that he kept on his person.

"Gonna be back for this one," Jasper patted his trusty JanSport, hanging from his friend's shoulder.

They looked at each other awkwardly.

"I…" Clarence started tentatively.

"I know," Jasper said, not at all sure what Clarence was trying to say, but Clarence seemed satisfied with that. "Feed the cats for me from time to time."

"Really?" Clarence grimaced.

"Really, you bum." Jasper hit him in the shoulder. "Or

I'll haunt your dreams, I promise."

"Jesus take the wheel—anything but that."

They hugged and held on to each other for a couple of seconds longer than teenage boys are usually comfortable with. Then, without another word, Jasper got in line for the security screening. When he looked around, Clarence was gone.

At the front of the line, an officer checked everyone's papers before they went through the screening. Jasper had observed him for the last ten minutes, so he couldn't help but be alarmed when he was the first traveler who actually got asked a question.

"Are you traveling alone?"

"Er, yes." *So far, so good.* "Is that a problem?"

"Please wait here," said the officer. "Someone will be right over to pick you up."

Is this where I run? Jasper closed his eyes and plunged into Accelerated Time. When he opened them again, everything around him had come to a virtual standstill.

The officer holding his passport still eyed him, so Jasper remained still. The question might be harmless? Could be routine for underage travelers, it was impossible to know.

If he ran now, he'd never be able to take the flight. He could make it out of the airport, but they'd check the security footage, and he'd be trapped in the country, forever on the run.

Running made no sense. Jasper let go of Accelerated Time. Moments later, a portly second officer approached the little desk and opened Jasper's passport. His clean-shaven, round face looked non-threatening enough.

"Jasper Durant?"

"Yes, sir."

"Please come with me. Don't worry, we just have a few questions." He slid Jasper's passport into the breast pocket of his powder blue short-sleeve shirt.

At the end of a long corridor, a bald, middle-aged man wearing a black suit on broad shoulders waited for them and opened the door to a white-walled room. He wore a generic airport security badge. Jasper couldn't tell what agency he was from.

"You'll have to leave your carry-on outside," said the rotund officer who had picked Jasper up.

Reluctantly, Jasper leaned his suitcase against the wall of the empty corridor. In contrast, the screening area and the airport had been quite busy. He entered the room with a queasy feeling in his rumbling stomach.

"Please sit down." The officer gestured to a small chair in front of a simple desk. It held one of those outdated computers you only see in government facilities, which calmed Jasper's nerves.

The officer sat down opposite Jasper. Baldy stepped into the room and closed the door behind him.

At the computer, the officer swiped the first page of Jasper's passport through a reader and looked at the screen.

His badge read Ricardo Cruz, from the DHS, the Department of Homeland Security. Despite his name, the man didn't look Hispanic at all.

On the wall behind the desk hung a picture of the president and a propagandist-looking DHS poster with a slogan picked from a random list of keywords: "Vigilance, Diligence, Security. Report Suspicious Activity Immediately. A Safer America, Together."

"Everything seems to be in order with your passport," Officer Cruz said.

Jasper suppressed a relieved sigh. He didn't expect his father to keep a forgery around, but he still couldn't explain why his name was Jasper Durant in there. His mother's maiden name had never been more than trivia to him.

"But," Cruz continued, "I'm afraid I can't let you leave the country. You see, I have a call waiting on this line here." He tapped the telephone on his desk. "Someone desperately wants to talk to you. A Detective Keane, who's convinced that you're not Jasper Durant, but Jasper Faulks, a fugitive from the law."

The officer turned the monitor around: a screen capture of Jasper at the police station.

Jasper's heart skipped a beat or two. He needed lies and excuses, escape and battle plans, fast.

A *click*. Jasper looked to the side. Baldy had locked the door and crossed his arms in front of his wide chest.

"Shall we talk to Inspector Keane?" Cruz picked up the receiver and pressed a button.

Jasper closed his eyes and sought the blackness. This time, instead of diving head first into a shifting blackness, he waded slowly into dark waters.

"Yess, Ssssir... Nnooo, I diddn't..." Jasper entered

Accelerated Time, but unlike previously, in a slow and controlled way. He closed his eyes and extended and contracted time, playing Cruz's voice like an accordion, pushing and pulling on individual sounds.

"Yesss, he's sittinggg rrright herrrre-uhhhh… But excuse me, I wassss expecting Inspector Keannnnnne… Who are youuuuuuu?"

For the first time since Jasper acquired his peculiar new talent, he felt like its master. He snapped back into Real Time, and the phone conversation continued. After a while of silently listening to the person on the other end of the line, Cruz's eyes widened, and he said, "I understand. Yes, sir. Right away."

Now! Jasper closed his eyes and stretched the moment as long as he could. It expanded before and around him. He opened his eyes and found himself in a still life version of the real world. The soft gurgling of Cruz's "Sirrrrr," directed at whoever was on the other end of the line, reminded him that life didn't pause, that it continued moving at a comatose snail's pace.

He got up and walked around the room. He could do whatever he wanted to the wax figure-like Cruz and baldy—tie their shoelaces together, flick their noses, take their guns. Or he could just leave before either of them could even blink.

"…rrrrrrrrrrrrr…"

No. He could still leave whenever he really needed to. Something unexpected happened in that phone conversation.

Jasper straightened the picture of the president on the wall and sat down again. It felt good to be in control. He slowed back down to Real Time to let the situation play out.

"…rrr." Cruz hung up. Nobody had noticed anything out of the ordinary. "Right." The officer put Jasper's passport on the desk and headed for the door without acknowledging Jasper's presence. "We're done here," he said to baldy. They left the room together, Cruz briefly glancing at Jasper with apprehension.

How could they simply leave him alone? *Done here? Does that mean free to go?*

Jasper slipped back into Accelerated Time.

Obviously, Keane hadn't been at the other end of that line. Had Uncle Martin intervened on his behalf? Was he cleared to fly? Better to sit on that plane to Zurich than hang around to find out.

Tick-tock, tick-tock. Who wants to stand around doing nothing when you have the power to do anything you want? A voice in the back of his head cautioned him. *Not anything. Only what you're already capable of, just faster.*

The lock—

A locked door would trap him regardless of speed. He pushed down the handle.

So far, so good. He took his carry-on and headed back down the empty corridor to the exit.

Around the corner, nobody. Another corner and he arrived back at the door to the security screening area.

He opened it and stepped into busy airport life that hadn't noticed his absence.

Passport and boarding card checks, people taking off their shoes, opening their laptops, emptying their pockets. The pre-flight theater was in the middle of its daily performance.

Nobody in the airport appeared to be moving at all, apart from a little boy who frantically waved goodbye to someone around the corner in the main terminal. His outstretched arm swayed slowly from left to right.

Outside the window, a jumbo jet inched forward mid-takeoff.

Move! A voice in the back of his mind.

Yes, *move*, so you won't be seen by the tick-tocks. Stay too long in one place, and it doesn't matter how fast you are, the world will see you, just like you see a hummingbird hovering in front of your window, even if you can't see its flapping wings.

Besides, he had a plane to catch.

Jasper stepped over the security rope. Gate 119. He looked at his boarding pass (*LX 41, LAX-ZRH, Gate 122*). *Keep moving.*

Three more gates. Two long queues had formed in front of the ticket readers, where two airline employees with frozen smiles scanned boarding passes.

Jasper walked right between the lines and straight onto the jetway, then into the airplane past the flight attendants who greeted the arriving first and business class passengers. With corridors too narrow to walk past anyone without touching them, he zigzagged through the middle rows.

He walked past his assigned seat in economy class toward the restroom. The door closed, but not locked, he slipped back into Real Time and waited for the sounds of people entering the economy cabin.

Nobody took notice when he got out of the bathroom

and took his place in row fifty-nine.

A brief snafu delayed the takeoff procedure. The flight attendants counted the passengers, patrolled the corridors, and put their heads together, but then LX41 took off only twenty minutes behind schedule and landed in Zurich thirteen hours and thirty-five minutes later.

Jasper had made it to Switzerland.

Now he only had to make it past border security with a flagged passport, find his way around a strange land without speaking any of the local languages, and rescue his father and his friend from the richest and most powerful man in the country. Easy-peasy.

After disembarking, Jasper kept his head down and made a beeline for the bathroom for more reasons than one.

Chapter Twenty-Seven

Late Dinner

Eva's life had almost gone back to normal since she had so narrowly beaten Father back to her room after sneaking out. Almost.

Adam droned on and on about how she should stay in her room and never, ever, ever go back down those stairs, silly girl that she was. By now, Eva's anger at his gloating had mellowed into annoyance. She tried to banish her memories of the strange place to the far outer reaches of her mind.

Her thirst for adventure quelled for the moment, she spent even more time with her beloved Rip Current magazine (*"Friends 4 Lyfe! See Robbie And The Gang Hang Out Backstage!"*). Soon, she surely wouldn't have to stay in her quarters all the time anymore. According to Father, new medicine was on the way.

Although he did seem a lot more stressed since *that* morning. When he had come into her room a little later, she asked what happened outside, that she heard something breaking, but he dismissed it.

Later that day, he arrived slightly out of breath with her lunch and asked if she ever heard noises outside at night or noticed anything else out of the ordinary. Hopefully, she hadn't left any traces during her foray.

Then yesterday evening, he made a mistake in their backgammon game and looked at his watch display twice as often as usual.

Tonight took the cake, though. She had never seen her father this ruffled, not even after her mother had taken Adam.

First, dinner arrived fifty-two seconds late. Eva had already begun to wonder whether she'd have to go to bed hungry.

Then the napkin was wedged between the plate with her food and the bowl with her medication instead of folded under the cutlery.

Father looked disheveled too: the laces of his right shoe tied asymmetrically, the tip of his belt not threaded through the second belt loop, the cuff of his black turtleneck sweater partially turned up on his left wrist, and if that wasn't enough—he hadn't shaved. He had never not shaved. Ever.

She reached up to touch his scratchy cheek, which brought the suggestion of a surprised smile to his face.

"I guess I was preoccupied." He looked into her mirror, adjusted the sweater cuff, and threaded his belt through the second belt loop of his black pants.

"New medicine?" she asked full of hope. "You said there might be good news soon. After your tests."

"No." He cleared his throat. "Not yet. The tests didn't go well." The disappointment on Eva's face softened his voice. "I'm sorry, I will keep trying. I'm trying everything. You know that."

"I heard the helicopter." Eva had been so sure it meant good news. Once, a long time ago, her mother had taken the helicopter to visit her.

"Yes." He hesitated. "A new patient."

"A patient? Like, a man who's sick?" She thought of the man in the bed downstairs. "Or a boy, like Adam?"

His expression darkened. "No. A girl."

"A girl?" A little disappointing, but could she expect Robbie to move in next door? That'll be the day. She never had a female friend before. "Can I meet her? Please, Father."

"She isn't well at the moment," he said, "and we don't want to upset her. I'm trying to help her, like you."

"Where is she now? Doesn't she need to go to the hospital?" Eva asked.

He smiled wearily. "Eva, *Schatz*, you know hospitals are not for us. She is our guest."

"Please, please, please can I meet her? It would be so nice to have a friend."

"But I'm your friend. When you're better, we'll see the whole world, *ja*?" He looked at his watch and swiped across the display a few times. "No backgammon tonight. Work."

Eva knew exactly where the girl would be, and Adam and his fears be damned, she'd pay her a visit. The prospect of new medicine had curbed her wanderlust, but without it? Listening to Adam's ranting and rereading encyclopedias indefinitely? No, thank you. What had been her daily routine less than a week ago now seemed like admitting defeat. Adventure loomed.

When Father left, she jumped out of bed. On her way to the door, she heard him fiddle with the lock outside, then stop. Instinctively, she dove back into bed.

Thanks to her overdrive mode, she had already wrapped the comforter around her when he opened the door again and said good night for the second time before deliberately pulling the door knob until the lock clicked shut. He had never done that before.

No way around it, despite nearly dying of curiosity, Eva would have to stay in tonight.

Now that's a good girl, going to bed like she's supposed to. Adam couldn't help but twist the knife. *Father would be pleased. You heard him, he is working so hard for a cure.*

Chapter Twenty-Eight

Bathroom Break

The sights, sounds, and smells of an airport toilet stall didn't make it easy to find a moment of serenity, but Jasper hadn't come this far to be derailed by a labored number two next door.

He blocked out the distractions, dove into the darkness of his mind, and reluctantly took a couple of deep breaths of fetid air. He opened and closed the door to his stall a few times to survey the surroundings. There could be no bumping into anyone and no slowing down, especially not in front of the cameras outside.

No way he'd risk customs and immigration with his passport. He had to charge for freedom, or at least the closest thing to it for now: leaving the airport undetected.

Another worry had stuck with him since he settled into his seat on the plane fourteen hours earlier. What if an invisible hand moved the pieces on the board and had put him exactly here? Maybe not *exactly* into a bathroom stall, surveying the scene like a peeping Tom, but in Switzerland?

Sure, there had been obstacles, but after every hiccup, things had gone his way. Spotting the police at Clarence's house, paying cash for tickets, Homeland Security weirdly backing off at the airport, the takeoff delay... All luck? All his doing? And if neither, was the invisible force benevolent or malicious?

It didn't much matter now. He could only move forward from here.

Another peek. Three men at the urinals stood with their backs to the room, a cleaner in loose gray overalls bent over in front of the sinks to tie a black work boot, his mop leaning against the wall next to a bucket of water. A broad-shouldered businessman exited the restroom, leaving the door to close on its own.

Now.

Fast and smooth, out of here in no time. No Real Time, rather. Jasper opened the door fully and scanned around once more before committing.

Go.

From the corner of his eye, he sensed a shadow on the ground get longer right before something cold pressed against his neck. He jerked forward instinctively. Lightning crackled behind him—a stun gun.

No grip... Jasper lost his footing and slipped on the damp floor, but the weapon had missed him. He scrambled to his feet, turning around.

The sole of a massive black boot closed in on his face...
Duck!

Just in time—but another slip—and back on the floor.

At the other end of the boot: the Bastard. *Who else?* The momentum of his kick carried the goon forward, leaving the leg supporting his weight trailing. The same left leg Jasper shot during his flight from the Passage of Time.

Adrenaline gave Jasper strength and uncharacteristic poise. He shifted all his weight onto his left leg, then kicked the cleaning bucket over. Reaching up, he grabbed the tick-tock near the exit door by his belt and pulled the man into the Bastard's path and himself upright in one motion.

None of the other tick-tocks had even turned around yet.

The Bastard, off-balance, planted his foot back on the floor into the puddle of soapy liquid and slid down hard, doing the splits on the shiny tiles while dropping the stun gun to break his fall with his hands.

Jasper lunged forward out the door, not looking back at the carnage.

Go, go, go... Out the door and into the arrival area. Passport checks, customs, baggage claim flew by, tick-tocks going about their business everywhere.

Duck, twirl, jump—Jasper ran for his life, past security personnel and surveillance cameras. If anyone saw him, he passed them too fast to notice a reaction. Let Maya dance, let the tick-tocks suspect whatever, a straight line would have to do for now. He allowed himself a quick glance over his shoulder at the final sliding door to exit the terminal. No Bastard, but he knew better than to let his guard down already.

He raced down a line of taxicabs to the front and entered the first, tumbling onto the backseat and out of Accelerated Time.

"Grüezi, hab sie gar net gesehen. Wo darf's denn hingehen?" The middle-aged Swiss driver put down his paper and silenced the radio. The friendly tone of his voice indicated he didn't question the unnaturally rushed intrusion, but Jasper

still didn't understand a word he said.

"Uh… English?" Jasper asked tentatively.

"Sure, good afternoon, velcome to Switzerland. Vere to?" The driver reached for the taximeter.

"Just drive," Jasper said.

"Dis isn't a TV show, my boy." The man furrowed his brow and let go of the little box on his dashboard again. "You have to tell me vere."

Jasper sunk into the backseat but kept an eye on the airport exit. Nothing stirred. *Yet.* "Uh, Davos, please, yes?" *Just go.*

The driver laughed. "Davos? Or maybe Paris or Rome? Dis is a taxi, *ja*?" He crossed his arms.

"The train station then." Jasper squirmed, trying not to stare at the airport exit doors too obviously. "It's my first time here."

"*Hauptbahnhof Zürich,* very well." The driver finally set the taximeter and drove off.

About time. They pulled into traffic with nobody following them, and Jasper's heart finally settled back down into his chest cavity. The invisible hand had shown itself to be a gloved fist after all.

The cab ride took twenty minutes. Against the driver's objections, Jasper paid him in US dollars. Overpaid him considerably, most likely, but from the spate of muttered German words that followed Jasper out the door—unkind things about Americans, as best he could tell—the man wasn't too happy.

Without looking back, Jasper entered the main station, assaulted by a plethora of noise, humanity, and confusing information. It felt more like an airport than the train stations he knew.

A group of middle-aged tourists stood in front of the giant timetable in the midst of a heated argument about whether to turn left or right to their platform, if their gesturing was any indication.

As his gaze went up to check whether Davos showed up on the railway schedule, he noticed the—of course— ubiquitous security cameras and immediately bent over to pretend-tie his shoe, happy he hadn't put on the "I *heart* LA" T-shirt earlier. He couldn't remember why buying that had seemed like a good idea at the time, but his carry-on had stayed behind in the airport restroom anyway.

With his money and his papers in his jeans pocket, at least he wouldn't have to risk stealing, but with gloved fists and invisible hands after him, he needed to change gear and get to Davos as soon as possible.

From the corner of his eye he surveyed the right side of the giant main building. Touristy shops, a ticket office, and— *yes!*—an exchange bureau. He kept his head down as much as possible without going full Hunchback of Notre Dame and made his way to the exchange bureau.

Avoiding eye contact and substituting grunting and nodding for talking, Jasper exchanged five hundred dollars for Swiss francs, a sum he deemed safely below the threshold of attracting attention in a city of rich people. Back outside, head still bowed, he ducked into one of the souvenir stores and bought a baggy sweater, a *Grasshoppers* hat (branded after the local soccer team), and mirrored sunglasses, hoping the combination didn't come across as the equivalent of an oversized trench coat with a popped collar.

Since the taxi ride, Jasper had gotten by without any talking, and thankfully, the ticketing machine could be switched to English to keep the streak going. In another stroke of luck, one too big for any invisible hands to play a part in, the hourly train to Davos would leave in six minutes from *Gleis 13*, so he wouldn't have to linger around the station and find out if the Bastard caught his scent again after the airport escape.

He took his *Billet* from the machine and headed for platform 13, head now held high in his new getup. On his way to the escalator, keeping to the edge of the giant main hall, the door to a maintenance room opened near him and a hulking silhouette in overalls took shape in the frame.

Jasper dove into Accelerated Time without hesitation and rushed forward. Everyone and everything around him froze in the now-familiar way, including what turned out to be an actual janitor emerging from the supply storage room.

Rats, damn paranoia. He had risked attention, even discovery, for nothing. But looking around, nobody's attention seemed focused on him.

Keep moving, keep moving…

He stayed in Accelerated Time all the way to platform 13, careful not to remain in the same place even for one moment. The EuroCity train stood by for boarding, but Jasper saw no way to transition to Real Time on the platform safely unseen, so he entered the train directly and hoped for more privacy inside. A bathroom offered respite.

Taking his seat in the main cabin a little while later, Jasper felt quite confident nobody had taken any notice. If he had learned anything since becoming a time bender, it was that people didn't notice the impossible, like bodies vanishing or materializing. You could land a UFO in a football stadium, and spectators would just keep on munching their popcorn.

In a town called Landquart, Jasper had to change trains. A smaller regional carrier serviced Davos directly. The transfer time was brief, advertised at six minutes, but as he stood on the platform—near the exit, with sunglasses on and hat pulled down—six minutes came and went. He couldn't understand the German announcement that blared over the PA system, but judging from the shocked groans of the other passengers, it wasn't good news.

Jasper scanned the crowd. Who would be most likely to speak English and forget him the instant they stopped talking? He picked a blond girl a year or two older than him who had disgustedly dropped her backpack at the announcement.

"Excuse me, I don't speak German. What's going on?" Jasper asked.

"Oh, uh, there's a, uh, delay," she stammered, taking a moment to adjust to the foreign language. "Someone…" She moved her thumb across her throat. "*Krrrrr…*"

"Killed?" Jasper asked, horrified. Surely even if someone had tracked him, delaying his journey wouldn't be worth killing an innocent person, but he couldn't help questioning the timing. *Paranoia.*

"I don't know." She shrugged. "Someone stood in front of the train."

Jasper thanked her and ducked into the shadows of the tiny train station of Landquart.

No invisible hand can arrange this. The impulse to run (*where?*) battled Jasper's firm belief that it would be too big, too sudden for someone to have arranged a death to delay *his* journey, of all things.

Still, he stayed in the shadows for the time being, but when a substitute train eventually pulled into the station to take the waiting passengers to Davos, he looked left and right, took a deep breath, and boarded it. *Caution yes, paranoia no.*

An hour later, they arrived in Davos, and Jasper had no reason to suspect the dozen other people getting off the train alongside him were anything but random fellow travelers. He slowed down, watching them scatter. Behind him, the train doors closed. Accompanied by a whistle from the conductor, it continued its journey, leaving Jasper alone on the platform.

A big sign proclaimed the name of the station "*Davos Platz.*" Although it was nearly 9 p.m. now, the sun had barely started to set.

I made it. Kind of. But not fearing for his life for a second prompted another question to nag him — *what now?*

Chapter Twenty-Nine

Sleep of the Righteous

Knowledge was power, they said. Whether true or not, Jasper possessed precious little of both as they pertained to the logistics of the task at hand—locate and free his dad and Maya from the clutches of a powerful man and his murderous associate who already targeted *him*.

He didn't even know whether to turn left or right outside the train station. Right, he decided, towards the hotel signs, although checking into one would be folly. Might as well just walk around with a blinking arrow pointing at him.

"Free Wi-Fi" signs taunted him from the windows of hotels and coffee shops, but even if he had a device, would it be safe to use? If Zeiger could reach Uncle Martin in his basement, poking around a network in his hometown didn't seem advisable.

He'd have to find another way. *No knowledge, no power— no problem.* At least he had time. Lots of it, in a way, as long as he didn't have to run for his life.

"What do you think I do with my time, my nails?" Maya had asked him once. He'd just have to find the right avenue to apply his talents and right now that meant finding a safe and comfortable place to sleep.

Despite being dead tired, he could walk on auto-pilot for hours, if need be, so he kept up a steady plod past hotels, restaurants, bars, shops, a soccer field, an ice hockey rink, and a bowling alley. Nothing caught his eye as a convenient hiding spot.

The streets became a little narrower, the shops—all closed now—smaller. Among them, a vintage furniture store, dimly lit inside, with a locked front door, but a high-sitting window to a side street left ajar.

It had to be a weekday night, although Jasper couldn't remember what day. Passersby were few and far in-between. A burglar scaling the wall would risk discovery, especially on the way out, but Jasper had no intention to *leave* through the window.

And no burglar could get a trash can to stand on, fidget with the window hinges forever, climb back down, move the trash can back to its original location, awkwardly scale the wall without help, fall down three times, barely (but successfully) suppress a torrent of curses, finally pull himself up, *and* return the window to the initial position in the two seconds of Real Time it took Jasper.

Phew.

The window let him into a small office room that led to the store. Inside, near the back, he found an ornate canopy bed covered in decorated pillows.

At the front, he dragged a wooden pedestal into the path of the front door and placed a large vase on the very edge, where the slightest tremor would knock it off. Afterward, he retreated to the bed and lay down on the pile of fancy pillows to sleep the heavy, dreamless, peaceful sleep of a jet lagged sixteen-year-old, all looming mortal peril be damned.

When the sound of a fake Ming dynasty vase shattering into a thousand pieces tore Jasper from his slumber in the morning, he felt the opposite of refreshed, despite six hours of rest.

Damn that biological clock!

He transitioned to Accelerated Time at once, fluffed the comforter back into shape, and slalomed around the returning store owner (and the shards on the floor) on his way out the front door this time. As long as one had room to maneuver, Accelerated Time really felt like a spectacular cheat code.

Outside, the unfamiliar morning breeze helped by the speed of Accelerated Time prickled Jasper's cheeks and blew away any remaining sluggishness. Life felt primed for a fresh start.

On the main street, vendors set up market stands with fruit, meats, vegetables, and flowers. A lively picture, but he didn't dare linger and weaved around the pedestrians. To have a closer look, he needed to transition back to Real Time in a secluded spot, not in front of the local butcher, so he kept on moving.

He had overreacted to the airport bathroom encounter. Of course they'd monitor flights from Los Angeles to Zurich, how else would he get into the country? He surely couldn't operate under the assumption that the Bastard waited around every corner and expect to get anywhere in his search.

Jasper's stomach grumbled, so he snuck into an ornately decorated bakery behind a book store off the main shopping street. He stole a few pastries and a can of cold brew coffee, feeling appropriately contrite about it. He could have transitioned back to Real Time before breakfast and paid for it, but the thrill of it had seemed irresistible for a second. Still, even gobbled down with a bad conscience on the stone steps of a shaded back entry to a side street parking garage, it might have been the best breakfast of all time.

With nobody in sight, he had let go of Accelerated Time for the feast. He couldn't keep moving all day anyway, and things like eating, studying your surroundings, or reading always carried the risk of dawdling for too long and becoming visible to the tick-tocks.

After finishing his meal, the magnitude of the challenge ahead kept him rooted to the stone steps for a while. A fresh start, yes, but still the same goals and obstacles. He needed more information about Zeiger, his estate, the company—everything, really—but if searching for these things on the internet drew attention to him, he needed an alternative.

Somehow, he doubted there'd be a friendly old lady running an ice cream stand around, who just happened to speak English, knew the Zeiger family for decades, and would spill the beans on a whim when an inquisitive teen from America showed up to buy a scoop of vanilla. That would make a good story, though. He crushed the cold brew can into a ball and threw it in a trash can from ten feet away. *Two points. Take that, Clarence.* Hopefully that hadn't been the highlight of the day.

He headed back to the main street in Real Time. If online research proved too difficult, then maybe a reconnaissance mission? Old school, *IRL*. Hitch a ride to the Zeiger estate—or steal a bike, if necessary—and have a look around, safely in Accelerated Time. That didn't sound unreasonable. The touristy bookstore next to the bakery surely sold a street map of this area. He could gauge the distance to Zeiger's property and take it from there?

But first, he had to find out the address. A paper phonebook would be a pleasantly analog way, but would a man like Zeiger be listed? No chance. He had to think outside the box, utilize his talent. Maybe snoop around the archives in the local hospital or paper?

The main street had turned into a real farmer's market at the hour, with people everywhere and grocers busy selling their goods. Horrible terrain for a time bender who couldn't afford to slow down or bump into anyone. Crossing the street meant being trapped in Real Time, but at least it afforded Jasper the luxury of a leisurely look around. He'd have to get the lay of the land sometime. The map could wait for ten more minutes.

"Erdbeere? Probier ruhig eine." A stout lady in a checkered apron shoved a tray of strawberries in his face. He didn't understand her, but the manner of presentation was universal language—take a sample. They looked awfully appetizing.

He picked the ripest one and moved on with a big smile and a nod, eager to get away from the tight crowd around this particularly popular fruit stand.

A fluttery, whirring noise unexpectedly stood out against the background clamor of market activities.

Jasper dove into Accelerated Time, careful not to move at all. He scanned his surroundings with minimal head movement but couldn't identify anything suspicious until he looked farther forward—and up.

A drone hovered around twenty yards away and ten yards up from where he stood, right in the direction he had been headed.

It didn't have to mean anything, just someone taking pictures or video of the market, but why risk anything? Jasper let go of Accelerated Time and turned around again, drawing his hat a little lower. The bookstore first then.

To his relief, the crowd dissolved in front of him and he picked up his pace. The street narrowed slightly before the final stretch to the bookstore, and this time he saw it right when he heard it—another drone. Or the same drone? It hovered up and ahead of him, right in his path to the store.

Jasper looked around but had walked too far to see whether the first drone still flew where he had seen it. This certainly looked like the same model. To his left, a quiet alley led away from the market. He'd circle around the market and then back to his original destination?

In the deserted alley, he transitioned to Accelerated Time and pressed himself flat against an older brick building, leaning his head against the cool stonework.

Take a deep breath. Not everything is about you.

But he found it hard to convince himself, when in the filtered noisescape of Accelerated Time, he could have sworn he heard a clap, followed by distinct humming.

The drone again!

He looked up. A narrow strip of blue sky—nothing. But the whirring noise, while faint, grew louder.

He completed a full three-sixty turn—to an empty alley.

Jasper shook his head. A couple more days of living like this would be enough for Uncle Martin's paranoia to seem mild in comparison.

With a little *thump*, the whirring noise stopped, and he felt a prick on the back of his neck. His hand shot up instinctively and pulled a thin hypodermic needle with a feathered tail from his nape. He stared at it, dumbfounded, as he felt himself tumbling out of Accelerated Time.

The empty alley around him still felt so tranquil, but for the voice in his head: *Run!* Run toward people, safety. Back to the market street.

Suddenly so tired…

No running, but one foot in front of the other. A trot. Jasper scanned the alley—still nobody—but his eyelids grew heavier. The outlines of objects melted under his gaze.

Rest, a nap—no!

His thighs felt duller and duller, but he trotted on in the direction of the market. Honking in the distance, people chattering, a glimpse of a fruit stand.

Just. So. Tired. Almost there, one more house—

A door next to Jasper opened in the blink of a weary eye. A shape flashed outside into the alley so fast, it could only be a time bender. Jasper raised his hands defensively, but even if he had still been in Accelerated Time, he couldn't have defended himself.

So tired. Weak.

Another prick in his neck, then darkness approaching faster. Strong arms picked him up and carried him into the house. The appearance of his attacker solidified for a brief moment—contemptuous, blue eyes behind familiar steel-rimmed glasses.

Unconsciousness took Jasper after a final thought: *it's not paranoia if they're really after you.*

Chapter Thirty

Room with a View

"*Hector v. Achilles! Big Chart Showdown! Who Will You Pick?*"

Father had picked an annotated translation of the Iliad for Eva, but cross-reading her Rip Current magazine frequently broke her concentration.

Couldn't the day be over already? She wanted another crack at more exploration, despite the close call last time. Father's strange behavior, a new guest? She simply had to find out more tonight. Until then, any distraction would do.

Car noise outside. What a stroke of good luck. She rushed to the window.

A black SUV pulled up, driven by a man named Singher, who had helped Father in the past.

She had met him a long time ago when Adam still lived here. He looked cruel. Eva suspected he might be mad all the time because he was really a tick-tock. Father moved in Accelerated Time with him around, unlike, say, with *Fräulein Ochs*, but Singher never really did much of anything as far as Eva could tell. He always had a hard time just keeping up.

Once she had asked Father if Singher was like him.

"Don't be silly," he had said.

But none of that mattered while driving a car. Being a chauffeur (*"a person employed to drive a private or rented motor vehicle"*) seemed to be the man's primary purpose. Eva only ever saw him from her window these days. Father would never let him in her rooms. At least she hoped so.

Singher drove faster than usual today and cut the sweeping corner around the main residence.

Eva ran into the bathroom, put the stool from under the sink into the shower, climbed it, and pulled herself up to the ledge under the only window that looked to the southwest. It could only open horizontally for venting up to a maximum of seven centimeters, but if Eva put her head down on the far-left end, she could peek through the slit to the right and see all the way down to the courtyard. A small part of the courtyard, really.

The SUV drove into and out of Eva's view before it reversed into an area right next to the building. She got up high on her window and pressed her face against the glass, hoping she'd remember to wipe it clean later.

Singher got out of the car, opened the trunk, and lifted a large package out of the back. No, not a package, a person, loosely wrapped in black tarp.

Eva's father came into view. Singher pulled the tarp back to reveal the head of a blond teenage boy. He looked asleep. Father gestured, and Singher carried the limp body outside of Eva's view.

First the stranger in bed downstairs, then a girl patient, now a boy? How could she make it until tonight without dying of curiosity? What if Father checked the lock again?

No, she would have to—

Count your blessings and go back to your book, that's what you should do. We're never going down there again, remember?

She sure did.

Down in the courtyard, Father closed the trunk of the SUV and looked around. Left, right, and up.

Eva pulled her head back. He couldn't have seen her. Couldn't! She dropped down from the window ledge to the stool, to the shower, her mind racing. Strangers, distractions, new medicine.

The air grew thick, and she started twitching—

She found herself in bed, looking out the window. The alpine afternoon sun bathed her bedroom in a glorious shade of orange.

Still the same day, according to her alarm clock. A little luck, at least. She got up and checked her bathroom. Had she taken the stool out of the shower or had Father done it? She couldn't remember. The window was closed now.

Everything else in her apartment looked unchanged, so she sat down in the office and picked up the Iliad. She'd have to play it cool with Father. Just another standard freeze, nothing to worry about. She had gotten very good at pretending over the years. Sometimes she pretended so hard, she almost believed it herself.

Father, clean-shaven, brought dinner on time tonight. He stayed while she ate in silence, making sure she didn't choke.

When she was done, he picked up the tray. "No

backgammon again, I'm afraid. The work continues. Good night, I will check on you later."

"Good night, Father."

He hesitated on his way to the door. "I know you're impatient, but I'm making progress. Maybe tomorrow there will be good news."

Progress? Good news? When father left her room, he lingered while the door closed. If he checked the lock, she'd be trapped again. She needed a distraction.

"Father?"

He pushed the door back open. "Yes?"

"Nothing," Eva said, "just, good luck with your work. I love you."

He seemed a little flustered at the overt display of affection and couldn't help but smile and give her a little wave as he left her room for the second time. The door appeared to close freely after he disappeared from her view.

Eva leaped from her chair and grabbed her improvised escape tools from the desk. She scurried to the door and stuck the coaster between the lock and the strike plate, then tapped the door handle with her pen to simulate the sound of the lock. She put her ear against the door but heard nothing outside.

Endless Real Time seconds passed before she dared open the door. Father had left. She stepped into the hall.

I know where you're going. You're breaking your word. You'll regret this before it's over. We both will.

"Oh, do shut up." She didn't have time to coddle Adam, she had some serious investigating to do. *Progress! Good news!*

He looked awfully cute, with that tangle of almost-blond hair, Eva thought. Not too tall, not too short, with just the right amount of pinchable baby fat on his cheeks. He really could pass for Robbie from a distance, even if she couldn't tell his eye color from her vantage point.

Of course the boy wasn't *her* Robbie. No coincidence ("*a remarkable concurrence of events that happen by accident but appear to have some connection*") in the world could be big enough for that. She lived in Switzerland after all, and he surfed in Los Angeles or toured in Japan, Portugal, or Argentina.

Not-Robbie, however, was on level -2 in the bowels of father's underground facility. But maybe he also sang in a band?

Eva had visited the same room before. The window was a mirror on the other side—*Not-Robbie* couldn't see her. Not that it mattered right now. He slept, just like earlier when she had seen Father's helper carry him in. She could see him breathe regularly.

Hopefully, Father could help him. And the girl he had mentioned. Eva hadn't seen her yet.

Good news tomorrow! Something was up for sure.

Maybe Father could even help the man at the far end of the room, behind the curtain, who she had seen before, similarly asleep. Or comatose?

Eva looked left and right down the deserted corridor. Father said he was going to be busy. Too busy for backgammon for two days running. *That* busy.

She so wanted to make a new friend. One like her or Adam, not a tick-tock. (She'd make an exception for Robbie, of course.)

But just the boy's presence alone surely meant he couldn't be a tick-tock. They had their own hospitals everywhere.

Eva waited for Adam to raise his usual objections, but he had been quiet since she snuck out. Still flabbergasted at her daring excursion, she suspected.

It couldn't hurt to check whether the door was locked or not, could it?

Chapter Thirty-One

A Friend Indeed

Jasper woke up on his back in a narrow bed, a brightly lit white ceiling above him.

Alive. At least that. Every heartbeat felt like a gong struck between his ears. His mouth was parched, his stomach rumbled, and all muscles in his body felt dulled.

But, alive, and alone for now. Just not safe, far from it. He wanted to check his neck where the dart had struck, but straps tied his wrists and ankles to a metal bed frame. A drip feed supplied an IV access in the crook of his right arm, while the index finger of his left hand stuck in a pulse oximeter. Out of the collar of what appeared to be a hospital gown (*gross!*), cables ran to a monitor behind the bed that silently displayed his vital signs.

He lifted his upper body, straining against the leather straps, and looked around the windowless room: a large mirror next to a door straight ahead, a counter with medical equipment, cabinets, and a light box with a chest x-ray on display to his left. The room continued to his right, but a curtain blocked his view. Probably more beds.

"Hello?" The moment the word had left his mouth, he thought better of it.

Shut up, you idiot. Who knew who would answer? What good could come of it?

Jasper made fists, again and again, trying to get the blood flowing. He turned sideways, wiggled back and forth, pulled on the restraints, but they could hold down stronger men than him.

When he looked back up, a young girl with long black hair had appeared out of nowhere right next to his bed and scrutinized him. She let out a peculiar little shriek.

What the hell? Adrenaline surged through him. He snapped back in his bed and yanked on the straps.

After the first surprise, she seemed sad at his reaction. He had problems focusing on her appearance.

Could it be? He closed his eyes and dove into Accelerated Time. Thankfully, the IV didn't contain any opiates. When he opened his eyes, the girl was in perfect focus.

"Ich wusste es, ich wusste es," she clapped her hands and giggled. *"Du bist wie ich!"*

"Excuse me?"

"I knew it, you're like me," the girl said in perfect English.

"Like you?" Jasper asked. "I don't even know who you are."

"I'm Eva." The girl formally extended her right hand. "Oh, sorry," she added when she realized he couldn't move. "I hope Father can help you. He's trying to help me, too. That's what all this is for. To help us, to find new medicine, a cure. Good news."

"To help me?" Jasper rattled his cuffed hand and feet. "Help me with what? I'm not sick. I came to Switzerland to look for my father. And a friend, a girl around my age. They were kidnapped, like me. Why do you think I'm tied up?"

For a split-second, the girl glanced sideways to the room-dividing curtain, but then focused a skeptical look on Jasper. "For your protection. Sometimes we can hurt ourselves. Like when we're in a bad spot when the spasms start or we freeze."

"Spasms? Freeze? I have no idea what you're talking about." But he had a hunch who he was talking to. "Look, I don't even know where I am, but you're in danger too. The man who brought me here, he's dangerous. A murderer. Big guy, broad shoulders, white-blonde hair, steel-rimmed glasses, cold eyes..." He focused on Eva's face while he described the Bastard.

"Singher," she whispered.

"Is that his name, Singher?" Jasper asked, and she nodded. "So you know him, you have to help me escape."

"No, no, no..." The girl got anxious. "Father will help us. We just have to be patient. You should be my friend. I have waited for so long. And you look just like him, you know."

"Like who?" Jasper was fast losing patience.

The girl's face lit up. "Like Robbie. He's from California. Are you from California?"

Was she simple? She had to be, what, ten? His situation didn't appear particularly ambiguous to Jasper. "Yes, I'm from California..." The girl clapped her hands excitedly and let out another little squeal. "But what does that matter? And who's Robbie?"

"He's a singer in Rip Current, you silly."

"The boy band?" Remarkably, the situation still had

room to get stranger. Jasper recalled a torrent of glossy ads all over social media a few years ago, but the girls in his middle school loved K-pop at the time, so Rip Current had vanished from the feeds quickly. "Didn't they break up last year?"

"No, you silly." The girl's expression darkened. "They're friends for life. They all said it in the interview." She flashed mock gang symbols with her hand. First four fingers, then a capital L. "For. Life."

Cray cray. Jasper drew breath sharply. "I'm sure you're right. Look, I don't know what you're expecting from me, but I want to be your friend." He gambled on his hunch now. "The man who brought me here, this Singher, he's not our friend. And I know who he works for. Tranquillo Zeiger. That's your father, isn't he? And this is all his, isn't it? Help me escape, please."

"No, no, no…" The girl put her face into her hands.

"My father was kidnapped. My friend too. I need to find them. Untie me, please."

She shook her head. "No, no… This isn't what's supposed to happen!"

Had he overplayed his hand? "Eva…"

The girl ran away and didn't look back at Jasper before the door closed, leaving him alone again.

What the hell just happened?

As he tried to gather his thoughts, a small machine connected to his IV drip started beeping, then ejected liquid from an oversized syringe into the tube feeding his forearm vein.

No!

He struggled against the leather cuffs in vain. Moments later, he lost consciousness.

Wake up.

A voice. His voice? No matter. Jasper opened his eyes. Without a window or watch, he had no way to tell how much time had passed, but he remained in the same place, strapped down, trapped.

He blinked rapidly, trying to clear away the cobwebs. There had been a girl, Zeiger's daughter. And she knew the Bastard. Her reactions had appeared genuine. She didn't know he had been kidnapped. Who knows what she had been through, if his predicament was any indication.

Jasper stretched his limbs, and the leather creaked.

How much did she know? Anything about Maya? About Dad?

Again the creaking of thick leather bending and stretching repeated in the distance, fainter.

"Hello? Is anyone here?" This time he had no reservations about making himself heard. "Hello?"

A pause.

"Jasper? Jasper, is that you?"

"Dad!" After all this time, his voice felt like a warm embrace, even if it came from behind the curtain, far down the other end of the room. "I found you!"

"Yes! Yes…" His voice got quieter. "You found me. Are you okay?"

"Strapped down and hooked up to all sorts of stuff, but otherwise okay. How are you? And what's going on here?"

"Ah, it's complicated." His dad's voice sounded weary. "Where even to begin… How did you get here? You found me?"

"It's complicated." *Where to begin?* "I can bend time, too. It just happened. I found the safe in the closet and the Passage of Time, but it's destroyed now. Uncle Martin helped us find you. And Zeiger. But the Bastard, I mean the mercenary, Singher, I think, he caught me, and then I woke up here. There's something in this drip that makes me fall asleep. Dad, how are we getting out of this?"

"Jasper, listen, forget about me, you have to get out of here. If you can save yourself, don't come for me. It's too dangerous. Get to the American Embassy and call Floyd Greasley at the State Department in Washington. You can tell him everything, only him, but don't tell anyone else anything."

"Dad, someone's coming!" The door opened, and a thin middle-aged man with short black hair entered the room. He wore a black turtleneck sweater under a white lab coat and looked older than in the pictures, but Jasper recognized him: Tranquillo Zeiger. "What do you want with us? Dad, he's coming."

The man didn't slow his stride or say a word as he walked through Jasper's med bay toward the curtained-off back of the room.

"Jasper, do you understand? Remember, don't worry about me. I'm at peace as long as you are safe." His father's voice remained steady but couldn't completely conceal a hint of desperation.

"Dad! Dad! I'm sorry, I didn't know. I didn't know anything!" Jasper stayed quiet to listen to what his dad said to Zeiger.

"Quillo, that's my son, you can't do this. Not after all these years. Do with me what you want, but not him…"

But Quillo didn't say anything, and moments later his dad fell silent.

"Dad? Dad!" Jasper flailed in his bed, but the restraints wouldn't budge. "Dad!"

Nobody answered. Instruments beeped, and feet shuffled, followed by a drawn-out, sharp scratching sound, then another. Zeiger drew away the curtains separating four med bays in total, two empty ones between Jasper and his father, now unconscious.

Zeiger walked back to Jasper's dad, loosened a brake on one of the wheels of the hospital bed and pushed it toward the door.

Panic rose up the back of Jasper's throat, but what he could he do? At the very least, he had to say something.

"I know who you are, I know who you are," was all he managed, but the man just looked at him dispassionately and wheeled the bed with his father through the room. "I know you, you're Tranquillo Zeiger!"

Zeiger stopped the bed and walked over to Jasper. "It's pronounced Ts-aye-guh, not Zey-jer."

He fiddled with the controls of the infusion pump at Jasper's IV until it made a single beep.

Since Jasper was in Accelerated Time, he could watch the liquid advance at a goo-like pace through the tube until it mixed with the main drip, then went into his vein.

He couldn't hold on to a single thought before he fell asleep.

When Jasper woke up, he didn't have the faintest idea how much time had passed, but what difference did it make whether he'd die on a Tuesday or a Wednesday.

He had come so far, uncovered his parents' mind-boggling life story, learned how to bend time, survived being shot point blank, located his missing father in a strange country, only to end up in a hospital bed, defenseless against an automated drip and a few straps of leather.

You have to get out of here. His dad's reaction harrowed him. But all the time bending in the world couldn't help him escape his predicament. Or could it?

If a prisoner could dig an escape tunnel with a spoon, couldn't he wear down a couple of leather cuffs? He'd really only need one, and he was definitely stronger with his right hand.

He transitioned to Accelerated Time and found it waiting for him like an old friend. Apart from the now-familiar glow that made his surroundings seem more real than reality, nothing changed. Absolutely nothing. His room provided no frame of reference: no people, no noises, no clock.

He had to trust himself and went to work on the right cuff. A polished metal buckle fastened a two-inch-wide strap of thick, brown leather.

Jasper twisted his forearm to put some strain on the material, then pulled, twisted, and pulled again.

The leather chafed on his wrist.

Twisted and pulled. His skin stung from the friction.

Twisted and pulled. A trickle of blood formed on his wrist.

Twisted. And pulled. The cuff smeared the blood down his forearm.

He had no way to measure how much time passed, Accelerated or whatever. Hours and minutes? Minutes and seconds?

His right arm and shoulder felt limp, the skin on his forearm raw. Blood stained the edge of the leather a darker shade of brown. Maybe the strap was a smidgen more pliable, maybe not even that. He'd never be able to escape.

Earlier tears of pain had long dried when despair arrived. He looked at the IV drip with disdain. Sooner or later that damn pump would put him to sleep again.

Jasper recalled what his father had theorized, that the time benders had by now become the worst versions of themselves, their anxieties amplified over years of isolation in their own heads. Uncle Martin had turned into a paranoid, drug-addicted troll, Dad into an antisocial Luddite.

What had Uncle Martin said about Zeiger? A Nobel Prize-level obsessive, probing how far time benders could push their bodies. A brilliant mind who wanted to trigger time bending abilities in Jasper's mom, but also a real-life Dr. Moreau whom his mom avoided.

The reference had flown by Jasper at the time, but

thinking of the name now triggered snippets of late-night cable TV in his memory, of a mad scientist and abominable medical experiments. He shuddered.

Jasper recalled Maya's words, too. *When you find your father and there's parts of him missing, you'll understand.* He was powerless, a platter of meat waiting to be experimented on, harvested, killed. He let go of Accelerated Time. Why prolong the agony?

Something deeper than sadness and fear gripped him. Something primal, less acute than panic, angrier than despair. He had no word for it, not even a sound, but he would try to get close.

And so he screamed—louder, angrier, and for longer than he would have ever thought possible.

The release somehow expelled more tears out of him. He dried his eyes on his shoulder and looked up. The girl, Eva, stood back in the same spot next to his bed where she had appeared the first time. Instinctively, he slipped back into Accelerated Time.

"What do you want? Gawk at the crying boy?"

"No!" She sounded indignant. "I thought about what you told me."

"And?"

"I still want to be your friend."

"Now that's a relief." Jasper laughed bitterly. "I have friends. What I need is someone to open these." He nodded toward his cuffs.

"Oh no, you're all bloody." She sounded genuinely concerned and tenderly touched his right forearm. The raw flesh oozed blood. "What have you done?"

"What don't you understand? This is a prison! If you're not going to help me, please leave." He turned his face away, half wanting to be alone, half gambling on the effect it might have on the girl.

"Father says we have the power to harm ourselves, and he has to make sure we don't," Eva said. "He knows these things. He's only trying to help. It's for the best."

"Eva, I'm not sick, I'm fine. I have no idea what it is that your father is doing here, maybe he's trying to help *you*, but he's sure not trying to help *me*."

"No, no, I'm sure he is. He knows these things, even if we don't." She drew her lips into a thin line. "He knows everything."

"Well, does he know you're here, talking to me?"

She twitched and looked over her shoulder in the big mirror next to the door. "No, but he's busy. It's not only about us, he's also trying to help others." She glanced over to the other side of the room. "He's like a doctor. Just smarter."

"That was my dad behind that curtain. I know you saw him. My dad screamed when your father took him away. He told me to save myself, he was terrified. What's your father doing to him?"

The girl trembled. For a moment Jasper thought her facade would break, but he couldn't be sure. There had to be some next-level brainwashing going on. "You know what, just leave me alone," Jasper said.

"I don't know… I don't know what you mean. I only wanted to be your friend!" The girl covered her eyes with her hands.

"I am your friend! But friends have to be honest with each other, don't they?" Jasper softened his voice. He couldn't imagine what her life must be like. "Friends are honest, and friends help each other. Eva, I have to get out of here. You can come with me. We'll both get out of here, and you can come with me to California. Will you help me?"

She sniffed and dried a tear with her shirt sleeve. "I only want…" The door opened before she could finish, "…us to get better."

Tranquillo Zeiger wore a surgical mask and a long blue surgical gown spattered with blood. "Of course, love, that is what we all want."

"*Vater*! I didn't… I just wanted to…"

"*Ich weiss, ich weiss, aber jetzt geht's wieder in dein Zimmer. Du musst dich ausruhen,*" he calmly said to her in what had to be German, before putting his arm around her and guiding her away from Jasper's bed. "*Der Junge ist verwirrt, krank. Er ist hier zu seinem Schutz…*"

"Where is my dad? What have you done with my dad?" Jasper didn't expect an answer from Zeiger, but as the questions burst out, he feared this might be the last time he talked to anyone before he had to follow his father's path, wherever that led. And so the words just poured out of him.

"Eva, don't listen to him. I'm your friend, Jasper Faulks. I live in Los Angeles and I am sixteen. My dad vanished on my birthday, and I'm trying to get him back… I'm not sick. I was abducted, my friend Maya was abducted, my dad was abducted. This is wrong. I just want to go home, with them. Please."

"*Vater*?" Eva looked at her father, but Zeiger opened the

door and gently but firmly pushed her out of the room into the corridor.

"Wait here, our friend is confused, he needs to sleep," he said to her in English, then went back into the room.

"I am not your friend," Jasper shouted. "Not your friend!"

Zeiger pressed a button on the infusion pump. With a beep, the machine sprang to life again. Zeiger turned his back to Jasper and went to join his daughter in the corridor. "Let's hope he is better when he wakes up," he said as the door slowly closed.

Eva turned around and looked at him sadly. Her appearance shimmered, and she started to convulse. Jasper saw Zeiger pick her up right before the door closed and he remained behind alone, with only the memory of her tender touch on his forearm.

Jasper glared at the pump injecting its blue-hued concoction into the IV. In Accelerated Time, it crept along and hadn't yet reached the main tube. He knew he wouldn't wake up again. Zeiger had sensed his daughter's doubt. Such a ruthless man wouldn't let Jasper become a loose end.

He exhaled and tried to slow down the world around him as far as he could. *Stand still.*

Same old Jasper Faulks had no tricks up his sleeve, except this one. No super strength, agility, or special training. And no clear grasp of the extent of his time-bending powers. Like a new muscle, he tried to flex his power to its limit. The drug couldn't reach his body, he'd have to stop time itself.

But how? Even the fastest man in the world can't fly. He closed his eyes and squeezed the darkness. The floating shapes collapsed into themselves over and over, until nothing but a black sea of tranquility remained. He could go no further and opened his eyes.

The liquid hovered at the very edge of mixing into the main tube but stopped advancing. What did it mean for time to stand still? Could he hold out for help? Nothing around him gave any indication of Real Time passing.

He flinched at the IV. A light blue tentacle of liquid reached into the main tube down to his arm. It got lighter and lighter, mixing with the colorless main drip. It would take time to reach his vein, but it still flowed. Time had not stopped. Accelerated Time merely prolonged his helplessness.

That's all this talent is useful for: prolong the dread before death comes for us all. He should let go, let Real Time take its course. In moments, he'd be asleep, and it would all be over.

Dad, I'm sorry. I tried. Maya…

He owed it to his dad and Maya to hang on, to hold out for as long as he could. If only he could have convinced Eva to help him. Would she come back for him? Had someone else, maybe Uncle Martin, managed to alert the Swiss police?

As the blue liquid wafted into the main tube, its tentacle got wider at the mixing point.

Someone had to be on the way, knock down the door, rescue him! That's how these things went, no?

No. He operated in Accelerated Time—if the tick-tock police were going to rescue him before he fell unconscious, they'd have to be at the door in Real Time already.

Nobody is coming. Time to let go. Maya had taught him the first rule of time bending. Everything you can do, you can now do faster, but you can't do anything that you couldn't do in Real Time. And no matter how much time he had, he couldn't free himself from these restraints!

He took a couple of deep breaths and closed his eyes, ready to let go.

I can't let go.

He opened his eyes and looked at the IV drip. The machine had ejected all the sleep-inducing liquid into the main tube. Near the IV access in the crook of his arm, the fluid remained colorless, but it wouldn't be much longer until it reached his bloodstream. He already felt a little drowsy.

The wide leather cuffs with the shiny buckle held his wrist in place. The shiny buckle…

Could it be?

The unbendable metal prong had extended through the last hole when he had struggled against it until his forearm was raw. Now it was the second-to-last. He pulled with all his might. The cuff felt looser than before but resisted his weak move.

A tremendous weight fell upon his eyelids.

Maybe I can try it when I wake up?

No! He pulled again and again, and once more with the force of utter desperation, grating his skin off at the edge of the cuff.

Finally, his hand popped free. He brought the crook of his arm up to his mouth, bit into the IV needle, and yanked it out. Warm blood sprayed his face.

Shaking, he undid the buckle on his other wrist, then the strap over his chest, finally the ankle cuffs. He pressed the bed sheet on his right arm where blood oozed from his vein and sat up on the bed.

Alive, if nothing else. His midriff heaved as he cried as much as he laughed.

Chapter Thirty-Two

The Kraken

Jasper calmed his breathing and composed himself. He put the bloody sheet down, grabbed a clean corner on the other side of it, and blew his nose.

The blood loss had made him dizzy, or some of the sedative must've gotten into his bloodstream. At least the bleeding had stopped when the vein collapsed.

He got up from the bed. *Ugh.* Naked under the open back hospital gown. *Gotta think of something else!*

Maybe being unconscious for that hadn't been the worst thing in the world.

He steadied his first steps by carefully setting one bare foot in front of the other on his way over to the counter and cabinets. The name on the x-ray was Faulks Jr. Same for several pages of blood test results. Faulks Jr... Faulks Jr... Faulks Jr.... Pages and pages of it.

How long had he been here? And how to get out, wherever *here* was? He looked through the cabinets—gloves, needles, swabs, gauze. Useless.

Jasper put his ear to the only exit door. Silence.

The door handle felt solid and cool to the touch. He hesitated. Outside, he'd be completely exposed, mooning the world in his hospital gown. *How can these things not have any buttons anyway?*

There had to be something around here he could use as a weapon. Or at least some clothing. With his right hand, he held the ends of the hospital gown together behind his back, then opened a small crack in the door and peeked outside—a wide, empty corridor.

He stuck his head out and looked down the other side. Nobody. He stepped outside and carefully closed the door. A small sign on the wall next to it read "208." On the other side of the door, he could look back into the room through a two-way mirror.

Bastards!

The corridor ran for at least fifty feet in both directions, ending in a cul-de-sac on each side. Nothing but unfinished concrete walls, illuminated by a string of fluorescent lights down the middle of the ceiling. The white linoleum floor reflected the harsh light and felt refrigerated under Jasper's bare feet.

Doors lined both sides of the corridor in irregular intervals. He tiptoed to the next door on the other side, a little narrower than the one to his former room and without a window next to it. A small sign read "209." Jasper didn't open it.

The next door back on the opposite side was "210," identical to Jasper's, just empty. All the beds looked freshly made.

He moved on to "211" on the other side. It had a door made of metal and a small window at eye level. A thick sliding bolt secured the lock, and metal bars crossed the window on the other side.

The room had a proper bed that looked unused. Next to it stood a small wardrobe and a tidy, well-stocked bookshelf, on the other side a washbasin and a small mirror. If not for the barred window, he could have mistaken it for a tiny studio apartment.

Since the bookshelf was stocked, maybe the wardrobe was too? Jasper decided to risk it. Not out of modesty, but out of necessity. Nobody had ever successfully escaped from anywhere in an open-back hospital gown!

He tried to make as little noise as possible as he eased the sliding bolt aside and pressed the door handle. The door swung open silently.

He took a tentative step forward.

Like a coiled spring released, a crouching figure jumped forward out of the blind spot in the corner and charged him, head down and arms extended. Two fists held metal objects like brass knuckles and aimed straight for his chest.

Jasper swerved out of the way. Good thing he had been in Accelerated Time, otherwise these things would have hit him square in the ribcage.

"Maya!"

"You? Damn, you're fast." The girl lowered her fists. She wore a baggy green sweater and matching sweatpants. Her long black hair was drawn back in a ponytail.

"What were you trying to do? Electrocute me?" Jasper recognized what she had charged him with: defibrillator paddles. She had slung a whole mobile defibrillator box over her shoulder.

"Well, not you, Sherlock. I didn't exactly expect you to

walk through the door." She raised herself on tiptoes, looked past him and smiled. "But I am glad to see you, and more of you than ever before."

Jasper looked over his shoulder. He stood with his back to the mirror. Blushing, he grabbed the ends of his gown to cover his backside. "It's the latest fashion in Switzerland."

"So that's where we are. I thought so. Do you want to slip into something more modest before we leave?" She opened the wardrobe with stacks of the same green sweaters and sweat pants she already wore.

"Yes, please, by all means!" He couldn't hide his relief. Life is weird. It shouldn't matter, but somehow it did.

"I hope you're comfortable in panties," Maya said. "We can call them unisex if you want. Or you have to go commando, I won't tell anyone either way."

Oh boy. At least she turned around unprompted as Jasper put on the new clothes. He didn't share which of the options he chose. Instead, he told her that he had found himself tied down to a hospital bed in the same room as his father, and how he had met Eva and eventually escaped.

"How did you end up here?"

"The Bastard was waiting for me at the hacienda. Ran right into his spider gun. No idea how he knew." Maya showed Jasper burn marks on her arm. "Hurt like a mother."

"The laptop," Jasper said. "Uncle Martin said it would be a red dot on someone's map. I tried to turn it on that morning at your safe house. Shit, I'm so sorry."

"Well, you didn't know better at the time." If she was upset, she hid it well. "Anyway, next thing I remember, I wake up in a small airplane, but he put me right back to sleep. Then I wake up here. No idea how long all of that took."

"Did he mistreat you?"

"You mean apart from killing my parents and shooting, drugging, and kidnapping me?"

"You know…" Jasper squirmed.

"Are you asking if he raped me?" Maya asked.

"I guess. I didn't want to upset you."

"Just use your words. Not as far as I can tell, but I was unconscious for who knows how long." She shuddered. "What about you?"

"What? No. I think. Sheesh." The loose hospital gown still made Jasper's skin crawl.

"Good, but I meant how'd you end up in this place?" Maya asked.

Jasper filled her in until he remembered what he wanted to tell ever since he found out. "My father left the message for you in your home. He wanted you to come to L.A. He reopened the Passage and checked on the other time benders because he felt everyone was getting worse. I don't think Zeiger or the Bastard even knew of you or me, or at least that we were time benders, until we fought down in the Passage."

"Huh." Maya processed the new information for a little while. "That doesn't change what the Bastard did to my parents, though, but since I woke up in here with a band aid on my arm I haven't seen him anyway. That Zeiger fellow has been bringing me food, but he's not talking. At first, I thought I'd wait and see. If they wanted me dead, they would have killed me already, right? But then I saw this."

She pointed at some scratch marks in the concrete wall behind the bed. They were shallow but legible and spelled out "Murat."

"This was done with fingernails on bare concrete. Can you imagine? I figured I had nothing to lose and picked the lock to this in-case-of-emergency cabinet. Found this baby, it works." She flipped a switch on the defibrillator, and the paddles started buzzing. "We should go."

"Wait." Jasper put a hand on her shoulder. "I don't know what you're planning, but I'm not leaving without my dad."

Maya nodded.

"And I'm not turning around for anything or anyone else," Jasper said. "I don't care what happens to them, I just want to get out of here."

"You know the Bastard has to die," Maya said flatly.

"We all have to die at some point, but I won't be the cause of that," Jasper said.

"Fair enough." Maya turned the defibrillator off.

Together, they explored the rest of the corridor, finding two more cells like Maya's and other bigger rooms on the opposite side. All deserted. The two final rooms had shelves of medical supplies and storage space for spare parts, machinery, and clothes.

"Everything looks brand new." Jasper picked up a broom and inspected the bristles. "Never been used." He unscrewed the broom handle and weighed it in his hand like a club.

"Before you use that as a weapon, you might as well try to ride on it," Maya said.

Jasper blushed. "We can't all be ninja fighting machines." He put the broom handle back.

"Here, scalpels." Maya reached into a box and tossed Jasper a handful. Plastic safety flaps covered the blades. "Maybe we'll be doing the cutting this time."

Jasper reluctantly put a few in his pocket. They went back down the corridor they had come from. He stopped at his former prison cell and looked through the two-way mirror. The sheet was bloodier than he remembered. He touched his wrists where the cuffs had chafed his skin raw.

Maya took his hand. "They'll pay for it. For all of it."

"Let's move on." Jasper gave her hand a squeeze before he released it. "There must be a way out on the other side."

They kept going until Maya stopped and inspected a metal insert in the concrete that ran up the wall, across the ceiling, and down on the other side. "Remind you of something? There was another one by the supply room." She ran her finger up the edge. "Maybe we can pry it open? Explosives might come in handy if we run into the Bastard."

"Are you crazy? What if we accidentally blow this thing up? And besides, it's probably just electrical wiring. Why would there be explosives in the wall?"

Maya shrugged. "For the same reason they rigged the Passage?"

"Look, an elevator." Jasper had kept on walking toward a set of horizontal sliding doors typical of freight elevators near the end of the corridor. A small panel next to it had just two buttons. "What do you think, up or down?"

"Neither. What if there's cameras, and they just turn off the power? We'd be trapped," Maya said.

"Well, we're already trapped. We don't even know where we are, but I know my father isn't on this floor. Maybe there's a window on one of the other floors or a building plan or something like that."

"I'm pretty sure we're underground. Even in Switzerland, it's not this cold in summer."

Jasper opened the last door. "So, up then?" It was a staircase leading up and down. A sign inside read "-2."

Maya followed him in. Two flights of stairs up, they stuck their heads out of the "-1" door. More of the same. A long corridor, doors in irregular intervals. No more windows into those rooms, though. And no locks on the doors either.

"Do you hear the humming?" Jasper whispered, as they tiptoed past the elevator door.

"Air conditioning? We're closer to the surface."

"No." Jasper put an ear to the first regular door they reached. "And yes. Reminds me of something." He opened the door. "Servers."

The whole room was crammed top to bottom with black boxes. Blue indicator lights blinked everywhere, some rhythmically, some sporadically. Thousands of tiny fans hummed. The air smelled of warm plastic. Same in the next room.

"We should pull the plug." Maya traced the outline of one of the servers' power switches with her index finger. "What are the odds any of this is doing something good?"

"I don't think we should light a bonfire before we find my father and a way out of here," Jasper said. "Let's keep searching."

Dead silence greeted them in the soundproof first room on the other side of the corridor. Books, files, and folders—a library or an archive.

"Whoa! I wonder…" Maya reached for a folder.

"No time. Let's go." Jasper went back out into the corridor and down to the next room.

"Whoa!" It was Jasper's turn to be impressed.

A much bigger room than any of the others had a wall on the far end entirely covered by large flat screen displays, dwarfing Uncle Martin's setup. Four elaborate workstations stood in front of that, arrayed in a fan-like pattern, complete with multiple super-thin displays that curved around the seats. A fifth station on a raised platform oversaw the room.

Every single display showed dark shapes with strange attachments or patterns swaying in space or black ink. The room had no other source of light. Maya and Jasper stepped onto the raised platform. From there, the whole picture snapped into place. The screens formed a gigantic overlapping mosaic of a kraken, an almost three-dimensional representation of the mythical sea creature.

The central array in front of them showed the head of the kraken with two lifelike black eyes. A minimalist keyboard and an oversized touchpad were the only objects on the small desk in front of it.

Maya lowered her hand onto the touchpad. At the faintest touch, the whole room transformed.

The images of the sea creature and its ominous light

disappeared. A visual assault of worldly information fell upon Jasper and Maya—TV news channels, website feeds, internet discussion forums, stock market information, traffic cams, air traffic control, airport security feeds, numbers, columns, code… It was unfeasible to survey the different kinds of media and information on display, let alone the individual data.

"Quite a screensaver," Maya said.

"Uncle Martin wouldn't like this." Jasper sighed. "I bet you could remotely flush a toilet in the White House from here."

They had found the brain of Zeiger's operation. It made Uncle Martin's basement look like a glorified typewriter. He had been shut down with ease, from the exact spot Jasper stood in now.

"Tell me again why we shouldn't torch all of this." Maya patted the mobile defibrillator she still wore over her shoulder. "A little shock to the system."

Jasper ignored her and stepped off the dais. "This is too much information for one person, even if you have all the time in the world." The TV channels, all muted with closed-captioning turned on, appeared near-paused, advancing only frame-by-frame—a reminder they operated in Accelerated Time, just as Zeiger would be while controlling this incredible external brain. Stock market updates still scrolled by at a decent pace. "No wonder he's filthy rich. What could possibly surprise you when you know everything first?"

Jasper stopped at the final station. "Look, it's us." On the main monitor of the fourth station dozens of overlapping windows showed footage of corridors and rooms that looked like the ones they had just come from. One window showed the control room they stood in right now. "There are cameras, we just didn't see any of them." Jasper looked around. "I still don't see this one. They must be incredibly small."

Maya stepped off the platform and walked over to Jasper. "They must be super high frame rate, otherwise you would've just appeared here. Look." He pointed at a red outline around her as she moved. Once she stood still, the red outline disappeared.

"Just go back and forth again," Jasper said, "I want to see something."

Maya turned around and did as he had asked her.

"I think the computer recognizes when you move in Accelerated Time. See?" The outline around her had appeared again once she was moving. In another window, text code appeared. It looked to Jasper as if the program logged information. "It recognizes time benders."

"If this is equipped to monitor time benders, then why has nobody come? Why are they allowing us in here? We could've blown this whole place up by now."

"Maybe there is no they?" Jasper wondered. "Maybe it's just Zeiger."

"And the Bastard," Maya added. "Maybe he's in one of these?" She used the workstation's touchpad to click through the overlapping windows with surveillance footage. None of them showed any people, but the big bloodstain gave away Jasper's former room.

He remembered his futile hopes that tick-tocks would

rescue him. "Maybe nobody stopped us because our whole exploration here lasted only a couple of minutes of Real Time?"

Maya kept on clicking through the windows. Finally, they saw people. Someone carried a child in his arms.

"That's Zeiger and his daughter Eva," Jasper said. "But it's not down here, the corridor has windows. He must be bringing her somewhere else, that's why there's nobody here. Damn, if we knew where my dad is, we could make it out of here before he comes back."

"Don't forget the Bastard," Maya said. "He's still out there."

She used the cursor to move the window with Zeiger to the side of the screen, then clicked through more surveillance footage of empty rooms, storage spaces, labs until she stopped on one that showed a human being. A man in a hospital bed, eyes closed, covered to his neck by a white blanket.

"Dad… That's my dad! Where is that?"

Maya hovered the cursor over the window. A little text bubble appeared: "PACU 1 (312)."

"Room 312? Let's go." Jasper felt re-energized. "We can make it before Zeiger comes back."

"We should try to find an escape route before we go back down." Maya clicked through more of the surveillance windows, but Jasper already headed for the door.

"Let's get my father first."

Maya took another long look at the screen and pursed her lips. "Okay, let's go."

Chapter Thirty-Three

Karma Killer

Now certain they had the underground facility to themselves, Jasper and Maya wasted no time and hurried down the stairs again. They got out at "-3" and went straight to 312, not even bothering to check the rooms on the way beyond glancing through some of the windows in passing. X-ray machines, a CT scanner, a fully equipped operating room…

Room 312—*Dad!* An electronic lock with keypad secured the door—inactive, fortunately. Inside the small room, Jasper's unconscious father lay strapped to a gurney.

As far as Jasper could tell, his dad's vital signs on the monitor above him looked stable, with a steady heartbeat. His neck was thickly bandaged, and an IV fed into his right arm.

Jasper gave him a long hug. The familiar smell cut through layers of hospital, fear, sweat, and exhaustion. For the first time in longer than he could remember, Jasper felt safe, despite everything.

Seconds, or whatever passed for it in Accelerated Time, went by until Maya cleared her throat. Jasper turned around and saw that she had kept her distance.

"Dad?" Jasper gently shook his dad's shoulders. "Can you hear me? Wake up."

He didn't move.

"This might be a recovery room," Maya said. "He may be under anesthesia."

"I bet it's this damn stuff." Jasper reached for the IV drip.

"Wait!" Maya stepped up to the gurney. "Don't make another mess. Press here."

She had Jasper clamp down on the tube, then fiddled with the little valve on the thing in his father's arm vein before disconnecting the drip and the other cables.

Jasper opened the buckles of the chest, wrist, and ankle restraints. "Do you think we can carry him all the way?"

"We'll use the elevator." Maya kicked the brakes on the gurney wheels loose.

"But you said—"

"Yes. That was before I knew we were alone in here." She stepped around to the head of the gurney and pushed it toward the exit.

"Okay, but then we should hurry. The elevator works in Real Time." It would cost them precious seconds, maybe minutes. What could they do if Zeiger, or worse, the Bastard, came after them with real weapons? Throw their scalpels? Zap them with the defibrillator?

Maya turned the gurney around, so Dad's feet pointed down the corridor toward the elevator. She took off her defibrillator unit and hung it over the handle at the head of the gurney before stepping away from it.

"Here. Be careful the wheels don't come off. Remember how fast this is in Real Time. Take the elevator to ground level. I'll take the stairs and wait for you at the top. If there's time, I'll look for transportation."

"Sounds good." Jasper pushed the gurney down the corridor. "But what if—" He stopped himself. Maya had left in the other direction. "Maya, hurry! You said we have no time to waste."

"I'll catch up once you're in the elevator," she said without making eye contact and continued down the corridor to what had to be room 313. She put her hand on the door handle and mouthed to Jasper, "Go."

She stepped into the room and Jasper found himself, save for his sleeping dad, alone once more. The mass of concrete around him felt a bit heavier than before.

No.

He had tried to send her the other way before nearly getting killed in the Passage of Time. And when they had split up later, they had both ended up in this fresh hell. No more ego trips. Together they had saved each other in the Passage of Time, and together they would make it out of here.

"I'm sorry, Dad." He kissed his father on the forehead. "I'll be right back." He went after Maya, whispering to himself, "I hope."

Through the window, room 313 looked much like the others, just a bit more elongated, giving the person on the gurney at the end of the room more privacy. Jasper had to put his head up to the glass to be able to see to the back.

Maya stood next to the gurney. She'd put some black fabric over her head and had wrapped it like a shawl, covering her whole face, leaving only a narrow slit for her to peek through. Jasper had no idea where she had found it in the mere moments it had taken him to catch up.

She reached into her pocket and pulled out one of the scalpels they had swiped from the storage room earlier.

On the gurney lay a big athletic man with white-blonde hair, unconscious. His neck was thickly bandaged in the same fashion as Jasper's father, but the gurney's restraints hung loosely from the side rail.

The Bastard. Eva had said his name was Singher.

Jasper knocked on the window. "Maya, don't do it."

"Go away," she said calmly, and turned her attention back to the sleeping Bastard.

The window was surely another two-way mirror. She couldn't see him. The vents above the window allowed them to hear each other, but they were too small to be of any other use. He reached over for the door handle—locked, of course. He banged on the door. "He's not worth it, let's leave this place."

No answer.

He had no love for the Bastard, far from it, but the thought that his friend would slit an unconscious man's throat repulsed him.

"That's not justice." He sidestepped back to the two-way mirror and knocked on it. "Maya!"

She stood next to the bed, scalpel in hand, waiting. Her lips moved under the shawl, talking to Singher or herself, in any case ignoring Jasper.

"Don't do it. Let's get out of here." The world would be better off without the Bastard in it, but his stomach twisted. He couldn't just watch. And he couldn't just look away either, for all of their sakes.

"Maya, life is precious. Not his, yours. The best revenge is living a good life." He had heard that last part somewhere, probably butchered the quote.

Maya didn't look up. She finished her inaudible mantra, then calmly held the scalpel to the Bastard's throat. "The best revenge is revenge."

No. It would ruin her, ruin *them*, if she cut this man's throat in cold blood. There's no way back from that. But for the life of him, he couldn't think of anything intelligent to say.

"I *see* you." It was the best he could come up with.

Once more. "I *see* you!"

It got her attention. Her arm relaxed. Why did he even care so much?

"I love you."

Hold on, where did that come from?

It didn't matter now. She lowered the scalpel. Her chest rose and fell. Laughing at his silliness? Crying?

She turned to the mirror, took a few steps toward Jasper, and turned up the palms of her hands apologetically.

"I—" The word hung in the air, but she never got to finish her sentence.

In the back of the room, the Bastard rolled off the gurney and took the briefest moment to unfold his limbs before he charged her like a wounded bull.

"Behind you!" Jasper screamed.

The Bastard moved fast, even for Accelerated Time. Maya turned around and somehow managed to almost twist out of the way of his broad shoulders.

A square hit would've broken her spine before she hit the ground, but the Bastard only clipped her hips.

The force catapulted her into the air and sent her shawl and scalpel flying across the room. The back of her head hit the floor with a thud.

The Bastard had been put off balance by her swerve, couldn't halt his charge, and crashed head-first into a flimsy cabinet. He collapsed onto a heap of splintered particleboard and the contents of the cabinet, his personal effects: street clothes, underwear, a Kevlar vest, black boots.

"Maya! Get up!" Jasper banged on the mirror, but neither Maya nor the Bastard moved. Jasper banged on the door again and kicked the electronic lock. "Maya!"

No use, he'd have to break the mirror. He took a few quick breaths and clenched his right hand into a fist.

Here goes nothing.

The thump echoed through the corridor.

Nothing but pain, except maybe a broken hand. Certainly not a broken mirror.

The Bastard stirred first, slowly raising himself to his knees. It looked like he moved in Real Time—this was Maya's chance.

"Maya… Maya, get up!" Jasper banged on the mirror with his left hand. "You can do it, wake up!"

The Bastard moved to all fours and tentatively checked the thick bandage around his neck. He cracked a smile and smoothly got up as fast as he had been before.

"Maya!" Jasper kept on knocking on the mirror. "Get up. The door is locked. I can't help you. Wake up!"

The Bastard looked over to the door, then to Jasper. His

cold, watery eyes somehow found Jasper's even through the two-way mirror.

Finally, Maya moved too. If her nemesis pounced now, she wouldn't stand a chance.

"I have a gun!" Jasper yelled. "Let her go, or I'll shoot."

"Sure you do." The man's voice sounded weird, maybe caused by the surgery on his neck, but he didn't appear alarmed.

Still, the diversion bought Maya precious moments to get up. Thankfully, she had slipped back into Accelerated Time. Being slow meant being dead.

Singher looked at Maya. She shook out her arms and struck a defensive stance. He took a quick sidestep, sizing her up and placing himself between her and the door. Something on the floor right in front of him caught his eye. He bent over and picked up the scalpel. "I'll gut you like a fish, bitch."

"No!" Jasper stepped over to the door again, kicking and punching in despair. "Get to the door, Maya! Open the door!"

Crashing sounds came from the other side. The fight had started.

Jasper looked around for anything useful. Concrete, the corridor, windows, his father's gurney in the distance—nothing.

Yes. Something. The defibrillator.

He ran and grabbed the machine.

Maya wielded the tall IV drip stand like a lance, using her agility to evade Singher's slashing. The Bastard was careful to stay between her and the door.

Jasper turned on the defibrillator. A column of red LEDs lit up, accompanied by a high-pitched buzz. Did you have to rub the handles together, or was that only in the movies?

Something bumped against the door from the other side. Jasper checked the lock again, to no avail. Now or never. He sandwiched the electronic lock's metal casing between the defibrillator paddles and pressed the button. The electric charge fried the lock's circuits and released its grip on the latch bolt. Jasper dropped the machine on the floor and opened the door to the war zone.

Apart from a little nightstand on wheels, every other piece of furniture and equipment had been turned over. Maya still held the towering man at bay like a lion tamer. She dodged another slashing attack by leaping nimbly over the gurney and prodding Singher with the drip stand to keep a safe distance. She only needed a whip to complete the picture.

When Jasper stepped into the room, Singher halted his attack and took a step back.

Happy that the Bastard hadn't charged him right away, Jasper became acutely aware of being unarmed.

"Pocket!" Maya barked. She must have read his thoughts. He pulled out one of the scalpels and broke off the plastic safety cap.

"Finally." Maya seemed annoyed more than relieved at his rescue attempt. "We can take him, he's slower than us."

Jasper glanced at his scalpel. The blade at the end of the plastic handle was barely longer than an inch.

"Trust me. He's slow, you'll see him coming," Maya said.

Jasper looked over to the Bastard, who labored to keep

his composure. He sucked air and appeared to be scanning the room for an escape route. If he had been confident enough, he would have attacked.

Maybe Singher really couldn't catch them? But did she expect Jasper to stab him in the eye with this tiny blade? They had to incapacitate him somehow.

The Bastard didn't give them the luxury of strategizing any further. He somersaulted on the floor between them into the far corner of the room, away from the exit door. After unfurling himself next to the nightstand, he picked up a syringe from a small vial rack and jammed it into the back of his neck in one smooth motion.

Maya threw the IV stand like a spear, but Singher swatted it away with his other hand. His eyes bulged, and he inhaled sharply, but his features relaxed. He… laughed? It sounded strangely drawn out, a bit like Real Time sounds in Accelerated Time, but kept on speeding up. First it turned into to a normal laugh, then a staccato cackle, finally a series of high-pitched stings.

Jasper and Maya looked at each other, but he didn't have a chance to ask if she had any idea what happened.

The Bastard turned into a blur. A whiff of air brushed Jasper's cheek as Singher scooped up Maya.

A crunching sound prompted Jasper to turn around. Singher had rammed Maya into the remnants of the destroyed cabinet. With his left hand, he held her upright against the wall by her neck, leaving her feet dangling above the floor. His right hand still held onto the scalpel.

How can anyone be this fast?

Singher's contours shimmered. A blur slashed sideways

across Maya's midsection, followed by a spray of blood. The Bastard released his grip on her neck, and she fell face first to the ground on top of the pile of Singher's clothes. Particleboard splinters stuck in her back. Underneath her, a stack of white undershirts turned red.

Jasper didn't have an emotional response, let alone a plan of action. Everything had happened too fast. He might as well have been a tick-tock.

Singher turned his attention to Jasper and spiked the bloody scalpel on a piece of the cabinet frame still attached to the wall. "You're lucky Zeiger needs you alive." The voice sounded like an alien trying to figure out how to sound human. He cracked his knuckles.

The Bastard shimmered, then appeared in front of Jasper. He took the scalpel from Jasper's hand before he could tighten his grip.

Casually, the Bastard flicked it across the room and kneed Jasper in the gut right on the gunshot wound, which hadn't completely healed yet. Jasper cried out in pain and staggered backward, his knees about to buckle, but the Bastard grabbed a handful of his sweater and kept him upright. Everything happened so fast, Jasper couldn't even have blinked if the man had poked him in the eye.

"Time to sleep." Singher relished Jasper's despair. "Any last words?"

"Behind you," Jasper said.

"Horrible choice." The Bastard cocked his fist to deliver the knockout blow, but Jasper raised his arms and slid out of the baggy sweater to the floor.

"Hey asshole." Maya's voice took Singher by surprise.

He spun around as fast as his newfound extra gear allowed him, but she had already pulled the trigger of the spider gun.

The lightning web fanned out, ensnaring Singher without giving him time to dodge or evade. The massive electric payload struck instantly. He managed only a high-pitched shriek before collapsing.

Maya lowered the spider gun but kept her finger on the trigger. The Bastard twitched and convulsed. Foam oozed from the corners of his mouth as his eyes rolled into the back of his head and a big wet spot spread from the crotch of his hospital gown.

Jasper was still on the ground catching his breath. "Enough?"

"Yes, enough." She dropped the gun and helped Jasper up.

"Never mind me," Jasper said and coughed. "How are you still standing?" He pried his sweater from the Bastard's hands and put it back on.

"Actually, scalpels are horrible weapons. Sharp, but way too short. We should've taken the broom handle." She showed him the horizontal cut that went all the way across her stomach but didn't seem deep enough to be life threatening. "Just a flesh wound. And it couldn't have happened in a better place. Look." She pointed to the floor. In the rubble of one of the cabinets were wound dressing supplies and painkillers. "Could you pick all that up for me?"

Jasper wheeled the nightstand over, collected the supplies, and spread them out on top of it. "Careful with the painkillers. We can't have you stuck in Real Time."

"I'll be all right." Maya crossed her arms in front of her belly and grabbed a hold of the blood-soaked sweater seam. She looked at Jasper expectantly. "Do you mind?"

"Mind what?" Jasper asked.

"A little privacy?"

"Of course." He blushed and turned around. "How did you find the gun anyway?"

"Karma. Bumped my head on it when I fell on his stuff," she answered. "You can turn around again." She had put on an oversized sweater from the pile of Singher's clothes and if she was uncomfortable with that, she didn't show it. She walked around the overturned gurney to the rigid Singher. "How long do you think he'll be out?" She prodded Singher's limp arm with her foot.

"No idea," Jasper said, "especially not in Accelerated Time. It seems complicated."

"We can't have him follow us."

"He's unconscious."

"He'll wake up," Maya said. "He was impossibly fast at the end. We can't have him on our heels."

Jasper picked up the small vial rack from the nightstand. "I think it was this stuff that sent him into overdrive." Five small injectors were left. He took a couple and put them in his pocket with a shrug.

Maya took the other ones. "That doesn't take care of him, though. We—"

"We're not murderers," Jasper said. "I'm not having that discussion again."

"Okay, okay." Maya sighed. "What then?"

"Do you think you can lift him in your condition?" Jasper asked.

"My condition? You mean the one he caused when he tried to, and I quote, gut me like a fish?" Maya lifted her sweater to expose the hastily bandaged cut. "If you think I'll carry this monster out—"

"I didn't say carry. I said lift."

Chapter Thirty-Four

Encore

Her encounters with the boy had confused Eva. Father only ever wanted the best for her, how could he not? But did he want to help the boy, Jasper? It hurt to admit, but Eva doubted it.

She had to help him. She believed him when he said he was her friend. Those hazel eyes did not lie!

"Windows To The Soul… Can You Match These Eyes To The Band Members? Take Our Test!"

But what more than loosening his shackles could she do, especially with Father right there? Nobody noticed her going into overdrive mode, but now Father's attention was focused squarely on her.

At best, she could buy her friend time. He'd have to escape himself.

Eva thrashed about and pretended to spasm for a few moments before she stood completely still in the middle of the corridor, emulating her fateful condition, the freezing. Not much to her performance, she figured, you just didn't do anything.

It took little time until Father turned around to check on her. When he approached, she felt a stab of panic. Eyes open or closed? How rigid or flexible did she normally feel?

"Damn it, of course that has to happen right now." Father scooped Eva up in his arms but didn't say anything else.

Her worries seemed unfounded. After who knows how many times he's had to carry her around, he took the lead, and she really didn't have to do anything but go along.

The bare concrete walls passed them by as she tried to let her head bob in unison with Father's steps. This whole place, it felt wrong. Monsters in the deep, Adam had said of the fourth floor.

Thankfully, they went up, not down, in the freight elevator. Normally, anything mechanical took too long for Father's liking, but from the complete stillness of his movements, she concluded that he had transitioned to Real Time. Well, she was tall for nine years old. He probably didn't fancy hauling her up the stairs.

It took forever to reach her room like this, Eva realized with relief. Time enough for Jasper from California to escape. He shouldn't be kept against his will. She couldn't leave, but she had a condition. What did Father want with a healthy boy?

After he got out of the elevator, Father still had a long way to go—across the garage floor, through the main residence, and up the stairs to the third floor and her room. Hopefully, Jasper had escaped already.

When Father opened Eva's door, the coaster she had used to block the lock fell down. He grunted and kicked it out into the corridor. In Eva's room, he put her down on the bed.

Usually when she recovered, a glass of water and a snack waited for her on the nightstand, but Father threw a blanket over her and headed back out.

Did Jasper have enough time? No way to know for sure.

She coughed, then gasped for air. Did she usually come back like this? It certainly got Father's attention.

"What happened? Can I have some water?" she asked in Real Time to stall him further.

Father squinted. "You froze. What do you remember?"

"The boy. What's wrong with him? How will you help him?"

"This was a very foolish thing you did." He pointed at the door. "Sneaking out like a thief. We'll talk about this later. Remember, whatever you think you know, I do it all for you. And will continue to do so, despite this shameful display of ingratitude."

A faint buzzing came from Father's watch. He tapped the display, now in Accelerated Time, and his expression darkened further. "I have to go."

"The water?" She couldn't think of anything else.

"Hm," he grunted, but did get her a glass from the bathroom. "Stay in bed until I return. I'll know it if you don't."

"But Father—"

"No. Rest." He rushed out of Eva's room, his fingers flying over his watch display. Buttons on the electronic lock on her door beeped a few times before everything went quiet. The door had locked, for now and forever.

Never go back down, you promised! No, no, no... Father will punish us now; you just wait. Don't say I didn't warn you. All I ever wanted was for you to be safe.

Eva could have done without Adam's doom and gloom, but in her heart of hearts she couldn't imagine life without him. Hopefully he wouldn't lose his mind when he figured out that this new Eva would never again be content to spend her life in a locked room.

Chapter Thirty-Five

Final Destination

Jasper pulled the lever to collapse the gurney, so him and Maya only had to lift the Bastard about a foot high. Singher, drooling, lay tightly strapped down with the same kind of leather restraints Jasper and his dad had endured before.

Maya checked every buckle twice to ensure he wouldn't be able to escape regardless of how much Accelerated Time he'd spend struggling against them.

"There, his hand moved." She zapped the Bastard again with the spider gun. Jasper hadn't seen him move but couldn't begrudge her the satisfaction.

With Singher rigid as a two-by-four, they closed the door behind them and headed back down the corridor to Jasper's dad.

Jasper looked back at the helpless Bastard through the two-way mirror with a sense of satisfaction.

Unsurprisingly, his father hadn't woken up yet. Barely a couple of minutes of Real Time had passed since they left him behind. At least so Jasper guessed without a clock available.

"Back to the original plan?" He gripped the rail at the

head of the stretcher. "Or did you just want to split up for, you know?"

"No, I still think it's better if one of us goes ahead." Maya's smooth stride had Jasper wondering how she held up so well without painkillers. "We're sitting ducks in that elevator."

When they reached the elevator, Jasper hesitated to press the up button. Once the doors closed, they'd be stuck. Not only in there, but also in Real Time. At some point, Zeiger would check back on his special patients, either in person or via his security cameras.

"We can't carry him," Maya said, utilizing her mind-reading abilities.

"No." Jasper pressed the button. It lit up, but the doors didn't open. He put his ear to the door and heard a distant metallic creaking. The elevator was on the way. "Ugh, this'll take forever."

"I'll scout ahead." Maya opened the door to the staircase and looked back at him. "We'll make it, I'm sure." She headed up the stairs.

As if he needed the reassurance.

Jasper let go of Accelerated Time. No point in prolonging the wait. Accelerated Time gave him a heightened sense of reality, everything vivid, starkly rendered, but in Real Time, he felt more connected to his dad than he remembered.

He took his hand. It felt ice cold. How Dad must have wrestled with his gift. Somehow, he had made it work, a marriage, a family.

Uncle Martin, Zeiger, Singher, none of them functioned in Real Time, in the real world. Maybe Maya's parents had, but they had each other and hardly ever interacted with other people. Like Dad after Mom's death. When she had still been around, they had made it work too. They had been a happy family.

"We'll make it work again." Jasper squeezed his father's hand. "You'll teach me, and I'll be there for you."

The elevator dinged. Jaw-like doors opened just as Maya reappeared in the doorframe. Jasper dove back into Accelerated Time, but she had already caught him.

"Do boys get bored that quickly? What if I had been Zeiger?"

"You'd be a lot richer. And uglier."

She rolled her eyes. "I found us a way out. Ground level is a delivery area. There's an SUV. I don't think the stretcher will fit, we'll have to lift him."

"Can you drive? Maybe it's a stick shift?"

"Pff… Sure." Maya shrugged. "Get in the elevator. We'll figure it out."

Jasper pushed the gurney into the elevator. The options were 0, -1, -2, -3, and -4. "See you at the top." He pressed the top button.

Nothing happened. Was it slow to react?

He put his ear to the elevator wall.

Nothing. Not even a distant hum.

He pressed the button again. Multiple times. "It's not working."

"Press it again," Maya said.

"Dude, what do you think I'm doing?"

"Try the minus one. We can carry him one story."

Jasper reached for the "-1" button. With a loud, drawn-out *click,* the lights in the elevator went out.

"Get out, quick," said Maya. "We'll take the stairs."

With another *click,* the ceiling lights in the corridor went out too, leaving them in a blackness more void than mere darkness.

With a flutter in his stomach, Jasper pushed the gurney out of the elevator and stopped. He knew the door to the staircase was to his right, but he feared falling into an abyss with every step. Closing his eyes actually brightened things up.

"Jasper," Maya said and felt her way to his hand.

Emergency lights sprang to life and painted the ubiquitous concrete blood red. Jasper's eyes took a moment to adjust.

"C'mon." Maya tightened her grip on his hand and pulled him and the gurney forward into the staircase. "It must be some kind of emergency protocol. We should hurry." Upstairs and downstairs, the red light turned the narrow staircase into a glowing chimney.

"Let's fold up the undercarriage." Maya crouched next to the gurney and looked for the lever. She put her head down to hide it, but Jasper noticed that she flinched at the motion.

"You can't carry him," he said.

"Don't be ridiculous." She found the lever, but Jasper took her hand and stopped her from folding up the undercarriage.

"It's six flights of stairs. Show me."

She managed to lift her side up but had to set it down right away. She bent over and pressed both of her hands on her belly. "I'm sorry. The cut opened up again. Maybe we can drag him?"

"No, I'll pull him up," Jasper said. The gurney had pretty big wheels. "Onto the thing. You help as much as you can on the other side."

Jasper didn't wait for an answer. Step by step, he wobbled the gurney up the first flight. Maya added some balance on the other side. She must have hated not spearheading their escape, but it did feel good to go ahead instead of following for once.

After the first flight, he allowed himself a breather. Could you delve further into Accelerated Time to speed up recovery or healing? He'd have to remember to ask his dad. He put a hand on his father's shoulder and felt a twitch.

"Did you see that?" he asked. "He moved, he's waking up." Jasper patted his dad's shoulder. "Dad, wake up." His dad started to turn his head ever so slowly. "Look."

"Shh, did you hear that?" Maya tilted her head sideways.

They fell quiet and listened. Utter silence lingered until Jasper's dad opened his eyes and whispered, "Jjjjjjjjjjaaaaaaassssssss…"

"He's in Real Time, we don't have time for that, let's move on," Maya said.

"Hold on, maybe he knows something," Jasper said. "Dad, can you hear me?" He leaned in and turned his head sideways to put his ear close to his father's mouth.

"…sssssssppppppeeeeeeeerrrrrrrr…"

A short burst of fire flashed down at them from one story up.

Jasper looked straight at it from his new vantage point.

"Duck!" he yelled over the muffled sound of a silenced gunshot strangely drawn out by Accelerated Time into an unrecognizable thump.

The bullet flew by. It missed him by two feet, traveling toward Maya's head.

She ducked in the nick of time.

More flashes followed upstairs. Jasper gave the gurney a big shove. It knocked Maya aside and rattled down the stairs before the bullets could hit Dad. Jasper stumbled after it, and they piled up at the foot of the stairs.

"Zeiger!" Jasper scrambled back to his feet.

For the moment, the gunfire had stopped. The gurney had hit the wall hard but remained upright. Dad was awake now, but stuck in Real Time, judging from the slowness of his wide-eyed movements.

Jasper yanked on the gurney to bring it in line with the next flight of stairs.

"Not down!" Maya shouted, but Jasper saw the danger before she did. Zeiger rounded the corner upstairs with a submachine gun in each hand.

What next, bazookas? Escalating terror and sarcasm shared emotional space much like laughing and crying. What could he do, flee… *harder?*

Jasper grabbed Maya around her hip and pushed them off the wall behind him and onto the wheeled stretcher aiming downstairs.

A deafening spray of bullets hit the concrete wall where they had been standing mere moments earlier. Definitely no silencers on these new guns. The bullets also traveled much faster than the silenced one earlier or the ones Jasper had evaded at the Passage.

Zeiger had switched gears and marked them all for

death. Maybe they really had to flee harder.

Trying to steer their ride, Jasper abruptly shifted his weight to the right to make a U-turn around the corner. They almost made it, but lost traction.

The wheels had come loose under the stress of Accelerated Time. The gurney crashed sideways into the wall, and the whole undercarriage collapsed under the three of them. Jasper clambered to his feet.

Maya held her midsection as she got up right after him. Jasper's dad remained on what had become an overly heavy stretcher, still too slow to process or react to anything.

Jasper looked up, but Zeiger hadn't yet made it around the next corner.

"Go," he said to Maya. "Open the door." Just one more flight of stairs to the bottom of the staircase. Like all the other floors, this one had a heavy steel door too. The sign next to it read "-4."

Maya teetered ahead while Jasper reached under his dad's arms and interlocked his hands.

Zeiger rounded the next corner and fired again.

Jasper yanked his father off the stretcher and barely kept his balance as he dragged him out of the bullets' way and down the final stairs. A rain of slugs chipped away at the concrete.

Shuffling backward down the final steps, Jasper didn't check behind him whether Maya had managed to open the door. If not, death was certain.

He pushed on, and they finally stumbled out of the staircase and into the fourth underground story.

Maya slammed the door shut behind them, then

crouched under the door handle and held it up with all her strength, her shoulder supporting her hands. With metallic pings, multiple bullets hit the door on the other side, but the steel held.

"Chair," Maya said.

What? Jasper sat up and caught his breath.

"That chair. Give me the chair."

Jasper realized they'd entered one big room, not a corridor. Maya pointed at a metal chair behind a small desk near the door.

Jasper slid it over to Maya, who wedged it under the door handle and knocked it in place. She pulled on it to check that it stayed put under pressure before sitting down on the floor next to Jasper.

Silence.

"Where are we?" Jasper scanned his surroundings. The red light made it difficult to put the information together. A room, about twenty by sixty feet, with the longer side aligned with the corridors on the upper floors. It had a string of inoperative fluorescent lights on the ceiling, crossed at a right angle in the middle of the room by a metal arch. Next to the barred door to the staircase sat the familiar freight elevator with the horizontal doors.

"Cold storage," Maya said.

Indeed, this far underground, it was much cooler than in the rest of the facility.

A couple of desks stood against the short wall close to them, one with a computer terminal, without power and minus a chair, the other with strange-looking machinery that had binoculars on top. An ultra-modern microscope perhaps?

Glass-door refrigerators spanned all sixty feet of the long wall across the room, broken up only by a single door in the middle. There had to be tens of thousands of vials and samples in there. The short wall at the end was naked concrete, save for a large plaque in the middle, the inscription too small to read from their vantage point.

Jasper's dad continued to wake up. His movement remained Real Time-slow, but his eyes appeared alert. He slowly raised his arm and gestured for Jasper to come closer.

"Why don't you look around, maybe there's something we can use," Jasper said to Maya. "I want to talk to my dad."

"Is that wise? Zeiger could come back any time. I don't think a chair will keep him out forever."

"Maybe he knows a way out. Or I can help him access Accelerated Time again. Got any better ideas?"

Maya hesitated for a moment, but acquiesced. "I'll see what I can find."

Jasper let go of Accelerated Time. Maya immediately turned into a blur moving from one refrigerator to the next, but his dad finally extended his arm toward him at normal speed. Jasper pulled him to his feet and they embraced, finally in sync again.

"Jasper, you have to go. Now." His dad sounded hoarse but spoke quickly.

"Dad, I don't know how much you saw. We're four

stories underground and Zeiger is outside. We can't just leave. And I'm not leaving without you."

"I'm a tick-tock," Dad said. "Do you know what that means?"

"Yes, it'll come back. I had the same thing after I took painkillers. Uncle Martin said it was—"

"Yes, yes," his father waved dismissively. "I know about opiates and how it feels. That's not it. I'm a tick-tick now." He touched the bandage around his throat. "Zeiger did something to me. Probably the thyroid." He sighed. "It's too late now, every second counts, you're wasting time. You have to leave me and save yourself, go tell your friend."

Maya had been back for a few moments already and tugged on Jasper's sleeve before he could answer his dad. Jasper slipped into Accelerated Time. "He says Zeiger turned him into a tick-tock and we should leave, but I'm not going without him."

"Leave him and go where?" Maya asked. "There's no way out of here apart from the staircase and the elevator. This is the morgue. Literally. The door between the freezers?" She curled her lip in disgust. "There's like, big jars, with, you know…"

She squirmed and let the implication hang in the air. An icy cold crept up Jasper's back.

Maya continued, "Plus ten adult-sized morgue fridge drawers. All occupied, I checked. Full of square-jawed hunks like the Bastard. There's only two exceptions, both labeled. One skinny middle-eastern man with bloody stumps for fingernails. A tag on the door said M.H."

"Murat. One of the original time benders," Jasper said,

and Maya nodded. "And the other?"

"A boy, maybe eight or nine, dark hair." Maya raised her eyebrows. "The door had a single letter—A."

Eight or nine, brown hair? Jasper thought of Eva. "Damn, that must be Zeiger's son! 'A...'" He snapped his fingers. "'A' for Adam. The article—the Adam Zeiger Foundation!"

"The hubris to call them Adam and Eva." Maya gagged.

"What about the fridges here?" Jasper asked, eager not to keep dwelling on the chamber contents. *Jars!*

"Blood and tissue samples and whatnot. There's thousands. I saw my parents' names. And ours."

Jasper cleared his throat. He was about to ask if Maya had any ideas, but she shook her head before he could even say it. His dad softly touched his hand, and Jasper transitioned back to Real Time.

"There's gotta be a way out. Zeiger would never risk getting pinned down like this himself." Jasper's dad spoke as fast as he could while Maya did another reconnaissance tour of their de facto prison. "He came up with a backdoor to the Passage of Time before he agreed to booby-trap the entrance. You have to leave me here and find it."

"Dad, it's a dead end. That's the morgue over there. That Murat fellow is in there. And Zeiger's son."

"Oh no." Dad gasped when a loud clonk announced that the elevator had resumed service.

Jasper instinctively dove into Accelerated Time and met Maya, who had zipped over from the other side of the room, at the control panel. The only button on it, an up arrow, was blinking. The noises from behind the door sounded like a descending elevator.

"We can take him." Maya gripped the backrest of the chair she had picked up on the way over and lifted it over her shoulder.

Jasper looked around. "See any other weapons?"

"Be the weapon," Maya said. "You're the fastest time bender I've ever seen. When you pulled me out of the way of those bullets in the Passage, you were faster than me, your uncle, the Bastard, anyone. I bet you're faster than Zeiger too."

"I don't know." Jasper looked at his bare hands. "Zeiger had submachine guns, and he knows we're time benders. The bullets looked much faster than the ones I dodged."

Maya ignored him. "Crouch over there on the other side of the door. When it opens, I'll attack swinging. Go straight for the gun. Grab his wrist. Control the wrist, and you control the gun. With any luck, I'll whack him with the chair before he knows what's up."

Only a thousand ways this could go wrong. Zeiger had two guns, what if he fired before Jasper even got near him? He could be near the back of the elevator or behind some sort of barrier. What if he had help? He could also be faster than Jasper in the first place. It had been impossible to tell during the chaos earlier.

He kept his objections to himself. Maya looked as determined as he'd ever seen her. No reason to sow doubt, and he couldn't think of a better plan anyway. Crouching on the other side of the elevator door like a sprinter in his starting block, he tried to control his breathing, difficult as it might be.

Drawers… Jars…

They simply had to overwhelm Zeiger. Jasper dug his fingernails into his palms of his hands.

The elevator croaked and creaked in the distance as it crept down the shaft in Real Time. An excruciating wait, but Jasper didn't dare transition back to Real Time. Any fraction of a second would count in the fight. He looked over his shoulder. Dad was a non-factor. He had his back turned to them. Despite his running stance, he moved at a snail's path.

"What's on the sign back there?" Jasper asked Maya.

"It's in German, lots of consonants. No idea."

A long *ding* and the arrow light on the elevator control panel went out, but before the elevator door opened—

An explosion ripped apart the metal door to the staircase. Deformed remnants of the door and the chair rocketed through the room and smashed into the glass refrigerator doors. The blast knocked Maya over.

She fell to the ground in front of Jasper. Crouched on the floor already, he hunkered down and closed his eyes as the pressure wave washed over him like a hundred-thousand-watt hair dryer. His ears rang, and the smell of sulfur shot up his nose.

After the wave passed, he crawled over to Maya and cradled her head. She groaned.

"Can you get up?" Jasper asked.

He looked up toward the doorway, where a cloud of dust hovered in the air. Through the mangled doorframe and into the billow stepped a thin man dressed all in black. He wore large transparent safety goggles over a surgical mask and held submachine guns in both hands.

Zeiger was here.

Chapter Thirty-Six

Family Affairs

Zeiger's footsteps echoed through the post-detonation silence. Jasper and Maya huddled on the floor, but Zeiger kept a safe distance.

"I might have let you live, out of gratefulness for being such a perfect match for my daughter." He looked at Jasper. "But now, you'll have to make your organ donations post mortem."

Zeiger aimed his submachine guns at them.

"No, wait, I... I... I want to help Eva. Whatever she needs, I want to donate. Don't shoot," Jasper pleaded, trying to buy time more than anything. At point blank, and on his knees, Jasper had no hope of dodging the bullets, let alone pulling Maya out of harm's way. The end, *their end*, felt inevitable. His hand found Maya's without looking.

"Not good enough," Zeiger said.

A diminutive figure peeked through the dust cloud from outside the deformed doorframe—Eva.

"I want to help," Jasper said loudly. "I'm her friend. Isn't that right, Eva?" He let go of Maya's hand and pointed at Eva in an exuberant manner. "I'm your friend from California."

Zeiger's head whipped around to his daughter. *"Was machst du hier? Wie bist du aus deinem Zimmer gekommen?"*

"Father, what are you doing? You said you wanted to help them!"

"Eva, geh in dein Zimmer."

"No! I won't go back to my room." Eva vanished from where she stood and appeared next to Zeiger.

She had moved faster than Jasper could see, the difference between her and them at least as big as between Accelerated Time and Real Time. Maya pinched him, and he squeezed her hand in acknowledgement.

"Speak English so they can understand," Eva said. "You said they are sick, and you want to help them."

Zeiger grimaced. "They are sick. They're a danger to us, to themselves. *Eva, Schatz, alles wird gut. Geh in dein Zimmer, ich erklär es dir später."*

"I want to know now!" she shrieked. "I'm not leaving. He said he's not sick. And he's my friend. It's been so long since mother took Adam."

Jasper got on one knee. "I'm sure we'll find a way—"

"Don't move," Zeiger shouted, keeping his weapons aimed at Jasper and Maya.

Jasper obliged, but would Zeiger shoot them in front of his daughter? He hoped not.

"Eva, geh in dein Zimmer oder es gibt Ärger! Jetzt sofort!" Zeiger barked without taking his focus off Jasper.

Jasper didn't need to understand German to know what Zeiger wanted from Eva—to leave. Tears welled up in her eyes. She shuffled her feet.

Don't leave, don't leave… Jasper sensed her determination

wilting. He had to find a way to get her to stay. "Eva, what happened to your brother? What happened to Adam?"

"Shut up," Zeiger said, but Eva perked up.

"My mother took him. She used to visit us, and one day she took him, and they never came back. I couldn't even say good-bye. I miss him so much."

"Shut up, everybody shut up." Zeiger finally lost his composure. He lowered the guns and took a step toward Eva "Go to your room, now, or you'll wish you had." He shoved her toward the door with his elbow. "Go!"

Jasper stood and helped pull up Maya too. Whatever happened, they wouldn't die on their knees. He held onto Maya's hand.

Zeiger turned around again. "Back down on your knees, you two. Now." He aimed the guns at Jasper and Maya, but Jasper had one more arrow in his quiver.

"Eva, your brother, Adam, he's dead."

"No!" she cried out.

"Shut up!" Zeiger hissed, but Jasper continued.

"Adam is dead. Your father killed him, and his body is right in there." Jasper pointed at the door to the morgue chamber.

"Shut up, shut up, shut up…" Zeiger pulled the trigger on his submachine guns and didn't let go.

Automatic fire spat a hail of bullets at a rapid pace.

Fool.

Jasper tried to pull Maya out of the way, but only got as far as squeezing her hand when the dull *dup-dup-dup* of the bullets exiting the gun barrels mixed with another sound—a piercing, otherworldly high-pitched squeal, followed by stillness.

They should be dead already, but the bullets never reached Jasper or Maya.

A spasm of disbelief contorted Zeiger's face.

Little Eva stood between them, fists raised above her head. She opened them, revealing palms and fingers covered in burn marks as dozens of bullets rained to the ground.

Zeiger dropped his empty guns. "I tried to help him."

"Like you tried to help them?" Eva's voice sounded strangely mature now. She looked like a girl and had struck Jasper as naive for her age, but how old are time benders really? Uncle Martin said he had lived two hundred seventy-five years. Dog years.

"Is it true, Father?" Eva asked calmly. "Is he in there?" She pointed at the entrance to the morgue.

Zeiger nodded. "I didn't—" He couldn't finish his sentence.

Eva's appearance shimmered, then disappeared momentarily before it solidified again, her eyes now puffy, her dust-covered face smeared with tears. The door to the morgue blinked open.

"I hate you." She pushed her father. "I can't hear him anymore! And who are the others? And the babies! The babies! I hate you!" She pushed him again. And again. "I can't hear him anymore, he doesn't answer! He's gone! Gone! Monster! Murderer! I hate you, I hate you, I hate you—"

"Eva…" Zeiger tried to keep her at a distance without using force. "You know he was sicker than you, I did all I could. They were all sick. I didn't kill him. All I wanted was to help, help *you*, you and Adam—"

"Don't say his name. You can't say his name." Eva stopped chasing Zeiger around, and for a moment, the world stood still. Nobody dared breathe.

Eva looked at her father with eyes full of pain and wisdom far beyond her years. "Don't. Say. His. Name."

Then the screaming started. She stood in front of him, shimmering, shrieking like a tortured angel.

Real Time, Accelerated Time, whatever she could do, it twisted into an unidentifiable jumble. Like a vengeful spirit set free, glimpses of her appeared everywhere in the room, always returning to her father, prodding him sharply with an accusatory index finger, screaming in his ears. Jasper couldn't tell whether she sped up or slowed down or continually cycled through time, but the sound of her voice physically hurt, even at a distance.

A thousand angry Evas and their agony swooshed and echoed through time, bending reality, turning the room into a nightmarish tableau. The infernal noise signaled its own coming as much as echoed its leaving, to the point where it took effort to remember a world beyond. Jasper and Maya plugged their ears with their fingers.

Zeiger, at the center of Eva's purge of pent-up anguish, looked helpless, a lost man, but when his eyes met Jasper's, resolve returned to his face. He checked his smart watch and typed on the display.

With a sad smile, Zeiger looked down at his daughter, who intermittently appeared in front of him, still screaming.

Zeiger's lips moved, the words remaining inaudible. After he finished, he pulled a small pistol from the side pocket of his pants. His other hand reached into the blur in front of him and grabbed a handful of Eva's long, brown hair.

"No—" Jasper yelled but didn't even get to finish the single syllable before Zeiger's hand flashed up so fast Jasper couldn't see where the barrel pointed.

Eva's screaming stopped, and the sound of a gunshot rang out.

A clumpy red geyser spewed from a hole in the top of Zeiger's skull. The pistol under his jaw, with his own finger on the trigger, pointed straight up.

Eva's appearance had solidified. She stood right in front of him, unflustered.

Zeiger remained upright for an eerily long moment before collapsing into himself on the ground.

Eva looked at his body with disturbing calm, considering the circumstances. Had Zeiger made her watch him commit suicide? Or had he tried to kill her, and she had diverted the barrel? An easy task for someone who could pick bullets out of the air mid-flight.

It didn't seem appropriate to ask her.

Jasper still felt queasy from the turn of events when Eva kneeled next to her father's body. She turned his wrist around and looked at the watch display.

"Do you know what he did with his watch?" Maya asked.

Eva shook her head and turned her father's wrist to Maya and Jasper. "You should go."

Jasper and Maya looked at the watch display. A timer ran down from 00:00:01:76.

"What's going to happen?" Jasper asked.

"I don't know." Eva appeared strangely detached from the situation and smiled sadly. "But Adam was right, there was a monster in the deep."

Jasper watched the timer advance mercilessly. The shock about Zeiger wearing off, he now felt indignant that after getting rid of him and the Bastard, they were somehow still in trouble. He looked around.

Maya gestured toward the exit door and the staircase. "We can't just stay here."

"Eight flights in your condition? And what about Dad?" Jasper turned around.

His father was on the far side of the room, still running in slow motion into the cul-de-sac. He didn't have the slightest idea what was going on behind him.

Jasper looked back at the countdown and snorted in joyless laughter. It already stood at 00:00:01:01. "It doesn't matter, we'll have to ride out whatever is coming, we don't have enough time. Let's get Dad."

"Wait." Maya reached into her pocket and pulled out one of Singher's injectors. "More time?"

Jasper reached into his pocket and pulled out one of the injectors himself. *More time?* Yes, Singher's sudden burst of speed during their fight. But who knew what exactly was in these injectors? He looked at Zeiger's watch. The hundredths of a second were counting down fast: 00:00:00:45, 00:00:00:44, 00:00:00:43…

Jasper turned to Eva. "Singher injected himself with this. Do you know what it does? Does it make him fast?"

"I don't know. I've never seen him use it, but he was

pretty slow sometimes, like a tick-tock. Father said he's not like us."

"Maybe Zeiger created a time bender through medication and it wore off sometimes," Jasper said. "But we're already time benders."

"No risk, no fun." Maya jammed the syringe into the back of her neck. She closed her eyes, but nothing else changed.

"Are you okay?" Jasper put a hand on her shoulder.

The countdown on the watch reached the single digits. Jasper hoped for a lockdown or alarm sequence. After all, Eva couldn't be sure what Zeiger had been doing.

00:00:00:07, 00:00:00:06, 00:00:00:05…

Maya's shoulder quivered under Jasper's hand. Her eyes snapped on. "Do it! Do it, do it, do it!"

00:00:00:04, 00:00:00:03…

Jasper injected the liquid into his neck. He didn't even feel the needle going in. Blackness and fleeting shapes in the dark—he knew this place. Behind it waited more time… He dove in head first.

He opened his eyes to breathtaking stillness. The physical world revealed itself as a sandbox to play in, with his imagination the only limit to his power to manipulate it. He let go of the empty syringe. It hovered in midair. *What are the rules here?* "Is this time on pause?" he asked.

"Amazing, isn't it?" Maya said.

"Yes," Jasper said, "let's get Dad. Who knows how long this'll last."

They headed for Jasper's dad at the other end of the room.

"It's not really 'pause,'" Eva said. "We should leave." She set out for the exit.

Time didn't quite stand still after all. The syringe started dropping ever so slowly.

00:00:00:01 turned to 00:00:00:00.

Jasper and Maya saw it before they heard or felt it.

The doorframe-like metal band that ran up the walls and over their heads on the ceiling came apart at the seams, bending outward, reaching into the room with misshapen tentacles.

Behind it, the destructive force trapped in countless pounds of tightly packed plastic explosives released in a white-hot chain reaction, spreading from brick to brick, tearing apart the metal and concrete surrounding it.

Jasper and Maya jumped forward, right ahead of a pressure wave surrounded by a halo of compressed air.

It steadily, almost gently pushed Jasper back, but he had no chance of resisting the invisible wall.

Maya struggled to keep her balance as the wave forced her backward, too.

On the other side of the explosion, Eva was shoved toward where she had been headed anyway, the exit door, but she turned around and poked the pressure wave with childlike curiosity.

Strangely, they still didn't hear the explosion. The wave had to be moving at supersonic speed. Jasper realized it saved their lives by sweeping them out of harm's way.

On its heels rode utter destruction. A cloud of metal shards and concrete fragments formed along the path of the explosion. Behind that cloud, the explosives burned with the power of small suns, displacing the support of the whole underground structure.

As soon as the pressure wave pinned them to a wall, the metal and concrete would shred their bodies to pieces.

He looked up and next to the furrow that housed the C4, a significant crack already ran across the whole room, and widened farther in the tiny, almost immeasurable fraction of Real Time it took for Jasper to look up.

"Let's get ahead of this!" He took Maya's hand and ran away from the wave toward his father, still frozen in Real Time, fleeing from the last disaster with no way of knowing how dire the situation behind him had become. But only the concrete wall awaited. A dead end.

Jasper looked back at the explosion. It had cut the room in half. The cloud of debris in the middle got denser and started to spread out, gaining ground on the pressure wave. Bursts of deformed flames overtook the solid matters in places and charred, then consumed Zeiger's body.

Not too far away Eva moved her hand through a curious blaze like a child would move a finger through the flame of a candle. Yelling would be useless, so Jasper frantically pointed at the exit, but when she looked over to him, she simply smiled and waved in an unperturbed way.

Jasper raised his hand in a salute before the cloud blocked his view. *A final goodbye?* Back on his side, his dad stood right next to him, still like a statue, lunging forward to nowhere. They had no way to communicate.

Jasper put a hand on his shoulder, something he wouldn't notice until they all got buried by four stories' worth of concrete and stone. If Jasper let go of Accelerated Time now, he'd be dead before he could finish a single thought.

The pressure wave had almost caught up with them again. Maya took Jasper's hand. She looked at him, but neither of them had to say anything. They hugged.

He wished he could have smelled her hair and felt the softness of her cheek at least once without the fear of imminent death. They had enough time to outrun a pressure wave, but somehow it was never enough.

Better to be unaware. Dad didn't know yet that they had failed; he still ran, reaching for something. Reaching for what?

The sign? What was *Bioabfallentsorgung*? And why was it set off from the wall?

Jasper wriggled free of Maya's hug. A hint of embarrassment scurried over her face.

"The sign!" he yelled. "It's not a sign!"

"Of course! How could I be so blind?" Maya strained to reach the sign before Jasper. While he gently moved his father's hand down, Maya opened what turned out to be a hatch rather than a door. The sign swung down on a hinge and revealed a dark maw leading down at a steep angle. The opening barely fit a person, but the chute appeared to widen below. About seven feet down, lay a metal grate.

The pressure wave caught up and pressed them forward. For the first time, they heard some rumbling building behind it. Small rocks and shards of metal began to overtake the wave.

Jasper ducked, and a walnut-sized piece hit the wall over the hatch.

In the center of the room, the ceiling had cracked open even farther, taking the whole structure to the brink of collapse. Not that they'd have to worry about that between the pressure wave, the cloud of deadly debris, and the rapidly advancing firestorm behind it.

"Get in the hole!" Jasper had to shout to make himself heard. The noise swooshed and swished like at the edge of a hurricane.

"What about your father?" Maya asked as she climbed into the black hole in the wall.

"You pull, I push!"

"Okay, the grate holds." Maya moved inside the hatch. She reached up and Jasper pulled his father's arms forward to allow her to grab them.

Jasper tried to lift his father's body, but forces in this Super-Accelerated Time worked against him. He didn't move an inch.

"Push," Maya shouted from below.

"He doesn't move. Ouch!" A metal shard had flown by and cut Jasper's cheek before hitting the wall.

"Get in now," Maya yelled, "there's no more time!"

He refused to leave his father behind.

The pressure wave nipped at his pants, and dust prickled on his skin like nettle. Soon he'd be pressed against the wall with no chance of escape.

"Guide us, we're coming in fast," he called out to Maya

and stepped around his father, stemming himself against the oncoming pressure wave. He grabbed him around the hips and crouched, resisting the pressure until it built to the point of no return. When it almost took him off his feet by itself, he jumped with all his strength. "Now!"

Finally, his father's body became unstuck and they surfed the air wave head first into the hatch, hitting the back of the chute and piling onto the grate Maya already stood on. Behind them, the hatch swung shut and left them in the dark.

"How did you do that? Are you okay?" Maya sounded out of breath.

Jasper scrambled to his feet, unable to even take inventory of what hurt after the wild ride. What didn't hurt? "Yeah, I'm all right."

In the dark, he felt for his father's limp body and propped him up into a sitting position. No way to ascertain how he had held up. If he ever woke up again, all injuries would have been worth it anyway. The whole mountain still trembled. "Are you hurt?" Jasper asked Maya.

Before she could answer, the brunt of the pressure wave reached the hatch door and punched right through it. Small rocks and pieces of concrete hit the back wall and showered them from above. Licking, bright-red flames crawled down the chute.

Heat warmed Jasper's face. At least they could see again. The noise rose too, building toward an eardrum-splitting crescendo.

"We have to stop the fire!" Maya yelled. "It's slow, but it'll still burn us."

"You can't stop it, there's a lot more where it came from!"

Jasper saw only one way out. Well, *saw*… Hoped for it. He stomped on the grate. "We have to keep going."

"We're in a mountain! This is going down. That's the wrong way!" Maya said.

"Just do it, trust me." Jasper had no idea if it would lead somewhere, but they were far past the point of no return. The hatch door was torn to shreds and if they hadn't made it down here, they'd be dead already. "Come on, you gotta help me."

"Okay, then let's be smart about it, get a rhythm going. And let's get your father up."

They pulled Jasper's dad to an upright position and leaned him against the wall, then stomped on the grate in unison. It rattled but didn't give.

"It's solid, but it doesn't fit tightly. Keep trying," Jasper said. The flames got closer and closer. Their faces looked red from the heat as much as from the light. "Come on, faster! Faster!"

"No, stop. This is going nowhere. Ouch!" One flame had swooped down and almost licked across Maya's face. She sidestepped it, but it just hovered there for now as more and more flames crept down the chute. Maya dropped to her knees. "Why is there a grate here in the first place?" She felt around the metal edges.

Jasper kneeled next to her and traced the other side. "I feel something. It's like… a knob or a button. Do you want me to push it?"

"Push it!" Maya's voice broke as she had to evade another burst of solid flame.

Jasper pushed the button and the grate swung down,

revealing a steep-angled shaft below that led farther into the mountain.

A big fireball entered the hatch and glided down toward them at a frightening pace. The noise had turned into a sustained thunder as the sound waves from the explosion had finally caught up with them.

"Your dad! Hold on! Now!" Maya shouted.

Jasper looked up. She had hugged his father tightly and held his head to her chest. Jasper grabbed his father's legs. "Now!"

They jumped but didn't fall. They barely even tumbled, they slid, and within moments they outpaced the flames behind them, even the noise of the explosion.

A Teflon-like substance lined the smooth shaft. In pitch-black darkness they picked up even more pace, before their chute dropped them into a bigger tube that brought water from somewhere else in the mountain.

After the near free fall down the chute, the water seemed gelatinous, the irresistible current overwhelming. Jasper lost hold of his father's legs, felt encased, desperate for air. Forces pushed him forward, ahead of his companions.

He stretched but couldn't reach Maya or his dad. Blackness approached. Oxygen deprivation already?

Accelerated Time slipped away from him. The gelatin turned back into water, the smooth, but steady pressure into a murderous undertow that slapped him left to right.

He got forced to the top of the pipe, where he gasped for air, then got pulled back under water moments later.

No.

This was the world's most hazardous water slide, but

after everything that led him here, how could he let the elements defeat him like this?

Go with the flow.

In the faintest hint of light, Maya came into view right behind him. Judging from her movements, she had also been forced back into Real Time, but she still cradled his father's head in her arms.

A rush of pure affection for both of them stiffened Jasper's resolve and he slithered his arm through the current to grab her hand.

She stretched forward too, but the body of his father bounced off the top of the pipe, and they got turned around. So near, yet so far. At least now he could grab his father's legs.

A beam of daylight announced a forthcoming sharp turn, but the current pressed them straight ahead. He gestured to Maya, and they both bundled up around his father to protect him and their own heads from smashing against the pipe.

The gleam became brighter and the water pressure fell away for the briefest moment, allowing them to turn the bend safely. When the light grew brighter still, Jasper and Maya reached out and clutched hands right before accelerating again.

After a disorienting, liberating moment, the current finally ejected them from the pipe into a shallow Alpine stream at the foot of the mountain.

Jasper gasped, seized Accelerated Time again, and carefully disentangled himself from his father.

Maya had been separated from them after the fall and caught her breath before transitioning to Accelerated Time as well.

Jasper propped the flaccid body of his father up against a large stone in the shallow water and looked around.

They found themselves in a surprisingly peaceful place. A creek, meadows, trees, mountains—nothing betrayed the cataclysm going on… somewhere else. Apart from the pipe opening, no man-made structures marred the idyll. Yet he didn't dare let go of Accelerated Time.

He helped Maya to her feet.

"Is this it? Did we make it?" Their situation had gotten from bad to worse so often, Jasper didn't dare get his hopes up.

"I think so," Maya said. "And if the mountain explodes now, I don't give a damn." She wrung out her soaking wet clothes. Her silhouette appeared to glow from the late afternoon sunlight reflected by the stream's surface.

Jasper ached to hug her, but before he could muster the courage, she turned away to gather her hair into a ponytail, and the moment had passed.

"Do you think Eva got out?" Jasper wondered aloud. It was hard to fathom, but she'd had a worse day than them.

Maya shrugged. "If anyone could, it's her. How's your dad?"

"I don't know. It's hard to tell in this Super-Accelerated Time, or whatever you call it. He's just limp."

"Go ahead, check on him in Real Time. I'll take a look around, see where we are."

Jasper closed his eyes and transitioned back. The gurgling of the stream, the flowery smell of the meadow, the current swirling water around his feet, a light breeze of mountain air, it all came rushing in at once, refreshing, reinvigorating, almost overwhelming.

When Jasper opened his eyes again, so did his father.

High on top of the mountain, a cloud of smoke and dust rose silently against a clear blue sky.

"We made it." Jasper helped his dad stand up and embraced him. They both held on for a long time until the hug dissolved in affectionate shoulder slapping.

"We really did," Dad said.

"There was a hatch behind the sign. How did you know?" Jasper asked.

"A hunch. It said organic waste disposal. There's always a way out."

"I didn't know you spoke German."

"I speak seventeen languages." He laughed and patted Jasper on the shoulder. "I'm afraid there's a lot you don't know about me, but we'll have to change all that if we can find the time." He touched his bandaged neck wistfully and hugged Jasper again. "Thank you. You and your friend. Is she—"

"Maya," Jasper said. "Maya Misra. I think you knew her parents very well."

"Goodness yes, what a tragedy. I tried to contact her—"

"She got your message," Jasper said, "but she thought it was a trap. She came to L.A. to find the killer, but he found you first. Without her, we both would've been filleted in Zeiger's dungeon."

"No doubt." Again, Dad's hand sought his neck. "I still can't believe Tranq was capable of this. We were like family for so many years. Is he…?"

Jasper nodded. "Shot himself in the hubbub."

"Huh, never seemed the type." Jasper's dad furrowed his brow.

"Could have been his daughter in self-defense. He might've been trying to shoot her." Jasper shrugged. "But he probably also didn't seem like a homicidal maniac when you were friends. Uncle Martin's not right in the head either. You…" Jasper hesitated. "You changed. I read your notes. Maybe you all went crazy in your own way."

They walked over to a few bigger rocks at the riverbank and sat down. "Our condition, it can be an awful lot of time, with very little life. Especially when you're alone, like I was after your mom—"

"I was there," Jasper snapped.

"Yes, you were. And I'm sorry. Sorrier than you'll ever know." His dad put a hand on Jasper's leg. "I spent so much time with other things, I almost missed you growing up. But we'll make it work now. We will." He loudly sucked in the fresh mountain air. "I may not be able to bend time anymore, but I haven't felt this much like myself in a long time."

Jasper took his father's hand and they sat in silence for a little while until Maya materialized at a respectful distance. She tapped an imaginary wristwatch.

"Dad, what was it that I needed to know?"

"What do you mean?"

"The note. 'I hope I was able to tell you what you needed to know.'" His dad's quizzical expression prompted Jasper to add, "In the safe with all the Passage of Time stuff, that note. What was it that I needed to know?"

"Ah yes, the note…"

From the tone of his voice, Jasper doubted he really remembered.

"Look, your friend is waiting for us." Dad got up and offered Jasper a hand.

Jasper took it and let himself get pulled up.

His dad looked into his eyes. "What you needed to know? That I love you, of course, you dummy." He smacked Jasper's upper arm so hard it stung. "The rest you were obviously able to figure out yourself."

Chapter Thirty-Seven

A Warm Embrace

Singher woke up a happy man. It had worked, Zeiger had delivered. The transplant from Faulks made him a permanent time bender. And even better, the *Thyrofen alpha*, the synthetic miracle drug that had made him almost as fast as a natural time bender, still worked on top of it. In darkness, he drank time like a man dying of thirst. Only when he opened his eyes he remembered—the kids, the fight, the lightning gun, a wet crotch.

A blip on the radar. They were weak, *weak!*, and had left him alive. They'd regret it before their demise.

These restraints wouldn't hold him forever. He pulled on the leather cuffs.

The gurney swayed, and a deep, distant humming grew louder and louder. The floor trembled, and the humming turned into booming, then crackling.

Directly above him, the ceiling split, and flames reached through the cracks, before a large chunk of concrete broke free right above his head and glided downward.

A childhood memory intruded on his thoughts of revenge. He had helplessly skidded to the edge of the narrow switchback road, the sharp-edged gravel shredding his soft, young hands. From there he saw his mother falling, flailing, getting smaller. The mountain didn't do anything to kill her except exist.

Such unfathomable powerlessness. But that had been Singher's previous life.

Tick-tocks… Walking corpses, always dying, rotting in their bodies without knowing it. Disgusting. Born, barely alive, dead before anyone noticed. Fruit flies who couldn't look beyond the hour, beyond the day.

Now, Singher was so powerful, the mountain could come to him and he laughed in its face. His improvements had put him on the path to a different life—aware, maybe eternal.

Any tick-tock in his place would have been dead by now already. "Instant and painless," as the news would say, but Singher, a god among men, would never let go.

Not enough time meant death, more time meant life, power. Finally, he had as much time as he desired.

So he held on when he could smell the flames licking at his hair. He held on as the mountain came to him and a slab of concrete took over his whole field of vision. He even held on as the pressure slowly pushed the bridge of his nose into his head. He held on until he felt a last sensation, a soothing warmth that spread all over him. The embrace of Mother Earth? No, his bladder failing him for the second time today.

Chapter Thirty-Eight

A Walk in the Countryside

Eva walked at a brisk pace on the narrow strip of lush green grass that flanked the empty road leading away from the Zeiger compound. She had looked out the window down this street for years and never seen traffic apart from Singher's car or deliveries.

Her hands still hurt, but not as badly as before. The bullets had been very hot and required a firm grip to pick them out of the air. The sacrifice (*"an act of suffering or surrendering something valued for the sake of something else regarded as more important"*) had been worth it, though. Besides, skin grew back, just like hair.

She squinted. In the distance, a small blue light crept over the hill that marked how far she could see. A little while later, she could make out that it topped the roof of a white car marked with neon orange stripes and large lettering: *Polizei.*

Should she tell them what happened? They could help—but help doing what? With tick-tocks, everything would take forever. She didn't have that kind of time; she had to find someone, as soon as possible.

Her mother had never abandoned them, she'd only have

to find her house and explain what happened. Mother would understand that she had not really hated her.

The police car crawled closer. Eva didn't have much experience in the Real Time world, except with Mother and *Fräulein Ochs*. It would take hours, days even, to explain what had happened.

If only she had some of the medicine, that had made the boy, Jasper, and his friend, *not* girlfriend, almost as fast as her. Everyone should take it, so you wouldn't have to spend most of the day with the barest of necessities.

How would life be like among the tick-tocks? Jasper and the girl might be the only other people in the world like her.

Fortunately, they had made it out of the mountain too. Eva had seen them down in the valley, resting with Jasper's father where the mountain creek met the *Albertibach*, the local river.

Even if he inexplicably didn't like the comparison, Jasper reminded her so much of Robbie. Boys like them always found a way out of trouble.

What would Robbie say to her predicament?

"RIP CURRENT SHOCKER! Robbie's Family Home Ravaged By Wildfire!"

Natural catastrophes befell California all the time; everyone knew that. But his family would have fled in time, and they could build a new house. And Robbie would have been on tour in Japan, Portugal, or Argentina anyway.

Unless Rip Current really did break up. It seemed impossible, *"Friends 4 Lyfe,"* but if so, Robbie would have to find his own way, just like Eva did now. And who knew, maybe their paths would cross some time. Maybe Mother wanted to visit California some day?

Eva stepped on a patch of cool grass and glanced down at her bare feet. How strange, when had she lost her slippers?

The tickle at her soles made her feel free and alive, more alive than in a long time. More alive than…?

She waited for Adam to interject that "alive" didn't have a comparative, but he kept mum.

Adam… Sometimes the biggest shocks are the things she should have known all along. Even in German, no word existed for that feeling. She should invent one, then it would be in all the dictionaries and encyclopedias, and everyone else would have to learn what it meant.

She breathed deeply, the fresh air stinging her lungs as it inflated them to the brink of their natural capacity. It smelled fresh and flowery and piney and of something she had never smelled before. She decided it had to be musk (*"a substance with a penetrating odor secreted by the male musk deer for scent-marking and used in perfumery"*).

It smelled like everything; it smelled like the world.

She had almost reached the police car that still descended the hill blocking her view. Seeing the car up close, she didn't worry that the men would spot her. From the way it kicked up dust, it went quite fast in Real Time, and judging from the policemen's facial expressions, they only had eyes for their destination.

Eva looked over her shoulder. A gigantic cloud of dust and soot rose up in the far distance. She reached the top of the hill and stopped.

From here on, the road gently serpentined down into the

valley, before merging with a busier highway from the Southwest to Eva's destination—Davos.

It looked much smaller than she remembered it. Good. That would make it easier to find her mother's house. A couple of hours of Real Time should be enough to scour the whole city. Make that two and a half hours, with stops for snacks.

She pulled a crumpled thousand Swiss franc bill out of her pocket. She had read about inflation (*"a continuing increase in prices and reduction in the purchasing power of money"*), but hopefully she had enough for a slice of pizza and a few scoops of chocolate ice cream.

Chapter Thirty-Nine

The Business End

fter Jasper, his dad, and Maya had made their way from Zeiger's compound to the U.S. Embassy in Bern, Dad called his old friend Floyd Greasley at the State Department. The next second, they got the full spy treatment. Seclusion, sleeping on a bench at the embassy, new clothes, temporary passports, the works.

Jasper expected to be bombarded with questions, but the staff just made polite small talk. Dad spent a lot of time away from Jasper and Maya, and it didn't take long for him to get frustrated with his new condition.

"This is ridiculous. How does anyone get anything done like this?" was one of his more politely worded complaints when he came back to their holding room after one of his many phone conversations throughout the night.

His absences left Maya and Jasper with a lot of time to say little to each other between uneasy naps.

Jasper often thought of Eva. "What do you think," he asked Maya, "did Zeiger experiment on her like the others, or did he really try to cure her?"

"He was so angry when you exposed what he'd done, he must've cared," Maya said. "Or he was simply nuts. We may never know the answer. Why did he have my parents killed in the first place?"

"Maybe it was an accident," Jasper said. "Maybe he only wanted to abduct them, like my dad, and the Bastard messed up." He hesitated. These weren't exactly words of comfort. "Not that that's necessarily better. Sorry."

She waved his concern away. "But what was the point of it all? Create an army of Bastards? Time bending children for everyone? He had all that money, all that time—"

"And yet he turned into the absolute worst version of himself. And with him, that version was pretty bad indeed," Dad said, leaning in the doorframe. They hadn't heard him approach. "You two will have to do better than all of us, but at least you won't have to do it alone. Maybe Zeiger did it all because he could, and nobody in the world told him he shouldn't."

"That's… pretty profound, Dad. Was that in one of your two thousand books in the garage?" Jasper asked teasingly. "You know, the ones you read instead of spending any time with me?"

"Ouch," Dad and Maya said in unison.

"Okay, how about I get us a flight out of here?" Dad asked. "I promise you can point out more of my faults on the way home." He returned to the embassy rooms, leaving them alone once more.

Feeling emboldened, Jasper got up from his chair and sat back down next to Maya on the bench. He wanted to put his arm around her, but chickened out at the last moment, making the move slightly awkward. "I…" He paused. "I never asked you how old you are?"

She hesitated, like she had to think about it. "Eighteen, but that's only in Real Time. So, you know…"

What was he supposed to know? Whatever it was, the way she folded her arms in front of her chest signaled the end of that conversation. He clumsily shuffled a few inches to the side.

A while later, Dad spoke to Maya separately. He had arranged for flights and when the time came to leave for the airport, Jasper already suspected Maya would split from them. She wanted to return to Farmington Hills, the place where she had grown up.

"I… I'll see you again." She hugged Jasper, but it felt perfunctory. Sensing his irritation, she added, "I need closure, take care of a few things, do some thinking. But I'll be in touch!" She pulled his head down and gave him a kiss on the forehead. "Goodbye for now, Jasper, Jasper Faulks."

For a kiss on the forehead, it had felt long and tender, but he was too embarrassed to ask Dad if his mind played tricks on him.

Jasper took off his shoes (white sneakers the embassy had gotten for him along with some khakis and a light blue short-sleeved button-down that would have been right at home in Clarence's closet), stretched his legs, and made fists with his toes.

Business class rocked!

He looked at the back page of the Swiss broadsheet they

handed out in the lounge.

Eva had survived the explosion. One picture showed the girl with her mother and a Zeiger Industries spokesman at a press conference, others depicted scenes from the destroyed Zeiger compound.

Dad had translated the article for him before they had taken off. Zeiger's "private research facility" had been destroyed along with the main residence, servants' quarters, garage, and hangar. Local police worked under the assumption that a major detonation in the delivery area, possibly misrouted explosives from Zeiger's old demolition business, set off a chain reaction of gas explosions.

Assumed casualties were the magnate himself and his missing bodyguard, identified as Francesco Singher, an Italian national and former French Foreign Legionnaire from South Tyrol. According to sources, other staff had been given the week off.

Eva likely inherited Zeiger Industries, but what would happen until she came of age was unclear. Since the parents had never been married—persistent rumors spoke of a surrogate mother situation—the article speculated about an independent custodian being put in charge.

Jasper folded the paper and put it into the pocket of the seat back in front of him before diving into Accelerated Time and leafing through the Los Angeles Times he had also grabbed earlier. To a tick-tock, it would look like he didn't find what he was looking for, and naturally it didn't even have a sidebar about the Zeiger story yet, but Jasper read every single article. He couldn't remember ever reading a whole paper from beginning to end. Amazing what could be done with so much time.

He looked out the window at the plane suspended in midair, barely moving. In front of him on the screen, the movie appeared paused. Next to him, his father drank sparkling wine. Mid-sip, it looked like Jell-O in a champagne flute.

No, there would be plenty of opportunity to apply his talent in the future. Today, he would enjoy a pleasant flight home. He let go of Accelerated Time.

Dad leaned over and put the glass of champagne down on the edge of his tray where Jasper could reach it from his seat without getting up. "I'm just going to leave this here," he said and winked at Jasper. "Reparations."

The level of bubbly in his father's glass dropped a few inches in an instant. Jasper smiled blissfully and reclined in his plush seat, ready to take a very long nap.

Chapter Forty

All Ends with Beginnings

Jasper and his dad stood in front of a rinky-dink fence enclosing a dilapidated mobile home. Somehow, this mobile home had managed to snag a lonely spot overlooking a pristine little bay on the Pacific coast northwest of Malibu.

"Are you sure this is it?" Dad asked. "Looks abandoned."

"These are the coordinates Clarence gave me," Jasper said. "And look at that." Three huge satellite dishes stood on the roof.

Jasper opened the little gate adorned with a rusty "Keep Out" sign. He knocked on the door and transitioned to Accelerated Time. Uncle Martin pulled the curtain aside for a split second, his unshaven visage in the window. This had happened before. The man *had* been watching him and Clarence, but they'd never noticed.

Uncle Martin opened the door. "Last time I opened my door to you, I had to torch the place an hour later."

"Well, I'm happy you're alive too," Jasper said. "Dad's a tick-tock. Zeiger removed his thyroid, but he's dead now. The Bastard too." Jasper transitioned back to Real Time to force Uncle Martin to do the same. "We can fill you in on the details later."

"Later? What do you mean?" Uncle Martin said in Real Time.

"Hello, Marty," Dad said. "It's very good to see you."

"Tick-tock, eh? My condolences." Uncle Martin grimaced. "You falling behind on your reading?"

Dad nodded. "You have no idea. It's not all bad, though. We, I mean time benders, haven't been well. At least none of us who had to go it alone. You, me, Zeiger. Who knows about the others? Isolated in Accelerated Time, useless in Real Time. We've been thinking, maybe it does take a village. All alone, it's just too much time, not enough life."

"We have to stick together to get through this thing," Jasper said.

"What thing?" Uncle Martin asked.

"This thing called life?" Jasper asked tentatively.

"Catchy, but what are you saying?" Uncle Martin scratched his beard, sprinkling his washed out Lynyrd Skynyrd T-shirt with dandruff.

"We need your help," Jasper said.

"And you ours," Dad added. "There's still so much to learn, and now there's a next generation. Let's give it one more try. Like in the old days, just better."

"Are you saying we're getting the band back together?" Uncle Martin asked with a hint of mischievousness in his voice.

"Reunion tour."

"Greatest hits?"

"And all new material."

Uncle Martin hesitated for a moment and looked from father to son. "So, does anyone else know about this? Greasley? Your little girlfriend?"

"Only you. And my friend Clarence," Jasper said. "Remember, no secrets."

"Ugh," Uncle Martin groaned.

"He's a great guy, you'll see. If I've learned one thing, it's that there's a lot more to people than meets the eye. Give him a chance." Clarence was a genuinely great guy, but Jasper doubted Uncle Martin would come around to that point of view any time soon. Or vice versa.

"Well, we've spent years with much bigger assholes, ain't that right, Andy?" Uncle Martin asked, then laughed. "What the hell, I'm in." He disappeared for a second before reappearing with an overstuffed duffel bag slung over his shoulder. "Where are we going?"

Inside the mobile home, flames already started licking the curtains.

"Hi, Igor, how's it going?"

"Ah, still alive, Mr. Jasper, still alive. Just… these power surges… I don't know what's going on. It drives me crazy!" Igor lightly punched the open power control panel next to the elevator.

Jasper had made it a point to befriend the grumpy Russian-born janitor. Sure, in Accelerated Time, he could just sneak by him, but seeing how many times he'd be coming through here, better not to arouse any suspicion, so Jasper often walked through the lobby just to be seen.

Officially, Jasper interned at the new imaginary translation agency on the third floor. They had rented an office on the third floor, and his father had been busy setting it up for show, but they would never try to translate Chinese toaster oven manuals.

As fate would have it, three reserved parking spots on the second level of the underground parking garage corresponded to the office on the third floor. Curiously, they were right in front of an unmarked service room. When Uncle Martin had picked the lock, the service room appeared to have been unused for many years. And on top of that, upon closer inspection, one of the walls in the service room turned out to be false. Behind, a rotating alcove worked surprisingly smoothly considering it hadn't been used in over a decade.

On the other side of the mechanism, at the end of a long corridor of bare concrete and another rotating alcove, Jasper had been hard at work in Accelerated Time with Uncle Martin to get ready for today: the official unofficial reopening of the Passage of Time.

Dad had only wanted to rent the rooms upstairs and leave the Passage untouched, but for once Jasper agreed with Uncle Martin—secret endeavors needed cool headquarters. And with some refurbishment down here, they had everything they could ever want, whether it be a research facility and archive to continue exploring the nature and genesis of their condition, a safe haven from the tick-tocks, or simply a clubhouse that happened to house cutting edge home entertainment of thirty years ago.

And maybe, just maybe, even if they didn't cure cancer, something good would come from it this time.

Up on the surface, a new Metro station took shape where the city workers had cleared away the remnants of the previous entrance. Fictional gas explosions had become a mainstay in Jasper's life. The very real explosion hadn't destroyed the Passage of Time itself, though. The long corridor to the main lounge that had caved in functioned as a predetermined breaking point, and an emergency exit existed inside the Passage itself in case anyone got trapped on the wrong side of the cave-in.

There's always a way out.

Or in, obviously. The previous emergency exit had become the new main entrance.

Jasper couldn't wait to show everything to their tick-tock partners in crime. He smoothed the front of the new T-shirt he had bought yesterday, a plain white V-neck that looked classy and grown-up with his new jeans. This kind of adulting he could get behind. A pity Maya had never seen him in anything but horrible loaner clothes.

He stepped out of the rotating alcove and ducked under the retractable movie screen into the theater. Two adolescent black cats greeted him by rubbing their bodies against his legs and meowing. He bent down to pet them.

Uncle Martin sat in the first row and sucked on an e-cigarette. "Wow, this new 3D technology is amazing."

Jasper was too nervous for a witty comeback. "Let's keep it in Real Time for our guests today. Is everything ready?"

"Hey, would I be sitting here if not?"

"Probably. Yes," Jasper said. Credit where due, though. Uncle Martin had reconnected the power, set up the computers, and confirmed the habitability of the old quarters by moving right into his old room.

Jasper's dad stepped out of the alcove behind the screen first. Jasper sensed some trepidation, but as soon as their eyes met, he smiled and gave him a hug. "Who would have thought this would turn into the family business?"

Clarence followed, his eyes widening after a glance around. "Damn, sweet theater room. Original prints? Back to the Future? Indiana Jones? Is that a vintage 35mm projector?"

"Vintage!" Uncle Martin spat out the word. "The hell do you mean by vintage? That we're old?"

"Guys, can we save the bickering for the end of the tour?" Jasper asked.

"Tour? How long will this take?" Uncle Martin got up from his seat. "I have to monitor a few, er, developments online."

"Troll…" Clarence muttered while clearing his throat.

"Go," Jasper said to Uncle Martin. "I got this."

"Hey, do we need a name for this little project?" Uncle Martin asked. "Something heroic, like *The Fantastic 4* or *The A-Team*. Just not that, obviously." He walked past Clarence and poked him in the chest. "Think of a name, Einstein!"

"How about *Three Men and a Baby*, you eighties man?" Clarence asked, but Uncle Martin had already transitioned to Accelerated Time and didn't hear him anymore. "So unfair, I was proud of that one."

"How about we hold off on the squabbling for now,"

Dad suggested. "I for one want to get to the tour."

"Agreed, me too." Clarence reverentially brushed the spines of the film reels on the shelf with his finger as they walked to the back of the room. "Who knows where this strange enterprise is leading anyway?"

"The future, of course," Jasper said. "Always the future." He put Panther and Shadow on his shoulder, followed his friends out, and turned off the lights behind him.

Chapter Forty-One

Magic Hour

The thick manila folder had the hand-written title "Kruzman II 1990 (Rogue)" and bore a stamp of "Top Secret." It was the only item on a large mahogany desk apart from a simple pencil and a mobile phone.

The pant-suited woman looked at her digital watch: 8:33:01 p.m. Eastern Time. Soft light shone through the tall windows of her ground level home office. Magic hour, but she did not have eyes for her lush garden outside while amending a list of names on the first page of the folder.

Project Manager
> Kruzman (terminated)

1ˢᵗ generation
> Banerjee/Misra, Medha (deceased)
> Baumgarten, Alexander (deceased)
> Durant/Faulks, Renee (inactive) (deceased)
> Faulks, Andrew (inactive)
> Hakin, Murat (deceased)
> Higgs, Martin (active)
> Jupiter, James (active)

Misra, Nirav (deceased)
Greasley, Floyd (active)
Zeiger, Tranquillo (deceased)

2nd generation
Misra, Maya (active)
Faulks, Jasper (active)
Zeiger, Adam (deceased)
Zeiger, Eva (active)

The telephone rang. She picked up.

Her interlocutor did most of the talking, limiting her side of the conversation to "Yes, sir, my apologies." "Agreed, most unfortunate." "My understanding is that he managed to synthesize lightweight particles almost as effective as thyro-generated ones, but without access to his research we—" "Yes, we're doing what we can under the circumstances." "I suggest we monitor them for the time being." "He's been with us for years, I can vouch for him." "Unfortunately, we lost his trail years ago." "Yes, sir, I will."

She hung up and cleaned a smudge on the polished table surface with her cuff. She dialed another number and looked at her watch: 8:33:02 p.m. Eastern Time.

MILAN OBRADOVIC

is the author of *Jasper Faulks and the Passage of Time* and the upcoming sci-fi novel *Sky Skraper 1*. After growing up in Germany, he has made the Golden State of California his home for the last couple of decades.

Always grateful for the fruits of globalization, Milan enjoys French wine, Italian food, Japanese electronics, German cars, and American movies. He lives with his wife, his son, and his hard of hearing Miniature Schnauzer on the Westside of Los Angeles. Find out more and tell him how much you like his book at milanobradovic.com.

www.ingramcontent.com/pod-product-compliance
Lightning Source LLC
Chambersburg PA
CBHW030704190726
48286CB00001B/157